THE
COSTUMIER'S GIFT

From the award-winning author,
recipient of:

IndieB.R.A.G Medallion
Chill with a Book Readers' Award
BooksGoSocial Gold Quality Mark

Other books by Vicky Adin
whose writing has been compared with that of
Catherine Cookson:

Gwenna The Welsh Confectioner
Brigid The Girl from County Clare
The Cornish Knot
The Art of Secrets
The Disenchanted Soldier

THE
COSTUMIER'S GIFT

VICKY ADIN

THE COSTUMIER'S GIFT

Produced for Vicky Adin by AM Publishing New Zealand
www.ampublishingnz.com

Cover Image: Queen Street, Auckland, c. 1910
Sir George Grey Special Collections,
Auckland Libraries, 35-R26,
Auckland Libraries Heritage Collections

Other books by Vicky Adin (see p. 376)

Gwenna *The Welsh Confectioner*
Brigid *The Girl from County Clare*
The Cornish Knot
The Art of Secrets
The Disenchanted Soldier

To order copies of Vicky Adin's print books:
www.vickyadin.co.nz, www.amazon.com

Ebooks available from www.amazon.com, www.kobo.com, www.smashwords.com

DEDICATION

I dedicate this story to my best friend for the last fifty years, my husband Bruce, who sometimes leads a solitary existence when I am in writing mode.

ACKNOWLEDGEMENTS

Authors need a large family around them to bring a book to realisation. Not just a personal family who encourage, and who patiently listen to every twist, turn and problem and still bring coffee or wine when needed, but also a family of experts.

These skilful people read and critique, correct mistakes the author doesn't see, design the cover, prepare the layout and double-check every word and punctuation character to present a book as near to 100% perfection as any human being can achieve. Any errors that have been missed are my responsibility alone.

There are too many to name individually, but my special thanks go to members of my writing group, Mairangi Writers, for their continuing support and critiquing skills, and providing assistance with the historical details, and to fellow author Jenny Harrison who picked the story to pieces, searching for character faults and plot holes (author of Out of Poland, The Lives of Alice Pothron).

I'd also like to express my thanks to author Phillipa Nefri Clark, who provided invaluable feedback on the story and supplied information and advice on ways to promote my books to make them more visible in the book readers' world.

Thanks also to Kathy Servian Giannoulis who made the costume and took the photo of the woman on the cover, and to Julie Cave of French Mode Vintique for advice on historically correct mannequins. Thanks go to Kura Carpenter, graphic designer and especially to Adrienne Charlton, my editor-in-chief without whom this book would never have seen the light of day. She does all of the above and more.

A Short Guide to the Historical Characters

BRIGID'S HOUSEHOLD in 1903
(from the book *Brigid The Girl from County Clare*)

Brigid Price (née O'Brien) – lacemaker, from County Clare (b. 1868, aged 35). She had two daughters of her own, Lilly and Grace. Before coming to New Zealand from Australia, she "adopted" Jane and Laura O'Neill, sisters aged 8 and 10.

- **Lilly** Price (Brigid's first daughter, b. 1893, aged 10).
- **Grace** Price (Brigid's second daughter, b. Dec. 1895, aged 7).
- **Laura** O'Neill (Jane's sister, b. 1876, aged 27).
- **Jane** O'Neill (costumier at the Opera House, b. 1878, aged 25, Gwenna's best friend).

Sally Forsythe – Brigid's best friend and live-in companion whom she met on the migrant ship (b. 1862, aged 41).

Charlie Price (1914) – half-brother of Gwenna (from the book *Gwenna The Welsh Confectioner*)

Charlie married **Grace** Price and they had three children:

- Thomas Charles Price (**Little Tommy**, b. 1915).
- Jane Brigid Price (**Jaybee**, b. 1919, married Jack Ellingham and had one daughter, Elizabeth, b. 1945).
- Kathleen Grace Price (**Granna Katy**, b. 1928, married Robert Bridges (1950), and had son Michael, b. 1951, and daughter Susan, b. 1953, modern **Katie**'s mother).

GWENNA'S HOUSEHOLD in 1903
(from the book *Gwenna The Welsh Confectioner*)

Gwenna Price – confectioner (b. 1881 aged 22), Jane's best friend.
Hugh Powell – Gwenna's husband.
Charlie Price – Gwenna's half-brother (b. 1893).

- **George** Price (Gwenna's son from a previous marriage, b. 1900, married Florence Chitham. Their firstborn son, Geoffrey, was **Jared**'s grandfather).

1

1

LIVING IN THE PAST

April 2018

Katie had only herself to blame and now it was too late: too late for Granna; too late for her; just plain too late. Saddened, Katie shrugged the thought away. Life would never be the same again.

Her mother's death fifteen months before had shaken her. No, more than that, shattered would be a better term, but she doubted the old woman sitting before her, endlessly chattering about the past, even knew her daughter had gone.

"Janey, Janey. You're here," said Granna, looking through Katie to someone else. "Say hello to our Katie here. She's your ... oh dear, I can't remember now, your great-granty-something-or-other, she is, but you know her, don't you? Our Janey's ever so clever."

"Who's that, Granna?" asked Katie, knowing she wouldn't make sense of the answer if one came.

Part of her wanted to find out about the people Granna talked about, but none of it mattered. No one else cared about Granna or the past, and there'd be nobody to care in the future either, now Katie's life had gone awry.

"My Janey is so special," said Granna, continuing her conversation with no one in particular. "Her designs are superb. Oh my … is this for me?"

After Katie's grandfather died, roughly twenty years earlier, her grandmother had continued to live in their substantial and picturesque villa alone. A decade later, Granna could no longer manage on her own and moved in to her daughter's family home. But trying to hold her own family together and looking after her mother as her mind slipped further away from reality, became too much for Katie's mother's overworked heart.

Oh, why had nobody noticed, Katie lamented.

But Katie noticed things these days. She noticed the delicate bones in Granna's fingers, and the soft, papery skin riddled with dark lines under the loose flesh. Those once-strong fingers had been so creative and so gentle. Now they looked as if they would break if you touched them, except Granna was nowhere near breaking – at least not physically.

A bird tweeted out in the garden and Granna turned her head. Her dark velvet eyes glanced across Katie's face and momentarily held her gaze. Eyes that shone with love and purpose. In days gone by, you could get lost in those eyes, drawn into their protective warmth. Now, the depth that lived within them belonged to another era.

Putting Granna into the rest home had been the most difficult decision Katie had ever made. Her father had wanted nothing to do with the batty old woman, he'd said, and washed his hands of the whole affair. Katie had no such choice. Left with sole responsibility when her mother died, she could see no other option. Granna's safety was paramount.

Prone to wander, Granna had taken it into her head that she lived in her grandmother's old house and nothing anyone said could change her mind. 'I know where I'm going, Katie dear,' she'd say – but she didn't. Wherever the house in her mind had once been, the rest home was new and in a foreign-to-Granna area.

Now, cherished photographs covered every surface and filled her room. When she'd first moved in, the managers tried to persuade her to limit the number to those that would fit on one shelf and keep the rest in a drawer. They promised to change them regularly, but Granna would have none of it. She didn't say anything but simply took them out and put them where she could see them. Another time, they tried taking them away altogether but Granna had thrown such a hissy fit, they gave in.

One photo in particular always drew Katie's attention. The sepia tones had faded but the clothes and hairstyles worn by the two women were unmistakably Edwardian. One of the faces looking back at her was her own – the uncanny resemblance made her uneasy, but as it had no name on the back, Katie had no idea where she fitted in the family. Granna called the older woman Móraí, which sounded something like 'Morr-ee' to Katie's ear, but she'd never heard Granna call the second woman by name.

She made a mental note to look in her mother's collection and see if she could find anything with names. She'd put off going through the house and sorting her mother's possessions, but the time had come. Her father had a new love now and the woman didn't want the old stuff around.

"You should see those costumes our Janey used to make," said Granna. "The fabrics were glorious, but

Mam wasn't allowed to go to the theatre to see them on the stage until she was much older. Móraí was strict about that …" and off she'd go again telling a story, half in the present and half in the past, about people Katie didn't know and whose relationships didn't make sense. Convinced Granna mixed up the generations, Katie hadn't been able to work out which name belonged with which era. She couldn't even put a name to Granna's 'Mam'.

Although her grandmother didn't recognise anyone else, for some inexplicable reason, she knew Katie. Born on the same day as her, sixty years later, and named after her, they'd had a special relationship, until Katie'd gone off to university. Now she wished she'd paid more attention to her mother, and her gran.

The nurse came in. "Hello, Mrs Bridges, how are you today?"

Granna turned towards the newcomer and a polite smile creased her face. "Hello. Now, who are you? Have you come to see me? I do so like visitors, they are such interesting people."

"I've come to make you more comfortable, Mrs Bridges." Katie watched the nurse pat her gran's arm.

Granna wriggled in the La-Z-Boy chair and plucked ineffectually at the mohair rug she sat on. "I do so like this colour, don't you?" she asked. "It reminds me of roses."

Granna Katy had kept a beautiful garden once. The two of them had often wandered around it together while Granna named all the flowers. Katie's eyes rested on the deep-pink throw she'd given her gran. She, too, loved that colour.

"How is she doing overall?" Katie asked the nurse.

"Her memory of long-ago events seems faultless to me." But then, she couldn't say whether Granna was right or not.

"Very well, actually, for her age. She keeps active and goes to all the exercise classes, especially when there's music playing." Despite her memory loss, Granna was still a relatively fit and healthy ninety-year-old.

Katie smiled. She'd watched her grandmother more than once at these classes, dancing in her own world rather than following the instructor.

"And she still plays the piano," continued the nurse.

"I'm glad," said Katie. "She's a far better pianist than I'll ever be, even though she makes mistakes. The music seems to come alive under her fingertips."

Katie remembered the piano lessons with her gran at her house as a child, and the comings and goings of the other students.

"It's a pity she forgets what she's played almost as soon as she stands up from the keyboard," said the nurse.

Granna's voice interrupted their conversation. "I do so love my móraí. She's a wonder and such a great cook. She always makes my favourites. I can still taste those little biscuits that went with my tea. She'll be here soon."

"That's nice. There's a cup of tea coming shortly."

Granna unexpectedly got up from her chair. "We should go to Gwenna's Sweet Treats for tea. It's an age since I visited her. Grandma will get cross with me if I don't call. Now, where did I leave my gloves?"

While Granna searched the drawers, the nurse rearranged the rug on the chair, retidied the already-tidy bed, wrote something down on the chart by the door and pulled the window closed. "It's a wee bit windy at the moment. Do you think you should wait until it's died down before you go? How about doing some lacework instead? You can show it to her later."

Granna accepted the crochet hook and fine cotton thread and sat down again. Katie never ceased to be amazed her gran could move the hook so swiftly, in, out, over, under and around in a constant motion. She still created such intricate lace. The results weren't perfect, and she ended up with dozens of motifs and long edgings that would never get joined together, but Granna appeared satisfied with what she could see. "No, Janey didn't make lace, she was the famous costumier."

"Brothers!" growled Katie as she ended the call.

As usual, her eldest brother, Hugh, cited work issues and how busy he and Carol were with the kids' sport and music and whatever, as an excuse not to help sort through Mum's things. With her other brother, Tom, in Australia on business, everything fell to her – again, as usual. They were older than her by nine and eight years, and close together in age yet nothing alike.

But she wasn't mad at her brothers. She was mad at her father.

How could he even think of bringing *that* woman into Mum's house? Only a couple of years older than Tom, she still had teenagers at home. Katie wanted nothing to do with the whole sorry affair.

But how could her father have left it so long to clear her mum's things out? He'd not even touched her clothes; he'd simply shut the door on the room and left it all. Until now. When it suited him. And he'd left it for Katie to do.

"Don't be angry, Katie," said Tom. "Dad's a dreamer

and he needs someone to fill those dreams."

She walked into her mother's old room, threw back the curtains and stared out the window. She knew her parents' marriage hadn't been a good one and had deteriorated even more after Granna Katy had come to live with them. The pair had lived separate lives for many years: Mum saying she had the responsibility of Granna and couldn't go gallivanting off chasing rainbows, while Dad argued that getting out and doing the wishful things in life would keep them young. Full of madcap schemes that rarely paid off, Dad did enough 'wishful things' of his own to keep half the world young. No wonder Mum ran out of patience.

Katie turned from the window, putting her anger and memories to one side. She'd earlier packed the photo albums and other papers she wanted to keep, ready to take to the car. Now she had to tackle the personal possessions. Opening the door to the old-style wardrobe and seeing Mum's signature skirts and blouses hanging there, Katie knew Tom was right. Their dad was a dreamer and their mum the practical one who had held it all together.

Katie lifted all the clothes off the rail and roughly folded them into black plastic sacks. She would drop them off at the hospice shop later.

Then she tackled the drawers. Katie didn't want any of her mother's clothes, but she'd keep the odd piece of jewellery. Not the costume bits and pieces and fake pearl necklaces, but a few of the older, better-quality pieces. She put those to one side and continued sorting.

The bottom drawer jammed, and she got down on her hands and knees to see what the problem was. Spying something, she eased the drawer back a little and jiggled it until she released the package from its hiding place.

She looked at the battered cardboard box, tied with a dusty velvet ribbon which had once been green, wondering why her mother had kept it hidden. The ribbon disintegrated as Katie untied it. Inside, wrapped in yellowed tissue paper, lay a brooch in the shape of a cross, made from stylised strands of straw plaited together, and although black with age, it looked like it might be silver. She'd definitely not seen it before.

"Katie, is that you?" Her father's voice echoed through the house. "I saw your car outside."

Damn. She'd hoped to avoid seeing her father on this trip. "Yes, Dad." Katie slipped the box into her handbag and opened the door. "I'm in Mum's room."

Over a cup of coffee in the kitchen, she and her father hedged around each other.

"How's your grandmother?"

"She's fine, all things considered."

"I thought the old bat would have carked it by now."

"Nope. She's got staying power."

"Don't remind me. She should have gone a long time ago, if you ask me."

Katie's temper was starting to get the better of her, and the pain in her chest threatened to burst any moment. Why did her father bring out the worst in her these days?

"I'm taking Mum's clothes and things to the hospice shop later. Are you sure there's nothing you want?"

Her father shrugged. "I've got everything I need," he tapped his head, "up here. And anyway, I don't want anything of the past around. Get rid of it."

She swallowed hard, determined not to show how much she resented him replacing her mother so easily.

She gazed around the kitchen, seeing how the once-familiar touches were no longer there. The tea towel hung in a different place and the pictorial calendars Mum had liked were nowhere in sight. Her favourite china and her kitchen appliances had been put away somewhere and new coffee mugs were on display. Suddenly uncomfortable at being in another woman's kitchen, Katie climbed down off the bar stool and carefully washed and dried her coffee mug.

"I was hoping I could leave a few boxes of things here for Hugh and Tom to check and take what they like."

"Nah. Take it all away, Katie. If the boys wanted anything they should have got it by now." He too rinsed his cup, leaving it on the bench to dry, and looked out the window at whatever had caught his attention. "I've waited long enough."

She bit her lip, holding back a sharp retort. She'd always suspected things had reached crisis point before Mum died but how could he be so callous?

'Well, I'll be off then," she gabbled and rushed from the room. She couldn't, wouldn't, let her father see how much he had hurt her. Back in her mother's room she hurriedly scooped up the remaining items and carted as much as she could carry in one go out to the car. She raced back for the last load before her father got an attack of the guilts and offered to help her. She didn't want his help. She could cope quite well on her own – thank you.

Except she couldn't – not lately – she admitted, as the tears formed.

She'd single-handedly wrecked her career and her life.

Slamming the car door shut, she started the engine and backed out of the driveway without a second glance.

2

CONVOLUTED FAMILIES

February 1903

"What a delightful wedding, and such a perfect summer's day!" exclaimed Brigid as she removed her hat and patted her hair into place in the mirror. She straightened the St Brigid's cross brooch her grandmother back in Ireland had given her. It reminded her of home, but seventeen years on since she'd left, her family in Ireland were becoming a distant memory. Her adopted family here in Auckland were far more important to her these days. "But my, it's so warm, I'm near to melting," she said, dabbing her hanky to her overheated face. "And that newfangled electric tram was so overcrowded, I had to hold on for dear life as it jerked its way down Queen Street."

"I agree. The ceremony was indeed a joy," said Jane, taking Brigid's hat and hanging both on the hall stand. She'd been overjoyed when her best friend Gwenna, had asked her to design a second-wedding ensemble for her special day, and had incorporated Brigid's craftsmanship into her ideas. "I'm so glad to see the two of them wed at last. They are good together and deserve some happiness, but can I just say, your lace set off the dress perfectly."

"Ah, yes, but your design was the masterpiece," replied Brigid. "I'm so proud of you." Jane had achieved great success for such a young woman, and Brigid thought she deserved more accolades, and often said so.

"What's all this blether?" asked Sally, her Scottish accent still apparent. "If it's supposed to be a game of who can outpraise the other, you're wasting your time. Och! Ye both need congratulating. Y' did a fine job between you. Miss Gwenna's gown is the most glorious of affairs: elegant yet restrained. Just perfect for a wee widow. She'll get a lot of wear from that outfit."

Watching Sally, Brigid's best friend and companion, set the table for a late afternoon tea, Jane considered herself lucky to be part of the family she thought of as her own. As a young child, she and her sister Laura had met Brigid and Sally on the migrant ship taking them to Australia. Brigid had taken them under her wing and cared for them ever since. "Why couldn't Lilly and I go, Mam?" asked Grace, the youngest of Brigid's two girls. "We're well acquainted with Miss Gwenna, and everyone. And I love her sweet shop."

"Because children weren't invited. You are still only seven and there's plenty of time for you to go to weddings." Brigid kissed the girl's cheek. "Now tell me, what did you do with Aunt Sally and Laura this afternoon?"

"We've had a wonderful time," gushed Lilly, the bouncy, excitable girl who reminded them all of her father, who she'd never known. His ship had been lost at sea many years ago.

Brigid's beloved husband Tommy – fabric merchant to the elite, he used to describe himself – travelled the world bringing back exclusive fabrics for Miss Brigid's, the boutique where Brigid sold her intricate and bespoke lace to the most fashionable ladies of the town. She had lost the will to continue without him, but Sally insisted she keep working – she had two little ones to care for. Children who would never experience a father's love.

Jane just wished Miss Brigid's could be as flourishing now as it once had been, but Brigid and Sally were content and managed comfortably enough, while both Lilly and Grace thrived in the wholly female household. They loved their 'Aunt' Sally and their 'sisters', Laura and Jane, accepting the unusual and unofficial relationships without question.

While the women chatted, transferring cake from tins to plates and pouring the tea, Lilly kept talking about going to the park, the birds, the summer colours, the boots she'd seen, how mean Grace had been, and listening to the church choir. Sally and Laura looked on indulgently.

"So, can I, Mam? Can I?"

"May I, Lilly. It's 'may I'. Now, may you what?" asked Brigid, placing her cup gently back on its saucer and blotting her mouth delicately.

"Have the boots?"

Brigid's eyes softened at the eager look on Lilly's face, but never mind how she phrased it, the girl would not be pleased. "No, dear. I'm sorry, but you can't. Not yet awhile."

"But Mam!"

Wishing to avoid further argument, Sally changed the subject and asked Jane about her work at Abbott's Opera House. "What marvellous designs have ye done for this season? I remember when you designed that dress for our Breeda's twenty-first birthday. You couldna been more than eleven at the most."

14

"So do I," said Brigid. "I loved it and it became a favourite. You always were excellent at drawing, Jane dearest. And I'm so pleased to see you successful now."

Jane blushed. "But if you hadn't taught me sewing and lacemaking, and about shape and structure, I'd never have been able to do what I do." She paused, unsure how Laura would react this time. "I brought a few sketches with me, if you'd like to see them."

"Aye, lass, you must show us," said Sally. "But first tell me, what's the latest gossip around town?"

"The only gossip I'm interested in at the moment is the upcoming tour by Madame Melba, the world-famous opera singer," said Jane, thrilled by the opportunity coming her way. "I read she's due to arrive in Invercargill in a few days' time and is appearing in concerts around the country. It'll be early March before she gets to Auckland, but when she does ..." Jane paused, elated, "... both concerts are at the Opera House."

"That's grand," said Brigid, as delighted for Jane as she was herself. "I remember you saying the theatre closed for several months last year for renovation?"

"The refurbishments are finished now and, I have to say, are first-rate, and ready to receive such a revered performer."

"So where are these designs o' yours?" asked Sally.

The moment Jane collected her leather satchel, Lilly was distracted from her sulk.

"Show me, show me," she cried and rushed off to grab a stool so she could sit next to Jane.

"May I see too, Janey?" asked Grace quietly, sidling up to her.

Jane put her arm around the girl. Everyone else called her Jane, but with one extra syllable, Grace turned the reserved and cautious Jane into someone far more approachable and fun. "Of course." Jane smiled softly. "There's room for everyone and time for all of you to see."

Jane had started work in the wardrobe section of Abbott's Opera House a little after her sixteenth birthday. The skills she'd learnt from Brigid had given her a job repairing costumes, but her sketches had drawn the attention of the owner, Mr Abbott, himself.

People no longer called it Abbott's since he'd passed away, but Jane still missed her old mentor. He'd been the first person to give her an opportunity, and a place where she could hide the pain of the past amid the fictitious dramas of the stage.

Somehow Brigid persuaded him to let Jane accompany her on an extended visit to Brisbane the following year, to observe and learn more about design and fashion. How Brigid pulled it off, she didn't know, but since then, everything had worked out perfectly.

On her return, Mr Abbott came to the workroom and spoke to her, instructing the senior wardrobe mistress to use two of Jane's designs for the next show. And the next. Now, seven years later, Jane was the senior costumier, and all the clothes were made to her designs. She would remain forever grateful and loyal to his memory – and to Brigid.

"Will you be creating any of Madame Melba's gowns, Jane?" asked Brigid.

"No. Unfortunately. I'd have loved the opportunity, but she brings her wardrobe with her."

If she was not mistaken, Emily Nathan, who worked for J C Williamson as designer to the stars from Melbourne, would have been responsible for much of Madame Melba's wardrobe. At one time, Mr Abbott had hinted Jane could emulate her famous counterpart, but such an opportunity was yet to come her way. "I'll be taking careful notes, though. I might pick up some new ideas. Although it's not often I'm short of those. I worry more about how they'll fit with the production."

Jane loved the early mornings, when she could move around her top-floor workroom at the Opera House before anyone else arrived. She would compare progress against the numerous sketches pinned to the walls and inspect the elaborate costumes draping the mannequins. She could touch the rich fabrics laid out on the table ready for cutting and check the accessory trays holding the beads, threads and feathers used to adorn the finished outfits.

But the nights, when she let down her silky dark hair and dressed in her richly coloured, beaded silk wrap – making her feel like one of her exotic characters – was when she did her best work. With pencil in hand she would sketch gown after gown, suit after suit: sometimes total fantasy, sometimes glamorous, sometimes whimsical.

Where the ideas came from even Jane couldn't explain, and she often had no idea which design would work best for which show, but her pile of drawings had not let her down so far. Somewhere deep inside, she held the dream that one day she might become a famous designer, but meanwhile Jane couldn't be happier. On occasions, she even had the temerity to sell a few of the more fashionable designs under the name of 'Bernadette', particularly during ball season. A secret she kept to herself.

Jane lifted a sketch from the folder and passed it around. "I have so many drawings, I'm not sure where I'm going to use them all."

No one expected Laura to choose that moment to upset the cosiness which had settled across the room. "For goodness' sake, Jane, will you stop going on about your stupid costumes and think about something far more important!"

Laura had little time for Jane's career, or her sister's apparent contentment. She was far too driven by the need to change life for women in general to understand Jane's easy-going satisfaction.

"My work is important," argued Jane. "And I'm just as passionate about what I do as you are, but I don't need to shout and bluster to prove I'm good at my job."

"Well, that's a matter of opinion, isn't it. At least I'm learning to do something useful. All you do is make silly costumes for your silly theatre."

Brigid sighed. "Leave Jane alone, Laura. Neither of you are going to change the other, so stop trying." Brigid repeated herself most times the sisters got together, but nothing she said would halt Laura.

"I don't understand how she, or you for that matter, can't see sense," insisted Laura.

"Let's be careful about what we say, shall we, before we upset things any more," said Brigid, trying to calm things down.

"Tell me about your morning, Laura," said Sally, changing the subject in her usual manner.

"I was at a meeting." She left the sentence hanging, with the expectation someone would ask her about it. But nobody did.

"We had a nice surprise at the wedding today, didn't we, Jane?" said Brigid. "We had our picture taken. Just the two of us. I hope it turns out well. Sometimes the expressions on people's faces are a bit grim with all the waiting, but we were told the Box Brownie camera is quick and we could smile."

"I hope we can both get a copy," said Jane, a dimple appearing at the memory. It would be a photograph to cherish. Herself and the woman she considered her adopted mother, even if no more than a decade separated them in age.

"Don't you want a better life, either of you?" Laura was not easily dissuaded when she was fired up about life's injustices. "It's coming up ten years since women won the right to vote, and there's still so much more we need to do."

"Did we tell you, Laura? Our Lilly's been asked to sing in the choir," said Sally.

"One of us will have to walk with her to practice, of course," added Brigid.

"Lilly has the voice of an angel," praised Sally. "Takes after her daddy, she does. What with that Welsh lilt of his; he had a fine voice."

"Surely, she's old enough to walk by herself," said Laura, momentarily diverted. "Good gracious! She's nearly ten!"

"I wouldn't like to go walking on my own, not at her age," said Jane.

Laura turned on her sister. "What are you talking about? We walked everywhere on our own. We didn't have any option. Remember?"

"No, I didn't," retorted Jane, with a wobble in her voice. "I always had you with me, or ... or someone. And. Anyway ... I don't want to remember."

Jane moved to the far end of the room and stood staring out the dormer window, fighting to control her tears and her memories. Behind her, the conversation carried on while she reburied the past where it belonged.

"Laura," sighed Brigid, "why do you have to stir things up? You're very much aware that Jane hates talking about her time in Townsville. It's in the past. Leave her alone to cope the way she can."

"By hiding?"

"If pretending it didn't happen, or happened to another person in another life makes her feel better, then what's the harm? She's happy as she is."

"She's subservient and at the beck and call of the men who think they run that place. I wouldn't put up with it." Laura huffed and smoothed her dress into place.

"Maybe not. But she's successful. And it's her choice how she lives her life."

Still trying to smooth troubled waters, Sally agreed. "Maybe life could be better for some, Laura, but you must admit much has improved for women. Look at you, working at that law firm for Mr Devore and Mr Cooper, who's a judge now, and alongside that woman, and that Māori chap who used to work there? What's their names again?" Sally waved her hand airily.

"Do you mean Ellen Melville and Āpirana Ngata?" said Laura.

"Aye, that's them. So, see what I mean, lass? I ken not all employers and not all men are the same, and you must see some sad cases, but we do our best."

"Sally's right, Laura," added Brigid. "Not all women want to be suffragettes. Most just like the fact they have more choices available to them and are not so dependent on men. Or controlled by them."

"Except maybe the bank manager, eh, Breeda?" laughed Sally, who always called Brigid by her Irish nickname.

Brigid laughed too and reached across to squeeze her friend's hand, sharing memories of harder times.

"But ..." began Laura.

Brigid held her palm up. "We may not shout about it in the streets like you want us to, but quietly, behind the scenes, women are securing their future, and their children's. You can't expect everything to change at once, Laura, or upset the social structure in one go."

"I suppose you have a point," agreed Laura reluctantly. "And I am so lucky to be working beside Ellen. Have I told you she is only the second woman allowed to train to become a lawyer in her own right? I'm learning a lot and hope I can be as capable as her one day. And Mr Ngata, he was the first Māori to pass a law degree. He's such a clever chap. I'm sure he'll go far in parliament," she enthused before returning to her main argument. "But Jane could do so much better if she'd listen."

While the others had talked about Laura's work, Jane had kept her opinions to herself, but she had no intention of letting Laura tell her what to do. "Leave me to live my life the way I want, and I'll leave you to yours." Her voice was quiet but firm. "Now, can we change the subject?"

"Yes please, Laura," said Brigid. "We've all had more than our fair share of troubles and we deal with them each in our own way. Let's enjoy the rest of the day in a more peaceful and joyous manner, please?"

Laura grunted but acquiesced to Brigid's gentle words.

"Can we see Janey's drawings now?" asked Grace.

3

LEARNING TO LIVE AGAIN

May 2018

Katie hadn't told anyone she'd tossed her job in. She couldn't begin to explain it to herself, let alone anyone else. It hadn't made sense when she stormed out of the office, and it made less sense now. Nor did she remember how such a minor mistake had become 'the last straw', 'the one that broke the camel's back' – hated clichés in the marketing industry. But her back, or rather her resolve, *had* broken. At the age of thirty, she'd thrown in everything she had worked for.

She'd been skilled at her job, well respected by her peers, and thrived under the challenges, but that day instead of being her usual calm, reasoning self, she'd lost her temper with a junior, embarrassing both the girl and humiliating herself in the process. A feeling of dread had blanketed her shoulders, and her confidence drained away. All she wanted to do was run away and hide.

More than a month since she'd collected her mother's things, her days were now meaningless. She'd dropped the unwanted items to the hospice, but that's where her courage failed. Now, as she pondered over her photos, she struggled to settle to anything and doubted her ability to make a sensible decision – and she still hadn't looked at the paperwork and albums.

Only her visits to Granna Katy brought her any pleasure. With Granna, she didn't have to answer awkward questions, or justify herself. Granna simply wanted to hold her hand and talk, or sometimes to walk in the garden. Katie often didn't follow half of what Granna said, but the garden of the rest home was a delight. The shady trees, flower beds, shrubs, paths and strategically placed seating all helped obscure the high fences surrounding the property, designed to prevent the residents wandering. Granna could name all the flowers and often complained about the gardener doing something she wouldn't have done.

Katie started to take her camera on these visits and clicked random shots of Granna, seeing the odd resemblance to her mum or her brothers and even her young niece, in the tilt of her head or the way she looked at her. For as long as Katie could remember, she'd enjoyed taking photographs but had never been serious enough to show anyone. She rarely printed her photos, preferring to store them on her laptop, but flicking through some of the recent ones, she decided she might frame a few. Her brothers would appreciate them. Granna Katy might like one too. Her father wouldn't.

Thinking of her father brought to mind his impending marriage and how different his life would be with a new family from now on. She shuddered. Not for her. She didn't remember consciously deciding never to marry or have children, but neither had she felt the need for one person to fill her life. If anything, she'd been more worried about being tied down, like her mum.

She had enough family and lots of friends – even if she had avoided them since walking out on her job – to fill her life, and if her father was any sort of example, she didn't want a bar of it. She and her dad had never been close, but now the rift between them seemed too huge to repair.

Her role had required her to do a lot of travelling and she was on first-name basis with many of the so-called 'important' people in the industry; she'd even been one of them and had her fair share of relationships. She'd moved in with someone once but had not been brave enough to let her own place go, and moved back before she'd given the poor man a chance. Had it come from her disillusionment with her parents' marriage or from a disenchantment with all the men she'd gone out with?

Whatever the reason, she started to fall apart after her mother died. Not because she couldn't live without her mother, but because her world suddenly seemed hollow and worthless, and she couldn't make sense of it any more.

So, here she sat, with no idea what was happening to her or how to put her life back in order.

Frustrated by her thoughts, she ran her fingers through her hair, styled into the latest bob that naturally fell into place with a shake of her head. Unaware of her own grace and elegance, she uncoiled her long legs from beneath her on the long, white leather couch and padded across the lush carpet to the immaculate kitchen. The apartment overlooking The Viaduct had been furnished to her exacting tastes. She liked things clean and sharp, some would say austere, but clutter annoyed her.

She poured a glass of white wine and carried it back to the couch, placing it carefully on a coaster on the white, distressed side table. She picked up her camera again and scanned the images more slowly this time, studying the composition. A few more flicked by and one caught her eye.

After staring at it for a while, she reached for her laptop and brought the image up on the screen. In full size, the frame was even better to her eye. In fact, the photo was stunning, even if she thought so herself, and she'd captured the refracted light perfectly …

They'd been out in the garden and Granna had stepped first one way and then another, going wherever a fleeting thought took her. Her floral-patterned walking stick she used more as a pointer than a balancing tool, and she'd talked non-stop about the flowers she saw and the memories they brought back. She reached out to cup a late-blooming rose but couldn't quite bend down to check if it had that typical rose scent she talked of. Instead, she'd turned her hand slightly as if to pick it.

"No. One should not pick a rose at this time of the day," she announced as clearly and surely as if she had no symptoms of dementia. "You should pick roses in the early morning when the dew is still on them. Did you know that, Katie?"

Katie murmured a suitable response, but she didn't.

"And if you can't pick them early enough, leave it until the early evening and put them straight into a bucket of water. And don't cut them too short, do you hear me?"

"Yes, Granna." Although Katie was confused. It had to be well after four o'clock, so why couldn't her grandmother pick the rose?

"Excellent. You should learn something new every day, child," and away she strode, or as much as any ninety-year-old can stride. She stopped when she found a massive pink quill chrysanthemum in full bloom. "Look, Katie. Look at this 'mum'. Isn't it beautiful? So many little florets curving around each other to make up a whole flower head."

Katie couldn't remember what happened to Granna's stick but as she put out both hands to frame the flower, a ray of sunshine lit it up as if it stood under a spotlight on the stage. The skin of Granna's hand became translucent in the light, turning the edges of her fingers pink, and the character lines deepened into shadows. Light shafts appeared to extend from her fingertips, and the flower seemed to tilt its head to one side ever so slightly, as if drawing light or warmth from Granna's hands ...

Unbidden, a voice entered her head: you should sell that one online as a stock photo.

Katie instinctively turned to see who had spoken, knowing no one was there, but the thought wouldn't go away. She continued to browse through the rest of the images, adjusting them as she worked, and stored them in a separate file. An almost forgotten buzz of interest surged through her body as possibilities came to mind.

"Mórai!" cried Granna, looking more agitated than Katie had seen her before. "Mórai."

Looking up at something Katie couldn't see, Granna raised her arms like a child would to be picked up by an adult. Closing the door behind her, Katie swiftly crossed the room and sat on the stool beside her grandmother's armchair.

Wrapping her arms around her, she whispered, "I'm here, Granna. Katie is here."

Granna's eyes turned to her, and Katie could see the pupils change as if she was refocusing. "Katy and *Mórai*." A deep sigh escaped Granna as she turned her head to look out the window. "Can we go for a walk?" she said in a childlike voice.

"What a great idea. Take my arm; I'll help you up."

But Granna didn't need help. She was on her feet and rifling amongst her things in the wardrobe before Katie could untangle her handbag and camera straps from around her neck.

"Right, my girl. It's time for lessons."

Katie looked up, shocked at the total change of voice and demeanour.

In Granna's hand was a knitting needle.

Not wanting to upset her, Katie simply said, "Yes, Granna."

Granna Katy began to point to various things around the room. "What's this called?"

Katie couldn't think what response Granna wanted so said the most obvious.

"No, girl. No. In Irish. Now try again."

Katie blinked. She had no Irish words and didn't have any idea how to answer. Speaking, but not saying anything Katie could understand, and with her movements becoming more agitated with each gesture, Granna pointed to a vase, then a photo, the mirror and the bed. Or was it the quilt? Abruptly, she stopped. Her arms dropped by her side and the knitting needle fell to the floor as the energy drained from her.

Katie leapt to her feet and put her arm around her grandmother's waist before she collapsed.

After guiding her back to her chair and pouring a glass of water, Katie wasn't sure what to do. Should she call the nurse? But Granna seemed okay now, and colour was coming back into her face.

"Hello," she said with a gentle smile. "I've been expecting you. I do so like visitors."

Katie breathed a little easier. The Granna she knew was back, although which century she was in was anyone's guess. "How about we go for a walk?"

"I must do my hair," said Granna. "The photographer will be here soon. We have to look our best. *Móraí* said."

Katie picked up the hairbrush and gave it to Granna, who looked at it, then up at Katie then back again.

"Shall I do it for you?" offered Katie, reaching out for it.

"One hundred strokes," murmured Granna, putting the brush against the left side of her head and sweeping past her shoulder down her arm. She didn't notice her hair was short these days and continued to groom the long locks she could see in her mind.

A wistful, faraway expression softened Granna's features, and her eyes darkened to almost black orbs. She started to hum a tune Katie hadn't heard before, pausing in her brushing.

Katie quietly got her camera out of the bag. She shot dozens of photos while moving around Granna, kneeling before her or standing to one side or the other and taking close-ups of her hands or eyes.

"Come on, girls. Jane, Grace, line up behind me," said Granna, her voice strong again. "Hurry up. Stand there now. You too, Gwenna. I do wish Sally was still with us. I miss her so. Now Katy, you stand in front, there's a one. Don't move now. Wait till you're told. Just us girls together. That's grand, it is." Straightening her shoulders, Granna posed for the photographer in her mind.

Katie took her own shots in a burst, hoping for just the right one. "Thank you," she murmured, letting go of the breath she'd been holding.

On cue, Granna relaxed and slipped into her own world again.

Now all Katie wanted to do was get home and sort through the images as soon as she could. But more importantly, she had to hunt for that portrait Granna just posed for.

Time disappeared while Katie pored through the albums she'd collected from her mother's room, but she found nothing to help her identify any of the people Granna had named. What she found instead were photos of herself and her brothers when they were young. There were too few of her mum, who had obviously taken most of them, and no sign of her father. Memories flooded back and melancholia set in. Hours passed as the tears streamed.

Katie had never had any patience for people who needed 'mental health' days. She'd believed throwing herself into her work was the answer to keeping any unwanted thoughts at bay, but here she sat, blubbering like a child, and she didn't have any idea how to stop.

She let herself be overtaken by the grief she'd shoved aside for so long. Grief for her mother who'd left so many questions unanswered. Grief for the father she never had. Grief for the woman she thought she was but was no longer, and grief for Granna, who had become such a different person to the one she'd once been.

After days of moping and useless self-diagnosis, Katie decided she should search harder for that print Granna remembered in her mind but which Katie couldn't find in any of the albums. Putting them away, she pulled out the battered leather suitcase, hardly bigger than her designer tote bag. Inside lay dozens, possibly hundreds, of loose snaps. Some were tiny square prints, most likely taken on a Brownie; others were larger squares and some postcard-size studio images. All were old.

Over the next few days, she systematically sorted and grouped the photos spread out over the dining table. Some she identified, and a few had information written on the back, but most were nameless and useless. And that elusive picture in Granna's mind was still as elusive as ever.

From the pile, two photos caught her attention.

One was of the woman Granna Katy always called Móraí, and the other was of herself – or at least her doppelgänger, since the image was more than a hundred years old. The photographs looked like they may have been taken the same day as the one in Granna's room.

In Móraí's photo, a brooch was pinned to her lapel. The image wasn't clear, but Katie suddenly remembered the box she'd thrown into the bottom of her tote bag when she was clearing her mother's room. In her despondent and befuddled state, she'd completely forgotten about it. Fishing it from the depths of her bag, she held the brooch in one hand and the print in the other as the thrill of discovery swept through her.

A quick Google search on her computer revealed the brooch to be a St Brigid's cross. Katie knew she had Irish heritage, but little else. She was fascinated to read Brigid was a patron saint of Ireland. The cross had both Christian and pagan connections and was traditionally designed to protect the home from harm and had since become a recognised symbol of Ireland. St Brigid's feast day, on the first of February, people still made these crosses the traditional way, from straw or rushes, to mark the beginning of spring.

Katie smiled. "Well, well. Fancy that. Granna said I should learn something new every day, and I just have."

Not that it helped solve the riddle of Móraí; nor did it identify the woman who looked like her. She shuddered, feeling she was looking at her own ghost.

4

ONE OF LIFE'S HIGHLIGHTS

March 1903

After Laura's outburst, Jane kept away from the regular family Sunday lunch. Apart from being busy preparing for the arrival of Madame Melba, she didn't want to give Laura the chance to take her to task and upset her again. While more than a decade and a half had gone by, her mind still filled with memories of their youth in Townsville.

Poor Aunt Maggie. After their mother died in childbirth back in Ireland, Jane and Laura's father – an angry and violent man at the best of times, and more so when drunk – forced his sister Maggie to go with him to Australia to look after his girls. When things didn't work out as expected, life took a turn for the worse and his anger knew no bounds. Jane never admitted how much he frightened her.

Even though Sally told the girls their father was dead and buried, there'd been no funeral, no headstone, and no way Jane could be certain he wouldn't come back one day. His shadow haunted her, and Aunt Maggie had slowly lost her mind after that day.

That day. Jane could not have been more than eight or nine – had she had her birthday? She couldn't remember. They didn't celebrate birthdays then. But she remembered the fight between her father and Aunt Maggie. The terrible sounds echoed in her head still. And the blood. She remembered the blood. Laura had hidden her in the bushes, but she could still hear, and later she saw Laura throwing things into the pit in the back garden. She hadn't known what but didn't dare ask. She'd often wondered since what transpired, but it had all happened in another life. One she was trying to forget.

Jane pulled her thoughts away from the past. Right now, she needed to focus on preparations for Madame Melba's imminent concerts and the costumes for the next production after she'd gone. She couldn't let her work slip behind or risk mistakes being made.

Like most of New Zealand, Jane was soon caught up in Melba fever as the fabulous opera star from Melbourne toured the country. Two days earlier, along with many hundreds of other people, Jane had gone to the railway station to meet the diva. After news of her successful concerts elsewhere, the people of Auckland held high expectations for her two concerts at the Opera House, which, despite the guinea and half-guinea ticket prices, were filling fast.

"Isn't she simply splendid," said the woman pressed against Jane in the crowd as they craned necks and stood up on their toes to get a better view. Bands played as Mayor Kidd, the town clerk and the crowds of cheering and waving spectators greeted Madame Melba as she stepped off the train.

"Yes, indeed she is," replied Jane, ogling her lavish pink dress, coat and hat.

After being presented with a bouquet by the mayor's young daughter, Madame Melba gave a charming and gracious little speech before she boarded the coach taking her to the Grand Hotel in Princes Street.

Many people continued to wave as the carriage departed, but Jane couldn't afford to waste any time. She pushed her way through the crowds and boarded the electric tram to go back to the workshop. She needed to be ready well ahead of time if she wanted to watch Madame Melba arrive as guest of honour at a performance of *If I Were King* at His Majesty's Theatre that same evening, before going backstage to help with the costumes.

She couldn't wait to tell Gwenna all about it.

"Honestly, you should have seen it," said Jane when she popped in to have a cup of tea early on Monday morning.

"People packed both sides of the arcade leading up to His Majesty's, shouting and cheering and waving as she passed, and trying to hand her flowers. Her dress was divine. Impeccably fitted, midnight blue duchesse satin, covered in sequins and beads, with a matching headdress." Jane had noticed every detail. "But she arrived late and went straight to her box. Many of the audience were already seated before she arrived and didn't see her until the second act. We had such fun behind the scenes, I can tell you. Mr Hastings, in his role as François Villon, ad-libbed a line during his dialogue to acknowledge 'the sweetest singer this side of heaven'." Jane held her hand to her heart and sighed. "He said, 'if my eyes don't dazzle me, I see her now' and raised his glass. The whole audience rose as one and applauded. So did we backstage, but quietly. Oh, Gwenna, it was such a wondrous sight."

"What a marvellous story," said Gwenna, as keen as Jane on any gossip surrounding the star.

Jane took another sip of her tea. "We could see her from the wings, sitting up in her private box. I can't wait to hear her sing."

"How tremendous. I'm so pleased for you, truly I am, but you'll never guess my news." While delighted with Jane's story, Gwenna couldn't resist telling Jane. "Hugh bought me one of the half-guinea tickets to Melba's concert for tonight." She clutched Jane's hand. "I was so thrilled I forgot to tell him off for being extravagant," which had the girls laughing.

"It'll be well worth it, I'm sure," said Jane, swallowing the last of her tea. "Which reminds me, I'd better go. There's so much still to do at the theatre."

"Will you be her dresser?" Gwenna's eyes goggled at the thought.

Jane grinned and nodded. "Well, assistant. She has her own personal dresser, but I feel so honoured to have been chosen."

Thanks to the ultra-popular comedic farces usually presented at the Opera House, the venue was commonly recognised as the Home of Melodrama, which, in Jane's opinion, had lowered their standing in the theatre world. Now, with someone of the style and distinction of Madame Melba performing, it would be world-class again and a source of envy for all its rivals.

"We can have nothing go wrong," said the manager, as he hastened around the heads of department. "I want everything checked and double-checked before they arrive." The lighting team and stagehands had the toughest tasks as their efforts were crucial to the well-ordered running of the show.

Mr McConnochie checked his fob watch. "The musicians are due in three hours for rehearsal."

Jane listened to his instructions and nodded, replying, "Yes, sir," to each statement. Since Madame Melba was bringing her entire wardrobe and her dresser, Jane would not have as much to do with the diva as she had hoped.

Nervous tension spread throughout the theatre as the time neared for the entourage to arrive. Jane knew only that a 'complete concert company' was coming, but not how many, as the newspapers had reported that Melba was travelling with many family members, including her aunt and four cousins!

When the musicians arrived, Mr Paterson, Melba's business manager, brother-in-law and accompanist all rolled into one, demanded more from them than Mr McConnochie had, if that were possible. He checked the orchestra pit met his meticulous standards then inspected the dressing rooms to ensure they were adequate for Madame Melba, who would present herself later. "I will need an additional private room to change when we return this evening. And so will our harpist, Signorina Sassoli. The rest will manage."

Not completely satisfied, Mr Paterson insisted on changes to the placement of some of the black masking flats. Fortunately, the backdrop, set at mid-stage and depicting an Italianate garden scene, met his approval. As did the pedestal, with an enormous vase of flowers, set slightly off centre-stage left and softly lit from above.

Jane received more instructions, as Mr Paterson dumped the evening suits for the orchestra before her.

"Everything is to be cleaned and pressed," he demanded. "And speak to Signorina Sassoli about her gown. It is in need of repair."

Jane held her tongue at his rude, brus
"Sir," she answered curtly. Suddenly, she
had a lot to do. The hours passed in a flash
worked to meet Mr Paterson's additional den

Meanwhile, people had begun to line
several hours prior to the eighty-thirty start, waiting to
catch a glimpse of the famous diva or the well-dressed
patrons who could afford the ticket price. Many more
hovered near the doors in the hope of hearing Melba's
voice. But they were to be disappointed on one count
– Madame had entered unseen through the stage door,
with her personal assistants, and gone straight to her
dressing room.

Jane learnt there would be three changes of costume:
the opening gown and a character costume for the
first half, and a resplendent gold-coloured gown with
dazzling jewels for the second. She carried the costume
and accessories up to the wings for Melba's first change,
which would be in a curtained-off area in the corner of
the stage during the tenor's solo.

"I will need you to help me dress Madame in her
opening gown here in the dressing room, but only you.
She will arrive in time for her cue, not one minute
earlier," said her dresser. "Polly will wait in the wings
to adjust her hair should any strands become disturbed
when she changes into her character gown."

As Jane listened to Melba doing warm-up exercises,
she felt sure the sound would carry to the moon and
back, such was the power of that voice.

Finally, preparations were complete, and the crowd was
allowed in. Released from her duties in the dressing

om, Jane stood in the wings, eagerly awaiting the start of the concert. The orchestra tuned up in the pit, while the audience talked animatedly amongst themselves.

A hush fell over the hall as lights went down and the conductor appeared, receiving polite applause as he bowed. He tapped his baton against his music stand, and the first notes filled the auditorium. As the overture reached its climax, Jane heard a rustle and looked up in time to see Madame Melba step forward. At the signal from the stage manager, the curtain opened and she stepped into the limelight to tumultuous applause. The opening strains of her aria reached high into the gods, thrilling the patrons with the rich, smooth tone of her voice.

Jane and her two helpers listened in awe while they waited for the star to exit the stage for her quick behind-the-scenes change.

"Here she comes," Jane whispered to her team, holding her shoes, petticoats, headgear, and jewels, as the diva swept gracefully towards them. Minutes later Madame returned to centre-stage in a magnificent light-as-air silk affair, which floated about her during her character performance of Ophelia's mad scene from *Hamlet*.

Jane transported the heavily beaded gown Madame had worn for the opening back to the dressing room, taking care nothing was damaged as she went, then rushed back not to miss anything. The resonance of Melba's voice and skilful interpretation of the high trills was exhilarating. Peeking through from the wings, Jane watched the concertgoers, many of whom sat transfixed with opera glasses against their eyes for an entire aria. Goose pimples prickled her skin.

The interval was busy, helping Madame into the most exquisite gown Jane had ever seen. The rich fabric and ingenious design were especially flattering. Jane noted the construction and shape, making mental notes for her own work.

The second half sped by far too quickly, leaving everyone in awe and uplifted by her performance.

Disappointed when the concert finished, Jane watched as Madame Melba made her way back to her dressing room.

"Thank you, girls," said Jane to her team. "You've done your tasks even better than usual tonight and I'm very proud of you. I hope you enjoyed it as much as I did."

"We did that, Miss," replied one of the dressers. "I never knew such high notes existed afore. It were beautiful."

"Remember," said Jane as they gathered their coats, eager to tell their friends and family all about it, "we have to do it all again on Thursday. Now go home and get some rest. There's little to do tomorrow except some repair work. But then we've another season to prepare for, with Mr Musgrove coming up in May and Mr Rickards in June."

The following day, over a cup of tea with Gwenna, Jane read aloud from *The New Zealand Herald*. "Listen to this. The writer says the girl-harpist, Signorina Sassoli, impressed him with her gentle treatment of the sublime instrument, and the visiting flautist excelled during the cadenza from *Lucia*, but Madame Melba herself reached 'the hearers' hearts and left them spellbound'."

"All sounds a bit of a puffed-up way to say it, but he's right. The musicians were excellent, but she was out of this world," said Gwenna. "It's something we'll never forget."

"They've listed the whole programme but what it hasn't captured was the joy," said Jane. "He hasn't even attempted to describe the way bouquets were thrown, men whistled or how the applause deafened us all. Nor that each time they clapped, the lady curtsied to the crowd and how she acknowledged her musicians. She even introduced her harpist and threw hand kisses to every section of the house. She was amazing."

"She was superb," agreed Gwenna.

Jane hoped the second concert with its new repertoire, in three days' time, would go as smoothly. But whatever happened, the visit of Madame Melba would undoubtedly be one of the highlights of her career and, as Gwenna had said, something she would never forget.

In her spacious workroom, Jane checked her notes for the name of the forthcoming production, not that it mattered, nor what happened on stage. Her passion was for the way the fabric moved and its effect on the audience as the performers played their part. She had free rein with her designs as long as they suited the theme and complemented that of the overseas stars.

Jane sighed.

The one irritant in her otherwise fulfilled, if frantically busy life, was that so many of the stars – and lesser stars, if she was honest – brought their own costumes with them. Many times, Jane could have designed more flattering garments if she had been given the chance. Except those of Madame Melba's, of course. The diva's gowns were dazzling, with no expense spared. Jane could only dream of having the chance to design and make costumes like hers one day, but the more designs she added to her Bernadette range, the more she sold, which made up for any disappointments.

"Good mornin', Mith Jane," lisped gap-toothed Aggie, interrupting Jane's train of thought. Her best bead worker was always the first of the seamstresses to arrive.

"Good morning, Aggie. I've been meaning to tell you how pleased I am with the beading on that purple and pink concoction. You excelled yourself. We'll be able to reuse them, thanks to your cunning overlay."

Aggie blushed. "'Tweren't much, Mith Jane. It were a way to thave on the colourth that were gettin' low."

They continued talking about the supplies in need of replenishing, until half a dozen other workers arrived and took their places behind the treadle machines, the piecing table or at the accessory bench, and began work for the day. Within minutes, the place hummed with the chatter of voices and the whir and clatter of the sewing machines, and Jane's moments of quiet and retrospection were over.

"Miss Jane? Excuse me."

Jane turned to see Cecil, the odd-job boy, hovering. "You're early today, Cecil. Have you a message for me?"

Cecil usually appeared towards the end of the day when it came time to carry the finished costumes down to the changing rooms or when a new textile delivery arrived.

He shook his head. "No, Miss. Just ... um ... could I do summat up here for you today?" He hung his head, letting his mop of fair hair flop forward to hide his eyes, and knotted his fingers. Jane knew some of the burlier stagehands gave him a hard time for his gangly, effeminate ways, like a newborn foal finding its feet. Jane had taken pity on him more than once. Poor boy.

"Give me a few minutes and let me see what I can find. Meanwhile, grab a broom and sweep up any scraps and threads lying around and then sort the offcuts into colours."

A puppy-love grin lit up his eyes and he shuffled away to do her bidding.

"You're too soft with him," growled Paul, watching the boy go. "He needs to toughen up."

"I'm surprised at you, Paul. You, of all people, should understand what it's like to be picked on. But if you're unhappy here, I'm sure I could teach someone else to do the cutting."

Paul huffed and grunted, but they both knew his position was safe. He, too, had a great skill. He understood her sketches and could cut the cloth to fall precisely the way she wanted. In any case, she'd had the massive cutting table, which dominated the centre of the room, lowered specially to fit his stature. He pulled his waistcoat into place and smoothed his moustache, before picking up the shears, and began deftly cutting the silky fabric stretched out before him.

As usual, Jane's day passed in a blink as she checked the order of the upcoming season, that each show had its full costume list and the outfits were completed in the right time frame. She worked beside her girls in turn, overseeing every step of the garment's construction, conscious of every detail. In another area, costumes from previous shows were repaired or remodelled for another use. Around her, the long room buzzed. With a performance most nights of the week, plus a matinee, there could be little let-up in activity.

Cecil appeared at her shoulder again. "Mr Sir wants to know when 'e can 'ave the costumes." Cecil called all the directors, stage managers and production managers 'Mr Sir' so he didn't have to remember their name or actual position. If Jane didn't have the programme before her for every show, she would struggle too. Some of the personnel changed faster than the clothing. She was thankful for the regular appearance of Mr Musgrove, Mr Rickards and Mr Pollard and their troupes. At least she recognised a friendly face when she saw one.

Jane checked the watch pinned to her blouse. It was later than she thought. The seamstresses would be going home soon, and the dressers would arrive. She would have to stay for tonight's dress rehearsal to show them what needed to be done.

"Tell him half an hour, while I double-check everything. Then scoot back here and start taking them down for me. I'll be along shortly."

Downstairs, in the labyrinth of dark, narrow corridors, overcrowded dressing-rooms and packed storage areas hidden beneath the stage, resided a different type of misfit from those upstairs who worked the daylight hours.

Jane loved her sunny workroom and felt sorry for most of the cast and backstage crew who rarely saw the light of day. They worked and played in the dark hours, with only the cheerless yellow glow of the electric lamps – while the generator worked. Although superior to the gaslights and candle lanterns of not so long ago, the incandescent bulbs still cast eerie shadows, which only served to deepen the obscurity of those who wished to hide their true selves.

Entering the chorus girls' changing room, she squeezed between the bodies in various stages of undress to guide Cecil to the wardrobe rack.

"Hello, Cecil," called out several of the girls.

A few whistled.

"Can you do me a favour," said one.

"And me," added another.

Cecil always obliged. He much preferred being among the feathers and powders with the girls than with the backstage crew who teased him mercilessly for what they called his foppish ways.

After all the garments had been delivered to the various dressing rooms – in the opposite order to stardom, since the chorus fended for themselves, while the stars had their own personal dressers – Jane returned to help whoever needed assistance.

Jane enjoyed seeing her designs come to life. The chatter and banter never stopped as she slipped straps into place, tightened corsets and lifted dresses over heads. Few spoke to her directly, treating her as if she wasn't there. The quiet mouse who delivered the costumes, which turned them into someone else for a few magical hours didn't exist in their world of paint and make-believe, but she didn't mind.

Jane liked to live in her interior world with her thoughts. Talking was overrated, in her opinion.

With not a single jot of desire to be one with the women on stage, Jane's pulse lifted with the noise and shabby glamour of the dressing rooms. Mirrors gleamed, reflecting the light bulbs surrounding them as the minor players fussed with hairstyles, painted their faces with masterly skill and left the dresser-tops cluttered with their paraphernalia.

Much had changed since Jane's earlier days when the set and make-up were far more basic due to the dim lighting. In those days, the actors simply needed to dab powder on their faces and add a touch or more of rouge to look like parodies of themselves. These days, the latest Leichner greasepaint required a lot more skill. Layers of colour and shading were needed to recreate the natural shadows and highlights the harsher lighting stripped away. But she could not complain. Her budget was larger than ever and the fabrics more luxurious.

When all the costumes were fitted and the chorus lined up in a row ready for the call, Jane's satisfaction reached its peak.

"Thank you, Miss Jane," whispered the smallest and youngest.

Jane smiled at her in return as the girls disappeared along the corridor to fidget and fuss in the wings, waiting for the exact moment of their entrance.

Taking a seat in the third row of the near-empty auditorium occupied only by the production team, Jane took notes as the dress rehearsal unfolded. While she concentrated on how each costume performed, the music from the orchestra set her foot tapping in time with the beat, but she couldn't have told anyone about the storyline or the funny parts making others laugh.

Her job over for the night, Jane climbed the stairs to her workroom, checked the list for the next day and headed home. With the buzz from the start of a show flowing through her, she wanted to let it all loose in her sketches.

5

CERTAINTIES AND UNCERTAINTIES

June 2018

Sorting the photos from her mother's place had awoken something in Katie she'd never thought possible – an interest in the past. She had fallen in love with the softer filters and warm sepia tones of the old photographs and studio portraits. It added a sense of romance and nostalgia to the images, which some of the harsher black-and-white prints didn't have. She'd even experimented with a sepia filter on some of her own shots of Granna and had been impressed.

She spent hours going through them and downloaded an app for scanning old prints and had begun arranging an album. If only she could match a few more names to them, she could start drawing a family tree.

She knew she should be searching for work rather than playing with photos. Six weeks after she'd chucked her job, and eating into her savings, she couldn't shake the feeling of despondency and uselessness to do anything about it. She had submitted a small selection of her efforts to a few of the stock photo sites. Some had rejected her submissions, but a couple of others had accepted them, and her first payment had more than covered the cost of buying Photoshop. But it wouldn't be enough on its own.

Her mobile rang as she began to update her portfolio and submit a few more images to some other sites.

"Hi, Katie. How are you doing?"

"Viv. How nice to hear from you. I'm doing OK."

Viv, the manager from a rival marketing agency Katie had dealt with, had been at the office when Katie lost control. Katie was still embarrassed at how she'd behaved and still didn't understand the unexpected feeling of panic that had come over her. She never shouted at work, but she had that day, and Viv had seen it all.

"I've been thinking about you lately," continued Viv. "Would you like to catch up for a coffee sometime?"

Katie liked Viv, but they weren't friends in the true sense, and meeting for coffee wasn't a natural thing for them.

"What's on your mind?" Katie was hesitant to talk with anyone who knew her in her previous role. She didn't need people making judgements, and she knew Viv would.

"Things have gone to the pack at your old firm. The new woman isn't as good as you were, and I've no idea what to do about it." Viv paused. "I'm flat out here at the agency. You wouldn't be interested in a short contract, by any chance?"

"What, working for them?" Katie could hear her voice rising in alarm at the thought.

"Heavens, no. I wouldn't do that to you. No, I've received a web enquiry from a new client to help him advertise his product, and I don't have anyone to spare at the moment."

Katie remained silent. She hadn't realised how stressed she'd become until she'd quit, and while she didn't think she wanted to get back into marketing, a short contract might help her make up her mind and ease her financial problems. And get her involved with people again. Even she could see hiding herself away wasn't healthy. The thought scared her. She'd become so unsociable in the past weeks, making unconvincing excuses, that she was at risk of never going out again. "Why me?" she asked.

"Because product launches were your strength, and he wants to launch a product. Actually, all he really wants is help setting up a website and getting some photos taken. He's small scale at the moment. It shouldn't be too demanding."

Katie breathed an internal sigh of relief. That she could manage. "OK. I'll do it."

After deciding where to meet, Katie sat curled on the couch, smartphone in hand, watching the play of light on the ocean as the clouds rolling by temporarily hid the sun. For the first time, a plan started to form.

Rediscovering her love of photography was one of the more positive things to come from her self-imposed seclusion. She had to admit she had taken some remarkable shots, and the more she took, the better they were. When she wasn't sorting old photos, she was online picking up tips to improve her own attempts and how to edit them better. Viv's offer had given her an idea.

Katie arrived at the café in a far better frame of mind than she had been in for a long time. They ordered coffee and chatted about incidentals before Viv handed her a contract. Scanning it briefly while Viv outlined the basics, Katie nodded. Three months. Good terms. No ties. Katie had barely finished signing the forms when a man in his mid-thirties walked in, obviously looking for someone. Viv rose to meet him, introduced herself and led him towards their table.

"I thought we'd meet in a more informal setting to start with," she explained, "which is why I asked you both to come here today. Jared, I'd like you to meet Katie Anderson. Katie will be your consultant and will work directly with you. Katie, Jared Price."

The two shook hands, holding for a second or two longer than usual as they assessed one another.

Katie looked up at the curly-haired man wearing glasses and sporting a short beard and liked what she saw. "A pleasure to meet you."

"Likewise." His smile reached his eyes.

Katie thought they'd get on well together.

He shrugged out of his jacket and hung it neatly on the back of his chair. Viv ordered more coffee as Katie and Jared began talking about the initial concept.

"I'm a qualified pastry chef," Jared explained. "The bakery I work for makes the staples which sell well, with a few specialities on the side. I'd like to put my skills to better use, but I don't have an outlet to show what I can do."

They discovered Jared had begun his career in a hotel restaurant as a junior beside their executive pastry chef, someone with fixed ideas. He had watched and learnt and after a few years was promoted up the ranks, but they were never going to let him experiment, so he moved on. His second role allowed him greater freedoms, which he needed at the time, but Jared couldn't tolerate the bad-tempered chef's abuse. His current role limited his options.

"I'd like to branch out on my own but don't know where to begin. I first learnt to bake at home, I learnt to perfect pastry at my first job, and I learnt sugar-boiling from my grandfather. I want to put it all together, which is why I'm here. Can you help me?"

"We most certainly can," said Katie, delighted with the possibilities.

After their initial meeting, Viv said Katie could use the conference room at the office. Until she sorted out somewhere of her own, she had nowhere else to go. She wouldn't take him back to her apartment.

"So, Jared, do you have any ideas or specifics you want included?" asked Katie two days later when they met to establish a framework for the job.

"None. I'm in your hands. I can't start off too big or too quickly, and any orders I receive will have to be booked in advance. I can only do this in my spare time until – or if – all this takes off."

"Is that what you want to do – take orders? Orders for what, exactly? Or do you want to offer your services to another restaurant? Or create a step-by-step cooking class, or do in-house dining experiences? You need to set your goals before we go ahead with anything."

Jared just looked at her blankly for a few moments. "This is more complicated than I thought. I don't have any idea, if I'm honest." He took his glasses off and polished them. Without them, his eyes appeared darker, and gold flecks heightened their rich hazel colour. "Initially, I thought I'd take orders for special occasions."

Katie blinked and dragged her gaze away as Jared put his glasses back on. "Like wedding cakes and birthday cakes, you mean?" *He's disconcertingly good-looking*, thought Katie, trying to keep her mind on her role. Out of the corner of her eye, she could see Viv watching them intently through the glass walls. Her expression changed in an instant when she saw Katie looking, and she grinned and gave her the thumbs up.

"Yes, and no. I can do both, but there are probably hundreds of bakers offering a similar sort of service."

She looked up from her notetaking. "Have you checked out the competition?"

Jared shook his head.

"Well, I suggest you do that first of all, so you can gauge what you're up against."

"I think ..." He lifted his head so they were eye to eye.

A shiver travelled down Katie's back. She ran her fingers through her hair and patted it back into place.

"You've a real flair for all this," continued Jared. "You're making me reassess what I'm trying to do. Sounds like I'll need to give it a lot more consideration."

Katie smiled. "Only trying to help."

Deep in thought, he drummed his fingers on the desktop but just as Katie was beginning to find it annoying, he stopped.

"I come from a family of confectioners going back generations, but handmade sweets were almost a thing of the past by the time my grandfather entered the business. I just love the old-fashioned lolly shop idea – not that I want to sell lollies – but I'd like to create that kind of feel. Nostalgic, romantic, something special and exciting."

Katie was beginning to like this guy more and more as they talked. Not everyone appreciated things from the past – not so long ago, she hadn't either. She liked the fact that they had something in common.

"OK, it's a strong start, but who's your target market?"

He came near to laughing out loud but reduced it to a chuckle at the last minute. "People who eat desserts?" One eyebrow curled upwards with a question mark, giving him an impish appearance.

Katie grinned at his attempt at humour. "You've a fairly wide market then."

He returned her grin with a chortle. "True, but I suppose I'm thinking more of the busy mum who wants to spoil someone, or the young career woman needing to impress someone with something you can't buy in the local supermarket."

"In that case, the best idea would be to start with a website with photos of the sort of work you can do or are offering. We'll then link it to a Facebook page and a LinkedIn business profile." Katie kept talking while she jotted down notes for herself. "We'll create a booking page, but you will have to respond to queries pro-actively or people will go elsewhere."

When Katie looked up from her notes, she caught Jared studying her and instantly dropped her gaze. She tucked her hair back behind one ear. "Now, about the photographs," she hurried on. "Do you have any?"

"Nothing worthwhile. These are just some casual shots I've taken on my phone." He pulled the phone from his pocket and brought up a few examples.

"Send me these three," pointed Katie, after scanning the selection. "I might be able to fiddle something with those for some of the pages, but you need ones with exact examples of what people can order. You can expand the range as orders come in. Don't do too much too soon."

"Everything I make is fresh. It'll go to waste if I make too much all at once, but I ..."

Alarm bells rang with Katie as Jared talked. "You do have a food safety plan, or access to a licensed kitchen to make these things, don't you? You can't risk selling food from a home-based facility. I'm sure you need inspections and suchlike."

Jared paled as he realised his mistake. "Of course! I hadn't given it a thought. How silly of me. I should know better. I've read the rules."

"I think you'd better get that aspect sorted first. Meanwhile, I'll start looking for someone to build your website."

No sooner had he gone than Katie remembered she hadn't talked to him about her ideas for the pictures.

Viv popped her head through the doorway. "Dishy guy. How'd it go?"

"Quite well, I think, although he's not thought it through enough. There are gaps." Katie picked up her pen and notebook and slipped them into her carry case.

"I'm sure you'll help fill the gaps. Did he ask you out?"

Katie stopped midway through wrapping up the cable from her computer, momentarily surprised. Concerned she might give herself away, she ducked her head to avoid Viv's eyes, put the cords away and reached for her laptop. "No, Viv. And I wouldn't go, even if he did. He's a client."

"Only for three months," she grinned.

Katie returned the grin. Three months wasn't so long. "I'd be more interested in taking his photo. He'd be great as the face to sell a product, with or without his desserts."

"I'd do both. Imagine: Sunset over the water, scrumptious dessert on the table, glinting wine glasses – and a hunk. Sounds like a great combination to me."

"Viv!"

But the image wouldn't leave Katie's mind.

6

AVOIDING THE TRUTH

April 1903

The bell tinkled as Jane stepped through the door of Miss Brigid's lace boutique.

"Jane, how lovely to see you," said Sally, coming out of the downstairs room. Jane remembered it as the elegant showroom where Brigid entertained the wealthy ladies who came to buy handmade lace. "We don't usually see you on a Saturday. What brings you here, lass?" she asked, giving the girl a hug.

"I felt I owed Brigid an apology for my behaviour last time, and for not coming around lately."

Jane often marvelled at how strong the friendship between Sally and Brigid had become. They were, or had been, so different on the ship to Australia. In those days, Sally had been a brash and brazen barmaid; Brigid, the shy and gentle servant, was a caring soul, for all her tender age of eighteen.

"Whisht, girl, Breeda understands."

"She's so kind-hearted, we sometimes take her too much for granted. Anyway, I can't stay long. I'm expected back at the theatre. Is Grace here?"

While Jane loved all her diverse and unusual family, she and Grace were particularly close.

"Sorry, lass, no. She's away having piano lessons."

Disappointment lodged in Jane's stomach but she said nothing; instead she focused on what else had been nagging her recently. She looked up the stairs.

"Does Brigid do much lacework these days?"

"Not much. Not like she used to. We always had stock on hand when we needed it once. These days she only makes something for a specific order and then she fusses and frets, saying she's losing the knack. What happened to our brave Breeda to whom we all turned?"

"Maybe that's the problem. Maybe she's forgotten how to be Brigid, instead of mother, friend, carer and so much more to everyone else."

Sally nodded at Jane's words. "She won't tell you, but Phillip Harrison-Browne has written. He invited her to Brisbane to do lacemaking demonstrations, like she used to. He says he wants to promote the handmade lace aspect again, especially for high-end evening wear, but she refuses."

Jane shook her head sadly, remembering the strange, often difficult Mr Harrison-Browne who owned and ran the largest department store in Brisbane. He'd been Brigid's arch-rival once. Giving much with one hand and taking more with the other. He'd been furious when his mother outwitted him and set Brigid up in charge of Miss Brigid's instead. Fortunately, they eventually reached an amicable arrangement that suited them both.

"Why?" asked Jane.

"She wrote back saying she has a responsibility to her family to stay in Auckland. But I think she should go. It would do her the world of good and maybe give her some ideas for this place too. I've done everything I can. Would she listen to you?"

Jane fondly remembered their visit to Beatrice Browne, Phillip's mother, when Lilly was just a toddler. They'd stayed in a grand house on the hill where Mrs Browne had fussed over them while Brigid gave demonstrations and made lace for the department store. Their stay of several months had been successful in more ways than one. Brigid's lace was in high demand, but that was in the days when her husband was still alive.

"No. I don't think she'd listen to me either," replied Jane, wondering if she'd ever given Brigid advice. "But what a shame. All that talent going to waste."

In the seventeen years since Brigid had brought them all to Auckland, fashions and business had evolved. With the advent of ready-made dresses and machine-made lace, clothing had become more readily – and cheaply – available to the masses. New stores had opened to meet the demand, and 'bespoke' slid from favour as more and more households bought the latest Singer sewing machines and made their own clothes.

The fine silks and velvets Brigid's husband used to source from foreign lands had disappeared from the shelves, and only a few were prepared to pay the higher price Brigid's specialty lace demanded. But instead of diversifying at Miss Brigid's, she seemed to be giving up without a fight and allowing it to shrink. Something Tommy would never have allowed, and Jane found too sad for words.

"We need to think of something to encourage her to go," said Jane. "We can't just let her accept defeat."

"I agree, lass. Let's put our heads together and see what we can do – but we'd better go up now." Sally raised her voice and called up the stairs. "Breeda? Look who's come to visit us, Breeda."

The two women went upstairs to find Brigid teaching young Lilly to make lace. She sometimes felt sorry for the girls who lived in a house of sadness. Leastways, Jane sensed much of the old joy had gone, even though Brigid and Sally often laughed. Would nothing bring back the light when Miss Brigid's was the talk of the town and Tommy was alive? But then, who was she to judge their life, living, as she did, in the shadows?

"Jane. It's good to see you," said Brigid, getting up to hug her. "And I've got something for you. I've been keeping it safe." Brigid went to the dresser and picked up an envelope which she handed to Jane. "Go on. Open it."

Jane opened the unsealed flap and pulled out a photograph. A gentle smile creased her face. "You look so lovely in that dress. You should wear it more often."

"I've nowhere much to wear it."

"In which case, you should get out more," said Jane, seizing an unexpected opportunity. "If more people could see your handiwork, you'd be inundated with orders."

Brigid dismissed Jane's comment with a shrug. "I'm happy enough with things as they are. Now tell me what you've been up to."

Soon the teacups were rattling, and the women sat chattering over the small incidentals of life. The tour by Madame Melba was still the talk of the town, but months could pass with little change in Jane's life. Hidden behind the walls of the theatre, a different life cycle prevailed, one which Jane revelled in, but she enjoyed these talks with the people she loved most, and which took her out of her self-enclosed world. The two girls were always a source of wonder and frequently the topic of their conversation.

"I can't begin to comprehend where all the talent comes from," said Brigid. "Grace is doing so well at her piano lessons, I just wish we had something better for her to practise on. And Lilly loves singing in the choir." Brigid lowered her voice. "I'm thinking she should have extra lessons."

On hearing her name, Lilly, as usual, became the centre of attention. "What are you saying about me, Mam?"

"Never you mind, Lilly. Would you like to sing for Jane?"

"Oh, yes. I'd like that." She rummaged through some music and found what she was looking for. "I'll sing 'The Last Rose of Summer' from a poem by Thomas Moore, and music by Sir John Stevenson," announced Lilly, as her tutor had coached her.

Jane listened while Lilly sang the charming ballad. She did indeed have a fine voice, but Jane would not be encouraging her, in case she wanted to learn more about the theatre. There were too many unsavoury characters who came and went, and who took advantage of the innocent, as she knew only too well.

"Look, Jane. Look what I've done," said Lilly, when she'd finished singing.

Brigid smiled the beaming smile of a proud mother as Lilly showed Jane her latest drawings.

"They're very pretty, dear," said Jane, instinctively knowing Lilly didn't quite have the flair needed to do what she herself did.

"Can I be a designer like you when I grow up?"

"You can be anything you want if you put your mind to it, my love," said Jane. "Doesn't Laura always tell you that?"

The girl nodded. "I want to be just like you and Laura."

The women laughed. Jane and Laura were nothing alike.

After a quick hug with Lilly, Jane checked the clock, hoping she could dawdle long enough for Grace to return, but she'd run out of time.

As Jane walked up the newly asphalted Queen Street, ignoring the clattering of the electric tram as it sped past, she realised one of the reasons she'd gone to see Brigid was to seek her advice.

But she had changed her mind. She didn't want to worry Brigid.

For some time, Jane had been convinced she was being followed – yet whenever she turned around to check, no one was there.

7

LIFE-CHANGING MOMENTS

Later in June 2018

At the time, Katie had no idea how prophetic Viv's words about dating Jared would be.

"Katie, would you come with me to a restaurant tonight?" asked Jared a few days later. "I'd like to show you something."

Being a week night, could she consider it a date? He'd not indicated the invitation meant anything other than a business meeting, and she did have things to discuss with him. They hadn't had a chance to get together since their first meeting in Viv's office and time was passing.

"Sounds interesting. Where?"

He told her the place he had in mind and she baulked. "Can you afford that? I certainly can't."

"Don't worry. I've organised something with the chef. It'll only cost a bottle of wine."

Katie was still doubtful. A glass of wine alone was an exorbitant price, but she finally agreed.

At the appointed time, Jared met her in the foyer of the hotel and escorted her into the lift. Under her tailored wool coat, she was dressed in well-cut black trousers and a black and gold tunic top, both of which set off her height and colouring to perfection. She was a bit surprised to see Jared had on well-cut jeans with an open-neck shirt and had turned up the collar of his jacket. The look would be far too casual on someone else at such a place, but he pulled it off with a charm he wasn't aware he had. He was far too self-effacing to have noticed, but Katie decided he could easily model for some fashion magazine, he was so naturally good-looking. And his face wore an artless, nearly there smile all the time. A comforting warmth engulfed her, and she looked forward to spending the evening with him.

Stepping out into a barren hallway, like a hotel corridor, Katie instantly felt uncomfortable. "Where on earth are we going?"

"You'll see," he grinned and, after guiding her a few metres, opened a door. Almost in total darkness, the empty room looked like a private dining room. At the far end, she could see a small, well-lit balcony with views of the harbour and a table set for two. He led her through to find the patio heater turned up full to combat the chilly air. The night was clear, and a shaft of soft moonlight glinted on the dark water.

A few moments later, a man in a black suit brought them a bottle of wine in an ice bucket and, after a quick word with Jared, left again, only to return with a tray of what looked like confectionery and a capacious carry bag, before disappearing.

"What's all this about, Jared?"

"You'll see," he repeated.

Jared poured the wine, a perfectly chilled late harvest Riesling.

"To the future."

They clinked glasses and took a sip. The wine was sweeter than her normal choice but with a hint of citrus; Katie enjoyed the lingering taste. "This is all a bit weird," she said, putting her glass on the table and gathering her bag. "You'd better hurry up and tell me what's going on or I'm leaving."

"Please don't. Not yet. There's nothing untoward going on, I promise. But after you told me to sort out my goals and my market, as well as a decent kitchen to make my goods in, I've been doing a lot of thinking. I'd like your opinion, and I knew you wouldn't come to my place, so I pulled in a favour from a friend."

"Well, you're right on that score. But what's all this?" She vaguely waved her hand around.

Jared explained he'd once worked with the pastry chef at the hotel, and when Jared had outlined his idea and his difficulties, his former colleague friend had suggested this spot because they only used it for corporate functions.

She still didn't understand how he'd pulled it off. Perks like this didn't come easily.

"I made these," he said, transferring a couple of the confectionery morsels onto a plate. "They're miniature versions of some of the desserts I make."

Katie looked at the small oblongs which appeared to be over-sized chocolates.

He handed her a cake fork. "Taste one and tell me what you think."

Katie chose a chocolate and cherry concoction. The filling just melted in her mouth. "Ooh, yum. How do you do it?"

"Now that would be telling. But try it with a bit of this." He lifted the lid on a plastic storage container and withdrew some spun sugar strands and fine honeycomb-style shards. Carefully pulling away a few filaments, he added them to her plate. Then from another container he added a tiny taste of coulis.

The second half of the tasting morsel was even more delicious. She was hooked.

As the moon rose higher, they shared the rest of the tasting tray, experimenting with varying quantities and thickness of spun sugar, coulis, chocolate and other ingenious toppings, trying to decide which combinations worked the best. The contents of the wine bottle disappeared to match the experience.

When the dessert bites were all gone, Katie sat back with a sigh of contentment and raised what little was left in her glass. "Congratulations, Jared. They were amazing. I've never tasted anything like it before. So, there's our challenge. How to show off your food best when we can't capture taste."

"These are easy to make and some of them keep well. I could offer a few free samples, or add free samples with each order. Would that work?"

"It certainly wouldn't hinder, and it's a tempting option. I … well, I …" Katie felt uncommonly nervous about putting forward her ideas. "Would you object if I took the pictures? I'm thinking of branching out into product display photography. Maybe you and I could be test cases for each other? I'd have more control over the process that way, too."

Jared's face lit up and he extended his hand. "Done," he said, as he held her hand. A quiver ran up her arm at his touch, and she opened her eyes in surprise at catching a similar expression on his face. They continued to gaze at each other for a few seconds longer.

"Yes, well, that's all right then," said Katie, pulling back her hand.

"Does that mean we'll have to spend more time together?" He sounded far too gleeful for comfort.

Katie could only nod as she assessed the consequences of what she had suggested. He didn't have a kitchen, and she didn't have a studio or the right equipment. What sort of business team would they make if they couldn't come up with the basics?

"We've still got a lot of details to work out," she floundered, "and there's the website design to consider, but we could manage our time, either in short bursts to limit our commitment, or do longer sessions to avoid wasting time."

Katie felt she was rambling but Jared seemed fully engaged.

"I'd like to spend more time with you. Working out the details, I mean. I finish at two pm so would have the rest of the day and evening available any time it suits you. You might be interested in some of my background around confectionery and pastry making. Would any of it be useful for the website?"

Their conversation continued, tossing ideas back and forth, until the man in the black suit reappeared and gave the signal to leave.

"Are you driving?" asked Jared.

"No, I came by taxi. I wasn't sure how much drinking would be involved."

"In that case, would you let me escort you home?"

His offer was surprising, charming and quaint, all at once, and Katie didn't want the evening to end just yet either. Arguments against letting a relative stranger know where she lived rattled around her brain too, but she ignored them. The night was pleasant if a little cool, and she had an idea.

"That would be nice. Thank you, Jared. There's a bar close by. We could share a nightcap if you like."

His grin grew. "Yes. I'd like that, very much."

As the taxi weaved its way around the roadworks along the waterfront, Jared stared out the window at the lights and activity. "I love this city. I'm a fourth-generation born-and-bred Aucklander, and I love knowing my grandparents and great-grandparents walked these same streets and entered the same buildings I do."

He pointed to the ferry terminal. "That was built around 1912 and the Town Hall at the other end of Queen Street was finished about a year earlier. What an amazing street Queen Street must have been in those days. We've lost a lot, though – Victoria Arcade, His Majesty's. Too much. I wish their old shops were still there, but they got swallowed up into bigger stores a long time ago."

Katie had no knowledge of architecture and pretty much took the things around her for granted. She was still coming to terms with Jared's fascination with history. Most of the buildings she had worked in were uninspiring, modern, glass, designed-for-business structures with little to distinguish them.

"I've never given it much thought," she said. "I remember Old Government House as a ramshackle old building when I was there. That's part of the university now, isn't it. But the old clock tower's rather grand."

"My great-grandmother could tell a story about Government House," he said, "but the clock tower wasn't built until the 1920s."

She laughed, not quite able to believe he could rattle off such information.

The taxi ride was short, and Jared paid the bill as she clambered out and pointed to the bar.

Once they were settled, she with a brandy and he with a bourbon, Katie said, "I'm a fourth-generation Aucklander too, so go on. Tell me what other places I should know about that my ancestors would have been familiar with. Don't tell me all this was here back then?" She waved her hand in the general direction of the water, the wharves and the Basin.

"Not like that anyway. But they reclaimed this area a long time ago for industrial purposes. Have you ever had a bite to eat at Elliott Stables, or gone to the Civic Theatre or shopped in Smith & Caughey?"

"Yes, to all three."

"The oldest is Smith & Caughey, dating back to the 1880s, believe it or not. It's expanded since then, but it's on the same spot. Elliott Stables date back to about 1910 and were the stables to the hotel on that corner, but the Civic was a late arrival, coming at the end of the twenties. But let's not talk about old buildings and ancient people, I'd prefer to talk about new ventures and new people."

"Such as?"

"You."

8

THE TENUOUS JOYS OF LIFE

September 1903

Jane enjoyed her morning walk to work. Particularly when the spring weather arrived after the long, wet winter days, and on a day like today, when the wind dropped and the sun shone warmly. But, at times, she still had an uncomfortable sense of being followed. The suspicion had persisted since shortly after the tour by Madame Melba six months earlier. She just couldn't explain why. She'd not seen anyone, and no one had approached her. Nor had she received any messages. After a time, she'd begun to think she'd imagined it all. The steady rhythm of life in the workroom continued unabated, and she forgot her worries.

Energised by the lustrous rays of light filtering in, Jane decided to catch up on some running repairs and make a start on a new set of costumes.

"Mornin', Miss Jane."

Young Charlie Price's visit came as a surprise. He'd often be found on a Saturday hanging around the theatre doors at the start of a matinee, touting Gwenna's Superior Sweet Treats. He often did a good trade, too, earning himself pocket money in the process, but this was an unusual time to see him.

"Charlie? Whatever are you doing here at this time?"

"I wanted to show you what I've done."

He opened the bag thrown across his shoulder and pulled out a jar of lollies. "Have one," he said, presenting the jar to her. His eyes never left her face as Jane selected one and popped it in her mouth.

"Hmmm. Nysh," she mumbled around the lolly.

Jane remembered the day she had first met his sister, Gwenna. She had gone to view the paintings at the Royal Exhibition two years earlier to see what the latest fashions from overseas looked like. Gwenna had been helping with the refreshments. With only three years separating them in age, and neither of them considered a 'society lady', they'd spent much of the evening chatting, and soon become friends.

Gwenna had joined the Arts Society in an effort to establish herself as a businesswoman of note – despite her youth and circumstances. Unfortunately, while accepted within the society, Gwenna was rarely invited anywhere else. Her poor Welsh background did little to endear her to the English upper-class ladies, despite, or maybe because of, her notoriety after the incident during the royal visit.

Her stepmother Bethan had mistakenly stepped out in front of the royal carriage, bringing the parade to a halt, and her half-brother Charlie had the temerity to speak to the duchess and offer her some handmade lollies. It turned out well in the end. Although a critical article had been printed in the newspaper at the time, Gwenna's innate good nature and excellent sweets secured her a place at Arts Society meetings and exhibitions.

Under normal circumstances, the two women might never have met – living in different parts of Auckland, attending different churches and with siblings at different schools – but fate often extends a welcoming hand, as it had done at the exhibition. Since then, the families had become close. Lilly and Charlie were the same age and teased each other unmercifully, while Grace idolised him and followed him around in awe.

Charlie shuffled his feet waiting for Jane to speak. "Well? What do you think?" he prompted.

"It's very tasty, but what're you trying to say, Charlie?"

Jane looked more closely at the sweets in the jar, noticing some misshapen ones, and ones with mixed colours. Broken pieces filled the gaps.

"I made them," he said with pride. "This is my first batch. Well, the first batch Gwenna would let me share." His smile stretched as wide as he could make it and his eyes sparkled.

Jane expected him to burst into a jig with excitement. "Well, congratulations, young man. Gwenna must be happy to have a helping hand."

"I'm not so sure. She wants to know who will do the selling if we're all making lollies. I told her not to fret, I'd sell them in the thousands if only she'd let me bring my tray to the evening shows at all the theatres." He laughed at his own bravado, but Jane wouldn't have been surprised at anything young Charlie came up with. Gwenna always said he was full of bright ideas, some of which paid off.

"Aren't you a little young? You can't be out at night. You've still got school."

"Aw, Miss Jane. You're as bad as Gwenna. She'd always said she wouldn't teach me how to boil sugar until I was twelve, but Hugh persuaded her to let me try. And see, I can. So why can't I expand? I could make my own range ... and ..." He stopped mid-sentence. "But she won't let me." He sounded so downhearted Jane almost burst out laughing.

"Small steps, Charlie. Gwenna only wants the best for you. Finish school first, polish your sweet-making skills, then you can think about expanding. How's the shop doing?"

He shrugged. "Seems fine to me. Mam says they're rushed off their feet most days, but I'm not allowed to work there."

She put her hand on his shoulder. "You're a great lad, Charlie. You do more than your share of helping out, and you do a great job of peddling your packets of lollies. And one day soon you'll be the best trader in town. Now scoot. I've got work to do."

Never to be kept down for long, he grinned, put his jar of lollies back into his bag and said, "I'm off to show Miss Brigid and Lilly and Grace now. I wanted you all to be the first to taste 'em. I've got plans, Miss Jane. Big plans."

No more than an hour passed before she was interrupted again by an unexpected delivery.

"Miss Jane," said Cecil, carrying a bouquet. "There's a man downstairs. Sent these up, 'e did. Says he's one of them artists from His Majesty's and would you join him?" He handed Jane a card.

Confused, but intrigued by who would send her flowers, she opened the envelope. "But I'm not acquainted with any of their artists that I'm aware."

Meet me in the auditorium, or would you prefer I came to your home? Alexander Phipps

Shocked by the veiled threat, her legs trembled and her stomach turned. Someone *had* been following her! How else would they learn where she lived? And who was Alexander Phipps?

"Are you a'right, Miss Jane? You've gone awful pale."

She looked up from the card at the sound of the young man's voice. She stared blankly at him for a second or two before she could speak. "Yes, yes, I'm fine," she reassured him. "Thank you, Cecil." She took the flowers from him and looked around vaguely, wondering what she should do with them, while her mind ran rampant.

What would be the right thing to do, she wondered. Send him on his way? But would he go? And would he accost her later on her way home? Or should she meet him and find out what he wanted? Would he go then? Should she meet a man she didn't know, alone?

"Would you tell the gentlemen I'll be down in ten minutes." Cecil turned to leave. "And Cecil, stay close. I might need you."

Cecil nodded, a smile of understanding – and something else ... relief? – crossing his face.

Jane fossicked around and found a jar to put the flowers in while she gathered her wits. The minutes ticked by all too quickly and, after smoothing her hair into place with hands turned chill with unease, she descended from the safety of her workroom.

Jane rarely set foot the auditorium except when inspecting costumes during a rehearsal and was always surprised how dark and unwelcoming it felt when empty. Her footsteps clacked on the wooden floorboards as she entered from the wings and stood at the edge of the stage.

A man sat lounging in the front row, nonchalantly twirling his cane, one foot resting on his other leg. With his hat on and in shadow his face wasn't visible, but his arrogance was unmistakable. Reassured by a glimpse of Cecil standing out of sight behind the curtains, she tried to settle her nerves.

"You asked to see me," said Jane, her voice unexpectedly loud in the echoing chamber. "What can I do for you, sir?"

"Come." Extending his hand, the man waved her towards him. "Please sit with me. I mean you no harm. I just want to talk." His voice sounded surprisingly mellifluous and vaguely familiar.

Climbing down the narrow steps at the side of the stage, her head bent to see where she was going, she hadn't noticed the man approach her. He took her hand – a little too firmly – and she looked up. With his hat tilted back, she could see his face. A gasp escaped her lips, and she tried to pull her hand back but he wouldn't let go.

"Ah, I see you recognise me, even after all this time. I'm flattered."

Jane wanted to say so much, but fear and shame tied her tongue. Now in his mid-thirties and dressed in all his finery, he looked the epitome of a gentleman. Except Jane knew he wasn't.

"Aren't you going to say hello?"

"What do you want, Mickey?" she muttered through gritted teeth.

"To get reacquainted, my dear. And I'm Alex now. Alexander Phipps Esquire, at your service." He performed an exaggerated bow while still clenching her hand. "We parted too abruptly. And, too … Well, shall we say, I want to make amends. I was but a callow youth, yet to learn the ways of wooing. I have so much more to offer you now." He kissed the back of her hand and guided her to sit down.

Jane couldn't think straight; she was too flustered, too angry, too hurt to say anything. Every nerve tingled in readiness, should she need to flee.

"Speak to me, dear Jane. I've thought of you often in the years since we last were together."

She remembered him only too well, and the young seventeen-year-old counterpart inside her still yearned for him. She had adored him once, captured by his good looks and ready wit. He had reminded her of Jamie, Brigid's cousin, who had been so kind to her, who had looked out for her and protected her when she was but a child. She'd missed Jamie so much, with his Irish humour and flashing eyes, that all the unrealised emotion she held for Jamie was showered on Mickey. But she was no longer a child.

"I don't believe you," she snapped, trying to keep her runaway emotions in check. "You just up and left without a word, and now you turn up eight years later. For what, Mickey. For what?"

"I told you, to get reacquainted. I had no option but to leave then. The troupe was moving on, and I needed to tour with them if I was going to make anything of myself."

"You could have sent a message."

But she knew it wouldn't have made any difference if he had. He'd gone and she never expected to see him again and certainly not all these years later. She'd successfully put their romance, if that's what she could call it, behind her and hidden it in the recesses of her mind. She didn't want the past dragged up. She was a respectable, single working woman now. She didn't want him back in her life. Did she? It would raise too many questions and cause distress to too many people.

"I'm here now." He raised her chin with his fingers so he could look into her eyes. The laughter in them reminded her of why she had fallen for him. But he'd not reciprocated. She'd just been a bit of fun to him. "I'm here for a while with the current tour, and I hoped you might allow me to escort you around town." His smile still touched something deep inside her, but her head told her otherwise.

Controlling her bitterness and biting back words she might regret should Cecil hear them, she decided to be extremely polite. Otherwise she would not be able to control the angry tirade on the tip on her tongue once she started. "Thank you for your kind offer, but I'm sorry I am unable to accept. I'm a working woman and needed on the job. You understand what theatre hours are like."

"I do indeed, but I'm aware of places we could go after the theatre lights are dimmed."

How had she not recognised his voice when he first spoke? That voice, rich, warm, melodious, enticing: another thing about him which had beguiled her.

"I think not. Thank you, again, but no."

She stood up to leave, but he grabbed her hand. He remained seated while he looked up at her. A menacing grin lit his face. "I could always visit you at your lodgings, if you'd prefer. I'm sure your landlady - Mrs Greaves, isn't it - wouldn't mind."

A chill spread through Jane at his words. "You've been following me."

"Are you sure? Did you see me?"

She didn't answer but her frozen expression told him.

"No. I thought not. I was merely out walking when I saw you. I fancied I recognised you, so I made sure I was walking in the same place until I was certain. There's nothing sinister in that, now, is there?"

"But it's been months," she argued, uncertain of his intentions. One minute he seemed genuine and the next threatening.

"How could it have been me, then? I've been touring the country and only recently returned to Auckland." He ran his thumb over the back of her hand and sent a flutter up her arm. "My offer still stands. Like I said, I want us to become reacquainted."

Could she believe him? "I'm sure you could have your pick of the many glamorous girls of your acquaintance. Someone who would be more suited to your new station. Why pick on me, a plain costumier?"

"Because, I seem to remember, I rather enjoyed myself. And you're much more than a plain wardrobe mistress, aren't you? Now, be sensible and say yes." He kissed the back of her hand again, and his dancing eyes reminded her how much he had hurt her.

Dread seeped into her spirit at his persistence. "My answer must still be no."

He let her hand go and inspected his immaculate fingernails. She turned to leave.

"I've worked out your little secret. Shame on you."

She stopped in her tracks, her back still towards him.

"I know all about your little hidey-hole, and about Miss Brigid and Miss Sally. And we mustn't forget the young misses. Lilly and Grace, I believe. If you want me to keep your secret, then be a good girl and do as you're told."

9

REALITIES

July 2018

Katie bought herself some new equipment including a portable light box, some inexpensive backdrops, a couple of reflectors and a better lens. She experimented with both natural and artificial lighting and increasingly became more confident she could do a good job of meeting Jared's requirements. The one aspect they hadn't sorted was when he would prepare all the specialities he wanted to make and where she would take the photographs. They avoided the subject, even when the opportunity came up.

As Viv had predicted, she and Jared were going out, although Katie still refused to accept they were dates as such, reiterating her claim that he was a client and she would remain professional. She'd learnt her lesson early on in her career about mixing business with pleasure, and she'd promised never to put herself in that position again – ever. But meeting at least twice a week was testing her willpower.

Sometimes he took her to another café to show her how desserts were plated or displayed in cabinets;

sometimes they met in Viv's office, which made it much easier to control the conversation. Often, the afternoons would extend to an after-work drink or a dessert-eating experiment. At times, Katie asked herself whether these meetings were entirely necessary or whether they were an excuse to spend time together, but she didn't pursue the thought.

Either way, she was having trouble denying her attraction to him. So far, nothing about him irritated her the way it had with other men. She often caught him looking at her the same way she surreptitiously looked at him and wondered if he felt the same tug. Or was she imagining it all, and when the contract finished in a month's time, would he disappear into his world and she retreat to hers? She hoped not.

"The website is coming along and I'm generally happy with it," she said at one of their meetings in Viv's office, where she had the draft set up on a large screen. They worked through each page, with Katie making notes on the changes needed. Jared had a good eye for detail and his comments were perceptive.

"When we're confident about every point, we can do a grand launch, which, on a digital platform, is a little tricky and often unrewarding because you can't see the number of people who might attend, but the stats will tell us how many visitors you have. If we announce it on your social media platforms at the same time, we should get some traction. What I need you to do is make sure you tell every one of your contacts you have a new website and ask them to take a look and comment."

Again, the obvious questions of when and where she would take the photos were avoided. Her kitchen would be perfect, and she'd already hinted at the fact, but it would change their footing and she wasn't sure she was ready for a relationship. She stepped back.

"Is there anything else you'd like to add before I sign off on the final stage?" she asked, taking a sip of her coffee. It tasted just about as good as a barista coffee, thanks to Viv's excellent coffee machine and the beans she supplied.

"I'm not sure how professional this is, but I wonder if ..." He paused, copying Katie and sipping at his drink. "Nice coffee." She watched him wipe the side of his mouth and admired his long, graceful fingers.

"If what?" she pushed. "You'll never find out if you don't pursue the idea."

"It's just, Grandad taught me how to do things with sugar I never thought possible. He learnt sugar boiling from his grandmother and she from her father. I don't know how much further back it goes, but my history with sugar reaches back six generations. I'd like to acknowledge that history somehow."

The expression on his face was enough to melt any heart. Not quite pleading, but persuasive.

"I think it's a brilliant idea. People like personal insights into the what, why and who. How detailed would you like to go? Would you mention names or stick with 'grandfather' etc.?"

"My thoughts are I'd like to use names. They are all gone now, and they deserve to be remembered. I'll have to ask my father if he wants his name mentioned. He wasn't one of the sweetmakers. By the time he was ready to take over in the eighties, the business had been bought out."

Katie nodded. "It's called progress, I guess. But sometimes I think it's such a pity we have lost the personal touch, and old-fashioned family enterprises have trouble matching today's big-business model."

"True, but someone has to have the enthusiasm and determination to succeed and make it happen – like my great-great-great-grandma Gwenna. She was the first ..."

Katie interrupted him. "What name did you say?" She was sure she'd heard Granna talk about a Gwenna. But why would Jared be talking about someone Granna knew? Someone with the same name? And such an unusual name.

"Gwenna. My three-times-great-grandmother. She set up the first shop around the end of the 19th century. I've got a newspaper cutting from the royal visit in 1901 telling her story."

"Gwenna. I'm sure I've heard that name ..." Stalling for time, Katie started to tap her nails on the table. A new habit she'd picked up from Jared. "My grandmother ..." she began but stopped abruptly. She was about to tell him about Granna Katy! What was she doing, entering private territory; she knew better. She pushed her hair behind her ear and hedged. "I think, um, I remember hearing something about a Gwenna once. When I was a child."

But if she'd remembered correctly, then the question should be, was Granna Katy's Gwenna the same person? Surely not? The thought was intriguing.

"Great-grandma served teas in her sweet shop in Karangahape Road, and she had a shop in Wellesley Street for a while too. Gwenna's Superior Sweet Treats was a popular place in its day. Maybe that's how you heard about it."

"Yes. Quite possibly," said Katie, pretending she didn't remember as well as she did.

"It's a Welsh name."

"Hmm. Lovely."

"She would have been well known at the time."

Katie bit at her bottom lip while staring at Jared trying to see ... what? A resemblance to any of the men in the photos she'd been poring over? Trying to find the answer in those eyes drawing her into their depths.

"Interesting."

"Can't you ask someone?" he suggested. "There might be a simple explanation. Maybe this person visited her teashop once, or knew of a story handed down. There must have been hundreds who did."

"Yes, yes. You're quite right," she said, flustered. She dragged her mind back to the work at hand.

Sadness enveloped her. She had no one to ask – except maybe the man in front of her – but now wasn't the time to explain about Granna Katy. Not everyone understood the difficulties of dementia. Anyway, Granna deserved not to be harangued.

Unexpectedly overwhelmed with an enormous sense of loss, her eyes itched, and she flapped her hands to shake off the tension. And that inexplicable and alarming sense of dread she'd experienced leading up to her quitting her job closed around her. "That won't be possible, I'm afraid." Her head pounded and her hands trembled. She could feel the throb of her heart in her throat and felt close to panicking.

She busied herself tidying papers and removing the used coffee cups.

"Are you all right?" he asked, noticing her sudden agitation. When she didn't answer, he checked his watch. "Would you like to come for an after-work drink? You could tell me ..."

She stopped him mid-sentence. "No. Um ... thank you, but no."

More or less panting from shortness of breath, and nauseous, she packed up her bag.

She had no idea why this was happening again, but she had to get out of there. Now. "I must go," she muttered as she fled the office leaving Jared staring after her.

"What on earth is going on?" asked Viv, barking down the phone. "Jared tells me he hasn't been able to contact you. You're not answering his calls and he's not seen hide nor hair of you. What the hell are you playing at?"

"Calm down, Viv." Katie had been expecting this phone call and had already worked out in her mind what to say to steer Viv away from asking the questions Katie didn't want to answer.

A dark sense of hopelessness had blanketed her since she'd fled the office and she could barely get out of bed some mornings. She thought her anxiety had been because the boundaries between work and her personal life had been crossed, and she'd wanted to put some distance between them before she broke her own rules, but there was more to it than that.

She wasn't ready. She couldn't share the strain of her pent-up inner feelings, or Granna Katy's reality, with anyone, least of all someone she'd only recently met – although she had a gut feeling Jared would understand. They had an affinity, often laughing at similar things, and, bit by bit, they'd discovered they shared comparable views on social and political issues and were deeply interested in each other's work and what drove them. She didn't want to scare him away. But she felt too wretched.

While she talked to Viv, she paced the confines of her lounge and kitchen, tweaking a cushion, flicking her hair behind her ear, shifting an ornament a fraction – anything to keep moving, to stop herself from panicking, hoping her voice wouldn't betray her.

"I've been working on his website. It's done now and I've detailed a day-by-day marketing plan for him to follow for his social media posts. I'll send it through to you. All he has to do is meet with your photographer to take the pics and he can upload the images where the placeholders are."

Katie came to the end of her explanation in a rush, but Viv wasn't convinced.

"You are on contract, Katie. I expect you to finish the job, not palm it off to me or the client. He said you were taking the pictures."

That was the one aspect Katie was now desperate to avoid. Taking photos would put them into close contact, too close, and she didn't think she could keep him at arm's length if they worked in such a setting. She didn't want him confusing her life any further; she was struggling to cope as it was.

"I did think about it but decided I'm not professional enough. There's no reason your guy can't do it. I just think it would be more businesslike if you handed over the final plan."

"Businesslike!" Viv exploded. "Have you lost your mind completely? I offer you a fantastic opportunity to get your hand back in again and you chuck it back in my face! Well, Katie Anderson, I'm not having it. I'm far too busy and so is my photographer. Finish the job I'm paying you to do and then we'll talk."

Viv hung up before Katie could respond.

She lost track of time as she stood at the window staring at the view yet seeing nothing as her brain tried to sort her dilemma. The phone, still clutched in her hand, vibrated. Unthinking, she answered the call without checking the name of the caller.

"Katie?" said the voice she both longed and dreaded to hear. "Thank goodness you've answered. You've had me so worried. I'm sorry. Whatever I said to upset you, I'm sorry."

Undone by the concern in his voice, Katie battled the tears threatening to fall. "No need to apologise. It's nothing to do with you. It's something personal I can't discuss." Knowing her voice was shaking, she took a deep breath and turned the conversation. "Your website is complete, apart from the photographs. I have added placeholders which can be replaced with the final images when you're ready. I'll send you the link. I've also completed a marketing plan. Please study them and contact Viv should you wish any changes. I have full confidence you can manage everything yourself from now on."

Her hand was trembling, and a hollow somewhere near her stomach ached painfully. Viv would hit the roof again if she knew Katie was duck-shoving like this. She silently pleaded for him to accept what she'd said without question, but Jared wasn't going to let it go so easily.

"I'm still sorry for whatever's upsetting you, and you only have to ask, if I can do anything to help. But don't we still have business to attend to? We haven't worked on the history page we talked about, and you said you wanted to take the photos so you could control the process and outcomes. I don't think Viv could do that. Can we not find a way to work professionally together? Please?"

Damn the man. Why did he have to say please like that – and in that tone? If he'd remained pragmatic, she could have regained some control maybe, but Katie also knew she couldn't risk Viv cancelling her contract without payment. She couldn't afford it. She had no choice. "Very well. I'll take the pictures. I will give you a two-hour slot on Sunday."

"Sunday? That's days away. Can't you ..."

"No, I can't do it before then. Take it or leave it. It'll give you time to prepare. Where shall I come?"

Every muscle in Katy's body had tensed and she could feel her teeth aching as she clenched her jaw in preparation for his answer.

"Well, the thing is ..." He sounded hesitant. "I was wondering ..." She could hear fidgeting and uncertainty but had no idea what was coming next. "That night, after the sample tasting at the restaurant. We had a nightcap in the bar, remember?"

Oh yes, all too well.

"You told me about the first-class kitchen you didn't use."

Now her heart seriously began to race. Was he going to ask to come to her apartment? She had moments to decide.

"It sounded perfect. Views in the background, the right lighting, everything. By the time you'd finished, I got the feeling you were going to suggest we use it. But you've not mentioned it since so I wondered if you'd gone off the idea. So, have you? Because I really have no idea where else to suggest. I can't use my work kitchen, and my home ... well, I couldn't take you there."

Why not, Katie wondered. What was wrong with his place? Was he hiding secrets too?

"Katie? Are you still there?" he asked, interrupting the lengthening silence.

"Yes, I'm still here." Even to her ears she sounded deflated. Resigned. She had been going to suggest he came to her apartment – once. They worked so comfortably together, it had seemed the obvious solution, but fear of entering into the realms of a more personal relationship held her back, and the shadow of Granna Katy's illness came between them. Her self-doubt returned with full force and her decision-making ability deserted her, but what he was saying made sense.

Jared cleared his throat and tried again. "We could try hiring a venue with a kitchen, I suppose, if you'd prefer. But I honestly don't have the budget for it."

"Ten o'clock Sunday, and don't be late." She hung up before he said anything further as memories of her last visit to Granna Katy flooded her mind.

Filled with guilt that she'd not visited Granna Katy as often as she usually did, while she'd been busy working with Jared, Katie went twice in three days. The first time, Granna had not recognised her. It happened sometimes and, while Katie knew it had nothing to do with her absence, her guilt increased. But something out of the ordinary came from the visit. Granna decided her visitor needed a guided tour of her photographs.

Around the room she trod, back and forth showing one after another of her framed prints. Katie admired them all over again. The straight-faced, dour expressions and stiff poses of eras past were all due to the length of time it took for the camera action to take place. Later, once the Box Brownie had been invented and came into popular use, somewhere around the turn of the 20th century, the poses had relaxed and appeared more natural, but they didn't all have the sepia studio finish Katie loved.

Granna had several modern colour pictures of the family, but she rarely talked about the people in those and when she did, she often got the names wrong. She didn't recognise her husband's image after close to fifty years of marriage. Nor did she recognise her daughter or Katie's brothers. Why she knew Katie herself was baffling.

Drawn to the past, Granna's interest was in the oldest ones. "Móraí and Granty," she said.

Katie knew that one well. It always had pride of place on Granna's bedside table. Móraí was still nameless, but the other woman – the one who looked like Katie – had a title at last. Granty. But who was Granty? Hoping to find out more, Katie was about to ask a question but Granna wasn't listening.

"Young Móraí."

Katie didn't think it was a *young* Móraí. Something about the mouth looked different, but she wasn't going to argue.

"Mam and Da."

Katie practically fell off her chair as she leant forward to see the image clutched in Granna's hand more clearly. She was sure she'd never seen it before. It looked like it could be a wedding shot because of the outsized bouquet the woman carried, except she wore a flawlessly fitted dark walking dress with a wide-brimmed hat, and the man was in uniform. She desperately wanted to ask questions and try to tie all the relationships together but she knew she would be wasting her time.

"Mam and Lilly," Granna announced, thrusting another image before Katie's eyes.

This time, Katie pointed to one of the girls, who she guessed would have been somewhere in her late teens.

"Is this your mother?" The likeness between her and the one in the wedding photo was unmistakable, but something else nagged at Katie. She wanted to compare several of them side by side and study them, but Granna put each one back in its place. Except for a few, which disappeared into a drawer.

As Granna put them away, she must have seen another one further down. She extracted a frame Katie couldn't see from where she was sitting. Granna held it in her hand, staring at it for quite some time, trying to remember.

"Grandma." A slow sigh rather than a sound came from her lips. "Grandma Gwenna. She'll know."

There's that name again, thought Katie. Jared talked about a Gwenna and now Granna had said it again. But who was she, and what would she know? Katie was no nearer to finding out.

"Who are you talking about, Granna Katy?" she asked gently, but glazed-over eyes turned to meet hers. The photo was replaced and the drawer shut.

Katie fought back the urge to leap to her feet and retrieve whatever was in the drawer. She very much wanted to see that one, but Granna could get dreadfully upset if you touched her things, especially when she was in a certain frame of mind. Searching for names and faces would have to wait. And she was no closer to discovering who Móraí was either.

But it didn't happen on her second visit either. Granna was unusually quiet and seemed to be having trouble remembering words or how to say them. Katie wasn't sure what had happened, but there'd been a change.

"Katy." Her breath was no more than a whisper but, relieved that Granna recognised her this time, Katie bent down and hugged the old woman sitting in her chair.

"I'm here, Granna."

"I've missed you, Katy," said Granna.

Full of self-reproach, Granna's comment struck a chord and added to Katie's guilt. "I'm so sorry. I've been busy, but Katie's here now. Would you like to see some of my photographs?" she asked, hoping they might spark a memory and Granna would start talking about hers again.

Granna looked past Katie out the window at something only she could see. Katie wasn't sure Granna had heard or understood what she'd said. Thinking to attract her attention, Katie took her camera out of its case and tried to connect to Granna's old-style TV but realised she'd left her cable behind.

"Blast," she muttered under her breath. Tucking her hair behind her ear, she put her camera away again. When she next looked up, she realised Granna hadn't moved. She was still lost in whatever world she was in.

Outside, the skies were grey and overcast, but the rain hadn't started yet. "Shall we go for a walk, Granna? You can show me the flowers?"

Granna didn't turn her head. "The flowers are all gone. Gone to the graveyard, every one."

At a loss as to how to respond or what to say next, Katie stood up. "I'll make us a cup of tea, shall I?"

With no answer from Granna, she left the room and headed down the corridor to the visitors' kitchen.

Sometimes Granna's vagueness and the things she said upset Katie more than other things did. Today, she felt particularly vulnerable. She'd lost so much already, she didn't think she could cope with losing Granna too.

After calming herself, Katie returned with a tray.

"I've missed you," said Granna before the door had closed properly.

"I've brought you a cup of tea and a biscuit."

Granna looked at the cup being held before her and then at the face above her. "Katy, my dear. I've missed you."

Katie's heart crumbled. Whoever Granna was missing, it wasn't her. She wasn't in the least mindful of the day or, in reality, the week and had no memory of Katie's visits just days before.

Katie knew she'd been in denial about Granna's condition but there could be no doubt Granna was getting worse. Now she looked at her more closely, Katie realised how thin she had become.

"Here," she said. "Let me help you."

Checking the tea was cool enough, Katie put the cup handle in Granna's hand, covered the whole thing with her own and guided it to Granna's mouth. Once she'd sipped the first mouthful, she took a second and seemed more revived.

"There's nothing like a good cup of tea, is there, Granna."

"Let Katy help, Móraí."

It dawned on Katie then: the 'Katy' Granna was referring to was herself.

"Don't leave me, Katy," said a trembly, croaky voice sounding nothing like her gran.

10

INFLUENCE AND COERCION

October 1903

Jane fervently wished she could avoid seeing Brigid, who, she knew, would only question her, but she couldn't and wouldn't miss Lilly's tenth birthday tea.

Over the last month since Mickey had approached her, Jane had lost weight and her clothes hung on her already slight frame. The man haunted her every moment. Even when he was away touring, she sensed his presence. She lived in constant agitation and her work was suffering. She might have avoided any significant mistakes so far, but she knew she wasn't on top of her work. Nor had she been able to come up with any imaginative designs lately.

She discovered *he* – she couldn't bring herself to call him by name – had paid a backstage boy to follow her throughout the winter when he was away. Performing, he said, in Australia. He wouldn't accept that paying someone to follow her was wrong.

"Nothing ominous in that, is there? I don't want to lose you, now I've found you again."

Jane had given in to his veiled threats, too scared he might harm those she loved if she ignored him. So far, his advances had been circumspect. When in town, he invited her to dine with him most nights, insisting she wear one of her enchanting creations. Sometimes they attended a private club before a show. More often they went to late-night haunts, known only by those who lived their lives in the hours of darkness, where gambling and drinking were the norm. As the self-appointed shining light at these affairs, he filled the room with his swagger, which often irritated her as being false and excessive, as if he was still on the stage.

Nevertheless, the charm and wit that had attracted her in the first place was indisputable, and there were times when, despite everything, she felt drawn to him again. She promptly pushed those thoughts away. She could never rekindle what they had. Too much was at risk.

Why was he bothering with someone as lowly as her? What did he want from her?

Mickey ignored her questions, constantly praising her ability and her style to others, while she remained unaware of her allure. Uncomfortable with this additional attention, dressing in evening attire and being considered by others as his 'lady friend' did nothing to allay her concerns. Underlying his constant flattery lay veiled threats he would ruin her reputation and her career if she crossed him. One day, she feared, he would press his advances further, and she had no idea how to stop him.

"I'm here, Brigid," called Jane when she arrived.

Brigid popped her head over the banister. "Sally has just taken Lilly to get some paper serviettes. It's just a ruse, but it got her away from the house while I set up. You can hide your gift in the showroom until later. Then come on up."

"Is Grace here?"

"Of course. She's setting out the cutlery for me."

Putting the parcel where Brigid had suggested, Jane was pleased she'd have time for a few words with Grace without Lilly taking over.

"Janey, Janey," cried Grace, rushing towards her as soon as she appeared at the top of the stairs and wrapping her arms around her waist.

"My goodness," cried Brigid when she got a good look at Jane. "Are you all right? You're so thin. Even thinner than the last time I saw you."

Jane had considered confiding in Brigid but she couldn't burden her with her worries when Brigid had enough of her own. Since Jane's conversation several months ago with Sally, Phillip Harrison-Browne had become more persistent in his demands for Brigid to make lace for him once more. He'd also threatened to fetch her to Brisbane if she didn't agree soon.

"I'm well enough," Jane replied, untangling Grace's arms and bending down to kiss her. "I've just got a lot on at the moment. Sometimes I'm too tired to eat." She wasn't exactly lying, but she wasn't telling the truth either.

"Well, you just sit down and relax," smiled Brigid, "and let me feed you up today. We've more than enough food. You can take some away with you, it'll save you cooking. Now, you talk with Grace for a few moments while I finish what I was doing."

"My piano teacher says I'm doing very well, but I need to practise more if I want to be even better," said Grace, pulling a face in response to Jane's question. "I like playing the songs but the scales are so boring. Lilly hates it when I play scales and shouts out mean things to distract me. She likes to sing the songs but tells me off if I make a mistake."

"I understand, Grace, dear, but sometimes the boring things teach you the most. You will never improve without repetition. The more often you do something, the better you get. It's the same with me. Your mam taught me to sew and make lace, and she made me do it over and over again until I mastered the skill. That's why I can do what I do now. If you want to play the piano well, you must practise. Yes? Promise?"

"Yes, Janey. I will. I promise. I want to make music when I grow up. It makes me feel good. I don't want to sew and make lace like the others. Lilly is the one who's clever at sewing, and Mam's making lace again too."

Jane was pleased to hear such news. After their discussion, she and Sally had sat Brigid down and had a long heart-to-heart about how the business had slipped in the four years since Tommy had gone. How she wasn't being fair to Lilly or Grace, with a mother constantly in mourning, unable or unwilling to keep the spirit of Tommy alive and well by making a success of the business. A business she could hand on to her daughters. How she couldn't waste a precious and rare talent. How she was wasting her life.

Something they said had worked.

They succeeded in reinvigorating Brigid's interest in lacemaking, thanks, in part, to a few designs Jane had drawn for Brigid to make for Lilly as a birthday gift. But Brigid was still refusing to go to Brisbane in answer to Phillip's request.

Jane and Sally had plans.

"Right now, where are those two?" said Brigid, wiping her hands on a towel and removing her apron.

"It's all ready. And where's Laura?" Brigid never quite knew if or when Laura would turn up to any family event these days. She seemed more and more involved with her political activities.

No sooner had she spoken than they heard the bell tinkle on the outside door, and moments later Sally and Lilly appeared at the top of the stairs, followed by Laura.

"Look who we found on the way back, Breeda," said Sally.

"Hello, Laura. I was just talking about you, wondering if you'd come."

"You didn't think I'd miss this girl's party, did you?" asked Laura, smiling at Lilly.

"Well, hello to you all," greeted Jane. "And happy birthday, Lilly. You look lovely today. Is that a new dress?" Jane glanced at Sally who grinned back.

"All right, you two," said Brigid. "Enough. I know all about your schemes. But yes, I am pleased with the way Lilly's dress turned out, and I'm glad you inspired me to get back into lacemaking again. I admit I've let things slip, but without Tommy ..." Brigid paused, trying to control her sudden emotion. Waving her hands to wipe away the unwanted and mistimed thoughts, she took the serviettes from Lilly and set about arranging them.

"Come along now, it's celebration time," said Sally, steering the talk away from Tommy.

Grace played the piano while the women sang 'Happy Birthday', then Lilly was persuaded to sing, after which they played charades, musical chairs and had a treasure hunt. Exhausted from their activities, soon all the pies and cakes had been eaten and they slumped in their chairs – all except Lilly, who fidgeted and paced.

"Now, is there anything we've missed?" said Brigid,

pretending innocence. The time had come for Lilly to receive whatever gifts were coming her way, but she wanted the girl to learn how to wait.

"Well, if you don't mind, I do have something I'd like to show Lilly," said Jane. "I'll be back in a moment."

When Jane returned, Laura gave Lilly a supply of ribbons and pins for her hair, and Sally presented her with a pop-up doll's house with cardboard figures. Brigid gave her an exquisitely dressed porcelain doll.

"I love her. Thank you, Mam. She is beautiful and so are her clothes. You're so clever."

The girl's comment made Brigid blush, so when Sally and Jane looked at her with a 'we-told-you-so' stare, she fell about laughing.

"You win. I promise to do better. Or at least try to. Now, Jane," continued Brigid, "have you got something to show us?"

Jane handed across a flat parcel giving no hint of its contents. Lilly carefully untied the string and brown paper wrapping to reveal several pieces of sheet music of songs from the latest shows overseas – *The Wizard of Oz* was among them. Lilly knew the story well from the book she'd been given the previous year.

"Oh, thank you, Jane. I'll take them to my singing teacher."

"I thought you and Gracie could learn them together."

Lilly pulled a slight face at the suggestion. "She'd need to get better fast then."

"Don't be unkind, Lilly," chastised her mother, carefully rolling up the string and paper for another time. "Grace plays very well. Now off you go girls. You can play in your room."

Once the girls had gone, Sally poured a sherry for herself and Brigid. Despite the efforts of the temperance movement, not all women agreed with them. Brigid and Sally, in particular, enjoyed a glass or two of spirits now and then, but sherry was more acceptable in the afternoon. Laura was against it, of course, but said nothing, and Jane preferred lemon cordial.

Once settled, Laura said, "I just have to tell you, in Britain, Emmeline Pankhurst has formed a Women's Social and Political Union. I'm so excited. It's like our National Council of Women but women are still fighting for suffrage over there. Thank goodness we won that battle, but the NCW isn't the powerhouse it once was. The leaders are old or dead, and many say we don't have the support we used to. It's so disappointing to lose ground like this. I wish I could do something to stir them along."

"Don't expect too much from people, Laura dear," said Brigid. "We know New Zealand women are better off than our British counterparts and we're thankful for it, especially now we've got rights the older generations didn't have. The right to vote, the right to be financially independent and the right to a pension will make a huge difference to many poor women. But as I keep telling you, change takes time. You can't rush things, Laura. Now what else have you been doing?"

"I'm enjoying my work at the office and following Miss Melville's endeavours. She's going to start studying law at night classes next year. Mr Devore has arranged it all. I hope I show as much promise as her, then he might let me train too." Laura often expressed her desire to become a lawyer and, being slightly older than Ellen Melville, sometimes thought she'd missed her opportunity. "But at least I passed my matriculation like she did, and Miss Melville says we must keep working towards advancement for women. Even she says our movement is at a low ebb right now."

Sally and Brigid shifted in their chairs, thinking how they could distract Laura from her obsession with Ellen Melville and how unfair life was on women. Laura never talked about anything else.

"Did you cycle here today, lass?" asked Sally, already knowing the answer, since she'd seen her arrive.

Laura looked perplexed. "Yes, of course. I always ride. I do like to go to the Ladies Cycle Club outings. There's talk now about what clothing we should wear and would it be acceptable. I like the idea of divided skirts. It would make it so much easier and more comfortable."

"They would be quite different, indeed," said Jane, trying to take part in the conversation but often finding herself thinking of her own predicament instead. "I could design something for you if you wanted me to."

"Don't bother. I can order them from England."

Unperturbed by her sister's rudeness, Jane shrugged. "I've heard there's a new soft toy available called 'Teddy's Bear'. One or two of the cast who've been overseas were talking about it. It's made from a soft fur fabric and stuffed to look like a small bear, a bit like a ragdoll, I suppose. It's called Teddy after President Theodore Roosevelt, so I'm told. I'd love to see one."

When the topic changed to sewing, fabrics and laces, Laura made her excuses and left.

"Which brings me to the subject of Phillip Harrison-Browne," said Sally.

"Oh, don't bring him up again, please," said Brigid.

"Why not? Didn't you just agree to try harder, to make a success of the business – your business, the one you set up with the help of Mrs Browne? Well, if you are going to reinvent Miss Brigid's then you need to specialise again. And Mr Harrison-Browne has given you the ideal opportunity."

"But it means travelling to Brisbane, and I don't think I could cope with the journey."

"What rubbish!" exclaimed Jane. "You've done it before, and it's much easier these days. The ships are so much better. It's only a few days in comparison. Take Lilly with you for company. She's old enough now, and it would be a great experience for her."

"But there's so many ready-to-wear options and yards and yards of machine-made lace available, how can I compete?"

Sally wasn't giving up on this argument, not while she had Jane to back her up. "You did it once, Breeda. You can do it again. Thanks to you, your handmade lace became a sought-after item. Miss Brigid's canna be allowed to become a haberdashery just because you decide not to make lace any more. What's got into you, lass? Where's the Breeda I know and love gone? 'Cos it's time she came back." Sally placed her arms akimbo and scowled.

"Sally's right, Brigid," added Jane. "Evening wear is in great demand again, and the ladies are looking for anything different to what their neighbour's wearing. It can't do any harm. You can experiment with dyes, add some silver or gold thread, or beads – just try something, please?"

Eventually, Brigid gave in and agreed to write to Phillip and his mother. "But not until next year."

"I'd be thinking of the Christmas trade if I were you," said Sally. "Strike while the iron is hot, goes the proverb, and there's no time like the present."

The three women stared at each other. Sally determined; Jane expectant. Brigid's defiance wavered.

"All right. All right. I'll do it."

"About time."

The atmosphere changed in an instant, filled with a sense of relief and purpose.

"Well, if that's settled, I'd better be going," said Jane. "Sally will tell me should you even think of changing your mind."

"Not so fast, young lady. You're not getting off the hook so easily," said Brigid. "I want to know what is going on in your life. You have lost so much weight, you're looking more like a starving waif than a successful designer."

11

STRENGTHS AND WEAKNESSES

August 2018

At ten o'clock on the dot, a knock sounded on her door. Chiding herself for acting like a nervous teenager, Katie smoothed her loose-fitting knit top down over her jeans and patted her hair before opening it.

"Good morning, Katie," smiled Jared cheekily from behind a pile of boxes. "I'm here right on time at your bidding."

Her heart did a double take at how much she had missed his natural affability.

Returning his smile, she relaxed as she invited him in and showed him to the immaculate white kitchen. A row of tall cupboards ran along one wall, interrupted only by the gas cooktop, while a long bench on the open side gave the impression of continuing beyond the floor-length window at the far end. Fortunately, the day was sunny, and the light shone through the plate glass.

He whistled. "You weren't exaggerating. This is stunning."

Although the bench was already partially covered with various props, a vase of flowers and Katie's camera,

Jared found a place for his boxes and shrugged out of his jacket. He briefly held it up in the air, looking around for somewhere to put it, until Katie relieved him of it and hung it in the cupboard by the front door. By the time she returned, he had flipped open the lids to the boxes and was looking in her cupboards. For a split second, Katie tensed. She wasn't used to people rummaging around in her kitchen, but he looked so at home, so comfortable in his own skin and excited by what he was doing, she forgave him.

"What are you looking for?"

"Platters to put this lot on." His voice was muffled by the fact he had his head half in the tall cupboard looking on the bottom shelf. "Aha!"

He withdrew three platters Katie had forgotten she had. The elegant long platters with graceful curves at each end, which her mother had given her, had never been used. She remembered the day her mum arrived with them shortly after she'd moved in, saying the apartment was perfect and she should entertain more. She never had. Katie wished she could talk to her mum right now. She was so confused by life, she couldn't decide which way to turn and barely trusted herself to make any decisions. The life-changing one she made a few months earlier was leading her down paths she'd never considered, and doubt was her persistent travelling companion.

Jared had no such doubts.

Katie watched in admiration as he carefully plated some of the goodies from the boxes. Chatting away about what he'd made, the ideas he had for presentation and the trimmings he'd brought with him, Jared dragged her attention to the task in hand. "What do you think?"

"They look delicious. How long did all this take you?"

"A few hours. Not sure exactly, but I've been up since five. You did tell me not to be late." His grin told her he was teasing.

She loved that spontaneous grin. It lit up his face and reached his eyes, which held a ready sparkle.

"So, what happens next?" He waved his hand over the platters.

"I take some photos, I guess." She tried to act and sound casual, but in reality she was a bundle of nerves.

Jared watched while she experimented with a few tabletop backgrounds – scrunched up brown paper, coloured paper and cloths, a marble trivet, a wooden tray – and stood a range of backdrops up behind the platters to see how the light fell. She then put the light reflector on its stand and manoeuvred it until she was happy.

A couple of times he started to speak, but Katie shushed him. She needed to work in silence. After a time, Jared's presence no longer bothered her as she concentrated on her work. She took a few experimental shots, adjusted the reflector, put one plate in the light box, changed the background for another and took a few more snaps.

"OK. Can you put some more of your desserts on individual plates, and then I want to try some action shots?"

As he started to do what she'd asked, she pushed him to one side with her hip as she moved to try another angle, and his leg got in the way. The heat of contact made her blush. She hoped Jared couldn't see her face.

"Action? I didn't know desserts could move."

She chuckled. "Well, you're about to learn something new."

She straightened, opened the pantry and pulled out a container and then a sieve from a drawer. "Here, sprinkle some icing sugar over this one when I tell you."

Moving one of the rich chocolatey-looking morsels into view, she reset the lighting and bent to her task. "Now!" she instructed and rapidly took a series of shots as the fine particles fell.

"Now, can you mix up something which will run off a spoon? I want to take some with something drizzling down the side of that one," – she pointed to a wedge of something creamy looking – "and let's pop some fruit with it."

Jared pulled out a couple of containers filled with tamarillo and mandarin, and one with passionfruit, and did as instructed, swiftly mixing up rich, colourful sauces which dribbled perfectly. Then she wanted a mango syrup poured over a shot glass filled with layers of sweetness. Lastly, came Jared's pièce de résistance, his spun-sugar creations. After each session, as they changed the items to be photographed, Jared pressed Katie into tasting each of them. She hadn't wanted to get her fingers sticky, and it felt so natural for him to feed her with a spoon or use his fingers to pop a small morsel into her open mouth.

The two hours she promised him disappeared, and by the end of the session they'd opened a bottle of wine to use as a prop and sipped at it while they worked.

"The light's changed a lot since this morning," she explained as the afternoon lengthened. "We had the sun coming in here, before the clouds came over, but now I've got darker and diffused lighting to work with, which will need more adjustment. I might take some more shots later if we get any sun from the west giving us those slanted shadows." In her mind, she could see the images she was imagining when she could use the view outside her window as a backdrop and her desk lamp for backlighting.

"If we don't eat them all before then," he joked. "Are you still hungry? Shall I get us a late lunch?" he asked, checking his watch. He was a time checker, Katie decided. Was it something to do with him constantly timing the cooking phase for his creations, or was it a nervous habit, she wondered.

"No, thanks. I think I've eaten enough to last till tomorrow but don't let me stop you."

He flopped down on the leather couch beside her. "I'm OK. This is fabulous. You've got yourself a glorious spot here. I don't think I'd ever get sick of looking at this view."

"Thanks. I like it too – and no, I never tire of the view either. It changes all the time."

Moments passed as they sat contentedly staring out the window, his arm resting along the back of the couch while she sat with her legs crossed in the middle.

Into the quiet, Jared said, "I understand you'd only planned on a two-hour photo shoot today, but since I've already ruined your Sunday by taking up far more of your time than allowed, can I ask … would you like to run through the website's history page, or am I pushing my luck too far?"

Immediately, unsettled by his request, Katie uncrossed her legs, then crossed them again fighting to control her nerves. She'd enjoyed the shoot. Time passed much quicker than she'd realised, and they'd worked comfortably as a team. So why did she constantly feel the need to put distance between them whenever he suggested they spend more time together? Especially since, deep down, she wanted the opposite. *Damn.* What was she so scared of? She sighed inwardly. She had to make up her mind what she wanted.

"Yeah, OK. Might as well since you're here. What're you thinking?"

Jared rose, retrieved a sheet of paper from his jacket in the cupboard and handed it to her.

"It's only rough, but it's an outline of the business from the 1890s on."

Katie scanned the hand-scribbled page, taking note of the name Gwenna at the top, and scrolled over the following generations whose names also started with a G – George, Geoffrey, Grant – until she got to Jared.

"So why does your name not start with a G?"

Jared shrugged. "Dad decided there was no necessity to keep the tradition going after the business was swallowed up by a larger one. Pity, but then I suppose G Price & Family Confectioners is not a particularly modern way of attracting attention."

"No, probably not, but Gwenna's Superior Sweet Treats was rather charming."

"Are we into superlatives these days?"

"Always! Well, sometimes ..." Katie realised they'd not talked about a name before. The website was simply titled Jared Price Pastry Chef and that, she decided, would not help the marketing strategy. "So, what are calling yourself?"

Again, Jared shrugged. "I'm not clever with words. You got any suggestions?"

Katie stood up from the couch and reached into the coffee table drawer for a pen and notepad. Perching on the bar stool at the end of the bench, she started scribbling words.

"In one word, how would you describe what you make?"

Katie got a kick watching Jared's face crumple as he thought about what she'd asked. He had such an expressive face, you could more or less pick what he was thinking. The frown lines deepened, and his smile turned to a moue. He took his glasses off and polished them with a handkerchief, and stroked his beard, but then his face cleared and the natural expression, which made him look like he was about to smile, returned. "I make deliciousness."

"Actually, that's not bad," she acknowledged and could virtually hear his shoulders relax.

She added his word to her list and drew lines from one word to another until she had a combination. Jared watched over her shoulder trying to keep up with her mind-mapping.

"OK," she said finally, "here's my suggestion. Name the business – and the website – 'Dazzling Desserts'. We can add a statement on the home page, 'Handmade Deliciousness by Jared', and place it over a rolling screen of the best photos. It'll need click-through links to more images with order forms. What do you think?"

He nodded a couple of times while he let her words sink in. "I like it."

His nearness was unsettling again. She pushed her hair behind one ear.

"Hmm. So do I," she murmured, wondering if she was talking about his website or him. Opening up the mock-up page on her laptop, she started to type. "I'll make a few tweaks to the design now, while I think about it."

Jared paced the room, trying not to crowd her, but she was aware of him the whole time.

"I like alliteration," she explained, as she added words like dainty, delightful and delectable. "It's a subtle ploy because the words are spread over several pages, but the mind will begin to accept and then expect 'd' words to go with desserts. Come and see."

Still perched at the benchtop, they worked through the pages again, tidying up loose ends and finally agreeing they'd done as much as they could – until the customers started using it and any faults appeared.

"Hopefully there won't be any issues," said Katie, stretching, "but order forms can be tricky and people use them in so many different ways."

She slid off the bar stool and stood in front of the window, easing the aches which had developed from sitting at the wrong angle.

"Do you want to call it a day?" asked Jared, clearly concerned.

"No, I'm fine. My fault for sitting the wrong way. Let's move to the table to do the history page. Storyline or timeline? Which way shall we go?"

They talked about the pros and cons of each method but decided to go for a brief timeline as it required less reading. Katie began formatting the layout and typing in the details.

Three entries stuck in her mind:

1900 – Gwenna Price opens Gwenna's Superior Sweet Treats in Beresford Street, later moving to Karangahape Road

1921 – George Price becomes a full partner

1949 – Geoffrey Price becomes master confectioner at the age of 22 on the death of his grandmother Gwenna.

By the time she had finished loading the information

and checking it, she couldn't hold back any longer. "Was Geoffrey the grandfather who taught you how to make spun sugar?"

"Yes, he was. He died in 2008, and I've missed him ever since. I was away at the time and didn't get to see him before he went – much to my regret. It seems every other generation delivers the creative one, and the others take over the managerial and business side of things. My great-grandfather George apparently couldn't boil sugar to save himself, and my dad wasn't interested. There's a knack, but it's more than that."

"How do you know all this stuff about your family?" Katie was envious of his knowledge and wished she knew more about her past relatives. Especially now, when she had no one to ask.

"I've always known – maybe not the dates, I had to look them up. But the business was something my grandparents talked about all the time. Grandad was bitter about the whole thing because his father let the business be taken over, even though he kept making sweets for many years after. He went to work in his uncle's factory, manufacturing to a mass recipe until it, too, was taken over. He did what he had to but continued to experiment with his creations and taught me. By the time Dad came of age, great-grandfather George had died and Grandad was reduced to working on a conveyor belt."

"That sounds so sad and such a waste. But how did you find out the dates?"

"My dad still has some of the old business papers at home. I found newspaper articles, adverts and an old wages book; things like that. They were stored in a box in the roof space. I think they must have been Grandad's and were shoved up there after he went, and forgotten. Why do you ask?"

Again, she'd put herself in the position of crossing the work–personal divide. Admitting she knew nothing about her past would be letting Jared into her life. One half wanted to, the other half rebelled. But the part wanting to learn something more of her history was stronger. Maybe he could advise her.

"We never talked about the past when I was growing up. I never particularly cared before, but lately I've been looking at old photos and realised I have no idea who they are and I've no one to ask. Can you help me?"

Jared beamed – there was no other word for it. His grin was bigger, broader and cheekier than ever, and his eyes came alive. "How much time do you have?"

12

BIRTHDAY SURPRISES

Early December 1903

"Janey, Janey. You're here." Grace wrapped her arms around her favourite big sister.

"She's been ready, waiting for you to arrive for hours," Brigid laughingly explained, "never mind how often I told her what time you were expected."

"Can we go now?" Grace tugged at Jane's arm, too excited to let the adults get caught up in a conversation which would delay them.

"Yes, my love, we can. But let me look at you first. My, don't you look so grown-up in your new outfit. Brigid, you've excelled yourself."

Brigid's smile was slow but lit her face when she looked at her second daughter. "It's thanks to you again, Jane. If you hadn't pushed me along and given me the design, I would never have thought to make anything like it. So modern, yet classy, without making her look too grown-up just yet."

The pale peach frock coat with a collar, buttons down the front and sleeves with buttoned flaps, flared out from the waist over a matching dress with a handmade-lace yoke. Her dainty beige button-up boots almost touched the lower edge of the coat, making her look taller, and a little beret-style hat perched atop her dark curls finished the ensemble. No longer did she look like a little girl in a frilly short skirt, even if she was tiny.

"I don't think I had much to do with it this time," laughed Jane, knowing Brigid had worked long hours to complete the outfit since her trip to Brisbane with Lilly the previous month. "Surely reinstating your contract with Mr Harrison-Browne has had a lot more to do with your renewed confidence than any drawing I came up with."

Jane's confidence had been renewed as well after designing Grace's birthday outfit. She had started sketching again for the theatre and increasingly as Bernadette, her alter ego, the secret fashion designer. The extra pennies helped with her savings.

"It's early days yet," said Brigid. "We'll see how things go with Mr Harrison-Browne, but yes, going back to Brisbane, seeing what he's achieved and how marvellous his store looked, has given me reason to feel inspired again."

Many years earlier, from the late 1880s, when Miss Brigid's was gaining a significant reputation in Auckland, Brigid had a contract to visit the Harrison-Browne Department Store on a twice-yearly basis to demonstrate and take bespoke orders for her intricate lacework. The agreement had been beneficial to both parties, and Miss Brigid's became the talk of the town in two countries. Jane remembered how happy Brigid had been then. Brigid created more lace in that time than any other – enough to cater for both shops. The trips to Brisbane came to an end in 1898 when Tommy died, and Brigid went into a long, deep mourning.

"And you were right about taking Lilly with me too, Jane. She loved every moment. Did I tell you I met Phillip's son, Joseph?"

"Yes, but only briefly. Was he nice?" asked Jane.

"Lilly thought so, at least," said Brigid, hinting there'd been more to the meeting than she was saying, despite their youth.

Jane smiled. "We must talk more about it next time I'm here. I'm pleased to see you happy again."

"Aye. Our old Breeda is back, if you ask me," said Sally, coming upstairs from the shop. "She's working like a Trojan to fulfil the orders both for the Brisbane store and here. And she's got Lilly talking about it."

Grace tugged at Jane's sleeve, forcing her to look at the girl. "Are we going now?"

"Grace," Brigid said sharply. "Do not interrupt."

"Sorry, Mam." Grace hung her head but held on to Jane's hand.

"So, where are you two off to?" Sally was looking to change the focus back to Grace.

"Well, now, let's see ..." began Jane before Grace, practically bouncing with excitement, butted in.

"Janey promised me an ice cream *and* lollies." The spontaneous child still sometimes escaped the girl trying to act grown-up.

"Are you going to Gwenna's?" asked Sally.

"Of course. It's the best, isn't it, sweetheart?"

Grace nodded enthusiastically. "Can we take the tram too, Janey? I love riding on the tram, and it's such a long walk up to Karangahape Road.

"Yes, we can take the tram, but we don't need to go that far any more." Turning to the others, she added, "Did you know Gwenna has opened a second shop down the road from the theatre? They've been advertising in the programmes lately, offering half-time refreshments."

Both Brigid and Sally had heard about but not visited the new store.

"Trade must be good to take on that sort of risk," said Brigid. "Won't the one detract from the other, though?"

"I don't think so. It's a canny move, Breeda," said Sally. "Being in the right place at the right time. Her young brother Charlie knows all about it. Didn't he used to walk around with a tray hung around his neck or push a small cart around? He'd go to all the picnic areas and sporting games. Smart thinking. He sold lots that way."

"Yes, and he still does. I often see him at the theatre on a Saturday," said Jane. "He's growing into a fine young man."

"Can we go now? Can we go to the new shop, can we?" begged Grace.

"Grace! Don't be so impatient and use your manners. What did I tell you about interrupting when adults are talking?" chided Brigid.

"Yes, Mam. Sorry, Mam. But can we go ... please?"

The three women laughed.

"All right," said Jane, "but first, we are going to an exhibition at the Art Gallery. And then I have a surprise for you."

No amount of cajoling from Grace persuaded Jane to tell her what the surprise was.

"You'd better get going then before she talks your ear off," laughed Brigid. "Have fun."

A tram passed by as Jane and Grace stepped out of Miss Brigid's in lower Queen Street.

"Hurry. We can jump on this one as far as Wellesley Street," urged Jane.

Grace nimbly stepped onto the slow-moving tram, turning to offer a hand to Jane. Two blocks later they got off and walked up the hill to the Art Gallery.

Over an hour later, they emerged into the sunshine talking earnestly about what they'd seen.

"I liked the one with the ladies on the promenade," said Jane.

"Yes. That was nice, but I preferred the boat pulled up on the beach and the children playing."

"Why that one?

Grace shrugged her shoulders. "Just did."

"That's not a good enough answer. You have to understand why you like or dislike something. Why you make the judgement you do, otherwise you'll drift through life listening to other people's opinions and never know your own mind."

Grace was quiet for a few moments and skipped a few paces ahead as they walked down the hill again. She stopped and turned to look up at Jane. "I liked the colours, and the way they made me feel happy. I felt free with all the open spaces, and it stopped me looking at the dark rocks in the corner. I thought something could be hiding in them."

"Excellent thinking. For that, you deserve your ice cream."

Hand in hand, they crossed over Queen Street and walked up the opposite side of Wellesley Street. A bell tinkled as they opened the door of the tiny shop. Unlike Gwenna's of Karangahape Road, which offered Devonshire tea as well as Gwenna Price's handmade lollies, this store only sold ice cream, lollies and soft drinks. The room gleamed from all the jars sitting on the shelves lining three of the walls. A modern gaslight with several arms hung overhead making it easy to see everything on display.

Behind the counter stood someone they knew well. "Good afternoon, ladies. How good to see you today. I'm Charlie Price and I'm here to tempt your taste buds." In an instant, he offered them a tray with tiny pieces of fudge.

"Don't be silly, Charlie," laughed Grace, reaching out for a piece of chocolate fudge. "It's just me and Janey."

"Don't want to sample my wares, then?" he teased as he moved the tray out of reach.

"Of course I do. That's why we came in," replied Grace.

"Well then, Miss, for you are indeed looking very lovely today, let us conduct our business in the way I would treat all my lady customers." He winked at Grace who glowed with pleasure.

"Very well," she giggled. "I'm delighted to meet you, Mr Charlie Price. My name is Miss Grace Price, and I would like to buy some lollies please." She gave a little bob of a curtsy, trying hard not to laugh out loud. They'd long ago worked out that pure coincidence meant they shared the Price surname.

"And you, Madam," Charlie said to Jane. A quick look at his face told Jane he was struggling not to laugh too. "Would you care to tell me which of these you favour?" He moved the tray within reach.

Removing her gloves, Jane made her choice. "Thank you, Charlie. What a kindly gesture."

"Consider this your second kitchen, where all the treats come from."

His demeanour changed again as he put away the tray of tasting bits.

"So how did I do?" he asked Jane nervously. "It's the first time Gwenna's left me here on my own, and I wanted to try out my approach. Will I do? Will it impress the ladies enough, or the gentlemen coming in to buy something for their ladies?"

"You impressed me, Charlie," said Jane. "I think you will do well, but who runs the store when you're not here?"

Charlie wrapped up an ice cream wafer sandwich in greaseproof paper and handed it to Grace and then scooped lollies into paper twists while he talked. "Mam and my sisters take turns with Gwenna, just like they do at the tea shop."

Jane had only met Charlie's mother Bethan a few times at the shop, but she knew Gwenna was very fond of her stepmother. "This is delicious fudge, Charlie. I presume it's some of Gwenna's? Her reputation has travelled far."

"My sister Gwenna is indeed a master and makes the best fudge and lollies this side of the world."

"You're making a proud boast, Mr Price."

"But he's right, Janey," said Grace. "It is the best."

Another customer entered and as Charlie went into full swing with his welcome patter, Jane and Grace said their farewells.

Five minutes later, Grace was again bursting with excitement. Jane's surprise had been a visit to her workroom as part of her birthday treat. Brigid rarely let her daughter visit the theatre after hearing some of Jane's tales of misfits and troublemakers.

Grace dashed from rack to rack and table to table looking at all the bright, shiny baubles. "Janey, is it all right if I touch this dress?"

"Of course, my sweet. In fact, we can do better. Would you like to try it on?"

Grace bounced with joy. "Oh yes, please."

The dress was one of Jane's fantasy dresses made of multicoloured gauzes she had dyed in shades of deep purple, navy and green, decorated with silver sparkles. The facemask and headdress she was working on in the quiet of the empty studio would need to be as elaborate. She'd already hand-dyed heavy stockings to match, so the dancer would be head to toe in underwater colours, as Jane imagined them. Her late-night scribbles came to life when a body filled the contours of the design, and Jane's heart lifted at the sight. The concoction was perfect, if a little large for Grace.

"It's beautiful," said Grace as she swished and sashayed and danced about. The girl's laughter echoed through the room. A tingle ran down Jane's spine. She must not let Grace get too involved with the theatre. This was no place for the girl, despite her love of music.

Brigid was teaching the girls to make traditional Irish lace and to sew, and Sally was showing them how to run a business. Lilly's future, at least, lay there. Grace she wasn't so sure about. And now Brigid had finally accepted Phillip Harrison-Browne's invitation, maybe one of them would find a calling over there instead.

All these thoughts flashed through Jane's mind in the split second it took for Grace to leap into the air, spin and crash into a rack of costumes being prepared for the next production. Over it went, dragging everything on the adjacent rack to the floor as Grace rolled amongst the muddle. Behind, other racks rocked precariously as more garments slid to the floor to add to the jumble.

"Are you all right, Grace?" called Jane as she raced across to where Grace now sat nursing her ankle.

Grace nodded as a tear slid down her cheek. "It hurts."

"Oh, my dear girl. I'm sure it does, my sweet. Now let's get you out of this mess, and I'll go and find something to make a cool compress and see if I can borrow a stick to help you walk."

Jane reached out to help Grace to her feet and almost dropped the girl. Exposed by the disarray, a pair of men's boots peeked out from under a mound of fabric. An involuntary gasp escaped her lips. Still supporting Grace, balanced on one foot, Jane peered into the gloomy corner. "Who's there?" she called sharply, hoping her voice sounded authoritative enough. But only silence met her call.

With her pulse throbbing, Jane helped Grace to a chair and picked up the giant-sized tailor's square from the cutting table. She had no idea what she would do with it if confronted, but the feel of something solid in her hand gave her the courage to take a second look.

She prodded the nearest pile of clothing with the end of the square, but apart from some of it getting entangled, she made little progress. Taking a couple more steps into the heap, she reached out and prodded again. Finally, she put the square to one side and grabbed an armful of fabric and with a great heave pulled it away from the pile. She breathed a sigh of relief that no one was hiding underneath it all.

Instead, concealed in the furthest corner of the wardrobe, Jane could see a thin mattress and blanket rolled up next to a burlap sack. She'd had no idea they were there and wondered how long they'd avoided detection.

But she had a pretty good idea who had put them there in the first place.

"Sorry to bring her back in such a state," apologised Jane as she helped Grace up the stairs, "but there's no real harm done. A bit of a twisted ankle but she'll be right again soon enough. Won't you, poppet?"

"I'm sorry I damaged the dress, Janey."

"Shush now. It's minor and easy fixed. Did you have a fun birthday treat after all? That's far more important."

"Yes, thank you, Janey. I did."

Jane briefly explained to Brigid, who was fussing over the girl, how she had tripped over the long tails of the costume. "Can I help you repair the dress? Or do anything to make up for the damage?"

"No. Everything's fine. You don't need to do a thing, except make this one happy." Jane smoothed the girl's hair, her heart aching for her. "But I'll be on my way."

"Are you going to find out who those things belonged to, Janey?"

"That I am, lass."

Grace nodded. "I don't like to think of someone sleeping under your costumes."

"Neither do I, my pet," said Jane.

"What's all this about, Jane?" asked Brigid, frowning with concern.

"I found some clothes and a sleeping roll hidden in the corner of the workroom. Someone's been hiding there. I suspect it's a lad at the theatre. He reminds me a bit of Jamie in some ways. He's as soft and tender-hearted as your Jamie was."

Jamie. Her childish infatuation with Jamie had got

119

Jane into her current predicament by transferring her affections to the young Mickey, who now preferred to be known as Alexander Phipps. As a child, Jane hoped Brigid's cousin and her Aunt Maggie would get together and everything would work out right again in her world, but they hadn't, and it didn't. Such things only happened in fairy tales.

In despair, Jamie went away to work in the South Island, and they'd lost track of him over the years. Seeing the expression on Brigid's face, Jane wished she'd not mentioned him. Jamie was another disappointment for Brigid to bear.

Darkness had fallen by the time Jane let herself back into the workroom. This time, a boy lay curled up in the corner with an arm over his head. "Cecil," murmured Jane. "Is that you? What are you doing hiding there? Come out, for goodness' sake. What did you think I was going to do – eat you?"

Cecil didn't move to begin with, and Jane became more anxious. She touched his arm. Keeping his face turned away from her, he slowly straightened and sat with his head on his knees and his arms wrapped around his lower legs.

"What's the matter, Cecil? I promise you are not in trouble. Won't you tell me what's happened?"

At Jane's soft voice and encouraging words, he lifted his head. A gasp escaped her lips as the light revealed his bruised face. One eyelid and both his lips were split, blood had congealed through his hair and dried on his face and neck. He looked as if he'd been crying too, but she wouldn't mention it.

Cecil grabbed Jane's proffered hand and managed to stand, although he limped as badly as Grace had. She didn't ask any further questions, knowing he would tell her what happened when he was ready. Meanwhile, he needed a place to rest and clean up.

Jane borrowed some ladies' boots and a skirt from the theatre wardrobe. She gave Cecil her cloak and hat as a disguise and told him to go to her rooms ahead of her and wait. Jane knew the risk she was taking. Mrs Greaves would toss her out quicker than she could explain if the woman thought for one moment Jane had a man in her room. Poor Cecil: wanting to be a real man, but far too pretty and fair to fit into a workingman's crowd. He didn't belong anywhere, and Jane did what she could to ease his lot in life.

A short while later, Jane crept up the stairs to her lodgings, trying not to attract the attention of her landlady. Not usually one to break the rules, Jane's heart thumped loudly and she shook with nerves, afraid she would give everything away if she met Mrs Greaves. She felt bad enough sneaking out and returning at all hours, thanks to Alexander Phipps, without this subterfuge. Fortunately, her landlady had accepted her work at the theatre as the reason for her unorthodox and irregular hours when she'd first taken up residence so didn't pay her as much attention as she otherwise might.

"Now, lad. Let's be looking at you." Jane filled an enamel bowl with hot water and added some drops of iodine. Taking a cloth, she gently sponged his wounds. He would have to keep out of sight for a few days until the bruises faded. "Can you tell me what happened?"

"Got into a fight, didn't I." He flicked his eyes to meet Jane's.

"That's obvious. But why and with whom?"

"Protecting you. Like you asked me to."

"Protecting me?" squeaked Jane. "What are you talking about?"

"That man who's taken a fancy to you. You asked me to stay close, so I follow him and the other ruffian who follows you. Keep an eye on them, I do. It's why I were sleeping rough in the workshop," he explained. "Have done ever since that Phipps fella turned up. I can watch you more close like, and be there when you need me."

When he could get away from the theatre, Cecil had followed her everywhere and waited outside the late-night clubs, even when she was with Phipps. Jane was both flattered and embarrassed, but grateful. Knowing someone else knew and understood her fears was a relief – despite the fact he was only a lad.

"And …?"

"I were watching the youth who followed ya home when the man cornered me and asked what he was doing. I told him nowt. I didn't want him knowing I was looking out for ya, and risk him taking it out on you."

"That was probably wise."

"I could've handled the bully boy on me own, but when the bloke used his walking cane on me, I was a goner."

"Oh, Cecil. That's awful. Then what happened?"

"His boy joined in to see what was going on, like. He offered to beat it out of me."

He tried to grin, but after a painful 'Ow', grimaced instead. "I told him to try his luck and he took a swipe at me, so I hit him back."

As the two quite evenly matched boys fought it out, the man had cracked his cane down, first on Cecil's arm and then his leg, bringing him crashing to the ground.

"The bully went mad then and thrashed the daylights out o' me. I must have lain there a while, because when I stirred they were well gone."

Jane was appalled at his story and was of a mind to tackle Mickey about it, but worried it would make matters worse, both for her and for Cecil. He promised he would carry on looking out for her.

"No, Cecil. I can't let you do that any more. It's too risky."

"Don't you worry none, Miss Jane. They know nowt about what I was doing or why I was there. I wasn't thinking proper. I'll be more careful in future."

"You'd better stay here ..." she began. "No, well actually, maybe not. You need sleep. But you can't go back to the theatre looking like you do."

"I'll be all right. Promise. Do you want me to get rid of him for ya?"

Jane was too scared to ask what he meant by 'get rid' or which 'him' Cecil meant: Mickey or the other lad. Either way, she couldn't countenance any more violence.

"No. No! Don't do anything. Don't put yourself at risk. But I thank you for caring and watching out for me."

Cecil blushed.

"Thanks for fixing me up, Miss Jane, but I'd better go. I can't afford to lose me job."

"Where will you go?"

A smile touched his lips. "Same place as always."

Jane reached out to hug him then changed her mind. They danced awkwardly around each other until Cecil opened the door and crept down the edge of the stair, making not a sound as he left.

13

SEARCHING FOR THE TRUTH

August 2018

Never for a moment had Katie thought looking for her ancestors would be as complicated and time-consuming. Neither did she expect to get engrossed with it, but she was utterly absorbed.

Before he'd left, after the photo shoot, Jared had logged into his online tree and shown her what he had collated. Some of the information had come from the family knowing the names of their grandparents and great-grandparents; some had come from hints and links on the family search websites. Either way, he had an impressive tree stretching back to George Price who had brought his family to New Zealand in 1881.

She'd scribbled down everything he said and was now trying to put it into practice. The story he'd told her of the names starting with G being handed down the line from George to Gwenna, and on through three more generations until Jared, made sense now she was looking at her own tree ...

"Be careful when you're adding siblings," he warned. "They can run away with you, especially with blended families. Not that they called them that back then. But look here ..."

He showed her Gwenna's page with a full sister, a stepbrother, two stepsisters and a half-brother. "By the time you add in all their spouses and their children, you end up with huge branches, which have nothing to do with the direct line. It's easy to get sidetracked."

He also showed her what to do when one name appeared on the records but people commonly used another. "Like great-grandma Gwenna who married Hugh Powell, but kept her Price surname. Her son George wasn't Hugh's, so George took the Price name."

"How did you know he wasn't Hugh's son?"

"Timing mostly. Hugh was twelve years older than Gwenna and went away to the Boer War. And there are stories of a first marriage and a sudden death, but I've not been able to prove anything one way or the other."

Nor had there been any further children from her marriage to Hugh, so George Junior's line dominated the rest of the entries, but a shock awaited her when he clicked another link. The page he'd brought up had been for Gwenna's half-brother Charlie Price.

"I only went so far with this page because it's not my direct tree. Charlie was much younger than Gwenna but he was involved in the business, so when a few hints kept popping up, I saved them. Some people become so obsessed they follow every twig on every branch, and the system picks up the hints. They certainly help lazy souls like me, who only follow a direct line. I haven't the time for any more."

The entry showed Charlie had married a Grace at the start of World War One in 1914. "I can't find a maiden name for her so I have no idea who her parents or siblings were, but I did find four children."

Katie scanned down the sidebar following Jared's pen: Thomas, Jane, Susan ... and stopped in her tracks. On 10 February 1928, a girl named Kathleen had been born.

"But that's my Granna Katy's birthdate, and her maiden name was Price too," she blurted out before realising she'd never told Jared about her grandmother.

"That's certainly quite a coincidence, but don't read too much into it. There are hundreds of people with the same name born on the same day all over the place."

But not in Auckland, thought Katie, *and not with a Grandma Gwenna*.

So, what did all this mean? She was suddenly itching to get started on her tree. But first, she had to complete Jared's website.

The photos had come out better than Katie had hoped, and Jared was as impressed as Viv.

"I might think about employing you as a photographer if this is what you can turn out."

"And I just might take you up on your offer if it's going. Thanks, Viv."

Viv left Katie and Jared in the conference room to finish loading the website and test everything one last time before the launch.

"Are you ready?" Katie asked when she was satisfied.

Jared nodded, but she could tell from his body language he was anxious. When had she started to notice the little things that gave him away? Overly polishing his glasses, checking his watch, pushing his glasses up his nose, folding and unfolding his handkerchief or whatever piece of paper was near ... and rocking his chair.

"Let's run through the checklist again, shall we? To be certain."

He rested his chair back on all four legs. Using her fingers, she counted off the tasks needing completion until they agreed everything they could think of had been covered.

"The two most important things we need to be certain of: Are all your social media sites linked and posts scheduled?"

He nodded.

"And the menu cards and flyers are printed? There's not much more we can do, then. Not until the stats come in – it could be a few weeks yet before we see any hits. The search engines have to find new websites, but with the SEO set up the way it is, I have my hopes set on seeing some soon and, hopefully, orders will follow."

"Thanks for helping me set all those links up. I would never have thought to join half of them."

He got to his feet and leant on the back of the chair facing her. "But there is still one issue?"

Katie raised her eyebrows, tucked her hair behind her ear and waited.

"A kitchen."

"What? What are you talking about?"

"I haven't told my employer what I plan to do yet. I still need the income, so I can't use my workplace. I checked out all the rules about getting a licence for my home kitchen, and there's no way I can make it work there. And I can't risk taking on a lease until I'm more confident about how successful it'll turn out to be."

Katie was momentarily stumped. No kitchen was a problem: a big problem. There was little point in launching a website to take orders if he couldn't fill them. She clicked on her search engine and randomly looked up kitchen hire. A few more clicks and a page came up that interested her. "What about something like this?"

Jared moved around behind her and peered over her shoulder.

"Looks like there's some shared spaces you can hire short term or even hourly. Would they work?"

"Where would I be without you?" he said casually. "I hadn't thought about hiring short term as a possibility. I didn't know they existed."

Katie tried not to read anything into his words, but his nearness was off-putting. They studied the options, the text details and the locations and finally picked one. She filled in the request form and sent it off.

His expressive face relaxed and that almost-smile of his reappeared. "I think you might have solved my problem, once again. Thank you."

"Let's wait until you hear from them," she said. "Coffee?"

Jared nodded.

While Katie was making the coffee, she kept thinking what other options there were to kick-starting Jared's new business.

"I'm not much good at all this, am I?" he said. "When it comes to desserts, I'm in my element, but all this, this organisational stuff just escapes me."

"It's not everyone's cup of tea, I admit. But we can't do much more right now."

They'd finished their coffee and Katie was tidying up ready to leave when his phone dinged.

"Wow. They were quick." He read through the email. "They've answered all your questions about prices, space size and hours, and it looks a goer." He closed his phone and pocketed it. "Will you come with me to visit the place? If I like one, I can sign the contract there and then, and it's mine anytime I want it. I'd value your opinion."

"I'm not sure I'd be much use," she hedged, clearing their empty mugs from the desk. "I don't know a thing about kitchens, or what you would need and how you work. So now the roles are reversed."

She loved it when he smiled.

"Maybe, but it's a start-up company, like me, and I need your reassurance they are legit. You know about contracts and things. You could handle the business side while I choose the kitchen. Deal?"

How did he manage to persuade her to do what he wanted so effortlessly?

She laughed. "All right. If it makes you feel better."

Two hours later, they were back in the office, contract in hand, decisions made.

Viv joined them shortly after, carrying a bottle of bubbles and three glasses. "I think we should celebrate since I hear everything has fallen into place so well. I told you Katie would handle your account to your satisfaction."

"She sure has." Jared was talking to Viv, but his eyes were on Katie.

"And the work has been finished well within the time frame. I hope you're satisfied with the service I've provided. I pride myself on outcomes."

"She's been amazing."

The unexpected praise and inferences didn't sit comfortably with Katie. "This is a bit outside the norm, isn't it, Viv? I don't remember celebrating the end of a project like this before."

"Well, you have never been in a position like this before." Viv placed herself between them and held out the bottle to Jared to open. "Would you do the honours, please?"

Jared expertly popped the cork and filled each of the glasses. Viv placed one in front of Katie and raised her own. When Jared lifted his, Katie had no option but to stand and raise her glass too.

"Thank you for choosing my company," declared Viv, "and here's to a successful launch." Katie gave her a puzzled look, which Viv ignored.

"To Katie," said Jared.

"To success," she replied.

"To us," added Viv.

After the first sip, Katie put her glass down. "Looks like the only thing left to do is push the GO button. Are you ready?"

Jared placed his glass on the table, rubbed his hands together and went to stand beside Katie. She opened the site and set the cursor on the launch icon.

"Go on, you do it."

Jared clicked the mouse and his new venture was launched. "Yessss," he said and punched the air. Viv clapped.

Jared raised his glass once more. "I couldn't have done it without you," he smiled at Viv before turning to Katie. "Either of you. Thank you – for everything. But I guess, from now on it's all up to me. I have to figure out how to do the rest on my own."

"Not entirely on your own," purred Viv, moving closer to Jared and clinking her glass against his. "If you have any questions, do come to me. I'd be more than happy to help."

If she gets any closer, thought Katie, *she'll push him over*.

"Thank you, Viv. I appreciate the offer, but I wouldn't want to put you to any trouble. I think we'll be OK." He winked at Katie but Viv was having none of that.

"It's no trouble at all, Jared. Not at all. Now Katie's contract has finished, I will take over."

Feeling deliberately ignored and shoved aside, Katie wondered what would happen next with Jared. She had thought something more would come of their growing attachment, now they were no longer client and consultant, but maybe the timing was all wrong. She would miss his help with her family tree, but he had his new business to focus on and wouldn't have time to waste with her.

Pull yourself together, she chided her inner self. A work contract had come to an end. Time to move on.

14

MISJUDGEMENTS

December 1903

Still vexed by Cecil's story and determined to put an end to whatever Mickey called this nonsensical dalliance they had entered into, Jane was taken aback when he arrived unexpectedly at the theatre the next day.

"He's downstairs, Miss Jane," said Cecil, handing her the note.

"Thank you, Cecil. I think it's time to put a stop to this." She only hoped she had the strength to follow through with her intentions and not be swayed again by his magnetism and memories of what had once been precious to her.

"I'll be watching, Miss Jane. Never fear."

Jane was moved by Cecil's loyalty. His cuts and bruises were healing but Jane could still see evidence of the beating he'd taken because of her.

Putting her palm against his face, she said, "Don't do anything rash, will you? But I will feel better knowing you are near. Wait until I call."

Jane gathered her skirts and descended the stairs to the corridors below. This time, Phipps had called by the stage door and hovered in one of the principal dressing rooms. Before he became aware of her presence, Jane watched him smugly preening in the mirror. How could she have been so deceived? This man thought only of himself.

Her anger at what had happened to Cecil reached boiling point, and any remnants of the naïve and gullible girl of the past disappeared in an instant. Seeing this man through fresh eyes, she realised how much she'd been manipulated and controlled. "What do you want?" she demanded.

He spun away from the mirror and his mask of chivalry fell into place. "Jane, my dear. Why the sharp tone? Have I done something to upset you?" He attempted to lift her hand and kiss it but she snatched it away. "Am I still the callous Mickey of the past to you? Can you not yet see me in a new light as the endearing Alex who cares for you?"

"Spare me your hubris. Why did you come here?"

Various expressions crossed his face as he tried to figure out why the usually passive woman had turned so aggressive. Eventually, he directed a smile full of forgiveness and understanding her way. "Forgive me, but I am mindful of why we lost each other all those years ago, so I came in person to tell you I am going away. I have been engaged for a lengthy season of performances in Australia over the festive season and beyond, but do not be distressed. I will write to you and we shall rekindle the flame when I return, my love."

His performance was magnificent. She had to give him that. No wonder he was sought after by theatrical managers and audiences alike. In other circumstances, she could have admired his skill, but now they served to inflame a different emotion to the one he intended.

"You are presuming upon a relationship which does not exist. I wish you good fortune in Australia, but do not return on my account. What has gone has gone and will never resurface. Good day to you."

She turned to leave, but he grabbed her arm. This time his facial expressions were less congenial as he struggled to control his temper.

He bent over her, forcing her to lean away from him as he hissed into her ear. "No one dismisses me like that, especially not a slut like you. All these months, I wasted my time with the niceties of courtship. I tried to be kind. But you, you stiff-necked shrew, wouldn't bend. Well, no more. I want what's mine and I shall have it."

He released her with a shove, sending her stumbling until she tripped and landed on her front on the chaise longue. She untangled her skirts and petticoats and turned in time to see him lock the door and begin to remove his jacket and cravat as he approached her.

"I seem to remember you had a liking for me once. Well, let's see if I can arouse that passion again."

"Leave me alone, Mickey," she growled through gritted teeth.

"Oh, I would have, if you'd been at all nice to me, but no longer. You are mine." He unbuttoned his trousers.

"Don't you dare ..."

He pounced, pushing her shoulders back against the velvet covering and fell on her, forcing all the breath from her lungs. She tossed her head from side to side as he began kissing her face and neck. She pounded and flailed him with her hands until he grabbed her wrists and held them tight with one hand above her head.

"Vixen," he grinned. "So you like it rough these days, do you?"

He grabbed a feather boa lying nearby and bound her hands, while his knee held her in place. He looped the end of the boa around her neck so it would tighten if she fought to free her hands.

"Get off ... I'll scream."

He put his hand on her throat and pressed; his smile was chilling. "I like a girl with a bit of spark in her. I find it quite invigorating. Can't you see? But I suggest you'll be better off if you don't fight me."

She lay there, eyes bulging at the evidence of his words, but fear kept her silent. She was struggling to breathe, let alone scream. And if she screamed, Cecil would hear. Mickey would kill him, or do him serious harm, if he tried to rescue her.

He released her throat and she coughed, gasping for air. Changing position, his hands lifted her skirts and he ran his fingers like feathers up the inside of her thighs before ripping away her stockings and pushing her chemise up. She gasped at his touch and flinched. "No. Don't."

"Such pale, soft skin." He began to stroke and gently pinch the soft skin as she writhed under his legs holding her down. "Keep still, whore. You wouldn't want this lovely flesh damaged, now would you?" He continued with his play until every nerve end was on fire, and at the point when she thought she could stay silent no longer, he plunged into her, tearing tender skin as he thrust again and again.

She sucked in more air and bit her lip in an effort not to scream but couldn't prevent the tears falling or the involuntary cries. "Stop. Please?"

A knock sounded. "Are you a'right in there, Miss Jane," called Cecil. "I thought I heard you call."

Mickey growled and with a final thrust lay still on top of her. "Send him away," he rasped in her ear. "Or I'll deal with him."

Mickey raised himself on one elbow and pressed a hard fist into her stomach.

She expelled air. "Yes, Cecil," she gasped. "I'm fine. You can go now."

Mickey's face took on an evil, grinning mask and his eyes burned with fever. "Wise move. Maybe I won't hurt him after all – this time."

He pulled away and stood up, staring down at her. She couldn't find the strength to drag her eyes away from his brooding presence.

"But when I come back, you and I will continue where we left off. Do you understand me?"

Frightened by 'that man' but unwilling to burden Brigid, Jane turned to her trusted friend. Nevertheless, she couldn't tell Gwenna everything either. She simply couldn't.

"Shh, Jane, shh," said Gwenna soothingly while she patted her friend's back. "Sobbing like this won't solve anything. You've got yourself worked up into such a state, I can't understand what you are saying. Now, here, drink this and start at the beginning." Gwenna handed a cup of black tea with honey and a splash of brandy to Jane and waited for her to calm down.

The tea helped, and tucking away her sodden handkerchief, she wiped her eyes dry with a fresh hanky supplied by Gwenna.

After a few deep breaths, Jane began telling her friend the tale of her love affair with Mickey all those years ago.

"I was young and naïve, but I truly loved him then and was heartbroken when he left without saying a word."

Gwenna understood all too well how Jane had been captivated, having been similarly besotted with her Johnno, which had only turned to heartache. The difference was she had married her love before he died in suspicious circumstances and left her with his son to raise.

"After he'd gone, I buried myself in my work," explained Jane.

She had become as one with the theatre and then one day her designs were noticed. The years passed, and Jane's passion for the costumes had long since assuaged the pain of youth.

"And then he turns up again a few months ago wanting to ... court me."

She told Gwenna how, on the one hand, he'd showered her with flowers, gifts, flattery, and nights out, and on the other, he'd had her followed and issued vague threats of ruining her if she didn't comply. Between sobs and long pauses, Jane confessed.

"I wanted to believe he would love me again like he once did but, in my heart, I knew. I was holding on to a false hope. Ours was a one-sided affair for which I paid the price ... I have no idea what he is playing at, but I'm sure he wants me as his mistress ... I could never ... not again ..."

There! She said it. She'd admitted her shame. She shook her head to dismiss the unspeakable thought, dabbed at her eyes again and took several deep breaths.

"Then I found out he'd been responsible for the boy Cecil at the theatre being beaten up and then, today ..."

"Go on. Today?" urged Gwenna. "What happened today?"

Gabbling as fast as she could, Jane recounted what had happened.

"He … he … forced …" She couldn't finish. "I ran, gathered my things and ran. I'm so frightened, Gwenna. What am I going to do if he comes back?"

Outraged, Gwenna covered Jane's clenched hands in her own in an effort to comfort her. "Well, he'll have more than one of us to contend with if he does. He's a right no-gooder, that's for certain. But for now, forget him. Hopefully, he'll think about it while he's away and won't bother you again. Why would he? You made it plain you wanted nothing to do with him, so why would he risk you rejecting him all over again?"

"Because it makes him feel powerful to have control over me."

"He does not control you," argued Gwenna.

"If he tells people about our … that I … Oh, Gwenna. I'm so ashamed. My reputation will be ruined, and I'll lose my job and my very existence." Jane dropped her head into her hands, but she was sobbed out.

Gwenna wanted to say something, anything to help Jane fight back, but she knew Jane was right. Society was a fickle thing. Men could get away with so much, but women who stepped outside the mould others made for them were looked down on and talked about.

Being part of the theatre wasn't quite as respectable as other careers, but Jane's talent gave her credence. In any event, if he chose to spread rumours around town that Jane was his mistress, then or now, even if she wasn't, she would lose what good name she had, whether she deserved to or not.

"We'll think of something. Don't despair, dear friend. Don't despair."

Life at the theatre became so busy Jane managed to push her anxiety to the back of her mind most of the time, but the possible consequences of Mickey's attack dogged her until she was certain no further shame could be added to her life. While immensely relieved, she still wasn't performing to her usual standard.

Demands from the actors and actresses, the visiting stars, the directors and the managers were non-stop in the lead-up to the Christmas season. She spent many nights working until the small hours and was struggling from lack of sleep. She'd not had time to visit Brigid or see Grace at her piano recital, but neither had she been sketching new designs. A part of her brain seemed to have shut down months before. Whenever she tried, she ended up balling the paper in her hand and tossing it in the bin.

Cecil was now her constant shadow, never mind what hour of the day or night she walked to and from the theatre, but she worried about him too. What if 'that man' returned and saw him and had him beaten up again? Her head spun in circles, full of questions with no answers, and endless doubt gnawed at her. Gwenna wrote reassuring notes and sent Jane lollies through Charlie, but they'd not talked since the day of her confession several weeks earlier.

Only a matter of days before Christmas, with three more shows to clothe before Jane would finally have a chance to catch up with the family, Cecil came to see her in the workroom. Saying nothing, he handed her a newspaper and pointed to a small notice practically lost in the middle of the page, except for the headline: POPULAR ARTISTE FOUND DEAD.

Jane glanced up at the boy wearing a satisfied grin and back at the paper, rapidly reading the few facts:

Mr Alexander Phipps, a well-known thespian of some repute, was found dead this morning in Kings Park, Sydney. The authorities believe he fell from his horse sometime during the night and hit his head. His horse still stood nearby.

She handed the paper back, dazed and unable to believe her nemesis was gone from her life. It seemed so sudden and too good to be true.

"No need for you to worry your head about him no more then, is there, Miss Jane." Still grinning, Cecil tapped the side of his nose.

She stood looking at the boy for some time, wondering if he knew something he wasn't telling her, but it seemed such a ludicrous idea since Mickey had died in Sydney and Cecil had never left her side. If it hadn't been for his suggestion he could 'get rid' of the problem for her, Jane would never have considered it a possibility. She frowned at Cecil, trying to read something in his eyes, but could sense nothing from his silly grin.

Numb with shock, Jane returned to her task of tacking an adornment to the costume on the tailor's dummy without clearly seeing what she was doing. Unthinking, she pricked her finger and blood bubbled from the tip. She stared at it in fascination for some seconds before quietly collapsing in a heap.

She awoke a few minutes later, propped up by Paul, her cutter, Aggie fanning the paper over her face and Cecil encouraging her to have a drink of water.

"You shou'd go 'ome, mith," said Aggie, her lisp more pronounced at seeing Jane faint. "You're not your

140

uthual thelf, haven't been for months, and we've been right wuwwied about you."

"Aggie's right," added Paul, helping her to her feet. "Go home. We can manage here."

Jane nodded, knowing she was incapable of doing anything of any consequence. Her head was pounding and she felt dizzy. "I'm sorry to have let you down."

"Nonsense," said Paul. "You haven't done any such thing. Everything is in order, ready and on time, as usual. You have worked yourself to a standstill these last months. Have you not noticed how thin you are?"

Jane glanced down. Her wrists poking out below the cuffs of her blouse were more bone than flesh, and her skirt sagged on her hips.

"I haven't been eating well."

"Miss Jane, will you let me walk you home?" asked Cecil, pushing her to a decision.

Accepting her colleagues were right and she did indeed need to rest, she knew where she wanted to be more than anywhere else. She thanked them for their concern and reassured herself they could manage without her.

"Would you walk with me to Miss Brigid's, please Cecil? I'm not feeling ..." she said, before subsiding exhausted into her chair.

Brigid and Sally were aghast at the state Jane was in when Cecil brought her to their door in a carriage, paid for by Mr McConnochie no less. Cecil filled them in on what had happened, whispering so Jane would not hear. "She called him Mickey."

Brigid's manner changed and her face froze.

"Mr Sir, the manager, says she's not to come back until after Christmas," said Cecil as he took his leave.

The two women brooked no arguments and put Jane to bed. There she stayed a full 36 hours, sleeping solidly without her usual nightmares, thanks to a tonic Brigid gave her. They took it in turn to watch her, forcing her to rest. When she awoke, they brought her enticing yet easily digested meals. Grace or Lilly read to her, with strict instructions not to tire her out or annoy her.

Slowly, the whole sad story was repeated. This time, she did tell Brigid the whole truth.

Brigid's face hardened. "We shall never mention this again. There is no point in you reliving it, and he's received his comeuppance. I just wish you had told me he was back a long time ago," chastised Brigid gently. "A trouble shared is a trouble halved."

Brigid and Sally understood more than anyone else could. They'd been Jane's strength and comfort the first time he abandoned her.

Brigid had handled the whole sorry debacle with aplomb. "Hush," she said, whenever Jane tried to talk about Mickey's unexpected, and unexplained, death. It seemed all too convenient. "Don't concern yourself with that man any more. He doesn't deserve any consideration whatsoever. I will never forgive him for what he did to you. We are all better off without him in our lives, however it may have come about."

With the gift of days off and her strength sufficiently restored to get up, Jane wanted to help and insisted on doing the Christmas decorations. She set a pine branch in the small dormer window and, with the use of some sticky mucilage spread over the needles and a layer of salt, Jane created a look of snow. Regardless of the fact

Auckland was in the midst of summer and the days were hot, many of the Christmas cards and decorations showed snowy scenes befitting the 'home' country.

Lilly crocheted a dozen mini snowflakes which Jane strung on the branches with red ribbon bows. Candles adorning the sill completed the pretty picture, which could be seen from outside. The mantel she adorned with similar snowy branches alongside the many cards they'd received. Handmade stockings hung from pegs on either side in readiness for Christmas morning.

"It looks grand, Jane," said Brigid. "Thank you."

On Christmas Eve, Jane, Brigid and Sally took Lilly and Grace to visit John Courts department store where, for the first time, a unique 'Christmas Wonderland' with a real-life Santa was on display within an enlarged toy department, and a 'Magic Cave' designed by the American decorator, Frank Carr.

The girls oohed and aahed with joy, and the three women gazed in awe at the spectacle and the resplendently decorated trees – still a relatively new trend. None of them had seen anything quite so magical before.

On Christmas morning, the girls were up early, eager to see what Santa had brought them in the night. Lengths of ribbon, an orange, a handkerchief and lollies fell from the upturned stockings to squeals of joy. Lilly received a sketchpad and a packet of Crayola crayons while Grace was given a teddy bear, which Jane had spotted amongst the toy display.

After they had tidied up, Brigid, Lilly and Grace attended the early service, while Sally remained behind as usual, promising to keep an eye on the lamb roast and welcome Laura when she arrived. Jane had protested she wished to attend church as well.

"Not today, Jane. The uphill walk will be too much for you. You mustn't overdo things," ordered Brigid. "Rest, Jane. Rest. God will understand."

The time passed as Sally set the table with the best china and all the extras needed for a special occasion, while Jane arranged fresh ferns and pōhutukawa flowers and lit the festive candles.

After an excellent meal, they pulled the crackers, exchanged personal gifts and laughter filled the room. Jane couldn't imagine any better way to spend her day than with the people she loved most: Brigid, the talented, humble and warm-hearted soul who took everyone's troubles on her shoulders; Sally, the resourceful schemer with a sharp eye who would protect the family with her life if needed; the delightful Lilly who was determined and inventive, and would go far in life; beautiful Grace, the tiny, talented girl who held a singular place in her heart; and Laura, her sister, bonded by blood and memories, who for once was in high spirits and hadn't spoilt the luncheon with dire warnings of male oppression.

After they'd done the dishes, returned the table to its normal position and packed away all the leftover food, Brigid said, "It's such a sunny day, why don't we take the ferry across the harbour for the afternoon? Do you feel up to doing that much, Jane?"

"I'm quite restored, thank you. And yes, I'd love to take the ferry."

After reaching a unanimous decision, the party meandered the short distance to the ferry terminal. Three-quarters of an hour later, across sparkling water under a perfect blue sky, they arrived in Devonport.

The women strolled along King Edward Parade under the shade of their parasols and rested on the waterfront seating, while the girls paddled nearby. Everyone was treated to an ice cream, but all too soon, the time came for the day to end.

"Brigid, it's been a lovely day, and I can't thank you enough for the care you've showered on me," said Jane. "But I must get back to my workroom tomorrow."

"Must you, Jane? Can you not stay one more day? You need to rest, you are so thin and pale still. You must regain your strength."

Grace's arms snaked around her waist. "Please stay, Janey, please. I like it when you come to stay."

Jane kissed the top of her head. "And I love being with you too, my sweet, but I have work to do. I honestly can't stay, Brigid, but thanks to you, I'm strong enough to return. Holidays are a busy time at the theatre, and I mustn't take advantage of Mr McConnochie's generosity any longer."

After disembarking from the ferry, they walked slowly back up Queen Street together. Laura collected her bicycle, saying she was off to visit friends, leaving the rest of the family to enjoy an evening of games.

On Boxing Day morning, Jane bade farewell and headed to the theatre in Wellesley Street, rejuvenated and reassured by the love of her adopted family. She desperately wanted to talk with Gwenna about the latest developments. She wasn't sure whether the news of Mickey's death had reached her yet – but Gwenna would be busy. Lolly shops were one of the few establishments allowed to open on Christmas Day, and Gwenna would never let an opportunity pass. Today would be another busy day, with several picnic events planned. She would have to wait a day or two.

Jane climbed the stairs to her workroom, glad her stressful year was coming to an end. To her surprise,

Cecil arrived moments after she'd taken off her bonnet.

"Are you feeling better, Miss Jane?"

"Thank you, Cecil. Yes, I am, but why are you here?"

His embarrassed shuffle and incoherent mutter about keeping an eye on her still answered her question sufficiently for her not to press him.

"I fawt you oughta know, Miss." He shuffled some more, grinned and flicked his hair from his eyes. "In case you fawt it were a trick 'n all, but that fella met 'is match a'right. But it weren't no accident."

Jane paled and flopped onto the chair, hoping she wouldn't faint. "Are you talking about ...?" She couldn't say his name.

Cecil nodded. "Story's rife all frough the featre. He'd come rushing over 'ere to escape some bloke in Melbourne who were mad at him over some sheila ..." Cecil stopped, turned bright red and stammered. "I mean lady, Miss. He were a right one for the ladies. No sooner were he back in Australia but word got around. Silly fing to do. Why'd he go back?"

"Because his ego was bigger than his brain," said Jane. "He had an offer of a big role."

Cecil shrugged. "Rumour 'as it, this other fella 'eard he were back and followed him and clubbed him one, and made it look like an accident. Either way, it's true, Miss Jane. He's gone."

So, Mickey had got his comeuppance. Terrible as it seemed, the news of his murder sat more truthfully with Jane than being thrown from his horse. She shuddered with revulsion. She'd had a testing few months, which had sapped both her energy and her creativity.

1904 could only be better.

15

THE LOSSES MOUNT

September 2018

Granna's sudden deterioration frightened Katie. She hadn't expected it to be so rapid. She had reported the time Granna had mistaken Katie for her younger self to the nursing staff, but each time she visited since, Granna appeared more disoriented than usual.

"It's quite normal," replied the supervisor. "You're fortunate she has connected with you at all. Some reach the point where they don't recognise anyone any more."

Tears stung Katie's eyes. She tried to find words to express her guilt for neglecting her grandmother over the past few months when the frequency of her visits had dropped off. "Should I have come more often?"

"It wouldn't have made any difference, my dear." The nurse showed Katie to a chair and sat beside her. "And you call more often than most. Don't blame yourself. There is no pattern to how well a patient responds. But I believe your success rate has been quite outstanding. You obviously have a very close bond."

Katie nodded. "We did once." She wiped her eyes and straightened her back, not wanting to hear the answer but determined to ask the question. "What happens now?"

"That's up to you. You can keep visiting as often as you usually do, with the understanding she may not recognise you at all or be upset by your visit. But she may still remember something about you that feels familiar and comfortable, and enjoy your visits. Or you can space your visits out if it helps you cope better, or cease visiting altogether – although I wouldn't recommend stopping completely. We will continue to care for her, whatever you decide."

She thanked the supervisor for her time and the pamphlets outlining the stages of the disease with tips on what to do and how to cope, and went to Granna's room.

"Hello, Granna, it's me, Katie. I've brought you some flowers."

"Hello, Katy. What a lovely little girl you are."

Momentarily, Katie thought Granna had remembered her. Her words had been clear for once, but the look on her face said otherwise. She was still away in another time.

Katie fiddled around putting the flowers in a vase and setting them on the bedside table.

"Aren't they pretty? Early daffodils, narcissi and freesias."

Granna turned her head. "Pretty." At least, that's what Katie interpreted. Sometimes her speech was more affected than other times, and it could change within moments.

"I've got something for you to look at."

Katie had made up a digital book with several of the old prints she'd found and added some of the new ones she'd taken. Pulling up a chair so she could sit next to Granna, she held the book across Granna's knee and pointed to the page, naming those she could.

Although silent and showing no sign of recognising anyone, not even ones of herself, Granna followed Katie's finger, tapping each image in turn. After a while, Granna showed some agitation and wriggled in her chair. Her hand vaguely flapped in the direction of a group of frames. Katie closed the book and put it on the floor and went to pick up one of the pictures. "Shall we look at this photo?"

Granna started to grunt and squeal so Katie replaced it and picked up another, but Granna became more agitated. "Hold Katie's hand, Granna. It'll make you feel better."

She was trying to remember some of the tips she read. Always repeating her own name, keeping her voice calm and not asking questions in need of an answer, but although her head could follow the instructions and understand the purpose for them, her heart was crying.

A few minutes later, Granna calmed down and appeared to be dozing. Unable to restrain her tears any longer, Katie tiptoed out of the room and hurried along the corridor to escape into the spring sunshine.

The last month had tested Katie's every fibre. Hugh had phoned to complain about their father, blustering about the horrible teenage brats his new wife had brought into the house. "Why did you let him, Katie?"

She'd exploded. "Why did I let him? What about you? You're his son, couldn't you talk to your father 'man to man', or whatever men do, and get him to see sense?

I can't bear to think about it. How dare you make it my fault."

She'd hung up on him and hadn't talked to him since, but for once she was not going to back down and be the first to offer the olive branch. Damn him!

Tom had been more understanding. He, at least, made time to see her on one of his stretches back in the country, after she'd told him about Granna.

"Sorry I'm not much help, Katie. I can't stand those places. And I've lost touch. I'd already left home before she came to live with Mum. But she seemed OK to me whenever I went around for Mum's family dinners."

"Well, she isn't now. And there's no point in you going to see her. It would only agitate her more. She may not have much longer. If she keeps going downhill as fast as she has in the last three months, she'll be lucky to see the end of the year."

After Tom commiserated with her, the conversation turned to his business and the issues and successes he'd had, and how much travel he was doing. "It's as well I don't have a family to worry about. They'd never see me. I do phone the old man from time to time, so he knows I'm alive, but I'm not sure he's worried one way or the other. He's got a new family now."

"Don't tell me about it." The bitterness rankled. "Drink?"

Tom nodded and while Katie opened a bottle of wine, she admitted she'd changed her job.

"Doing what?"

"I've gone freelance," she said nonchalantly, afraid to admit she had no specific job. She'd been forced to find some one-off jobs to keep money coming in. Thankfully, Viv had spread the word she was available and took great photos, but nothing so far inspired Katie to work full time.

"And?"

"Early days, but OK. I did a contract with a marketing company, and a couple of other little things for the same company, plus some photo shoots. I've been selling some of my images. Do you want to see?"

She switched on the TV and ran the slideshow she'd set up, letting it continue in the background.

"I want to get into photography for a living." Of that, she was certain. Although she hadn't worked out how she would achieve it yet. Spending time with Granna, working through the old photos again trying to match them up, and researching online took up all her time.

"Well, if these are anything to go by, you most certainly should. They're stunning."

Gratified by her brother's response, she told him about some of her successes, which, although small, boded well for further opportunities. And being paid for her stock images had boosted her confidence.

"I hope it all goes well for you, Katie. I really do. Stick to your guns, girl."

As the evening lengthened, she relaxed and managed to avoid talking about what wasn't going so well. "Do you know anything about the family tree?" she asked as they sat on her leather sofa after dinner.

Tom shrugged. "Don't think so, why?"

Legs curled under her, and pushing her hair behind her ear, she took another sip of wine. "Granna has a lot of photos of people I don't know. She has occasionally referred to them as Móraí or Mam and Da, and there's a Lilly, a Janey and someone called Gwenna. Any of those names ring a bell?"

Tom pulled a face as he thought about her question. "I'm not certain, but isn't Mórai an Irish word for grandmother?"

"How the hell do you know that?" But it didn't matter how, she opened her laptop and tapped a few keys and up popped the answer. "It is! Well, would you believe it. Another new thing learnt today, just like Granna says."

"No need to thank me," chuckled Tom. "But since you asked, I heard it one time when I was in Ireland."

"Ha ha, funny boy." Katie held a soft spot for Tom and theirs was an easy relationship – unlike Hugh, who reminded her of their father. "And thank you. It's a help. At least I've discovered which generation she's likely to belong to. But I still have no idea what her grandmother's name was."

"Well, another thing about Irish families is they often name their children after the parents, which really confuses things, or back in the day, after children they'd lost. How macabre is that! To be named after a dead sibling. What's Granna's middle name?"

"Grace," she answered automatically. *Grace*, she thought, doing a double take. Wasn't there a Grace in Jared's tree? Thoughts of Jared gatecrashed the evening, and Katie's comfortable chat with Tom was ruined.

Viv called several times during October. Twice she'd offered her a few days' work, which Katie had been grateful for financially, but it felt like charity. She didn't want to get back into marketing, and the jobs Viv offered were basic, fill-in office stuff anyone could have done.

The other times had all been about Jared. She seemed to know a lot about what he was doing.

"The stats on his website are quite good," said Viv, sounding unusually upbeat. "He's had people looking and picked up a few orders. Well done. Has he been in touch? He's not mentioned you recently, come to think of it. But he said he was pleased. Did he tell you? Probably not, he's far too busy."

Katie didn't want to talk about Jared.

He'd phoned her a couple of times, full of enthusiasm after the first few stats had come in, and asked her to meet him. "I'm quietly confident this is going to work out for me," he said as they met over a drink. They talked about his website, the desserts he'd made and how well the hire kitchen had worked out, but the conversation soon fell flat. As if they had nothing to talk about, which had never been the case before.

"I've had some success with some of my shots being accepted as stock photos," she told him. "And Viv is pleased with them, so I might branch out in that direction. I've started doing a website for myself."

He'd said the right things and congratulated her, but that conversation petered out as well. He'd not mentioned anything about whether the history page had been viewed or asked how her family tree research was coming along. And she'd not raised it either. Viv had pointedly told her how much she was doing to help Jared expand his market and how busy he was.

"Yes, Viv. He did tell me," said Katie, remembering how the evening had ended dismally.

"Really? So, cough. What's the goss?"

"There is no goss, Viv. He phoned me. He told me he was happy. I told him I was happy. We said goodbye. That's it."

"That's it? Oh, dear, it seems such a shame to let a

153

hunk like him disappear out of your life."

"I'm not sure he ever was in my life, as you put it. He was a client. I couldn't date him then. And there's enough going on in my life without me needing to look for a relationship where there isn't one."

The moment she said the words, Katie knew she was lying to herself. She *had* hoped for something with Jared after the contract was finished, but nothing came of it. He'd made it quite plain he wasn't interested. Now she hoped Viv wouldn't pry too much into what was going on in her life.

She had never shared her problems with anyone, and she couldn't start now. Especially Viv. She was a good colleague but not someone Katie would confide in.

"OK. Whatever you say. Bye."

What was that all about, Katie wondered, dismissing it with a shrug.

For a long while after she'd ended the call, she sat staring out the window. She did it a lot these days, as if she was in a holding pattern, not quite knowing how to move forward and determined not to look back.

She visited Granna every day, but the visits were becoming shorter as the weeks passed and her condition slipped further. Katie held her hand, talking gently about her photographs, and explaining to her grandmother about the research she was doing into the family. Knowing Granna didn't understood a word about ancestry or records or hints and links, she hoped a name might spark Granna's memory and she would say something helpful.

"My mother's name was Susan. That's the name you gave her. Did you know anyone else called Susan? I don't see any photos of Susan."

Katie kept repeating names, hoping against hope for some recognition. "I like the name Grace. It's your name too. You and I are both Katie, but you are Grace. I wish I was Grace. My middle name is Jane. Plain Jane."

Katie let curiosity get the better of her and took a peek in the drawers, ignoring a faint sense of disloyalty. She showed Granna a couple of pictures, holding them side by side. "These women have such lovely hairstyles. Today's styles are very plain in comparison. You had lovely hair once, I remember. Shall I brush your hair? Who used to brush your hair?"

One day, a small smile briefly lit her grandmother's face, but apart from a couple of grunts, she said nothing.

Other days, Katie talked about the clothes they wore, or the brooch – the St Brigid's cross – still wondering who the Móraí was who had first worn it. Thanks to Tom, at least she now knew the woman was probably a grandmother, but from which side, and what was her name?

And who was the other woman – Katie's ghost?

When she was with Granna, any thoughts of Jared stayed away. Only when she was at home working on photos or her ancestry pages did he come to mind. His passion and knowledge of his past kept bumping into her psyche. She wished she could phone him and ask questions about what she'd found or the difficulties she was having. But pride, stubbornness or fear of rejection held her back. Either way, she knew she was being her own worst enemy.

One morning in the first few days of December came the phone call she'd been dreading.

"I'm sorry, Miss Anderson," said the disembodied voice on her mobile. "Mrs Bridges passed away about half an hour ago."

The voice expressed their condolences and outlined what would happen next. Katie wasn't sure she took much of it in, but she let the woman talk without interruption. Getting out of bed, she padded through to the lounge and stared out the window. The sun was rising, washing the city with a golden glow of light on what promised to be a glorious summer's day, at a time when the light had gone from Granna.

"Thank you, I'll come soon," she assured the woman and hung up.

She picked up her camera and stood there for several more minutes watching the sun rise higher, casting pink, yellow and orange bands of light across the increasingly blue sky. With her finger on the shutter button, she shot several bursts, hoping she had captured one that conveyed her feelings right now. She wanted to treasure the morning as a tribute to her grandmother.

Somehow, she got through the procedure at the care home, which had contacted the funeral director, and telling her brothers. She went through the motions, letting her business persona take the lead while her inner self remembered.

She couldn't regret Granna's passing, but she would grieve, as much for what Granna had lost as for herself. Her grandmother's last few weeks had been awful to watch, but she'd led a full and interesting life right up until her mind started to fade.

Tom was away overseas again, but he'd answered his phone and promised to be back in time for the funeral.

"I'm sorry I'm not there for you again, Katie. I'm sure you won't need my help with the arrangements, but I'd like to help you grieve."

Katie nodded at the phone and then croaked a suitable 'thanks' before hanging up.

The phone call from Hugh had left her seething. "I didn't know she was so sick. Did she leave us anything?"

Katie coldly reminded him he had never visited his grandmother to find out for himself how she was. "I'll text you when the funeral is," and hung up before she said something she might regret.

Her mother had held power of attorney over Granna's affairs and while it had passed to Katie when her mother died, she had little idea of what was entailed. All she knew was the care home fees were paid directly from Granna's account and nothing had changed. There'd been nothing else for her to see to until now. She'd paid for the little luxuries Granna liked whenever her perfume or other toiletries were low, and brought her favourite chocolates. Granna needed nothing else.

She also phoned Viv to cancel the contract currently lined up. "Could you find someone else, please, Viv? I'm sorry it's short notice, but my grandmother died this morning and I can't face it right now."

Viv had effused. "Of course, of course. Don't you fret about it for one minute. So that's what's been going on. You were caring for a sick grandmother. You could have told me, I would have understood. So would Jared."

How did Jared enter the conversation? thought Katie but promptly dismissed it as a complexity she didn't need. "I can't talk about it now. But thank you. I'll be in touch – maybe next year sometime." She ended the call before Viv could say anything further.

The funeral director came to her apartment and talked her through the process, asking questions, which Katie answered as best she could and with as few words as possible. "It's to be a small private funeral. Just family," she said. "Her favourite piece was 'The Robin's Return'. I'd like that played in the background. No, I don't expect any speeches. I'd like roses. She loved roses."

He confirmed the burial site was in order and the wording for the notices, then tried to persuade her to speak. "I'm sure there will be friends or people from the home who will attend the service who would like to hear about her life. Some of the staff maybe?"

"Other people are welcome to attend, but she lived in a dementia home. She has no friends still alive that I'm aware of. So my answer is still no. I said all that needed to be said to my grandmother when she was alive. I have nothing to say to anyone else."

"You can't deny others the right to speak," he pressed, more than likely looking to charge a larger fee for his time, thought Katie uncharitably.

"Right? What right? If they didn't say what they wanted to while my grandmother still understood, there is no point saying anything now."

If her brothers wanted to say something, they could, but what? she wondered. Then she realised her father and his new family would probably turn up. She could hear him: 'I came for you, Katie, love. To be here for you.'

She groaned. How would she get through the funeral service without losing her cool?

Not for the first time, she felt totally on her own. Her mother's death was bad enough, but the last twelve months had been the worst time in her life . She could only hope the new year would bring her better fortune.

16

AS THE YEARS GO BY

January 1913

Every year, Gwenna and her family picnicked on Cheltenham Beach for the annual Anniversary Day sailing regatta celebrating the founding of Auckland in the early 1840s. The bay, curving round to the shelter of the trees at the far end, offered an expansive panorama and the best views of the sailing yachts. With their sails filled by the breeze, they were a spectacular sight as they tacked back and forth across the glistening waters of the course.

Anniversary Day had been a public holiday ever since and the one day Gwenna allowed herself to take off. This year Jane and Grace had been invited.

"It's not often my sisters and our families get together, so I'm glad you could join us," said Gwenna as she and Jane sat on the blanket on the sand.

Gwenna's family situation was even more complicated than Jane's, but at least the four women and two men all had either a mother or father in common. She loved watching the way the larger family interacted with one another, and a small part of her regretted she and Laura hadn't been close enough to share sisterly chatter, like Gwenna's siblings. Grace and Lilly hadn't been as close as they could have been either. Lilly had long since gone to Brisbane to work in the Harrison-Browne Department Store and was now married to Phillip's son Joseph, while Grace – lovely, beautiful Grace – had grown into a talented and capable young woman.

"I wouldn't have missed this for the world," said Jane. "Thank you for including me."

They watched the older children splashing around in the water with some of the youngest, but there were so many Jane couldn't keep up with them all.

"Have you noticed how much time Charlie and Grace spend together?" Gwenna commented.

"They've always got on well, haven't they? Right back from when they were children, there was always a spark."

"It's hard to believe he'll be twenty next month."

"I see Charlie's not missing any opportunity to sell some of your sweets either, and he's got Grace helping him." Jane pointed to where he was offering some bags to people he passed as he and Grace wandered amongst the crowds.

"I can always rely on Charlie to be my best salesman," laughed Gwenna. "It's in his blood."

"Do you think there will be anything more than friendship between them?"

Gwenna looked towards the two, deep in conversation. "I hope so. Don't you?"

Jane made a suitable sound in agreement but didn't trust herself to speak. It had long been her wish.

As she grew up, Grace had become a constant visitor at Jane's cottage, which she'd bought in the hope of expunging her memories after her ordeal with Mickey a decade earlier. But memories have a habit of returning. Never mind how many changes Jane made, they plagued her still, but she couldn't talk about them. Her designs were her only outlet.

One day, Grace had brought Charlie with her and Jane became their ally.

"It's easier to talk here than at Mam's, Janey," Grace confided. "I'm sure you understand."

She did. Brigid didn't miss a thing, as Jane knew only too well. She hoped something would come of their friendship, but she had to make sure she always put all her designs and her journals out of sight in case Grace turned up unexpectedly and discovered the secrets she'd kept hidden for so long.

Jane remembered how she'd scrimped and saved until she had enough to buy her cottage. It had taken longer than she'd hoped, even with the additional income from her increased role as Bernadette, designer to the Society Ladies of Auckland. It had been worth the subterfuge, though, and she loved her little home.

Until a ghost appeared.

"Lunch everyone!" called Gwenna's stepmother, Bethan, giving Jane some respite from her memories.

Jane could not believe how many people rushed from whatever they had been doing on the sand, in the water, or under the trees. Hands grabbed a Glamorgan sausage or two, sandwiches, cakes, slices of bara brith, Gwenna's famous fudge and so much more. All of it delicious. Everyone contributed to the picnic, bringing their own baskets full of food and drinks, but they relied on Bethan to supply the specialities no one else could compete with.

"Thanks, Mam," said Gwenna, putting an arm around her stepmother. "How would we ever manage without you?" She kissed the woman's temple and gave her a squeeze. Bethan looked as though she'd been handed the Crown Jewels.

Jane revelled in being a part of it, while still fraught with guilt for deceiving them all. At least the festivities took her mind off the fact she was totally unworthy of their love or friendship.

A few weeks short of a year after she'd moved into her cottage, there came a knock at the door. How she didn't collapse on the spot was a miracle, but the young man who stood facing her was the spitting image of Mickey at the same age. Except this rogue was coarse and roughly spoken.

"Who are you?" she stammered, hoping she was wrong.

"I fink you know who I am," he said, inspecting his filthy fingernails in the same way Mickey used to. At least Mickey's had been clean. He'd always been fastidious and nothing like this scoundrel. "My father told me all about you and your little secret togevver."

"What do you want?" her voice not much more than a whisper.

"He said if ever I fell on 'ard times, I was ta knock on your door and y'd help me out. Well, times are 'ard."

She had, of course, refused him and sent him on his way. But he returned time and again, threatening to destroy everything she had worked for.

"You should spare a fellow a coin or two when he's down. Be charitable. I'm not asking for much. I'd 'ate for you to lose your little 'ouse now, wouldn't I, but a 'and now and then wouldn't go astray."

He'd come from Sydney, he told her when questioned, where he'd lived with his mother until she died several months before.

"You're a strapping lad. Can't you find work for yourself and a place to live? Your father would not approve of this sort of behaviour."

"What would you know 'bout my father? He were never 'round long enough to be any use to anyone." He spat into the gutter.

Jane empathised. This lad had been born several years before she'd met Mickey. Which, in her mind, further served to prove what a terrible person she was, lacking any sense of judgement and allowing herself to fall for him in the first place.

But she couldn't help feel sorry for a boy who had been neglected by his father and not well cared for by his mother. Sometimes, the intonation of his voice reminded her of Mickey and she pitied the lost soul. Maybe a little helping hand from her would make his life easier.

But the hand became greedier and greedier as the years passed, and his threats became more menacing until she feared for her safety.

She never knew when he would turn up. Sometimes he came every week for a month or two, then he'd disappear for several and she'd think she'd been reprieved. But he always came back. She'd not seen him in more than six months until he'd turned up again the previous night.

He always came at night – and late, after she'd returned from the theatre. She never let him in, and he never forced the issue either. But last night he arrived drunk and had pushed his way inside. He'd left sometime in the early hours, but this time he had genuinely frightened her.

Gwenna's raised voice dragged her back to the present.

"Do you remember me talking about the Ford motor car which travelled from Wellington to Auckland last November?" said Gwenna, whose love of cars was well known.

"How could we forget?" laughed Hugh. "You dragged me along to stand in the crowds in Queen Street to welcome them."

"Yes, well. But what a great feat they achieved," she said in their defence. "Only eight and a half days and through areas that had never seen a car before. In places, there were no roads and they had to build or rebuild bridges along the way. Just goes to prove how worthwhile a car can be."

"What are you leading up to, Gwenna?" growled Hugh, who'd guessed what she would say next.

"When I saw the first car travel the streets of Auckland, I vowed one day I would have one of my own."

"But you've got a delivery vehicle?" said Bethan, who was thinking of the shiny black horse-drawn delivery cart Gwenna's father had bought and spent so much money on emblazoning the sides with G *Price & Family Confectioners, Auckland*.

"This won't be a delivery cart, Mam, it's for me to use."

"Now why would you be wanting such a smelly, noisy thing?" Bethan shook her head in bewilderment.

"Yes, tell us, Gwenna," grinned Hugh.

"Because for the first time, I can afford one. I'm delighted to announce G Price & Family Confectioners has finally turned sufficient profit and all debts are paid off. I now fully own the house and the business and have money to spare."

"Congratulations," shouted voices, but loudest was Hugh's.

"It might have taken you over twelve years to achieve your goal, my girl, but I never doubted you would do it. I am so proud of you, and so proud to have stood by your side throughout your journey."

The look of love that passed between them was not missed by anyone watching.

"So, I can buy my car?"

November 1913

"Mam!" screamed Grace, running up the stairs.

"Whatever is the matter?" Brigid hurried to meet her daughter, wrapping her arms around the girl.

"There's hundreds of men on horses blocking Queen Street in front of the wharves. I was trying to get the ferry to Devonport, but they frightened me so much I didn't go. I hope Mrs White won't mind."

"Oh, dear. I had hoped it wouldn't come to this," said Brigid, who didn't agree with the strikers, but neither did she agree with the farmers being recruited to act as special constables. Pitting people against each other would not solve the problems, but the strike was getting out of hand.

It had spread throughout the country as unions backed up their fellow strikers from the Huntly coal mines. The month before, in the ruckus over working conditions, a miner had been killed and a policeman shot. She hadn't totally followed what had happened, but deep in her heart she knew desperate measures were only needed by desperate men. She just hoped there wouldn't be too much violence.

"It'll be all right, Grace. I'm sure it won't matter if you miss one music lesson. I'll send Mrs White a message to explain. Once the police have broken up the strike and the men disperse, the streets will go back to normal, you'll see. Meanwhile, why don't you play something for me?"

Grace sat at the piano and started playing Beethoven's 'Moonlight Sonata'. Within moments, she had disappeared into the music. Brigid, who had heard her play this piece often, thought how splendidly she played today, as if the notes were telling her a bigger story. No sooner had she finished than she followed it up with Reber's 'Remembrance' which brought tears to Brigid's eyes. The deep-seated ethos touched her to the core, despite serious classicists considering the composition light and frivolous.

Sally returned home as Grace finished. Removing her hat and hanging it on the hatstand, she began talking eagerly. "You should see the streets out there, our Breeda. Och, it's chaos, I tell ye. Chaos. It looks as though the police and those farmer blokes ..."

"I think they're being called Massey's Cossacks," said Brigid, not truly understanding why.

"Yes. Them. Is that what they call them? Gracious me. Well, they're everywhere blocking the way to the wharf."

"I saw them too, Aunt Sally," said Grace, turning sideways on the piano stool and sitting on her hands.

"Well, don't you fret none, lass," said Sally cupping

the girl's face in her hands in passing. "There's calm out there now but it looks like a stand-off to me. I didn't linger. I came straight back here wanting to show you this."

Sally unfolded the newspaper and spread it out on the table. She turned the pages until she came to a full-page advertisement by Milne & Choyce for the latest corsets. Together they read the articles about the pros and cons of the various styles and brands but particularly focused on the piece about the front-lacing Gossards corsets.

"I like these," said Sally. "Lacing is better than those ugly hooks and eyes and gives so much flexibility, especially if you can do it yourself. They'll make a difference to the way women dress. Now what do you say to me meeting with Miss Milne and seeing if we can come to some arrangement?"

"What sort of arrangement?" asked Brigid. "What are you up to now, Sally?"

"Just a little extra boost." The women laughed at Sally's attempt at a joke. "But seriously, Bree, if we can show how your lace bodices or insets could enhance a gown, and in turn the corset could enhance the figure, then maybe we can share the rewards between us. I want to display one of them in our shop."

Brigid never argued with Sally about displays. She had a knack with window dressing and people were always stopping to look, which was an advantage, as competition had increased severalfold in the years since she'd begun. The larger department stores with their multilevel, multidepartment, one-stop shopping – the likes of Smith & Caughey, the Court brothers George and John, Milne & Choyce and others – was having a huge impact on her little business. Unfortunately, she had to admit, the days of small shops like Miss Brigid's were numbered. The trips she had been making over the years to Brisbane had shown her the truth of her situation. Despite her reluctance, returning to the Harrison-Browne store had made a difference to both her way of thinking and her approach to Miss Brigid's.

"Whatever you say, Sally. Do your darnedest. Meanwhile, I have lace to make."

She had never quite recaptured the hectic days when Tommy was alive. Now that so much could be bought from overseas and through catalogues and advertisements, the customised touches were not so much in demand.

To keep the business going she had added a prodigious range of haberdashery and millinery supplies which brought in a different clientele, expanded the needlecraft selection, as well as stocking gloves, scarves and handkerchiefs, amongst the other bits and bobs her customers requested. Nevertheless, Phillip – *darn him* – and Jane had been right. Her lace had seen an upturn with the demand for evening wear, particularly among the older age bracket who could afford to regularly attend the theatre, concerts, balls and fancy dinners.

Suddenly, Charlie rushed up the stairs where Brigid sat making her lace while Grace began her studies and Sally tended the shop. "Are you all right?" He knelt on one knee beside the table where Grace sat and took her hands in his. "I was so worried when I heard." He turned. "And you, Miss Brigid, have you had any bother?"

"Everything is well, Charlie. But what's brought you here at such a rush?"

"I heard about the trouble in the streets with the watersiders' strike and thought you might have been caught up in it."

"I'm fine, Charlie," said Grace in a quiet voice. "They did give me a fright earlier when I tried to take the ferry, but there's been no bother here."

He turned back to Grace, worry etching lines into his forehead. "This wasn't the way I planned it, but I can't stand it any longer. I want you with me always. So, Miss Grace Jane Price, will you please say yes and consent to be my wife?"

Still clutching Charlie's hands, Grace leapt to her feet, looked expectantly at her mother with eyes agog and held her breath waiting for Brigid's approval. The nod came and Grace squealed.

She threw her arms around his neck. "Mr Charlie Price, I do believe I will."

17

TESTING TIMES

December 2018

Christmas songs greeted Katie in every shop. Glittering decorations hung from every conceivable space and lined virtually every street and mall. Advertising spurring people to buy, spend, spend more, and be happy, assaulted her senses.

She had no interest in Christmas cheer and watching the mad rush to obey what marketeers like her pushed into tired brains sent waves of panic coursing through her. There would no Christmas frills in her house this year.

Word had got around about her grandmother's passing – she assumed, thanks to Viv – and she was answering endless phone calls from people she'd once called friends and colleagues. She tried to be the gracious and polite receiver of such calls but in reality the insignificant people mouthing meaningless platitudes tested her control. All she wanted to do was curl up on her sofa, stare out the window, drink her wine and be left alone. But that clearly wasn't going to happen any time soon.

Her father decided to be all sympathetic and understanding, while the witch, Babs, her so-called stepmother, also called offering sympathies and invited her for Christmas drinks. As if!

Hugh was as bad when he rang. "Why were you so rude to Dad? And Babs for that matter? She's OK, you know."

Humph, she sniffed, he'd had a change of heart, but she shouldn't be surprised. Hugh was always Dad's man. "I wasn't rude. I simply said no thanks."

"Well, that's rude when you've been invited to share Christmas with them."

Katie took a deep breath and counted to ten. "Hugh, I am not in the right mood to celebrate anything. And it wasn't Christmas, just drinks. I don't need false cheer and awkward familial events right now. OK?"

"But Katie ..."

"But nothing, Hugh. I'll be in touch." She was getting good at hanging up on people.

The next phone call came minutes after. She readied herself for another onslaught.

"Well done, you," said Tom. Katie expelled the air in her lungs and burst into tears. "Hey. I didn't mean to upset you, I meant it as a compliment."

Silence.

"Hey, sis ... are you there?"

Katie mopped the tears with a handful of tissues grabbed at random from the box on the side table – something she normally detested – and thoroughly blew her nose. "Hi, Tom."

"Whoa, that's not my sister's voice. Where did she go?"

"Sorry. I'm a bit shattered."

"Understandable, kiddo. But listen. I'm here if you want to talk, meet up or go out or whatever you want. With my work and lifestyle, you don't collect people much, so I understand what being alone is like."

"Thanks, Tom. You're a pal." Another pause. "There's something bugging me, though." Katie pulled Granna's old pink rug over her knees and fiddled with the tassels, pulling away strands of fluff.

"What, hon?"

"In many ways, Granna Katy was lost to us years ago, but she became my rock after Mum died. I didn't realise it at the time, but Mum's life scared me; always at the beck and call of everyone, with nothing to call her own. She didn't have any hobbies or friends to laugh with. Her life was all work and worry. When she was alive, I rarely needed her – I was so busy with my career – but she was always there. But then she wasn't, and it was as if no one noticed. Dad moved on. Hugh continued the same as usual, and you're away so much, you couldn't possibly know what her life was like."

She took some deep breaths and barrelled on. "To me, Granna Katy wasn't just some mindless and, if you believe Hugh, useless old woman who should have passed away a long time ago. She was my link to what had gone before us. Our history, our connection to this world ..."

Katie broke off, not knowing if Tom was getting the thread of what she was trying to say or not.

"I understand you miss Mum, but honestly, Katie, life goes on. You can't throw your life into turmoil every time someone dies."

So, he hadn't got it.

"It's more than that. But I guess it's something I need

172

to work through on my own. Thanks for trying, Tom. Love you."

And she hung up on him too.

The morning of the funeral, she rose early and took a long shower trying to wash away the tiredness dogging her every movement. She felt calm, though, and considered it a plus. She couldn't avoid today – although she'd said her farewells, cried her tears and had spent hours collating the pictures she thought captured Granna as she saw her. Somehow, she had to show them Granna wasn't gone. Only her body had gone. Her spirit, her legacy, her past lived on, in them. Not that she expected anyone to understand.

Except Jared, came the unbidden notion.

She hadn't thought about Jared for ages. In fact, she'd deliberately tried to banish him from her mind. He hadn't called, so whatever she imagined might have been possible would not happen now. Too much time had passed.

She dressed in an elegant drape dress in rose pink to honour her grandmother. She touched her face up with some powder and lipstick, avoiding any eye make-up, and smoothed her hair into place. Simple white sandals, a small white handbag stuffed with all the hankies she owned and the St Brigid's cross she'd found in her mother's things pinned to her dress completed the outfit. She'd taken the brooch to a jeweller and had it cleaned and the catch repaired. It gleamed now in the mirror, reflecting the shafts of sunlight from the window behind her.

Giving herself one last look in the mirror and

instructions to remain composed never mind what anyone said, she left her apartment and drove to the funeral home. She was the first to arrive by a long way. Well over an hour lay ahead before they could expect anyone else to make an appearance.

"On your instructions, we have closed the casket," said the funeral director. "Are you sure people won't want to view the deceased?"

Clenching her jaw, Katie reminded herself to stay calm. "If they couldn't visit her when she was alive, they don't deserve to see her now."

The chapel was small, catering for less than fifty people, which suited Katie. She took her seat in the front row and waited. Three tiers of tall candles on either side decorated the small platform across from her. The flames flickered in a slight draft, and the sizeable bouquet of pink roses, artfully displayed in a crystal vase, sat on a pedestal in the middle. In front, the bier waited to support Granna when she was carried in. The silence was suddenly filled with music as the sound system was turned on and still Katie sat, hands on her lap, knees together, heels together, eyes forward, holding herself erect.

She became aware of people moving around her. Tom sat beside her and placed his hand over hers. "Dad's here."

She didn't look around.

"He decided he'll sit at the back. He's got Babs and one of her kids with him."

Katie remained mute.

Tom checked the crowds. "Hugh's arrived, and Carol's keeping their lot in line. There's a couple of nurses, a man, and a woman in a suit."

Minutes passed. The funeral director and his attendants began their duties, handing out the service sheet as more people arrived. The photo she thought captured Granna the best filled the entire front page. Her name, Kathleen Grace Bridges (née Price) was printed at the top, and the two dates marking the passage of her time on earth at the bottom. Inside, the facing page held the formalities required and named the music to be played. Katie had allowed the director to include one short poem, 'Letters from Heaven', and a thank you. While she had arranged for refreshments to be served after the committal, she would not stay. Small talk was beyond her ability. Her life was one staccato moment after another until she could free herself from this time warp.

She hadn't noticed Tom get up until the music changed.

The casket was being carried in by Tom, Hugh, Dad, two people she didn't know and Mike! She'd forgotten all about Uncle Mike and his two boys. How could she have been so thoughtless? Mum's brother lived in Perth and had done for decades. The last time she'd seen him was at her mother's funeral. He'd come alone and had not stayed long, citing family and work for returning home the next day. She supposed Mike had seen his mother while he was here, but Granna had forgotten so much by then maybe she hadn't recognised him. Katie couldn't ever remember seeing him visit Granna, but she'd deal with this embarrassment later. She forced scenes of her mother's funeral from her mind and concentrated on what was happening before her. The sounds whirled around her as if in a vacuum.

Half an hour later, they carried the casket out and

placed it in the hearse waiting at the door. No one had taken up the funeral director's offer for anyone to speak. He had read what needed to be read and said the words needing to be said. All of it washed over Katie.

She stood by the hearse, not remembering how she got there, tall, erect and trying to control the trembling. People threw rose petals and whispered to themselves. A few spoke to her and she let a faint smile answer them.

She felt so totally removed from everything as though behind a glass wall or in a gigantic air bubble. She looked at the people she knew, from her work, from the dementia home, her family, and some she didn't recognise, wondering who they were and why they'd come.

Tom took her elbow and steered her around the side of the building. "I'd take you home, but I don't think you should be alone. You look so utterly done in."

He put his arm around her and for a few moments she rested her head on his shoulder and let some of the tension slip away. Tom was good for her.

With her head turned to one side, away from the people still gathered around the front of the chapel waiting for the hearse to move, she thought she'd started hallucinating. A man stood hidden in the shadow cast by a substantial pōhutukawa tree in full bloom ready for Christmas. For a split second she thought she saw Jared but persuaded her tired brain it couldn't possibly be him. Never mind how much she wished it.

She turned her head away and looked up at her brother. It did feel nice to have someone taller than her to lean on. "Thanks, Tom, but honestly, I'm OK. I just need a breather. I'll come and find you in a minute or two."

She watched Tom walk back towards the main door and disappear around the corner. He would talk to everyone and thank them for coming and be the grieving grandson. He could also keep Dad and Hugh in line. Maybe she didn't have to go back in, maybe she could …

"Katie?"

She turned around. She wasn't hallucinating after all. He stood no more than two metres from her. His usual, nearly-smiling face wore an expression of deep concern. She took in every detail, soaking in his presence, grateful her wish had been fulfilled. A sense of relief flooded through her, and her body yearned to lean against him and let him take away the pain, but her feet wouldn't move.

Jared voiced her thoughts. "You have no idea how much I've longed for the moment when I'd see you again."

18

PLEASURE AND PAIN

January 1914

True to her word at the Anniversary Day Regatta the year
before, Gwenna ordered the car she and Hugh had chosen
– a Ford Model T two-seater Roadster. She'd had to wait a
while for it to arrive but in the meantime had taken driving
lessons. When it finally came, everyone was invited to see
it. In fact, everyone in the street turned out to watch and
inspect the vehicle from one end to the other.

"Give me a hand here, there's a good fellow," said
Hugh to his brother-in-law Tom as he began to unclip the
large domes holding the hood in place. "We need two of
us to get the top up."

The fold-down top created considerable enthusiasm
with lots of oohs and aahs as the men pulled it into
place. Charlie undid the levers on either side of the
fold-back windshield and demonstrated how it operated.
"Depending on whether it is raining or not."

The speedometer, gas lamps, on-board generator and
the three oil lamps were interesting discussion points for
the men, while the tubular horn soon became a toy for
the young boys.

"George! Will you stop that," snapped Hugh to his stepson. "You should know better and it's only encouraging the others. Now behave!"

They all stood in awe as Gwenna climbed into the driver's seat, attired in a new driving skirt and jacket designed by Jane, topped by a wide-brimmed hat with a scarf tie and leather driving gloves. Hugh cranked the handle several times, the engine fired and, to much applause, Gwenna drove up and down Karangahape Road, demonstrating her mastery of the vehicle. The 30-inch wood-spoked wheels and whitewall treaded tyres rolled effortlessly along the newly surfaced road.

Bethan was impressed. "It's much nicer than I thought it would be," she conceded.

By New Year, Gwenna had become a recognisable figure tootling around town, meeting people and attending functions, but she'd promised there would be no surprises at this year's regatta.

The day began with a misty rain and light winds, and some of the early races had seen sails flapping around the masts, but by eleven o'clock when the flagship *Warrimoo* set sail from Queen's Wharf, the wind had steadied. The sun shone brightly and the sparkling waters were ready for a great day's racing.

"Let's leave the men studying the paper for all the details about the boats doing whatever they do in a race," said Gwenna, linking arms with Jane. "You and I can take a walk, and you can tell me the latest gossip."

Jane covered her friend's hand with hers. "To tell you the truth, Gwenna, apart from saying thank you, yet again, for including me in your family picnic, little has happened lately," lied Jane.

A lot had happened, and had been happening for more than five years, but she couldn't – just couldn't – tell anyone. "The shows are going well still, despite the announcement the Tivoli Music Hall in London is soon to close. The increased competition from these moving picture shows that have come about can't be helping."

"Oh, tosh. You're family to me. The day wouldn't be the same without you. I must try and find the time to attend more of your theatrical events. I do so love the theatre, but honestly, the shops are doing well, I'm rushed off my feet some weeks trying to meet the demand. How I ever thought I could do anything without Hugh – and Charlie – is beyond me, but that's ancient history now."

Gwenna glanced over her shoulder. "And will you take a look at those two." She nodded towards Charlie and Grace who were busy selling bags of lollies to every comer. "He's even got Grace selling lollies on her own without him standing by her side all the time."

"Whatever happened to the tray and cart Charlie organised for George?" asked Jane.

"I love my son dearly, but he is nothing like Charlie. George hated every moment he was out selling. He came back having lost some or had bags pinched or was short-changed. He moaned so much, Hugh and I decided he would do the business more harm than good. So he stays and works in the kitchens and packing room. He's not much better at boiling sugar either."

As they talked, they made their way through the crowds and off the beach and walked along the roadway until they found a seat under the shade of a tree.

"Has he been any help to you with the exhibition at

the domain? How is it going?"

Gwenna shrugged. "A little. At least he has an eye for display and can stack and pack things. The opening day of the exhibition last month was a near disaster. It rained. Of all days. So people stayed away, and instead of the fifteen thousand they said would come, only about four thousand did. But thankfully, the summer has improved, and we've got another three months before it closes. Trade has picked up, and I've opened accounts for customers further down the island and from the South Island, so it's been worth it for me. My stepbrother Eli has done well with his furniture too, so Alice tells me. Have you been?"

"I've wandered through a couple of times. But I don't enjoy the fun fair activities, and I've hardly any need of the mechanical or agricultural displays! It's interesting to visit and they've done a sterling job with the buildings and setting it all out. It seems popular. Have you got any of your products on sale at the tea rooms?"

"I most certainly have. I arranged it early on. I didn't want to host the teas but they have lots of my treats available. What about the concert hall and art gallery – are they having an effect on theatre attendances?" asked Gwenna.

"I don't think so, but then I have nothing to do with the box office. All I care about is how many costumes they need on any one day. And the number hasn't dropped off any." Which was true on so many levels, but she was struggling to keep up the pretence and meet the workload.

"Which brings me to what I wanted to talk to you about, my dearest Jane. Would it be too much if I asked you to design a new dress for me for Charlie and Grace's wedding? If you're not too busy, of course. You're looking so tired these days, I wonder if you're doing too much."

Jane was unbelievably busy. To make the money she needed to pay off her blackmailer, she had increased the number of designs she sold. Not the ones she dreamed up for the stage, nor those she sold under the name of Bernadette, but designs for the most fashionable ladies about town in need of more than one ball gown, or their daughters desirous of a gown like no other for the debutante balls. She'd created a mystical name for herself – Mademoiselle Maree – and as before, advertised in the paper. The response was greater than expected, and she sold dozens through a private box number. Over time, word spread, and dressmakers and department stores were writing, asking for her designs – including the famous Harrison-Browne store, she noted. Soon she began to make more money than she needed and more than she earned working as the costumier. Her savings grew.

But never mind how busy she was, she would never turn down any request from those she loved. "Of course, Gwenna. Nothing is too much trouble for you."

"Only if you're sure, because I've heard some excellent things about Mademoiselle Maree if you'd prefer? But she couldn't be as brilliant as you."

Jane's guilt mounted, but once the topic of the upcoming wedding was raised, the two women might as well have been somewhere else. The beach, the picnic, the crowds, the activities and the sight of the majestic craft sailing on the Waitemata faded into insignificance.

Jane hoped 'The Ghost' would stay away from Grace's big day. She was sure Brigid would recognise the man, just as she had.

In all the bustle, Jane stood to one side admiring the young bride and her effervescent husband. In the twelve months since Charlie had proposed, so much had changed in the world that Jane wondered if life would ever be the same again. The unrest in Europe had escalated to the point where, a month earlier, a state of war had officially been declared, much to the consternation of many. But New Zealand would go where England went. Charlie was determined to do his duty and had been one of the first to volunteer. He wanted to join the Royal Navy, having seen HMS New Zealand when it had toured the country the previous year, but the powers that be wouldn't allow him. Instead, he would be leaving with one of the first infantry contingents in a matter of weeks, if not days, depending on orders.

Grace and Charlie's wedding day was both a happy and sad occasion, one that brought them together and tore them apart. Jane could only hope their love would survive whatever the future held.

The day was notable for her too. As she surveyed the guests, Jane felt justifiably satisfied with her designs worn by Brigid and Sally, and those worn by Gwenna and Bethan, as well as her own simpler gown. They were a match in elegance and refinement for anything bought from the most fashionable stores, but then she smiled to herself: many of them were her designs anyway. She allowed herself a small thrill.

Grace's wedding ensemble was Jane's showpiece, and she couldn't have been happier with the outcome. The narrow, belted dress, with three pleated drapes to one side, made the tiny girl look taller. Finishing a little above the ankle with secret gores to make walking easier, the tasteful deep-violet gown, trimmed with a white V collar and pointed cuffs was the perfect combination of celebration and solemnity. Only the extravagant bouquet Grace carried gave any hint the outfit was bridal. And the matching brimmed hat adorned with gauze and flowers completed the picture.

Charlie looked very smart dressed in his dark green twill uniform with red trim, lemon-squeezer hat, red hatband and khaki puttees of the local infantry battalion. He had insisted on a professional photographer, regardless of the fact his brother-in-law Tom was there with his latest Box Brownie taking 'happy snaps', as he called them, of all the smiling faces. As with so many like him, Jane thought Charlie looked far too young and innocent to be involved in war, but nothing anyone said would make any difference. Gwenna's Hugh, who had fought the Boers, had remonstrated with him at great length about the horrors and stupidity of war. 'Wait until you're called up, lad. There's no need to rush things,' but Charlie hadn't been listening.

Brigid was in her element organising every detail. Gathering people together for photographs and making sure Tom had time to get similar shots kept her busy. The photographer had set up a mini studio in the corner of the hall with a backdrop, flashlight and reflector. Charlie's entire family – his mother Bethan, his sisters and their husbands, his estranged half-brother and his wife, along with Brigid's extended household – were in attendance, so a lot of people had to be included.

Lilly had returned from Brisbane with her husband Joseph, and their son Phillip Harrison-Browne Junior.

"Mam, it's so lovely to be back amongst my own family again," she gushed. Tall and elegant, Lilly was still as excitable as she had been as a child. "Grandma Browne is wonderful, and I know how lucky I am. She supports me in everything, but she's not you."

Brigid remembered Mrs Browne fondly. Twenty-five years ago, Phillip's mother, once her employer, had become her mentor and gifted her Miss Brigid's after it became established. She owed her livelihood and prosperity to Beatrice Browne. "How is she?"

"A little frailer these days, but in good fettle. And she doesn't stand any nonsense from Papa Phillip."

Brigid smiled to herself. Beatrice Browne had never stood any nonsense from anyone. She was a woman who knew her mind and made sure things turned out the way she wanted them, even if the men hadn't quite cottoned on to what she was doing.

"I've my own little department in the store these days," said Lilly, who had worked in the successful store over several years whenever she and Brigid visited. It had come as no surprise to the parents when she and Joseph wed. "I handle all the laces and trims and buttons and bows and everything the well-dressed woman desires. I've got some great plans, but Grandma Browne tells me to bide my time. Papa Phillip, who is apparently just like his father and won't let go, and Joseph who is a carbon copy of young Phillip, according to his grandmother, argue all the time. But my time will come." Lilly did a little twirl and gave Brigid a wink.

"You are incorrigible," said Brigid, the love in her voice taking any misunderstanding away.

"And I need more of your marvellous lace, Mam dearest, so please get your fingers going faster."

Jane had not attended Lilly's wedding, which had been held in Brisbane at the request of the Harrison-Browne clan. Only Brigid and Grace had gone to be fêted and honoured. Jane had often wished she'd been braver, and sometimes regretted her decision, but at least she had the photographs. Watching the photographer now, she thought about the ones she held the most precious.

There was one of Grace and Lilly together taken the Christmas before Lilly married, and one of Brigid by herself at Lilly's wedding, and the one of Brigid and her at Gwenna's wedding a long time ago. She would add today's photo of Grace and Charlie to her list.

"Jane," called Brigid, shaking her from her musing, "who is that young man over there? He seems familiar somehow. Do you recognise him?"

All the joy drained from Jane's body as she looked where Brigid pointed. She hoped she was wrong and Mickey's son had not turned up to upset things, but there he stood, in uniform. As soon as he caught her eye, he tipped his hat and disappeared.

"No. I don't think so." Jane's voice sounded odd to her own ears and she coughed to cover her lapse.

"Oh well, never mind. He's gone now. Come along and get your picture taken. Charlie's disappeared, so I thought we three should get ours done."

Jane smiled her broadest smile. She couldn't think of anything better than to share the limelight with Grace and Brigid, her two most favourite people in the world, and have a new photo or two to add to her collection.

"Now, Tom," said Brigid, withdrawing from the tableau, "can you take one of Grace and Jane on their own please, while I check on the catering."

Jane could not believe her luck.

19

RESCUED AND PERPLEXED

December 2018

At the sound of Jared's voice, Katie crumpled, and with two strides he enfolded her in his arms as if she belonged there. He'd never held her before, and she clung to him as the soft murmurings he whispered into her hair soothed her. "You're safe. Be calm. I'm here."

After a few moments, he eased her out of his arms and handed her a hanky. She mopped her eyes, glad she'd not put on any mascara.

His hands still held her elbows as he looked into her eyes. "Do you want to go back inside? Or get out of here?"

"I should go ..." she flicked her hand idly towards the funeral chapel.

"No. No 'should'. You shouldn't do anything to please anyone except yourself. What do *you* want to do?"

"Um. Well, I can't go without saying goodbye or ... something."

"If that's what you want to do, then do it. I'll wait."

Katie turned her head towards the building. They were in the car park at the back. No one could see them. She was tempted to simply leave. Had anyone missed her? Tom would, she admitted. But he'd offered to get her away from it all if only she could be with someone.

"Have you got any paper?" she asked, making up her mind. She rummaged in the bottom of her clutch bag and produced a pen.

Jared patted his pockets and came up with a receipt. "Will this do?"

She nodded and rapidly scribbled a note. "The man you saw me with before is my brother, Tom. Give him this, and then, please, get me out of here."

Jared nodded and headed off to do his errand. He was back in a matter of minutes. "All done. He read your note and said he'd call you later. Let's go."

Katie had no idea where she wanted to go, so Jared drove around the sights of Auckland. Through the domain, where ancient trees offered shade and where, sitting on the steps of the War Memorial Museum looking at the view across the city and harbour, hand in hand with Jared, she could let her mind wander.

Back in the car, they drove along the waterfront to admire the sparkling waters of the Waitemata. From time to time, Jared searched for her hand and squeezed it briefly, a quick glance and a smile soothing her frazzled nerves. They picked up an ice cream at Mission Bay and ate it while walking along the path beside the wall.

"You don't have to explain anything to me, my sweet girl," said Jared as Katie tried to justify her silence. "We'll talk when you're ready. Meanwhile, the distractions resume."

They continued their drive to Achilles Point lookout, letting the wind ruffle her hair. He held her this time while she rested her head against his shoulder.

"I'm glad you're here with me," she muttered as he lightly kissed the top of her head. "You ease my soul."

Back into the city to Cornwall Park and One Tree Hill. Captured by the magnificent view, they climbed the steps to the monument and turned full circle, taking in the expanse of the city.

"This park was once part of a farm owned by Sir John Logan Campbell," Jared told her. "He gifted it to the people of Auckland during the royal visit of the Duke and Duchess of Cornwall in 1901."

Jared continued to explain about historic Acacia Cottage being Campbell's, and the Parnell Rose Gardens being where he had built the house he and his wife lived in, and about all his brewery and timber interests and roles on numerous boards and committees.

"How do you know so much about him?" asked Katie.

"Just interested, I suppose. He's been called the Founding Father of Auckland many times, so I read up about him."

Jared deliberately avoided any talk of the funeral or family and kept to neutral topics, but standing in front of Campbell's resting place, and before the obelisk in honour of the Māori people Campbell so admired, reminded Jared of his great-grandmother Gwenna.

"She must have met him or at least known of him. He was made Honorary Mayor during the royal visit. There's a family story all of its own wrapped up in that."

"You must tell me sometime."

Katie's mood had improved enormously since they had left the funeral home, and she no longer wanted to burst into tears every other minute. She relaxed in his company, as if she belonged with him.

Jared's chatter about the beauty of Auckland and its history had fascinated her. More so, when she realised Granna Katy, and those before her, would have visited these same places and knew and loved the same, if slightly different, city to the one she knew. As had Jared's ancestors. She'd never given it any thought before, but all of a sudden, she felt anchored to this place that was such a huge part of her life.

They made their way back to the car and Jared drove slowly through the park to the main exit, keeping his eyes firmly on the road. "At the risk of sounding like I'm suggesting you should 'come see my etchings', I do have a framed newspaper article at home of the event involving Gwenna and the sweet shop during the 1901 visit. You're welcome to come around and read it any time."

Katie burst out laughing. "Where on earth did you drag that old phrase up from?"

"I like old things," he retorted.

"Are you suggesting I'm an 'old thing'?"

Caught out by his own tongue-in-cheek comment, Jared spluttered. "No, of course not. Not at all. It's just …"

"Yes, just what exactly?" she teased. "Are you trying to take advantage of a poor girl by suggesting something improper?"

The tables had turned and Jared laughed. "Only if you want me to."

In that moment, Katie did want more from Jared than he had offered before. She swallowed, looked straight ahead, too tense to look at him and in the most prim and proper old-fashioned voice said, "Mr Price, I do believe I do."

Two days later, she sat by herself in the lawyer's office. Tom had been called overseas again on business and wasn't sure he'd make it back in time for Christmas. Hugh only wanted to know how much he'd get from Granna's estate, and her father had the good grace to say nothing and keep away.

Jared had offered to go with her. "Katie, I hope I've made it plain enough, I'll do whatever you want. Anything to make you happy." Which included staying away.

The night after the funeral, they'd gone to dinner at the cosy bar near her apartment where they'd been before.

"We need to sort something out," Jared had said.

Concerned by his change of tone from bantering to solemn, Katie wondered whether she should have left well alone. If he wanted a relationship he'd had plenty of opportunities to say something sooner. The business contract had ended months ago, and apart from one uncomfortable get-together and a few awkward phone calls, only now had he appeared again.

Despite her brain writing the script ahead of time, Jared seemed as natural as ever. He parked the car, took her hand as he guided her across the road and chose a table for two in a corner away from everyone else.

She picked at her food, unable to quell the fluttering in her stomach and ready to burst into tears again, she gulped at the excellent red wine he'd chosen.

"Katie. Please understand, I want to make you happy. So don't take this the wrong way, but I need to know where I stand."

She started to say something, but wasn't sure what to say beyond um, well and yes.

He stopped her before she put her foot in it again. "What's going on, Katie? When we were working together there was a definite spark between us. Yes?"

Katie nodded.

"I wanted to nurture that spark, but you always pushed me away just when I thought we were getting somewhere. Now you tell me you want something more. The thing is ..." he paused and took a gulp of his wine. Katie wondered why he looked so nervous. "Viv says the opposite."

"Viv? What's Viv got to do with this?" A memory of some of the things Viv had said niggled at her. She was always commenting on what Jared was doing, and whether Katie knew, and whether Katie had seen him. Had Viv chased him herself?

"A lot. I kept getting messages from Viv saying you wanted her to handle some parts of the account. She'd call me at odd times to talk about a lot of nothing and then start asking if we could meet. And always in the evening after work."

"Was this while we were working on the website?"

"Yes – and since. Lots of times since. After the second or third time, I began to wonder what the point of the meetings was. She'd always arrive slightly late, and in a rush, and gushing about her busy life and how she missed having a night out with someone interesting. She'd order a bottle of wine for us to share and it seemed rude to leave, but all she wanted to do was, well, flirt I suppose is the old-fashioned way of putting it. If I'd followed her lead, we'd be a lot more than business colleagues right now."

Throughout the explanation, Jared's nervous habits of polishing his glasses or folding the paper serviette increased.

"Go on ..." said Katie, fuming at Viv's behaviour and how she'd been fooled.

"Whenever I asked about you, or how things were coming along, she fobbed me off with excuses. You were tied up, or involved with another client, or, as we got closer to finishing the website, you had handed the project back to her to finish. I got the distinct impression she was telling me you didn't want to see me ever again."

No wonder their drinks evening hadn't gone well. Each of them had received the same message from Viv – neither one had wanted to see the other.

"Well, it's not true," defended Katie. "But there were a couple of times when my grandmother took a turn for the worse and I needed to focus my attention on her."

"Why didn't you tell me? About your grandmother."

"It would have been unprofessional of me. You were a client. My personal life should not interfere with business."

He reached across the table and took her hand, smoothing his thumb back and forth across her knuckles. That spark they'd talked about ran up her arm and she couldn't stop herself looking into his eyes.

"I'm not a client now, and I would have understood. And you knew it. Didn't we have the beginnings of something more than just business?"

Katie nodded.

"Then why, Katie? Why did you push me away?"

The time had come. Either admit her attraction to him or tell him to go away for good. "I don't know. Or rather I don't know how to explain it."

"Try me." He sat waiting for her to continue.

She took a deep breath, took her hand away from his, and held hers tightly in her lap. "I always wanted to be a career woman, dependent only on myself, with no plans to get involved with anyone who could hurt me or cause the sort of messes I saw within my family. Something went wrong with my plan earlier this year, and I tossed in my whole career. I'm still not sure why, or where I'm going or what I'll do next. I'm a mess of my own making. Viv offered me a short-term contract which I took because I needed the money. But then you came along and ..." She stopped short, wary of saying anything more in case she was misreading the situation.

"And what, Katie?" His eyes burned into her, pleading for the right answer.

But then again, maybe she hadn't misread anything. "I liked you – a lot – and enjoyed being with you."

She saw his shoulders relax a fraction and that nearly-smile of his softened. "So what happened to that idea?"

"I didn't think it fair to burden you with all my problems and worries when you were starting out on a new career all of your own, and I couldn't ..." Utter sadness enveloped her, and she didn't have the strength to carry on. She couldn't trust herself in a relationship when she'd ruined so many before. And she couldn't face losing anyone else. "Sorry. Just forget everything I said." She gathered her bag and, forcing back the tears, got up from the table and ran from the bar.

Jared caught up to her as she got to the door of her building.

He stood squarely in front of her, blocking her way, one arm folded around her as the other cupped her cheek. A thumb wiped away the tear trickling down her face. He said nothing but leaned forward and gently kissed her, tenderly at first, then more insistently. The spark lit the flame and her body tingled. His message was one of empathy, of coming home. Her arms crept up his chest around his neck and when their lips broke contact, he hugged her, unwilling to let her go.

Moments passed. She turned her face towards him seeking his lips for a second time.

Passion flared.

"Trust me, Katie. I'd not do anything to hurt you. Please don't shut me out of your life any more. There's something special between us already, and I want there to be something more."

She took his hand and led him to her apartment ...

"Miss Anderson?"

The lawyer's voice called her back to the present. She wished she had allowed Jared to come with her, but maybe it was better he wasn't there. She had a lot to sort out in her head before she could share this with anyone.

Still, she couldn't quite believe how caring and understanding Jared was, giving her space when she needed it, but also being her rock. How could someone become so important in such a short space of time? She was falling in love with him, but fear of ruining everything still held her back.

"Do you understand all the details of your grandmother's will?" asked the lawyer.

She stared at the man blankly for a second or two, letting his words sink in.

A year before Granna Katy had given up her home and gone to live with her daughter, she had drawn up her will 'while still of sound mind and body', emphasised the lawyer. Katie realised her grandmother must have guessed or possibly been diagnosed at the onset of dementia. For whatever reason, Granna had been thorough in tying up her assets. She had organised for the investment from the sale of her house even before it sold, instructing the lawyer to meet her payments to her caregivers, whoever they may be – now, or in the future.

Granna had also allowed for the possibility she might outlive her children and protected her estate accordingly. Skipping her own children, Granna left it to her grandchildren with instructions the money be used for education or housing purposes only.

"Yes. I think so," said Katie. "My brothers and I are to each receive an equal lump sum payment. My two cousins in Perth, who I don't know, by the way, will receive the same amount, but if I fulfil the other requirements of my grandmother's will, I will receive the remainder of the estate."

Mrs Kathleen Grace Bridges had been a much wealthier woman than Katie realised. She knew Granna was comfortably off but never imagined long-term investments could amount to so much.

In the years following her husband's death, she had invested their savings wisely and the shares and dividends had proved more than successful. Somehow, she'd avoided the market crash of 2008 by selling her shares in time and putting her money in the bank, which, the lawyer told her, was still earning interest today.

"Yes. That is correct. There are three clauses to address. Your grandmother requires you firstly to set up and manage three independent, self-funding, annual lump sum grants available only to female students."

Katie listened while he explained the criteria for the grants and the process to set them up formally and legally. The second clause prescribed the cataloguing and archiving of numerous design sketches, which she knew nothing about, and the rules around making them available to museums and art galleries. Her head was spinning with all the details and ramifications. But the final clause made no sense to Katie.

"In addition, a lump sum payment matching the bequests made to yourself, your brothers and cousins, is to be made to the youngest female descendant of her firstborn daughter, one Elizabeth Ellingham, for the purposes of advanced education."

"Who's she?" asked Katie, totally confused.

"I'm unaware of her identity, sorry. Mrs Bridges did not advise me. It seems that is something she expected you to discover. It will be necessary for you to have incontrovertible proof of this person's lineage, of course."

Again Katie nodded, wondering how she was supposed to find this person she didn't know existed.

"Once you have fulfilled those requirements," continued the lawyer, "the balance of the not inconsiderable estate is yours."

Katie had no idea where to start. Straight away, Jared came to mind. He could help her untangle this mess, but there was no point talking to the lawyer further. She needed to think.

"Thank you. You've explained it very well."

"There is, of course, probate to be gone through before everything can be finalised. The designated lump sum payments can be paid out as soon as I receive probate, but, I repeat, the other conditions stipulated in the document will have to be met before the bulk of the estate is paid. You do understand, don't you?"

"Yes."

"In the meantime, any accounts associated with the funeral or tidying up her affairs can be sent to me.

I will pay them according to her instructions."

"Thank you for your time."

They shook hands and he handed Katie an envelope with a copy of the will and passed her a small leather suitcase, which he said he'd been holding for Mrs Bridges for many years.

Katie walked away from his office utterly bewildered but far richer than she ever dreamed possible – richer in knowledge, richer in understanding and richer financially.

20

ON THE HOME FRONT

March 1915

The war soon impacted on the lives of those left behind. With so many men having left their jobs, their homes and families to fight against the enemies of England, the women were forced to step into their shoes.

"Isn't it wonderful?" said Laura. "Women have a chance to prove how capable they are now. And they will, believe me, they will."

"I'm not sure I'd call it wonderful, dear. There's nothing wonderful about war," said Brigid, "but I'm sure lots of women will be more than capable of doing their share of work. It's more that I'm not sure what *I* can do to help. I still have a family to care for and a business to run."

"No, I can't see many women needing lace for a while," said Laura, "but the men will need bandages and other supplies. You could help that way. There are groups who get together and pack boxes to be sent over to them. Lots of volunteer nurses and medical people have already left and more are in training."

"Shush, Laura. Not so loud. I don't want to upset Grace. If she thinks for one moment Charlie could be lying injured, or worse, somewhere totally foreign, it will affect the baby."

Laura dismissed Brigid's concerns. "Grace is made of much tougher stuff than you think. But all right, if it keeps you happy, I won't ask her to do anything. But there are hundreds of women now working in all walks of life. Lots of them have taken over the factory work, but there's all the farming to do, and growing vegetables. You could organise fund-raising events."

"Could I start a peace movement instead?"

Brigid felt so old sometimes, and far too often spent her time pretending life was as it once had been. Losing Tommy had stripped Brigid of her self-confidence, and she lived in fear of losing more of those she loved, or one of them having to go through the pain she went through. Every day she watched Grace following the news, checking the casualty list and praying Charlie would not appear. So far, no one they knew had been on the list, but the casualties were mounting.

Sally, as usual, was her rock. "Breeda, my dear. You can't change what can't be changed. But neither do you have to get involved in anything Laura wants you to. Strange as it may seem, Jane is as busy as ever. People need entertainment to take their mind off things. Maybe we should go to the theatre."

Brigid declined the offer. She was happy at home, listening to Grace play the piano when she was in the mood and to care for her when she felt down. But something in Laura's words rang true. She could help in some way. Maybe knitting socks, but, no, Sally could do that. Her time would be better spent appealing for people to donate goods and money to the cause. She only had to decide how best to achieve her goal.

Pregnancy suited Grace. She was blossoming, despite her worries about Charlie. "Do you think we can get a message to Charlie when the time comes?" she asked.

"Of course, dear. Laura tells me it's quite easy to send a message through to the troops," she assured the girl, although unsure of her facts.

At a time when people needed to be together, it seemed the busyness of war kept them apart. Jane had not called around in some time. Instead, Laura had become the more regular caller. She was so involved in 'the war effort' she needed to share her enthusiasm with everyone, but eventually the lack of interest from Brigid and Sally had sent her looking for support elsewhere.

"Quick. Send a message to Jane. She has to be here," said Brigid as soon as Grace went into labour. Sally donned her bonnet and hurried to tell Jane the news. At fifty-five, she was showing her age and slowing down, although she hadn't admitted anything to Brigid. She decided to take the tram, even though walking the relatively short distance to Wellesley Street would usually be quicker.

The two women arrived back at the house breathless and anxious. Jane had insisted on walking, which she claimed calmed her nerves. But on arrival, her nerves seemed anything other than calm. "How is Grace?"

"Doing well, all things considered. The midwife is in with her," answered Brigid.

A few moments later, sounds of Grace groaning reached their ears, along with the remonstrations of the woman attending her. "Stop that noise. Think of what the men are going through in battle. I bet they aren't complaining like you."

Jane was shocked. She yanked the door to Grace's room open and stormed in. "How dare you speak to Grace in that manner!"

Jane knelt beside the bed and took Grace's hand. "My darling girl. Take heart. You will come through this with the grace you are endowed with. Remember, you are loved by so many who think of you as their precious one. Now, breathe slowly. In and out. There's a good girl. Do as the midwife tells you."

Jane refused to leave Grace's side, never mind what the midwife said. She knelt on the floor, holding Grace's hand throughout every contraction, encouraging her to be brave, to understand there was a priceless gift at the end of her ordeal.

Eventually, the gift arrived. Amid screams of pain, shrills of protest and squeals of joy, Thomas Charles Price was born. He made his appearance on 14 July, the same day they learnt the first of three hundred wounded men from Gallipoli would arrive in Wellington. Charlie was one of them.

Frustrated at not being able to travel to Wellington to meet Charlie, Grace and her bevy of 'mothers' waited in a state of turmoil at the station for the specially outfitted Red Cross train to arrive.

Grace had earlier voiced a string of 'what ifs', worried how she would react if his injuries were horrific or frightening or life-threatening or any other consequence of her vivid imagination. They had no idea of the extent of his injuries.

"If any of it were true, he wouldn't be about to step off the train, now would he?' assured Brigid, herself a nervous wreck as to how Grace would cope with both a new baby and an injured husband.

"Don't fret, dear girl. I'm sure you would have been told about anything unusual," said Jane, secretly crossing her fingers behind her back. Superstition was rife in the theatre, and she had long since picked up the habits of wishing for luck against the odds.

Gwenna seemed the only one focused on fact. "Charlie is blessed with the good luck of the Irish, like you, even if he is Welsh. He will get off the train and look for you with love in his heart. And what a gift you are giving him in return."

"Aye, lass," said Sally. "Together you will manage whatever the future holds."

Slowly, they watched the train emerge along the tracks. The smoke rising from the stack puffed grey and black, and its whistle pierced the air. The women instinctively moved closer together, determined not to be split up by the pressure of the other nervous relatives wanting to catch the first glimpse of their loved one.

Inch by painfully slow inch, the train came to a stop along the length of the platform. The band started playing, and the officials stood ready to welcome the returning soldiers. There would be a formal welcome at the Town Hall later.

Doors were thrown open, and people started calling the name of their beloved. First off came some of the stretchered men, the ones most damaged by their wounds. Wails of despair from the men's families reached their ears. Relief flooded through those remaining.

Uniformed men started to appear at the top of the train's steps to look up and down the platform, searching for a familiar face. Every person on the platform stared back, trying to understand their injuries in preparation for when their man came into view. Relief and joy replaced worry as each soldier recognised someone and, as he stepped down, the crowd moved to allow him passage.

"There," pointed Jane. "There's Charlie."

He looked gaunt. Haunted. At least that's what Jane saw. Grace and Gwenna only saw him alive.

"Charlie. Charlie," they called. "Over here."

Gwenna reached him first, but after a quick hug, she stepped to one side. Wiping the tears from her eyes, she watched as Charlie and Grace came together, almost in slow motion. In one hand Charlie carried a bag, the other arm rested in a sling.

"Charlie. I'm so glad you're home," she said in a whisper, thankful he didn't look too badly injured. "I'd like you to meet your son. Thomas."

"Grace, my darling." He kissed her on the forehead. "What a fabulous welcome. A man couldn't hope for a better homecoming. Thank you all for coming," he said, casting his eyes over Jane, Brigid, Sally, Gwenna and Hugh before returning to Grace.

Hugh reached to take his kitbag from him. "Good to see you again."

Charlie nodded and put his now free arm around his wife, holding his baby. "It's good to be back."

To Jane, his voice sounded flat. He was saying the right things, but the Charlie she knew was not the man standing in front of her. Something was missing. Only time would tell, but she hoped the old Charlie would soon return.

His sisters and the others were waiting impatiently for a better time to welcome him, he was told. They had stayed away to give Charlie the chance to say hello without becoming overwhelmed.

"How thoughtful."

"Shall we go home now?" asked Grace.

"Home." Charlie's voice sounded distant, and the way he said the word 'home' had nothing to do with the place he lived but more of a vague notion of what being 'home' now meant.

21

LOVE AND LAUGHTER

December 2018

Katie awoke on Christmas morning, stretched and smiled at the man lying beside her. Wanting to avoid putting pressure on their newfound intimacy, Jared had not stayed over until the previous night. Katie had dreaded the thought of waking up on Christmas morning on her own – even though she'd done it plenty of times in her adult life. This year, there were too many memories and too many shadows. She needed a major distraction.

"Good morning," said Jared, sitting up, "and Merry Christmas."

He proved to be the perfect distraction. His kiss lingered on her lips long after he'd leapt out of bed. "Race you to the shower," but this morning she didn't care. Today would be a day of total indulgence.

While she showered, Jared took over the kitchen. By the time she joined him, he was putting the finishing touches to their breakfast. French toast, complete with berries, liqueur and cream, looked the most scrumptious she had ever seen. He poured two glasses of sparkling wine, dropped in a couple of strawberries and handed one to Katie. "Here's to the end of one story and the start of another."

She clinked her frosted-up glass against his, in total accord with his words as they sipped the wine.

"Now eat."

The first bite was pure deliciousness. "Oh yum, but I'm going to get so fat if you keep feeding me like this."

He leant towards her and kissed her nose. "You'll do me in any shape or size."

Katie blushed and returned his gaze, trying to determine the meaning behind his words, but he just grinned, filled his mouth with food and pointed with his fork for her to eat up.

So much had changed, and in such a short time, she had difficulty believing she was the same person.

Not long after Granna's funeral, Jared broached the subject of her emotional state of mind. He'd asked some tactful questions, and she'd hesitantly told him why she'd quit her job back in May and how she had shut herself away since.

"You can't keep going the way you are. You've admitted you aren't sleeping or eating properly, and your mood changes, tears and lethargy I think are signs of something more than grief. Not least to say the chronic self-doubt you have. It's not good for you."

The doctor diagnosed mild depression, saying he wasn't surprised, given all she'd been through. Katie never once considered herself a candidate for mental illness and was staggered how easily it could creep up without warning. The doctor gave her some ideas how to change her lifestyle to help combat her anxiety, suggested she took a course of St John's wort since she didn't want medication, and gave her the contact details of a therapist should she need further help in the New Year.

Once Katie realised the problem, she made changes to her routine and felt much better for it. And knowing Jared was there to support her reshaped her whole outlook. She was still aware of her fragility but each day was better than the last.

"See, I told you, you should have had me in your life a long time ago, then none of this would have happened."

She laughed, and teased him. "How do you know you didn't make it worse?"

"Because you're laughing."

She hadn't been quite so keen on laughing last week, though; she'd had too much to digest.

Jared had been waiting for her when she'd left the lawyer's office ...

"You OK?" he'd asked, seeing her deep in thought and biting her bottom lip.

She nodded, relieved to see him. "Just lots to think about."

They'd walked hand in hand back to her apartment.

"You do know how envious I am of you living around here, don't you?"

She'd not yet visited Jared's home, which he'd said was a small, unassuming townhouse with no outlook and little in the way of frills.

"Envy away. But yeah, it's great."

"The best thing about my place is all the old photos I've got hanging everywhere. When you sort out the ones from your grandmother, you'll see what I mean. Have you looked at them yet?"

Katie shook her head. "And now I've got this to deal with," she waggled the narrow suitcase she carried. "The lawyer said he's been holding it for years, ignorant of its contents."

"Sounds intriguing. Best thing then, in my opinion, is for you to open it as soon as you get home and see what secrets it possesses. Call it therapy, and then you should get stuck into sorting those photos."

She hadn't told Jared the contents of the will, and he hadn't asked. She needed to absorb what it all meant first, but her curiosity had been aroused by this old leather case.

"OK. I'll look at it this afternoon. It might distract me from all the other things clogging my mind."

He squeezed her hand. "Good girl."

At another time in her life, she'd have considered a comment like that patronising, but now she took it as moral support.

They arrived at her building, and he kissed her goodbye. "Sorry. I've got to get back to work. Got a living to make and meet all the orders from that website 'somebody' designed. It's working a treat. You OK for a while?"

"I'll be fine." She smiled, believing she could cope better now, knowing he was only a phone call away. "And I'm so glad it's working out well for you, Jared. I truly am."

Once inside, Katie had thrown open the windows and stood admiring the view, which always amazed her. She loved her apartment, but hiding away in it had to come to an end. She had much to be thankful for.

Katie had phoned Jared later that afternoon – not because she was feeling low, but because she was bouncing with joy. "It's full of diaries and journals and sketches and, oh so much. I'm sure the answers are here somewhere," she squealed.

"OK, OK, calm down. What is full? What diaries? What answers?"

"The suitcase. Oh, Jared, it's incredible. It seems Granna's story hasn't ended after all. And there's this gorgeous beaded shawl wrapped in layers of ancient tissue paper. It's so old and fragile I'm scared to touch it, but it must be important."

She reminded Jared how she'd needed to clear Granna's room in a matter of days to make room for another poor person who'd lost touch with reality. The notion had scared her.

"After I'd dropped Granna's clothes and other personal items at the op shop, I pushed the rest into the hall cupboard. I've just pulled them out again and sorted everything into what to keep and what to give away. And I found more photos."

"Any names?" asked Jared.

"Not so far. I haven't finished sorting and there's a lot of reading to do to fit it all together. But there's one photo in particular I want you to see."

"Fantastic. So, get on with it. See how far you get and I'll be over later."

True to his word, Jared arrived later that evening. Katie met him at the door, draped her arms around his neck and kissed him. Taking him by the hand, she pulled him through the doorway as he kicked the door shut behind him. Laid out all over the floor were photographs in assorted sized frames and of various ages.

"I think I've put them into some sort of tree, but I can't be certain."

She handed Jared a hand-scribbled list of names with lines and arrows all over it, hastily trying to explain what she thought.

"So, which one did you want me to see?"

Katie handed him a picture of a woman holding a bridal bouquet and a man in uniform flanked by two women – one of them was Katie's lookalike. "Isn't it delightful?"

Jared looked from Katie to the photo and back again, his jaw dropping in surprise. "I've seen this before. I've got it. I'm sure it's the same, and I know who the bride and groom are. And the woman on this side. But who is *she*?" he said, pointing to Katie's double.

Katie's jaw dropped open this time. "You have? You do? I haven't got a clue."

"This is weird. I think I'd better come over a lot more often and we'll sort it out together." …

Now, a week later, he was here with her on Christmas morning and everything was perfect.

Jared cleared away the breakfast things while Katie wiped the table and put the mats away and brought their coffee cups over.

"I've a present for you," he said as she began to load the dishwasher.

"Oh, that's naughty." She stood to face him and pretended to be stern. "We agreed no presents."

"But I couldn't resist." He winked.

"Me or the present?" Katie couldn't quite believe what she'd said. She wasn't normally so forward but she felt so comfortable with Jared, it came out before she thought about what she was saying.

"Let me think on it," he teased as he leaned forward and kissed her. "Mmm. You. Definitely you. More bubbles?"

"No, thanks. One glass is more than enough for a morning, Christmas or not."

"Then how about going for a walk? It's a glorious day."

"Sounds like an excellent idea."

Puzzled by his change of direction, she wondered when, or if, she should tell him about her gift. If one can break the rules, so could two.

She watched as he gathered his overnight things together and placed his bag by the door. "Shall we go?"

"Sure. I'll just grab a hat and my sunnies and pop some sunscreen on."

When she was ready, they called the lift but Jared pushed the button for the basement where he'd parked his car.

"I though you said we were going for a walk."

"We are, but I like the walk along by Kohi and thought we'd go there."

Katie knew the path he was talking about. It followed the beachfront from Mission Bay, past Kohimarama Beach to St Heliers. "It's a bit far to walk there and back, so we'll park along the way."

Katie could see sense in the suggestion. Jared tossed his bag in the back as she got in the passenger seat. Watching the scenery go by, Katie hadn't noticed which route he took until he pulled up in front of a set of three townhouses.

"Here we are. That's my place at the end."

"This is a surprise," said Katie, unsure why Jared had decided to take her to his place, today of all days.

"I've got something to show you."

Jared's place was just as he described, plain and lacking much in the way of colour or extras. To Katie's eye, it looked as if the room had been tidied and cleared of personal touches and all the other doors were pulled shut, but she didn't stop to wonder why. The walls told a story of their own.

"Start here," he pointed to the framed newspaper cutting dated 1901. Katie read in awe the story about stopping the royal cortege and giving the duchess a bag of lollies, which put Gwenna's Superior Sweet Treats in Karangahape Road on the map. Katie was amazed at the level of detail in the article, including a list of names.

"No wonder you've followed your family history. What an awesome story."

"But this is the photo I wanted to show you."

Katie turned to the framed sepia print on the adjacent wall as Jared stepped out of her line of vision. She stared, unbelieving at what her eyes told her. "But ... I don't understand. It's the same one I showed you. So what does all this mean?"

"I told you I knew three of them. The bridal couple are Charlie and Grace Price. Standing next to Charlie is his sister Gwenna, but I still have no idea who the other woman is. But maybe this will help."

He handed her a small package wrapped in Christmas paper from the table behind him. "Go on. Open it."

She sat on the couch and ripped the paper from the parcel. In an instant, her gift of a personalised business card holder and a box of new business cards seemed trite.

"Is this the photo you've been searching for?" he asked. "The one you told me your grandmother talked about?"

Katie nodded. "But how ...?" she stammered, overwhelmed and unable to take her eyes from the newly framed, very much restored – and until now – elusive photograph her grandmother had posed for.

Jared sat beside her on the two-seater. "So, there's Gwenna," he said, pointing to the woman on the right. "I'm certain of that. And this one is Grace. The slightly older woman in the middle, I'm sure is the one you keep calling Mórai. So we still need to identify the one who looks like you and the little girl in front. Am I right?"

Katie had no doubt the young girl standing in front of Mórai was her Granna Katy, just as she had described on that memorable day. How Jared had a copy, or recognised it, or found it, was a mystery still to be unravelled, but Katie didn't care. Another link in the chain of discovery had been handed to her.

22

DEATH AND DISASTER

November 1918

While the war still raged, two deadly influenza virus strains swept through the world, killing millions. One strain arrived in New Zealand. Within two months, families already suffering from the ravages of war found their lives further decimated by the pandemic.

As the list of war casualties mounted higher and higher, adding up to figures most people could not digest, dying of the flu seemed incomprehensible. Until the tragedy became personal, and families were hit by yet another catastrophe. Piercing screams of grief could be heard echoing through the streets, seemingly at every hour, bringing people out of their houses to ask, "Who is lost this time?"

The theatre had been forced to close for a time, along with hotels, banks and schools and many other public places, as the government desperately tried to control the spread of the disease. Despite the efforts of the thinly spread and overstretched medical personnel and the well-intended government interaction, hundreds more died every day. Many were quickly buried in mass graves.

On top of those Gwenna's family had previously lost, Bethan Price, mother to Elias, Louisa, Janetta and Charlie, and stepmother to Gwenna and Tillie, also succumbed to the disease.

They would never forget 23 November 1918, when the highest number of deaths from the flu were recorded on any one day. It came less than twelve days after the ceasefire was announced and the armistice signed, signalling the end of the war. But such news didn't help when thousands lay dying – and men in particular. Armistice celebrations had been banned in an effort to keep everyone away from public spaces. But still the contagion spread.

Jane murmured a few words of comfort to Gwenna as she stood by her at St James's Church in Wellington Street. This wasn't the first time Jane had attended this church in recent times, but this funeral seemed harder to take. The pain she saw in the eyes of those around her upset her more than she expected. Internal tremors shook her body as she tried to withhold her tears and offer solace, instead of adding to their burden.

Gwenna dabbed her hanky to her reddened eyes. "It's so unfair. Why, why should we be punished like this?"

"It is, dear friend. It is most unfair. But don't think of it as punishment. It is no one's fault. Try and take heart, you are needed by so many." Jane thought her words ineffectual against so much misery but knew not what else to offer.

Standing alone, surrounded by Charlie and Gwenna's extended family, each of whom had someone missing from their lives, Jane fought to maintain rigid control, a handkerchief clutched in readiness should a rogue tear fall.

Only at night, in the privacy of her cottage, did Jane let go of the emotions she hid during the day. Where she railed against the damage done to those she knew and loved as she paced, crying and shouting, cursing against the inhumanity of war.

The war years had done so much harm to so many and as she reflected she named each and every one, family by family.

Too many.

Gwenna's husband, Hugh, who had been put on Home Duty, partly because of his age but mostly due to his previous war record, suffered badly. He'd been left with painful memories, which had worsened over the last four years and manifested in unusual ways. Although he tried to control his reactions, he could never be sure when a noise would send him scurrying for cover, or headaches would confine him to a darkened room for days. Only Gwenna could calm him.

Charlie had not responded well to his injuries either. The damage to his left arm was permanent, and it was of little use. He couldn't lift or carry, and he would never again make sweets. Jane constantly worried about him and Grace. He had lost his trademark sparkle, more often morose or silent. He spent most of his time with his brothers-in-law, Hugh and Tom, much more than with Grace and baby Thomas, and never talked about his plans for the future any more.

So many lost. So many wasted lives.

She thought of Cecil. The news of his death had devastated her. She would never forget his loyalty. Her pain deepened and she shed more tears. He'd been one of thousands conscripted back in 1916. She had worried about him from the start, knowing his proclivity would not endear him to the men, but enemy fire had taken his life long before his penchant became an issue. Not since her childhood had she experienced such anguish.

During these terrible years, life continued much the same for Jane within the confines of the theatre world, and the demand for entertainment kept her busy.

Music hall, pantomime and vaudeville, shows which made people laugh, were all the rage amid the sorrows of war. Now, with the additional tragedy of the pandemic, light relief was a tonic for innumerable broken hearts and minds but with materials in short supply many of the performers made do with existing costumes. Jane's job was to keep them together and, with the addition of a few accoutrements, make them look different from the last show. Creating new and evocative costumes was a thing of the past, and as more and more staff became involved in the war effort, the workload fell to Jane.

Outside the theatre walls, her life had been a series of joys and worries. After Charlie returned home mid-1914, he and Grace had gone to live with Brigid and Sally, in the small rooms above the shop. Early the following year, Brigid announced she was giving up the business. They had all been shocked and had argued with her, but she remained firm.

"The war has changed so much and more change is yet to come, I believe. I can't hold on to the past any longer. Miss Brigid's has been overtaken by larger firms with more to offer, so I've sold. Laura pointed out I could help with the war effort, with fund-raising and other duties which are far more important than lacemaking, and I've come to agree with her. Grace and Charlie and little Tommy need a larger place to live, so I shall buy a house more suitable for the family's needs."

In many ways, Jane wanted to applaud. The old Brigid she remembered from her youth had returned. And the more she felt needed, the stronger she became. Sally, on the other hand, seemed to shrink. Jane wasn't quite certain how old Sally was, something like six or seven years older than Brigid, but she could have been mistaken for someone far older. There didn't appear to be a specific complaint pulling her down, but rather a chronic malaise. Whatever the problem, the shop was proving too much for her, so they decided to sell the property and move on.

Now, three years later, they lived a far more contented life looking after the family.

"Hello, Jane, dear," said Brigid as Jane entered the kitchen after the funeral. "Are Grace and Charlie with you?"

"No, they stayed behind to spend some time with Gwenna and the others."

The impressive five-bedroom villa with a wrap-around verandah, in Devonport, had worked perfectly for the family. Brigid and Sally used the smaller back bedrooms, while Grace and Charlie occupied the one at the front. The remaining bedrooms waited to be filled with the family Charlie and Grace planned. The kitchen, with access to the verandah, was large enough for a dining table for the family, two comfortable armchairs and a sofa, where Brigid and Sally spent most of their time, sitting next to the coal range.

"How did things go?" asked Brigid who had stayed behind to look after Tommy, now toddling around the kitchen playing with his toys.

Jane shrugged. "As well as could be expected, I suppose." She fiddled with the braid on her dress and looked at the overly ornate vases filled with peacock feathers and other dated paraphernalia that had come with the house. "Such sadness fills everyone's hearts, I wonder if we will ever truly feel happy again. It breaks my heart to see Grace watching Charlie, hoping for some sign his natural spirit is returning, but seeing nothing beyond utter dejection. He's been back with us now for over three years, and I don't see any sign of him returning to a normal life."

"Neither do I," admitted Brigid who bustled around making a cup of tea and putting cake from the tins onto a plate. "But something has happened recently. Grace is playing the piano more and seems brighter in herself somehow. But she's not confided anything to me."

Jane lifted young Tommy onto her knee and started playing tickling games with him. His giggle helped raise her spirits. "Where's Sally?" asked Jane, noticing her absence for the first time.

"Resting. She tires so easily these days. Has Grace spoken to you?"

"No, but I've noticed a change in her, too." Jane turned to Brigid, "Could she be with child, do you think?" hoping it might be so. Tommy needed someone to play with.

"Now you mention it, maybe she could be. I hadn't thought of that. How remiss of me."

Jane didn't consider it at all remiss. Brigid had more than her fair share of distractions to cope with.

When Lilly's husband Joseph had been killed, Brigid wanted to go to her without delay, but civilians were not allowed to travel. She had to trust Lilly to the care of the Harrison-Browne family, knowing Beatrice would look after her as best she could, given her age. Which was just as well. Lilly's relationship with her mother-in-law was distant at best, and she would never receive any consolation from a woman grieving her only son. Astonishingly, Phillip allowed Lilly to continue working in the department store. If anything, he saw it as a duty to remain open and provide goods the populace needed. A continual stream of letters from Beatrice and Lilly eased Brigid's mind, until the day Lilly wrote, a few months later, saying Beatrice had died of a heart attack. The losses mounted and the cracks in Brigid's heart multiplied.

She'd had kept busy with her war work but, still cloaked in worry over Lilly, she couldn't possibly be expected to think of everything, in spite of them being under her nose. Or maybe, because she saw Grace and Charlie and little Tommy every day, she could see for herself how they were.

"What will happen to all your Patriotic Committee work, now the war is officially over?" asked Jane, putting Tommy down and accepting the cup Brigid extended.

"Some of it will wind up quite naturally but, as Laura says, many of our troops are not home yet, nor will they be for some time. They still need our help and will do so long after they return. Those poor men. So sad."

Jane grew used to Brigid's constant reference to Laura. Her sister had reached into Brigid's desire, or need, to help people, and in return she had become Laura's champion. Sally too assisted the cause by knitting endless socks for the soldiers. Jane admitted her sister worked hard. She'd stirred up many a women's group to do good deeds, prove their worth and fight for their rights. Laura was committed to her beliefs, but they weren't Jane's to share.

"After that," continued Brigid, "I think many organisations will develop into something similar. Women have become so used to doing something worthwhile and are thankful for the conviviality and friendship they've found through their committees, they won't want to give it up in a hurry." The front door slammed. "Sounds like they're back." She rose to refresh the teapot.

Grace appeared through the door, looking as if the world had come to an end. Jane was on her feet and had engulfed the girl in her arms before she could say a word. "Come and sit down."

"And drink this." Brigid handed her a cup of tea sweetened with two spoons of sugar. "Is Charlie with you?"

Grace nodded. Automatically, the women looked towards the door, expecting him to come in and tell them what had happened since the funeral to upset Grace so much.

"Where is he then?"

"Packing. He's leaving."

After a moment's shocked silence, Brigid recovered her senses. "Not if I have anything to say about it," she said, fired with a mother's passion. She headed towards the door obviously intent on speaking to Charlie.

"Wait a moment, Brigid," said Jane. "We don't know why, for how long, what started it or anything. Don't risk making the situation worse by riling him."

"When did you learn to be so sensible?" said Brigid, picking Tommy up on her return.

"I must have picked it up from you," Jane quipped. Brigid had always been the level-headed, positive influence in their lives, but sometimes her fiery Irish blood complicated matters.

Hours later, after a lot of tears, the occasional burst of anger, much pleading from Grace and a painful confession, Brigid and Jane discovered Charlie's intentions.

"I'm no use to anyone as I am," he admitted, after initially refusing to discuss it. Most men refused to talk about their war experiences, leaving the women to guess the horrors haunting them. Eventually, he conceded Grace needed an explanation. "This damned arm – forgive me, ladies – but this blasted arm of mine is useless, and so am I."

Word by word, sentence by sentence, Charlie's troubles were laid bare. "I've tried. I've talked to Hugh about how he copes. I talked to Tom, who's been like a father to me and always put me right before. I talked to Eli about how he changed from sweetmaker to cabinetmaker and what difference it made to him – inside. I've talked with the doctors. None of it's helped."

Endless pots of tea were made, only some of them drunk. Silence settled in the air when no one knew what to say to ease Charlie's anguish, but once he began, they let him talk at his own pace.

"I can't see what I can do with my life. Not now I can't make sweets like I always dreamed I was destined to. And now Mam is gone. Who is going to replace her and help Gwenna? She can't manage with two of us lost to the business."

In between sentences, restless and agitated, he paced the floor and rubbed his eyes. "I live on a miserable army pension and the goodwill of others." He turned to his mother-in-law. "You especially, Miss Brigid, and I'm thankful. Don't get me wrong, but even Gwenna invents things for me to do." He started pacing again. "I feel so useless. I *am* useless." He punched the wall.

He stopped pacing to look at his son, now peacefully sleeping in his cot. "Grace tells me there's another child on its way. So something has to change. I have to change, or I'll go mad."

Brigid and Jane silently acknowledged their guess and welcomed the news of another child.

"But isn't that all the more reason why you should be here, with us?" argued Brigid. "Won't the love of family help?"

"It will, but not until I sort myself out. I've been given a place at Queen Mary Hospital in Hanmer Springs in the South Island. I leave tomorrow."

23

DISTURBANCES

January 2019

"What!?" demanded Katie, an icy chill settling over her.

"I'm sorry." Jared tried to touch her elbow and comfort her.

The familiar spark of electricity when he touched her inflamed her skin, but now it felt like a mockery of all they had been to each other. She pulled her arm away.

"I should have told you about my daughter before, but ..."

The view from her window was as magnificent as always, and she wanted to be out there, in the wide-open spaces and away from the truth now upsetting the balance between them. She wanted to run. Run away from everything and everyone who hurt her.

"I love you, Katie. And have done almost since I set eyes on you, but I didn't think ..."

She had longed to hear those words, but after his confession, they seemed hollow. "No. You didn't think," she interrupted. Her voice cold and distant. "Explain to me, just how would my not knowing about an ex-wife and a child help our relationship?"

The last two weeks had been the best weeks of her life. The whole Christmas–New Year week had been a glorious round of joyfulness, matched only by the fireworks exploding from the Sky Tower to mark the start of a new year – a new life.

They had explored Auckland, finding new places to walk and talk, picnic and swim. They wined and dined, loved and laughed. With Jared around, she let her grief for her grandmother find its natural place. He made her happy. He held her when she was down. He kept her distracted. He gave her the gift of family. She loved him.

Not that she had told him yet. And just as well too.

"I think you should leave now."

As tears began to roll down her cheeks, she sat on the couch, tucked her legs under her and turned away from him.

The cushion next to her sank as he sat down, and she saw his hand creep towards her, close but not quite touching her.

"I admit I was wrong, but I'm not going anywhere. I'm not letting you push me away again. I want you, Katie, and I believe you want me too. We can work this out."

She wriggled and tucked her legs in further so she wouldn't touch him. She couldn't let him ignite the flame of wanting or she'd succumb to his charms far too soon. She needed to think.

"I can't change the past, but I do want to create a future, a new future with you. I won't say anything more until you ask, but please, Katie, don't shut me out. Please."

He shifted in his seat and settled into the corner of the couch away from her.

They sat in silence for an indeterminable time until cramp crept in and she needed to move. Carefully unwinding her legs so as not to touch him, she stood and stretched. Without looking at him or saying a word, she went to the bathroom and stood under a steaming shower for an eternity, or longer, sorting her emotions.

When she emerged, he was still there, where she'd left him.

He stood as she moved closer. With his back to the window, the shadow over his face did nothing to hide the anguish in his eyes. The nearly-smile flickered between almost and not at all. His brow creased and he constantly pushed his glasses into place but, true to his word, he didn't speak. His eyes did all the pleading for him.

"Why tell me now?" she asked.

Over breakfast, still sitting unfinished on the kitchen bench, he had told her the story. He'd been young, coming up nineteen, when he'd met the girl who stole his heart. She was a bit older than him, but when she discovered she was pregnant, he insisted they marry. She was the girl for him. Life changed when their daughter turned five and his ex decided to find work.

Katie hadn't listened to any more. She hadn't wanted to hear the details. Learning he had an ex-wife and a child, a practically grown-up child at that, was too much to take in.

In her heart, she knew Jared was right not to have told her the night they first got together after her grandmother's funeral. She hadn't been ready. She wasn't sure she was ready now, but why choose this moment?

"Because my daughter is arriving tomorrow."

Katie nodded. In her head, she argued the pros and cons. He'd had no choice. He had to tell her today or spend the rest of the time lying about where he was and what he was doing. At least he hadn't lied.

But why couldn't he have told her before? Wasn't that lying by omission? She knew the answer before she asked the question. He wanted to protect her. He always put her first. He was good to her, for her, but she couldn't shake the feeling of being let down.

"Grace and I have a solid relationship," he said. "She's a great girl and I think you'd like her. But I won't ask you to meet her until you're ready."

Katie continued to stare at him, saying nothing. He looked uncomfortable under her scrutiny but waited for her to say something. Anything.

"What happened?"

"My ex hated the late shifts I worked back then and wanted me to get a proper job, one where I worked regular hours. But I couldn't change careers and she couldn't, or wouldn't, understand why. She found a job and got more and more involved, saying she loved being with the people. Over time, things went from bad to worse, and one day she left. She'd found someone new and she took Grace with her. End of story, really. Except part of the settlement was a week about with Grace. I did change my job then so I could be with her, which is why we are great mates now. I never missed a week, never mind how hard it got."

Neither of them had moved from their stance, a few metres apart. Tension prickled the air. Katie's head told her he had done all the right things; her heart hammered out a different rhythm.

"Is her name Grace?"

"Yes. I've always loved the name, and I love her more."

"Nice name. There's a Grace in my family somewhere. Granna's middle name was Grace."

"I've a Grandma Grace too."

Another nod. Now was not the time to get involved in family trees. "You'd better go then."

Jared tilted his head to one side. "I'll call you."

"No. I'll call you, when I'm ready. If I'm ready." She wasn't going to let him off the hook easily, even if her heart was breaking.

After he'd gone, Katie cleared away the breakfast and fastidiously tidied and cleaned the apartment, putting anything of Jared's out of sight until not a trace remained. Not even a faint whiff of his deodorant. Her mind was numb and she kept it that way, refusing to think about anything to do with his daughter, their relationship, their future – anything.

Instead, she returned to her photography. She'd got into the habit of taking her camera with her wherever she went, hoping for that perfect shot. She knew it would be a struggle to make money as a freelancer without an awful lot of effort. While a steady trickle of money arrived each month, she needed to do more to make a success of it. While money wasn't an issue any more, thanks to Granna's inheritance, she still wanted to make this work for her own sake.

She kept adding images to stock sites, working out which ones attracted the most attention and paid the most. She had to understand what people needed the images for. Only the very best of her shots of the city received clicks, and most of her bird and scenic shots got lost amongst the myriad of similar images. Her most popular ones were those of Granna: hands, half-face, with flowers, her eyes, blurred distant images, those she'd converted to faded black and white or sepia.

She trolled through websites looking at how people used images, visited the book outlets and studied book covers, googled photographers and what they offered, and began to build an idea of what she liked before flicking back to her own collection.

One of her favourite photos of Granna appeared before her eyes, and all the sadness washed through her again. But she felt calmer, not so wracked with grief, and able to look at the image with love and gratitude to have had such a wonderful grandmother for so long.

Granna's love was still giving. Katie had been shocked by the revelation at the lawyers and she was still taking it all in. And there were those conditions to meet, but she'd not told Jared any of it.

Am I the one being deceitful now? she thought.

She'd kept a secret from him, just like he'd kept one from her – and for the same reason. The truth added complexity to their relationship, and they weren't ready. Neither of them. But if they were to trust one another, they had to be honest. And she wasn't.

Burying herself in photographs, both new and old, and working through her family tree, Katie let the next couple of days drift by. Many a time, she'd wanted to pick up the phone and ask Jared something but changed her mind. She needed more time, and his focus was on his daughter. He didn't need her complicating things.

As she moved Granna's framed pictures around, trying to date them from the clothes or who was with whom, she was bothered yet again by what her eye told her and what the online records told her.

The suitcase the lawyer had given her contained several scrapbooks of fashion sketches, and as many scrapbooks with tickets and programmes and other mementoes, but nothing to identify the owner. She also had a series of hand-written journals – but not about the ordinary things in life. They were more like recordings of major events, with long, detailed descriptions and explanations, and listing names that meant nothing. Katie couldn't work out who the author was either. At first, she thought they were Granna's, but they all predated her.

As Jared had taught her, she worked backwards from herself, to her mother and father, and then their parents. She abandoned her father's side, knowing none of the photos in Granna's possession had anything to do with them.

She added her grandmother's name and dates to the online tree, and her grandfather's. His side she ignored as well. Within moments, a bunch of hints appeared. She clicked on a couple, which took her to a string of records – birth, electoral rolls, marriages and deaths – but she wasn't sure if they were connected or not. None of the names fitted with any she knew. A man, Thomas, and a woman, Jane, who weren't old enough to be Granna's parents, yet were still a lot older than her. A child, Susan, had been born in 1923 and died a few months later. But why had they come up on Granna Katy's page? Katie's mother was called Susan. Could there be a connection?

Jared had told her to watch out for naming patterns, but he also said to double-check each record before confirming it as true. 'So many times, people with the same name, who lived around the same time, come up who aren't connected.'

Her problem, she discovered, was most of the people were identified by their relationship rather than their name, and those who did have a name weren't identified by a relationship. The longer she looked, the more confused she became.

She held the image of the three women and the soldier in her hand, the same one hanging on Jared's wall, and stared at it, hoping something would jump out and give her a clue. He'd told her the bridal couple were Grace and Charlie Price. Standing next to Charlie was Gwenna, his sister, which matched the mysterious photo in Granna's drawer. At least, she'd solved one little mystery.

The woman on the left, beside the bride, was Katie's double. Whoever she was, she was important to the family. She often appeared in the family groups. Katie had put a pile with her in them to one side. Next, she focused on the woman called Grace.

She crumpled the scribbled family tree she'd started and got out a new sketch pad she'd bought and started again.

A few minutes later her mobile rang. For a split second, she hoped it would be Jared until she remembered she'd told him not to call her. She briefly wondered if he would respect her wishes or ignore her foolishness, and couldn't decide what she wanted him to do.

"Hello, Viv." Katie was still smarting from the underhand trick Viv had tried to pull with Jared. Although they hadn't been a couple at the time and she'd had no claims on Jared, especially then, she still believed Viv had gone behind her back.

"Katie. Happy New Year," said the overly cheery voice. "I hope you've had a fabulous break."

Katie's hackles went up. What did Viv want this time?

"I've been meaning to call for ages, but you know, work and Christmas things, the time just disappeared."

"That's OK, Viv. I've been pretty busy myself."

"You have? I'm glad to hear it. I've been worried about you."

Katie frowned. What was the woman talking about?

"Your behaviour was a little erratic last year, I have to say. And, well, I got talking to a friend of mine, and ... anyway, she said you were probably suffering from depression, what with having to look after your grandmother and her dying and everything. But it could be something more than that. Even bi-polar. You really should seek help, Katie. It's an illness, not a crime."

How she didn't lose her temper and tell Viv precisely what she thought of her interference, she couldn't say. "I'm perfectly fine, Viv," she answered as calmly as possible.

"Sounds to me as if you are in denial. Truly, Katie. You need help."

What! Katie ground her teeth and gripped the phone so hard she was at risk of breaking it. "I don't think you know me well enough to tell me what I should do. And I don't need your kind of help. Thanks all the same."

Why did she not hang up?

"I saw Jared a couple of days ago." The voice changed and became a purr as rapidly as she changed the subject. "Such a lovely man, don't you think? Aren't you talking to him? No? What a pity. Him being such a catch too."

What was the woman playing at?

"How nice for you, Viv, but I must be going."

"Don't go yet. I haven't told you the best news. He was with a lovely young woman. I was most impressed. But she was far too young for him. It won't last. He needs someone with more experience."

Katie came close to laughing. How could anyone be so blatant. "Someone like you, you mean?"

"Well, since you suggest it. Quite possibly. I was wondering ... could you give me ..."

Katie wouldn't give her the time of day. She didn't need her any longer.

"Viv. Let's get one thing straight, shall we. Jared told me all about your little trick, and whatever game you think you're playing won't work. And the young woman he was with? She's his daughter."

Katie heard the gasp as Viv drew air.

"Even better, then," the hard, calculating businesswoman voice returned. "I only called to make sure he wasn't being sucked in and feeling sorry for you in your pathetic state. I needn't have bothered."

Katie stared at the phone long after Viv had hung up, unsure whether she wanted to laugh or cry. Crying won. Despite everything, Viv had hit a nerve.

24

RETURN TO HAPPINESS

June 1919

The household was in an uproar dealing with the imminent birth of Grace's baby and the expected return of Charlie. After six months at the hospital treating men with post-war psychological problems, he was coming home. He'd promised he'd be there in time to meet his second child.

"Is he here yet?" yelled Grace between contractions.

"It doesn't matter whether he is or isn't. He's not coming in until this baby is born. Just get on with the business of birthing, girl, and we'll deal with the father later." The midwife was a no-nonsense sort, but kinder than the one she had when Little Tommy was born.

Baby Jane Brigid Price, who would be known as Jaybee, was born less than a day before her father came running from the ferry and arrived, dripping wet from the winter storm, on their doorstep.

"Am I in time?" he shouted through the kitchen door while he scraped his boots off on the verandah and hung his hat and coat on the outside pegs.

Brigid held the door open for him. "Congratulations,

Charlie. You have a daughter," she said, watching him closely, wanting to see which Charlie had returned to them. "Mother and child are resting, but they're both grand. Welcome home, lad, welcome home."

He entered the warmth of the kitchen, his eyes quickly scanning the room.

"It's just as you left it, Charlie," said Brigid, noticing how he took in every detail. "And as cosy and welcoming as a kitchen should be. It's grand to have you home again."

"I'm pleased to be back."

"It is so good to see you, Charlie," said Jane, reaching to hug him and seeing something in his eyes which had been lacking before. Although clearly happy to have returned and keen to see his wife and daughter, there was something else: an eagerness Jane hoped meant the old Charlie was at last home.

She remembered the sound of that word 'home' when he disembarked from the train on his return from the battlefront. Maybe it had taken him this long – close to four years, nearly as long as the war itself – to find its meaning again.

"Are you well?" she asked.

He took Jane's hand in his good arm and twirled her around. "Miss Jane, not only am I well, I am a new man, ready to take on the world. I have plans. Big plans."

Sally clapped her hands, Brigid crossed herself and said a silent prayer, while Jane grinned as her heartbeat changed rhythm, thanks to the huge lump in her throat.

"You've given us the best news any one could have hoped for. Now go, tell your wife."

According to all the newspaper reports, the country had lost roughly 17,000 men to the war, without counting the 40-odd thousand casualties, many of whom would possibly die, and around half as many again were lost to the pandemic. Many were buried in mass graves, never to be known again, and too many soldiers returned home to find they had lost loved ones on the peaceful soils of New Zealand to an invisible killer.

The resultant shortage of capable workers when coal shortages were at their worst meant the economy plunged. Charlie wasted no time. "Some of the men have injuries far worse than anything I have," he explained. "My eyes were opened at the hospital. If I felt useless, some of the other men were positive wrecks. I soon learned to stop feeling sorry for myself. I can talk and I have two good legs, two good eyes and a good right arm. Some of them might never return to normal. They need to learn a new way of living. I needed a new way of thinking."

Charlie paused, looking for the right words to tell Gwenna and Hugh, and Grace and all the others, what he planned. "We can help. I want to expand the business and diversify into bulk production. If we have a manufacturing arm, we can employ some of the people I met at the hospital. We can help these people. I'm sure we can. What do you think, Gwenna?"

Charlie's ideas required a bit of innovation but nothing that couldn't be achieved.

"I can see such great opportunities ahead."

His infectious enthusiasm convinced Gwenna, who'd needed little persuasion. She was just happy to see the old Charlie again. "As long as you run that side of things, so I can still make my range of sweets and run the two shops," she said.

"My compliments," said Hugh, shaking his hand. "It's a brave move and very generous. But you've a few challenges ahead, thanks to the coal shortages. It's making life very difficult. Transport is almost at a standstill, and electricity is a bit hit-and-miss these days too. Supply is hard to get and harder to keep."

"Nothing that can't be overcome. But the on-and-off-again peace celebrations – once they make up their minds which dates to go for – will give impetus to the economy, and we'll need workers."

"Let's hope they can run the trains and have enough electricity for the illuminations," laughed Hugh.

"People will make their own fun and hold their own celebrations regardless. We don't need any of the high-ups to tell us what to do," said Charlie.

"At least the war is now officially ended since they signed the treaty on the 28th," said Hugh. "Six months since the armistice, and it's taken this long to get a peace agreement. Better late than never, I suppose."

Charlie nodded. "Hopefully now, those Germans can get hauled over the coals for what they did in those concentration camps. Made me sick, it did. Glad I wasn't there to experience it first hand, but what unbelievable horror." He shook his head.

Before long, the talkative Charlie had found suitable premises, purchased the right machinery, set up a series of conveyor belts and started employing people, some able-bodied and sound-minded, others victims of war.

"Do you intend to change the name of the business?" asked Jane the next time she met Gwenna to talk about the rapid reorganisation occurring.

"No. And Charlie doesn't want me to. All he wanted was to expand the business. Not only has he given people employment, but he's also created a role for himself. It's incredible to see those men feel useful again. It transformed their whole attitude – and Charlie's. I don't know what title you would give him. Ideas man? Absolutely. Manager? He does that and more. He talks with people all day, adapting the functions to make the place run more smoothly, but he also keeps an eye on all the orders, making sure they are processed properly and despatched to the right place. Honestly, Hugh and I can't keep up with him."

"It's so good to see him happy again," said Jane.

"Isn't it? Hugh's happy too. We have more delivery vans working than we ever imagined, and having so much of the work done by machinery means we can employ people who otherwise might not find work. There's plenty of simple tasks for the more disabled to do."

The difference in Charlie within a matter of months was immeasurable. He had a ton of energy, and as the year rolled into the next, the business grew exponentially. He and Grace were back to their normal, easy-going partnership, which pleased Jane more than anything else, and he adored the little ones.

Jane's life returned to its usual rhythm in her theatre workroom. With new staff, except for Aggie the beader and Paul the cutter, who had been rejected for service because of his deformity, Jane was back in her element. But not with the same passion. Since the Opera House had become the recognised home of vaudeville, Jane's enthusiasm for the different styles of costume was low. The world had moved on. She had not. And she missed the loyal, reliable Cecil far more than she admitted to anyone.

In her spare time, Jane was spending more and more time visiting the people she loved. She'd not seen or heard from Mickey's son since Grace's wedding five years earlier. She had no idea which name he carried, and as he was Australian, she might never find out what happened to him. Hopefully, he was gone from her life forever, but a certain sadness lingered, thinking he would probably have been lost amongst the war dead.

Bernadette and Mademoiselle Maree had done little during the war years. Nobody had needed fashionable gowns then, but maybe the time had come to put them to work again.

25

RECONCILIATIONS

January 2019

Katie woke up lying on the floor feeling stiff and foolish. She'd cried herself to sleep after Viv's call; now the first person she thought of was Jared. She propped herself up against the wall and dialled his number. The photos and sketch pad lay scattered around her. "Are you free?"

"For you, always. What's up?"

The sound of his voice set her heart racing, but the relief she heard in his voice made her feel terribly guilty. He was hurting too.

"Viv called."

"And what charming things did she say this time to upset you?"

"How do you know I'm upset?"

"Because you are. I can tell by your voice."

"I'm not really."

"Yes you are."

The conversation seemed so banal Katie could hardly believe they were having it, considering how important this call was to their future. An unexpected wave swept over her, and she thought she was going to burst into tears again. She bit her lip and said nothing.

"Right now," he said into the silence, "you're staring out the window believing you are in control and fighting the urge to let it all go. Right?"

When did he get to know her so well?

"Something like that." She tried to sound light and finished with a tiny laugh.

"So, if you're upset, does this phone call mean you want to talk or ..." He took a deep breath. "Are you drumming up the courage to tell me to clear off for good?"

She could hear the tension behind his words. The next thing she said was make or break – again. She kept doing this to herself and to him. The time had come to make changes and take control again. "I want to talk." She lifted the phone from her ear and could still hear the whoop.

"I'll be there in five."

She was standing by her door as he walked out of the lift. He swept her into his arms, lifting her off her feet, and covered her neck and face with kisses as he twirled her around. By the time he put her down, she was laughing.

"You are so good for me," she said, running fingers through his hair and down his neck, before running them across his lips.

"I told you so," he grinned.

With arms still around each other, they moved back into her apartment and he kicked the door shut behind them. This time he kissed her deeply, letting his lips convey how much he loved her. "I've missed you," he murmured into her neck.

"I've missed you too ... Can we start again?"

"I'm willing, if you're sure." He tilted her chin.

Katie nodded.

"I love you, Katie Anderson."

"And I love you too." Wrapped in his arms with love shining from his eyes, the words slipped easily from Katie's mouth. At last, they were the right words said to the right person.

He looked around the apartment at all the papers, the loose and framed photos and notebooks scattered over every surface and whistled. "I've never seen this place other than immaculate. What's going on?"

"I'm going nuts," she said with a laugh, half-jokingly.

"So, that's what you want me for, is it? To help sort out this mess."

"Well, yes – and a couple of other things."

He raised one eyebrow and looked at her quizzically. "And what are the other things in need of sorting?" he teased.

His nearly-smile was now a total smile lighting his entire face and buoying his every move.

She loved him so much, she realised, but she had to tell him the truth before they could move forward. She pushed herself away from him.

His face fell.

"What's the matter, Katie? Why the sombre face all of a sudden?" He hung his arms loosely by his side and kept folding his fingers into the palms of his hands.

She could sense his heart thumping from where she stood and could plainly see the twitch in his temple as he clenched and unclenched his teeth. "I was hurt and reacted badly because you'd hidden something ..."

"And I'm sorry," he interrupted, spreading his hands in supplication. "I said I'm sorry. I should have told you ..."

"Yes," she said, not letting him finish his sentence. "You should, but that's not what I'm talking about. I'm sorry too."

He waited, as she hedged and fidgeted. The seconds passed agonisingly slowly.

"It's my turn to confess. I've hidden something from you too."

The expression on his face showed surprise and something else – wariness?

"Sorry, can we sit down," she said, on edge and uncomfortable. She fingered her hair forward and then tucked one side back behind her ear. "I'll get us a drink."

"I'm OK for now." He followed her into the kitchen.

"I'm not. I need something to do to get me through this."

"This is starting to sound serious. Should I be worried?"

She opened the fridge, pulled out a bottle of wine and collected two glasses from the cupboard. After filling both, she handed one to Jared. "In case you change your mind."

Leading the way, she crossed the lounge and curled up in her usual position on the couch, putting a couple of photos from the table onto the floor.

Jared sat at the other end of the couch, where he'd sat the last time tension had kept them apart. "What's this all about, Katie? You're being very mysterious."

"My grandmother – or rather what I've discovered about my grandmother." Katie took a deep breath and gathered her thoughts. "I've come into an inheritance," she said, telling him about the smaller lump sum. "And I have to set up some grants, which are going to take some time to organise, and dedicate them to people who I've only a vague idea about, but have to find. And then find some long-lost descendant, and I have no idea where to start."

By the time she'd finished explaining about the will and the archiving of the old design sketches belonging to some obscure fashion designer, Jared looked solemn.

He stood up and refilled their wine glasses. "Wow. That's some revelation."

She kept back the information about how those conditions were linked to the bulk of her inheritance and how much money was involved. She had a gut feeling it would change their relationship if he knew about that part too soon.

"The lawyer wasn't helpful about the people concerned, but the original Grace Price you told me about is one of them. Plus a Janey and an Elizabeth," she said.

Katie sat with her elbows on her knees rubbing her hands through her hair as if it would put her brain into some sort of order. She accepted the refilled glass from Jared and took a sip.

"Well, we know who the first Grace Price is, at least. Do you want help finding the other two?"

Katie nodded. "Yes, please. But first, and while we are on confessions, something Viv said ..."

"I think it's time I had a conversation with Viv and stopped this once and for all."

"No, not that. Well, yes. She might still come on to you, but that's not what I'm talking about."

Jared sat down beside her and put his arm over her shoulder. "What then? I can't believe you are so out of sorts in just a matter of days. Can't live without me, huh?" He kissed her temple.

The corners of her mouth creased up into a silly smirk and fell back into place. "Ha ha, funny man. And you're closer to the truth than I care to admit."

"Go on, admit it. I don't mind if you tell me you can't live without me."

This time she did smile. "Maybe I can't." Katie could feel her anxiety rising and fought to hold it in check. She hated the sensation. "Viv said ..." she began, and then finished in a rush, "my behaviour was irrational, I was pathetic, and in denial about it all and needed help."

Exasperated, Jared threw his arms up in the air and leant against the back of the couch. "That bloody woman! Doesn't hold back on anything, does she?"

Katie turned her head to look at him, her face partially hidden by a veil of hair. "But is she right? What do you think?"

He sat up, moved the hair away from her eyes and looked intently at her. "I think you are the most amazing, wonderful person in the whole world."

She pushed him playfully in the shoulder. He rolled away and ended up kneeling on the floor in front of her.

"Be serious, Jared. I'm worried. I know I've behaved oddly at times and I have this heavy feeling that comes over me that clogs my thinking, and I can't stop crying and ..."

"OK. Serious now. I think you've let things get on top of you again. The doctor you saw before Christmas said you were suffering from depression and anxiety. So OK, now you can deal with it – but our latest setback won't have helped. Are you still taking the St John's wort?" Katie shook her head. "Is that wise? I'm no expert but seeing another doctor won't do any harm. I don't know. Maybe you need to get out more, or exercise and talk to people – if not me, then a counsellor – take some suitable medication, if necessary. Although, I think that should be a last resort. But more importantly – sort out all the mysteries bugging you. And ..." – he lifted her chin – "this on-off nonsense between you and me has to stop. I love you, Katie. I want to be with you. All the time, not just when you decide it's suitable. OK?"

Ridiculous tears welled in Katie's eyes again, but these were tears of joy rather than hopelessness. He loved her. Nothing else mattered. "I love you too, but what about ..."

He wiped away the stray tear rolling down her face with his thumb. "I didn't say there weren't obstacles, only that we should deal with them together. Can I get up now? My knees are killing me."

Despite her low spirits, she laughed. He always made her laugh. With exaggerated moans and groans he got to his feet and reached for her hand pulling her up against him. "Well, Miss Katie Anderson, do you agree?"

"I think so, yes." Safe in his arms, she closed her eyes and let herself dream for several moments.

"Good. 'Cos there's one more snag."

She looked at him, and her spirits sank again. What now?

"Grace."

She'd wanted to talk about it all then and there but Jared had other ideas.

"We eat first. I'm starving and I bet you haven't eaten properly in days. Let me just text Grace." Minutes later, he popped his phone back in his pocket. "She's cool. Blobbing out on movies, popcorn and chocolate."

247

"On her own?" Katie asked, surprised by her reaction. She'd loved doing those things too, except maybe not the popcorn. She'd preferred pizza and wine, but she'd been in her twenties by then, not a schoolgirl.

"Grace is utterly self-sufficient. She'll be fine."

He turned her kitchen upside down looking for some decent food to cook but, in the end, they went to the bar on the corner.

"Tomorrow we buy you some groceries," Jared growled as they strolled, holding hands, along the walkway. "You have to take better care of yourself."

Once they were seated, had ordered some more wine and chosen their food, Katie was more like her old self again. Jared had that effect on her, but now he seemed on edge.

He stared at his hands for a moment or two, then took his glasses off, fished for a handkerchief and started polishing them. "To think we might never have found each other if I'd been more IT and business savvy." He put his glasses back on, folded his handkerchief and put it away and took her hand. "And to think I nearly lost you."

Sometimes she had no idea what to say. She'd never known a man to wear his heart on his sleeve like Jared, except maybe her grandfather. He was always telling 'his beautiful Katy' he loved her. Fortunately, the arrival of their main course arrived, saving her having to reply.

"So, which problem first?" he asked, tucking into his steak. "Your grandmother or Grace?"

Katie shrugged. Both seemed insurmountable to her.

"OK. Well, since I think your grandmother's issues will require a lot more space to work on and both computers going at once, I guess it's Grace."

Through mouthfuls of food and with a lot of fork-pointing, Jared explained the situation. "I had no idea my darling daughter had sorted out what she wanted to do and did all her research before telling me. She found out whether she could leave home without getting into trouble, decided where she wanted to live and where she wanted to finish her last two years of school. Only then did she announce she wanted to live with me."

Katie did a double take. She hadn't expected that.

He spread his open hands towards her, giving her the chance to make comment.

"When you said she was coming, I thought you meant for a visit. Not that she lived with you. There was no sign of someone else living at your place." Realisation hit Katie like a bucket of cold water. "You'd tidied everything away, hadn't you?"

Jared nodded. "I didn't mean to mislead you. The time didn't seem right for lengthy explanations. This is her final year at school. She says she intends to go overseas for a while before going to uni. I'm not so keen on the overseas bit. We'll see, but that's her current plan."

In many ways, Grace sounded just like Katie had been at her age: focused, knew what she wanted from life and did it. How did she end up such a mess, she wondered. And how would she get on with a teenager who knew the rules and made up her own mind? The thought scared her. She'd never had anything to do with children of any age.

"So where was she when you were with me?"

"She'd been to visit her mother for Christmas. She just got back."

Jared explained how, after he'd separated from his wife, the task of raising Grace as part of two families took its toll on the girl. Especially after his ex remarried and had two more kids.

"Grace never got on with her stepfather. He wasn't nasty or anything, she just said he treated her differently, and life was easier if she stayed in her room. She was a different kid when she was with me. We spent all our time together when I wasn't working."

"What about when you are working?" asked Katie, wondering if she'd be expected to pick up any slack.

"Grace sorts herself out in the morning, which means I can spend more time with her at the end of the day if she's around. She's a busy teenager with a busy social life. She's made some great friends."

"What about when you're baking for yourself as Dazzling Desserts?"

"She's come with me a few times to the hire kitchen. She's a big help folding the boxes and making sure I've enough supplies and writing down stuff when my hands are sticky. She's a switched-on kid with some helpful ideas of her own. I was rushed off my feet in the lead-up to Christmas."

For a while the conversation turned to their routine, his work, his new website and the orders coming in.

"I'm starting to get sick of the early-morning starts at the bakery. I needed a break so I put the website orders on hold for two weeks. I'll start again Monday."

"That's not an ideal way to start a new business," she murmured.

"Maybe not, but being with you is far more important."

Warmed by the feel-good vibes he radiated, her head was trying to sort out how any of it would work. Him. Her. Grace.

His eyes burned into her across the table. "I love you," he said, "and I want us to be a couple, but you have to want me as much, even with all my extras and foibles."

Katie laughed. Sometimes he used such funny words. "I think I'm the one with all the idiosyncrasies."

"Nah. That's just you being you."

"Grace's presence is a bit more than a snag, isn't it?" said Katie, thinking there wasn't room in her one-bedroom apartment if they agreed to move in together. But she didn't think she could live in his two-bedroom townhouse with an unknown teenager either. Seemed like love couldn't conquer all.

"Just something else to work through," Jared reassured her. "But it's nothing we can't do together."

He pushed his plate away, finished his wine and sat back. "That was very good. I can see us eating here a lot more often. The last couple of times were a bit fraught, methinks."

"That's putting it rather mildly," said Katie, remembering when she ran out on him the night of her grandmother's funeral. The night their relationship truly started. Was it only a month or so ago? She felt she'd known him forever. "But I agree. I like this place and my meal was delicious."

"Let's walk."

He held her hand as they headed in the opposite direction to her apartment and took in the lights and sounds of the city as darkness fell on a warm summer's evening. Laughter followed them from diners still enjoying their meals under restaurant verandahs or youngsters dodging people as they raced ahead of their parents. A cruise ship inspired talk of possible travel options, places to go, things to do and experiences to enjoy. They did a circuit of the wharf and headed back, taking in the sight of the harbour bridge with its lights.

"Feeling better?" he asked as they paused to lean on the rail to look at the yachts, launches and various other craft moored in The Viaduct.

"Yes. Thank you. You're a lifesaver."

"Are you telling me you're ready to take the next step?"

"I think so. But all I can see are difficulties."

"In which case, we need to remove those difficulties. Starting tomorrow. Fresh food. Fresh ideas. Fresh approach. Are you up for it?"

"Yes, sir. I do believe I am."

They linked arms and set off for her apartment. As they got back to her building, he stopped by the entrance and checked his watch. "I better not come up tonight. I need to get back to Grace. She and I have a lot to talk about. She doesn't know about you either."

His kiss said trust him, love him, believe in him. Her heart wanted to beat in rhythm with his, yet her mind said she would always come second in his love.

26

CELEBRATIONS AND CALAMITIES

May 1921

"Happy birthday, George darling," said Gwenna, after welcoming everyone to the function. The hired hall she'd spent hours decorating, with the help of Jane, Grace and Louisa to celebrate her son's 21st birthday, pleased her immensely.

"Happy Birthday," echoed the crowd invited to witness George's formal ascent into adulthood, raising their glasses to both him and Gwenna.

Toasts were made, congratulations offered and backs slapped. As Jane wandered around the room, stopping to talk to people she knew or offering a tray of Gwenna's treats, snippets of conversation reached her ears.

Two topics seemed to dominate – Anzac Day, the public holiday on 25 April commemorating the landing at Gallipoli, and the growing recession. A lot of the land farmed by the returned soldiers had proved to be marginal, leaving them struggling with debt and low returns.

The air was thick with smoke from the cigarettes most of the men smoked, and the hum of their voices grew louder the more they drank. Jane smiled and nodded at those talking politics and moved on. She had no interest whatsoever but she knew Laura would be in the midst of it somewhere. Sure enough, her voice reached Jane's ears.

"Isn't it wonderful? The New Zealand Federation of Country Women's Institute has just been formed. After all the work they did for the cause during the war, they will be the backbone of this country. Mark my words."

She turned away hoping Laura hadn't seen her and passed another group discussing sport and the forthcoming tour by the Springbok rugby team, while another group were in awe of George Bolt's flying achievements and his recent attempt at delivering mail by air.

Jane left them to their debates, continuing her circuit of the room until she returned to the kitchen where Gwenna was overseeing the supper arrangements.

"How's it going out there?"

"Fine. Everyone is chatting about what's good and bad in the world as they see it."

Gwenna chuckled. "I shouldn't laugh, but it's been a bit like that in our household lately." She finished giving the kitchen girls instructions for the sandwiches, pies and tarts ready to be put out for supper and took Jane's arm. "Let's get a drink and sit down for a while."

The Temperance Movement was still trying to ban the manufacture, distribution and sale of alcohol, and a bill had come close to passing at the general election a couple of years earlier, but, with the possible exception of Laura, no one in the room had any interest in their activities. A workingman deserved his beer, and the workingwomen Gwenna and Jane knew enjoyed a quiet glass of sherry or wine now and then and saw no harm in it.

They'd settled themselves at a table, surveying the crowd as Gwenna explained her dilemma. "Hugh and I are still struggling to decide what to do about George's pointless jealousy of Charlie. I always intended to give him a place in the business once he turned 21, regardless, and he does deserve one. But all he talks about is Charlie. Constantly going on about what Charlie has done, how lucky Charlie is, how much I praise him, which in George's mind somehow takes something away from him. It doesn't make sense to me."

"He's still young. He'll grow out of it once he tastes success of his own. But you've made the decision, haven't you? Didn't you say you were going to announce it tonight?"

"Yes, we are, a bit later, when the cake comes out. And hopefully we've come up with the right answer. But I still wonder what George will do. What he *can* do ..."

Gwenna had confided in Jane about her worries months before, and in the end, she and Hugh decided to separate the manufacturing side of the business from the retail side. Gwenna still liked to make her sweets, fudge and chocolate by hand, which proved to be a successful strategy for the two shops but would never meet the overall demand, while Charlie had turned the manufacturing section into its own success story. George would have a partnership in the retail side.

"Does George know?"

"No. We haven't told him. We thought we'd make it a birthday surprise." Gwenna smiled, thinking how significant it would be for George to be acknowledged in front of all his friends and family.

"What does Charlie think?" Jane asked. "Where is he, by the way? I don't think I've seen him yet."

"He's gone to get more beer – we're running low, apparently – but he thinks the role will be a boost for George. Give him a sense of worth."

Jane could understand the feeling. It had taken her a long time to have a sense of worth about herself, and Charlie's came from his efforts at the factory. One of his other successes was his ability to drive, with some minor vehicle modifications, in defiance of his damaged arm. It gave him much more freedom and he had his own car and delivery van with C Price Manufacturing Confectioners painted on the sides. Cars were a common sight now as the roads improved, especially around town, although Jane had heard some of the rural roads were often nothing more than muddy tracks and rough lanes. "Charlie must have been pleased with your decision, too. You're very generous."

Gwenna dismissed her comment with a wave of her hand. "Charlie deserved it after what he went through. And the factory was all his idea, in any case. He's proved it can be done, and the ex-soldiers he employs think he's wonderful. I would never have been brave enough to take on anything that big."

Jane begged to differ. "None of it would have happened without you in the first place, so don't put yourself down." She knew the struggles Gwenna had gone through to get herself established in a retail shop. Her success was huge for its time.

"I'm loving getting back to what I do best, though. Expanding the shop into bigger and better tea rooms is the best decision for me too. It would have been too much for just Hugh and me to manage on our own if I'd increased our capacity in the kitchen, even with the new electric ranges. And Charlie can fill in any gaps if I need anything extra. It all works out in the end."

Jane had forgotten Hugh was much older than Gwenna. He must be well into his fifties and due for the pension once he reached sixty, if he passed the means test. Jane didn't think he'd stop work, though; he was still keen, even if he did get short of breath. "What exactly is George going to do?" she asked, silently admitting she didn't like the young man. He was no chip off the old block, unless he took after his father's side, which Jane knew nothing about. He patently wasn't anything like his mother.

She caught sight of George across the room, talking to some men she didn't recognise, and decided he was the sullenest of creatures.

"A bit of everything, I suppose. He has to learn the business from the bottom up, just like I did. He likes doing displays and he's competent with the books, but I'll keep him away from customers, I think."

That was probably the most disloyal thing Jane had ever heard Gwenna say about her son.

"Now, enough of me, tell me what you've been up to," said Gwenna.

The two women laughed and giggled like youngsters, comfortable in each other's presence, as Jane regaled Gwenna with gossip from the theatre, but keeping some of the juicier bits to herself.

Yet Jane had her concerns. "There are so many places showing moving pictures these days, I wonder if live theatre will survive. When I checked the Entertainment Index, they listed three live theatre productions, two concerts at the Town Hall and nine moving pictures. *Nine!*"

"But didn't I hear there's a big overseas musical show coming from London later this year?"

"Yes, *Chu Chin Chow*, but it's going to His Majesty's. All the Opera House seems to be doing is vaudeville and music hall. Not to my taste, but fun shows, sometimes a little bawdy if truth be told. The audiences go away happy, often still chuckling as they leave the theatre. It's just I'm a little tired of the costumes. I can't let my imagination loose when the performers only want quick repairs."

Jane itched to tell Gwenna about her life as Bernadette and Mademoiselle Maree, but she still wasn't sure what she was doing was honest. She sold the sketches with full instructions on how to piece together the designs but left the dressmakers to work out the measurements to fit. As such, she'd managed to keep her identity a secret.

Unlike some of the commercial patterns advertised in magazines and newspapers which could be ordered from overseas, Jane's designs were more suitable to the New Zealand scene and climate. The whole process was done by private mailbox and postal notes so there was no chance people would ever learn her real name. From time to time, she secretly wished the ladies who wore her gowns could know who she was, but then again, she had never sought recognition.

"Why don't you try selling some of your designs?" asked Gwenna, as if she had just read her friend's mind.

"What?" flustered Jane. "What do you mean? I couldn't do that, could I? I mean, it wouldn't be honest, would it? I mean, I work for ..."

"Jane, stop. What's the matter? You're gabbling. I only suggested you could sell some designs. You're so gifted. You have the eye for what people want."

"But aren't I bound to the Opera House?"

"Of course not. The designs you do for them, yes. And it would be awful if another theatre company got hold of those sketches and used them before they did. But the sort of things you design for your family and friends are yours. You must have dozens of those. Your head is always bursting with ideas."

"True. And fashions are changing. I've seen some fabulous new ideas coming from America. Shorter skirts, straighter dresses needing less of the awkward boned underwear. I'd love to have a go at some."

"Well, go on. Have a go. Make up a false name, if it makes you feel better."

Jane turned all shades of pink, white and red as Gwenna talked. Surely, she hadn't guessed her secret, had she?

"I quite like American designs myself," continued Gwenna, unheeding of Jane's discomfort. "Did I tell you about my new car? It's a Dort from America. A five-seater, and it has a magneto ignition thingy making it so much easier to start. And lights ..."

Jane stopped listening about the car. She still preferred to walk or use the tram. Her frugal, busy lifestyle was paying off as her savings grew, but with one sentence, Gwenna had freed Jane from all her guilt over so many years.

With the changing fashions, numerous balls and race-day outfits in demand, maybe she could make a name for herself after all.

"I think it's time for some music, don't you? I feel like dancing," said Gwenna.

She walked over to the gramophone and cranked the handle before placing the needle on the disc and adjusting the sound horn. Crackly music began to play, drowning the voices of those nearest to it.

Clearly, Gwenna wasn't the only one in the mood for dancing. Before long, couples were swaying to the foxtrot and the very fashionable waltz or swinging around the room, skirts flaring and tailcoats spinning to the music of a polka or the Viennese waltz. The whole atmosphere became one of fun and frivolity instead of worry about things they couldn't change.

Somewhere in the middle of it all, Charlie returned and called for help to unload.

"Go on, George, go and help Charlie," said Gwenna.

"What should I? It's my party."

"All the more reason. If you're the host, you should display some good manners."

They stared at each other for a moment or two, and Jane wondered if he would defy his mother, but she was made of sterner stuff. He capitulated and stormed out the door.

Minutes later, the sound of crashing, men yelling and a woman screaming reached them.

"What on earth was that?" asked Gwenna.

They rushed towards the doors, and Gwenna tried to push her way through the crowd already cramming the inside doorway, straining to see.

"What's happened? Let me through, please," begged Gwenna. "Tell me what's happened."

Jane could just see Hugh on the other side of the open door in the light from the street lamp.

"It's nothing. Stay there," he yelled. "Everything's all right, Gwenna. I'll see to it. Take all the folks inside again."

With a bit of effort, both from those outside and from herself and Gwenna, Jane persuaded the people all was well and to rejoin the party.

"Just a few broken bottles. Nothing to worry about," said one of the men.

Gwenna sighed with relief and set the gramophone playing again. "Jane, would you go to the kitchen, please, and see if they are ready to set out the supper." She looked at her watch. "It's a bit early, but maybe if they have some food to distract them, I can find out what is going on."

A steady stream of women traipsed from the kitchen to the supper table and back bringing out trays of food. Faint sounds of disagreement reached Jane's attuned ear as she approached the door to tell the men supper would soon be served.

Hugh, Charlie and George would need to clean up and be tidy before the big announcement and speeches. Before she reached the outside door, which was now partially closed, plunging the entranceway into shadow, she heard the sound of muffled sobs.

"Grace?" Jane's heart beat wildly. Why had she not noticed Grace was missing? She looked into the corner of the foyer. "Grace? Is that you? What's wrong?"

"Janey. Oh Janey. It's all my fault." She threw herself into Jane's arms.

"What's your fault? And whatever it is, it can't be so bad you want to cry at George's birthday party."

"But that's the problem. I've ruined it," she wailed.

"Shh. There. Shush. Tell me what happened. Are you hurt?"

Jane eased the door open a little, hoping to glimpse whatever was still going on in the street. The sliver of light turned into a wedge relieving the gloom where they stood. Half a dozen men, standing in a group with their backs to the hall, appeared to be looking at something on the ground. Their voices were lowered and she couldn't discern any words. In front of them, Jane could see part of Charlie's car. The steps appeared wet but she couldn't figure out anything further.

The constant movement of Jane's hand rubbing Grace's back seemed to calm her. She smoothed her hands over her dress. At once, Jane could see stains. "Grace! You're bleeding."

Grace inspected her hands, turning them over and back, then looked down at her dress. "It's not me Janey, but … but, I caused it," she sobbed, bewildered.

Jane pulled the inner doors closed, pleased to see people busy dancing and talking again and no longer paying attention to the scene outside. She eased Grace onto the pew at the side of the foyer. "Tell me."

"Charlie had been gone so long I wondered why, so when I heard him call, asking for help to unload, I went to speak to him. Not that I thought I could help. He wouldn't let me carry anything in case, you know, in case something happened to the baby."

Jane nodded. Grace hadn't been well in the first few weeks of this pregnancy and she was under doctor's orders to rest.

"I wasn't thinking. I rushed down the steps and I must have tripped. George was in front of me and I ended up pushing him forward. I'm not quite sure what happened, but he fell and I fell on top of him. Someone helped me to my feet, Hugh I think, but George was mad and started yelling. 'Stupid woman! What do you think you're doing? Look at my suit. It's ruined!' I tried to say I was sorry. His suit did look ruined; I saw dirt and a hole in his trousers."

"We can fix it. Don't worry," Jane reassured the girl. "Then what happened."

"He turned on Charlie. 'Can't you keep your silly wife

in order?' he barked, and Charlie said, 'Keep your mouth shut, George. You're drunk. And don't speak about my wife like that.' Anyway, he lunged at Charlie, shouting he wasn't drunk, and abusing him. Charlie tried to lift a box of bottles when it crashed to the ground. It must have been the noise everyone heard. Someone went to help him, and someone else pulled George away. George took a swing at them and lost his balance and … fell … on the broken glass." Her voice faded to a whisper and she shuddered.

"Was it you who screamed?"

"Did I? I suppose I did. I bent down to help him. I stroked his hair, but there was blood oozing from his head. Hugh picked me up and pushed me inside, and then you found me."

Jane resisted the urge to ask how George was, or to rush outside and find out for herself. Charlie and Hugh would look after him, but it didn't sound good since none of them had reappeared. "Stay here, Grace. Don't move. Promise me?" The girl nodded in response. "I need to tell Gwenna and somehow keep the party going."

On hearing the news, Gwenna said, "I must go."

"You can't go now," said Jane, placing a restraining hand on Gwenna's arm. "Not yet. How about we announce supper, like we planned and get people eating and then see what's happened."

Gwenna lifted the needle from the gramophone, which brought all the dancing to a stop. As people wandered back to their seats or lined the walls, she walked into the centre of the room and rang a little bell. "I'd like to announce supper is served. Please help yourself to refreshments and we will continue with the formal part of the evening shortly." Her voice wobbled a bit, and Jane could see the tension in her face, but she carried herself well.

The timing was fortunate. As people began to move towards the supper tables at the far end of the room, Hugh appeared through the door. Gwenna rushed towards him.

"There's been a bit of an accident."

Gwenna nodded, biting her bottom lip to control the quivering. "I heard. How's George?" Her eyes scanned his face for a sign whether the news was good or bad.

"He'll be all right. His pride is more injured than his body." Gwenna breathed more calmly at the news. "Although he'll be a bit uncomfortable for a while. He banged his head when he fell, and, um ... well, there's some glass embedded in his buttock and leg," Hugh chuckled. "The ambulance has arrived. We'll take him off to the hospital. Once they pull the glass out and wash it clean, he'll be home before you know it. I'll go with him but it looks like the party is over."

Gwenna shook her head sadly. "I'll tell them all to go home once they've had supper."

As Hugh turned to leave, Gwenna reached out a hand to hold him. "Thank you, Hugh. Where's Charlie? How is he?"

"Just here in the foyer with Grace. Jane's there too. He's a bit shook up but not injured."

"What a night! It hasn't turned out at all how I'd hoped."

Hugh patted her hand still resting on his arm. "Never mind, love. George is OK. Nothing else matters."

"Gwenna." Jane tapped her on the shoulder. "Come quickly. We've got a problem. I think Grace is about to lose the baby."

27

Revelations and discoveries

February 2019

"I'll give it a go, Miss," said the stonemason when Katie asked for the installation of Granna's headstone in time for her birthday. "But with the holidays and all, it might be cutting it a bit fine."

"I'm sure you'll manage. Please. It's important."

Others might think her idea silly, but Katie wanted to share part of her day – and Granna's birthday – talking to her grandmother. She arrived with a planter box of potted colour and put it down in front of the headstone and sat on the grass beside it. "Happy birthday, Granna. I miss you, although your mind had gone from me long since. I wish I could say happy birthday and have you say the same back to me. I wish I could understand everything you want from me. I wish so much, but wishes don't always come true, do they? I'm a bit lost right now, if I'm honest."

On Jared's advice, she had gone to another doctor, who had given her a prescription but advised her to do a course of therapy beforehand. Her first visit was traumatic.

"I cried through most of it but came out understanding a lot more about depression and anxiety and the triggers – and the recovery process. You'd have been proud of me, Granna. You'd say I was taking control."

Since then, Katie had improved her eating, sleeping and exercise programme and felt a lot more invigorated – and thankful Viv had been wrong. The prescription sat in the drawer unfilled, but she was taking St John's wort again instead. All the things Jared suggested might help.

"You never got to meet Jared. It's something I will always wish had happened. You'd have liked him, I'm sure. He's the sort of person you approved of – kind, loving, caring. Determined. But I can't lean on him for the rest of my life. I have to put it into order before I can move ahead."

Katie plucked at the blades of grass beneath her fingers while she rested her chin on her knee. Since the revelations by the lawyer, she'd done a lot of research around what she might do with her life, and it came back to photography every time. She relished the idea she could make a career from something she enjoyed doing so much, and now she had Granna's money to protect her from the financial risk, branching out was a gamble worth taking. Although she still intended to make a success of it on her own without taking her windfall for granted. But it wouldn't be easy. Not these days. Not with so many people able to turn themselves into amateur photographers. There wasn't the call for professionals the way there used to be. Not unless she could come up with something unique.

"I can't promise I'm going to achieve everything you wanted me to, Granna, but I'm going to try really hard because ..."

She stopped to think why fulfilling her grandmother's wishes meant so much, and decided it had to do with understanding who she was. Which seemed ridiculous. She knew who she was, or had been. Maybe a new Katie was waiting to emerge.

After a while, she got to her feet and started walking around the cemetery. She'd not been there before Granna's funeral. In this older section, the headstones, at least those still standing, were more ornate, heavily inscribed and mostly neglected.

Granna had been very specific in her will about where she wanted to be buried. She had bought the plot decades earlier but strangely she wasn't interred with Grandad. Come to think of it, Katie wasn't sure where Grandad was buried.

What was it with old cemeteries and headstones, she wondered, as she paused yet again to read an inscription. Why did we want to check how old the person was, or look for a hint at what their life might have been? She was surprised on several occasions by both extreme old age and infants. The ones with babies affected her more than the older ones.

SUSAN BETHAN PRICE
15 June 1923 – 10 September 1923
Beloved daughter of Charles and Grace
Sister to Thomas and Jane Brigid (Jaybee)
An angel is given and an angel is taken
To be with God in Heaven

Only three months old. How sad, she thought, reading the weatherworn engraving with some difficulty. Then she read it again. She knew these names. She'd heard of these people.

She walked to the next headstone and read:

BETHAN PRICE (HUGHES)
DEARLY LOVED MOTHER OF ELIAS, LOUISA,
JANETTA AND CHARLIE
LOVED STEPMOTHER OF GWENNA AND MATILDA
18 SEPTEMBER 1856 – 23 NOVEMBER 1918

Exhilaration pulsed through her. Here were more names she'd heard of – or at least some of them – grandmother and granddaughter lying side by side. She took out her mobile and snapped a couple of photos before moving on.

Several more headstones carried a name she'd heard of. She reached the end of the row and moved to the ones backing onto the front plots. She found more stones to her right and some to her left. So many of the extended family were buried close by, it was uncanny.

"Thank you, Granna," she said aloud, gazing up at the sky. "You led me here to give me this last gift. You are amazing."

Realising that this treasure trove would help her put names to faces, and parents with children through the generations, sent flutters of excitement through her. She took dozens more photos and started formulating a plan.

As she turned to walk back towards Granna's grave, she glanced at the headstones on the other side of the path, her eye drawn to a tall monument and a name in bold letters:

JANEY O'NEILL
15 March 1878 – 4 December 1950
Mother Granty Sister Friend
Beside you 'til the end
Forever remembered by those who loved you best
Grace, Jane Brigid (Jaybee), Katy, Elizabeth,
Laura, Lilly and Gwenna

Katie stood staring, trying to interpret the message it conveyed. Was this the Janey Granna had talked about? It must be. Who else would have so many Price women listed?

But something wasn't right. Katie couldn't quite put her finger on it, but something didn't fit.

She took more photos then dialled Jared's number. "You'll never guess what I just found ..."

When she'd finished explaining, Jared advised, "Go to the office and ask for as much information as they can find. I'll take another look at what I have for Grandma Gwenna."

As she was talking, she'd made her way back to Granna's headstone and reread the inscription, thinking it an inadequate representation. Within moments, she made up her mind to add a small plaque and include all the names and connections who made up Granna's life. Once she'd proven her theory.

The lady at the office was very helpful and provided Katie with the information they held and handed her a printout of other plots she thought could be related. Katie hurried back and checked the additional graves, took photos and scribbled more notes. Some of the obscure comments Granna had once made, and the people written about in the journals, started to make a bit of sense, and names began to form a pattern in Katie's head. She needed a large piece of paper and her laptop.

Hours later, Jared arrived at the door smartly dressed, carrying a bottle of wine and flowers. "I'll take a guess you aren't ready," he said, as he strode through the apartment to her kitchen. "And how did I come to that conclusion? Because you were too excited about what you'd found." He located a vase for the flowers and sat them at the end of the bench. "Now, I haven't got all night to wait, so a quick toast, then scoot. Into the shower, and put on your glad rags. We've a date, birthday girl. Remember?"

Katie had the grace to look guilty. "I'm sorry. I lost track of time."

"Hmm. Likely story." He smiled, nodding towards the open laptop on the dining table surrounded by papers, her sketch pad and notebook, as he opened a bottle of bubbly. "I suspect there's a fella hiding somewhere you've not told me about yet?"

She laughed, easing the kinks from the muscles complaining about being stuck in one position for too long, and gratefully accepted a glass from Jared.

"To you, my darling Katie. Happy birthday and may we celebrate many more."

They clinked glasses, and he leaned forward to briefly touch her lips with his. "I've got a surprise for you later."

She wondered what bright idea he had this time, but from experience she knew asking would be a waste of time. He would tell her - or show her - when he was ready.

"And I've got some for you - but there isn't a fella lurking in the paperwork. It's a line of amazing women."

270

"Like you?" he said, nuzzling against her neck.

"Far more amazing than me, I assure you," she said, arching against him.

He stepped back before things got out of hand. He had other ideas for tonight first. "It's all to do with perspective, my girl, and you're looking at things from the wrong side."

He took her glass from her hand, set it down, turned her around and gently pushed her towards the bedroom. "Now get dressed."

Barely twenty minutes later she emerged wearing the gold and black top she'd worn when they had first tasted Jared's miniature desserts more than six months earlier. She knew it suited her. His whistle confirmed it.

He indicated she should do a twirl as he surveyed her from head to toe. "Perfect. Except for one thing. Turn around."

His hands crept around her neck and something dangled in front of her. Her hand went to her throat to touch whatever it was. From a fine gold chain hung a pendant with a series of interlocking rings made from gold, rose-gold, platinum and crystals.

"Jared, it's beautiful." She turned and wound her arms around his neck. "Thank you. I love it."

A hug became a kiss – a long, lingering kiss promising much.

"Hmm. If we stay here like this for much longer, we won't ever make it to where we're supposed to be." He peeled away from her and extended his bent arm. "Shall we go?"

She picked up her clutch purse, took his arm and allowed him to escort her down to the taxi. Minutes later they were taking the lift to the top of the Sky Tower.

"Are we dining here?" she asked.

"I thought you'd enjoy the chance to view the city we love from the highest vantage point and watch its constantly changing moods as day gives way to night."

"What a splendid thought," she grinned, taking his arm.

While they waited for their table, they took a walk around the observation deck, admiring the view, remembering the times they'd visited certain landmarks, and amicably disagreeing on their favourite.

The sun dipped towards the horizon as they took their seats. Jared ordered the wine and food, and time passed as they watched the amazing play of light and shadow across the harbour and the city as the restaurant revolved.

"This is fabulous. You spoil me rotten."

He took her hand across the table and ran his thumb over her knuckles, a gesture which had become a characteristic of their relationship. She returned his gaze, struck again by the way his glasses enhanced the depth of his eye colour.

"I'm glad we've got that sorted at last."

There'd been quite a bit of toing and froing about who should pay for what when they went out, but eventually they reached an agreement. Tonight, a treat was a treat.

Deciding to leave her discoveries of the day until they had time and space, they chose instead to talk about each other. As usual, Katie never knew where the time disappeared when the two of them were together. They talked so effortlessly, enjoyed the same tastes and experiences, and yet were different enough that they complemented each other.

With the meal finished and an after-dinner layered liqueur in hand, Jared raised his glass. "Now to my surprise."

"Another one? I've had two lovely surprises already." She fingered the pendant hanging from its chain. "My necklace, and this superb restaurant. What more could a girl want?"

"This." He reached into the inside pocket of his jacket and withdrew an envelope.

Katie took it and waited for an explanation.

"Go on. Open it."

She pulled out several sheets of paper. The top two held a list of names and dates. The third one was a family tree. She raised her head in surprise.

"It seems you and I might have a common ancestor. Our mission, should you choose to accept it ..."

She burst out laughing. One thing they did not have in common was a love of remake movies of old television shows and hackneyed action movies.

"OK. Enough of the action-hero talk – what's this about a common ancestor. Who?"

He winked and his almost-smile turned into a huge grin. "Looks like you're stuck with me for a bit while we find out."

"I think I can manage."

As it turned out, many days would pass before Katie found the time to look at her notes or the papers Jared had given her.

Since setting up her website offering product photography a few weeks earlier, she'd received several enquiries and had done one totally unexpected and lucrative shoot. Her latest assignment was different.

Someone had seen some of her images of Granna and taken the time to track her down. "I was impressed by your handling of the subject," said the woman. "It's just the sort of thing I've been looking for."

The woman explained she was the manager at a small but exclusive retirement village. "Some of our people are not quite living in this world, but they are still beautiful people with interesting stories to tell. I'd like your help in telling those stories."

Katie wondered if she had heard her correctly. It seemed too coincidental for someone who understood dementia patients, like Granna, to contact her. Without any hesitation, she agreed to visit the village to discuss the idea.

"I'm Rosemary Becroft. Welcome to Heart's Home Village."

Rosemary guided her around the complex where Katie recognised the high railings, specific door locks and wall planners for the staff to keep track of the health and welfare of the residents.

"So many of the families are at a loss as to how to talk to their loved ones when they're at their worst. I'd like to give the families a way of remembering the days when their relatives were an active and valuable part of the community – and the family."

The longer the woman talked, the more eager Katie became. After each resident passed away, Rosemary intended to offer the family the opportunity to purchase a photo album showing the best aspects of their loved one by tying their lifelong hobbies, interests and occupation in with the individual they had become.

"While they sometimes can't remember the person

they once were, the family can. It's more for them, in fact."

Katie was momentarily overcome and had to clear her throat and force back tears. "I totally understand," she croaked. "Forgive me. You see, my grandmother had dementia. She was exactly as you describe. She died in December, but it was her – and my – birthday a few days ago. She and I shared the date, and the photos I took of her have led me here. It's hard to believe it's possible."

Rosemary's face brightened with an enigmatic smile. "Sometimes the mysteries of the world are not to be questioned. I knew, the moment I saw the beauty in those images, you were the person I needed."

Back at her apartment, Katie phoned Jared. "The whole thing sounds too good to be true, but it isn't. Rosemary will get the relatives to write down their memories, anything from snippets to pages, which I'll turn into a storyline and fit with the pictures I take – sometimes with family members but mostly of the resident. It'll be like a coffee table picture book with a story."

"You sound really excited about it all. It could be a winner for you, that unique proposition you were talking about, but won't it bring back too many memories of your grandmother? Don't upset yourself, love."

"I'm not upset at all. On the contrary. I was a little bit at first, but now I've got the hang of what Rosemary is trying to do, I think it's a brilliant idea. I want to do this. To play my part."

Katie struggled to contain her enthusiasm as she paced the room, jotting down notes and letting her imagination run wild while she talked. "Oh, Jared. I've got so many ideas, I hardly know where to start. Wait. Yes, I do. I'll start with making up an album about Granna. It'll be my example. Then I can personalise the others from there."

She wrote up a list of easily transportable props she could use and checked online for a suitable wheeled case to carry her equipment. She studied the album she'd made up for Granna with just pictures of people, the one she'd used to prompt her memory, and refined her ideas on presentation. Then she started writing down memories of her grandmother.

She briefly thought of asking her brothers for their memories too but decided anything included in an album had to fit the family profile. If her mother hadn't passed away, the story would have been different. Together, they would have kept Granna's spirit alive, but her father didn't care and her brothers hadn't had the right sort of relationship. She wrote it down as part of her criteria. Only the adults who cared enough should provide a story, but memories from children would be a great asset.

Within the week, Katie was back at Heart's Home.

"I'm very impressed," said Rosemary as she flipped through the pages of Granna's album. "It's well laid out, thoughtful and I recognise some of those images. Beautiful. Just beautiful. I couldn't imagine a better memento."

Katie explained how each one would have slight differences in layout and presentation. "Depending on how long it is, or how many other members of the family want to be included."

Katie started work straight away and the more photos she took, the happier she became. She wandered around the garden, the lounge, the dining room, anywhere she might see a resident doing something they might once have done. Like Granna playing the piano – she didn't remember she'd taught piano to hundreds of students over the years, but she could still remember how to play.

When families visited, Rosemary engaged them in the programme, and after getting their permission, Katie included them in family group photos. A few had declined to be involved, but Katie still took photos of the resident for the rest home's records. One or two saw what she was doing and asked to be included. Word soon spread.

Remembering all the days she had struggled when visiting Granna – what to say, what to do, how to feel – Katie surprised herself at how much she enjoyed the work. The commonly understood phrase 'beauty is in the eye of the beholder' fitted. Her eye saw beauty in the old faces, the wrinkled hands, the outstretched fingers, and allure in the lost world of sad eyes.

28

THE END AND THE BEGINNING

February 1926

While the rest of Auckland, and New Zealand for that matter, looked forward with great anticipation to the upcoming tour by Anna Pavlova, the famous ballerina, Jane gave her little thought. Pavlova's troupe of more than sixty people – dancers, dressers, choreographers, make-up artists and an orchestra – would not involve Jane in any way, and it would draw crowds away from their usual entertainment choices. J C Williamson and His Majesty's Theatre had pulled off another coup.

Jane had seen it all. She had worked at the Opera House for more than thirty years. She'd witnessed the ups and downs and failures of many local and international performance companies, and seen the comings and goings of their managers – and theatre owners. She had seen the changes in theatre styles, firmly disliking the current fashion for vaudeville, and the advent and rise in popularity of moving pictures – including a local fledgling filmmaking effort by Rudall Hayward. His second full-length moving picture, *Rewi's Last Stand*, was well praised in the papers, and Jane had to admit she'd enjoyed it, but the rumours that talking pictures were the next great thing to come was a concern.

She would never remember how many costumes she had designed, made, altered and repaired, and still, life for her behind the scenes had carried on virtually unchanged, but she was losing heart. Especially now.

Jane rushed straight to the house the moment she heard the news.

In the spacious Devonport villa where Brigid and Sally lived with the family, sadness filled the empty spaces. The three women sat commiserating with each other on the latest tragedy to befall their precious Grace who had sunk into a heavy torpor of grief and was confined to bed.

"Life has been so cruel to them," said Jane. "For her to miscarry a second time is a terrible blow."

"It is that," said Brigid, mopping her reddened eyes. "Specially after losing Susan. I had hoped this baby would help relieve her grief."

"I can't imagine the pain a mother must experience at losing a child," said Jane, "but to lose so many ..." She couldn't continue. The vibrant, sensitive Grace they all knew and loved was a mere shadow of her usual self.

"More'n two years gone and I can still see her," said Sally. "Such a wee mite, with the most gorgeous big eyes."

"It's as well they have young Tommy and little Jaybee to keep them busy, but to lose three ..." Brigid shook her head, at a loss for words and unable to explain how deep her pain went.

To ease his own pain, Charlie buried himself in his work, so little Tommy's uncles kept a keen eye on the eleven-year-old – as they had with Charlie when he was a boy. Seven-year-old Jane, nicknamed Jaybee – short for

Jane Brigid – was an intelligent little miss with a love for plants and flowers. She was always asking questions about the hows and whys, and seemed content enough.

"Tea." Sally's voice pulled Jane's thoughts away from the children. She gratefully accepted the proffered cup and took a biscuit. Brigid was still complaining she was too thin. At least eating a biscuit would prove she did eat sometimes.

"We don't get out so much these days, Jane," said Sally. "It's good to see you. Now tell us what you've been up to."

"Apart from working, not a lot," said Jane. "I don't enjoy going out much either."

"I tell you what we do enjoy, don't we, Sal?" said Brigid.

"What's that, Breeda?"

"The radio. We enjoy the radio broadcasts. It keeps us up to date with all sorts of things, and we can hear some lovely music without having to go out to concerts and such."

Jane listened as the two women talked about their favourite programmes and how amazing it all was that they could have such things in their own homes.

"I prefer to read, but if you're interested, a few novels are being turned into moving pictures. *The Phantom of the Opera* has drawn quite a crowd, I hear."

"It's an idea you've given me, lass. Aye. And I *might* go to one of those moving pictures and see for meself one day."

Sally had successfully drawn their conversation away from Grace but, while Jane was taking part in the conversation, she couldn't get the girl out of her mind. Maybe if Grace hadn't given up the piano, she might have found solace in her music. But there wasn't much call for teachers during the war, and since then she'd been busy being a mother, but still …

"What can we to do to help take Grace's mind off her loss?" she said in a break in the conversation. "She needs something. And I don't think George's wedding will do it."

After much discussion, Grace decided to spend the winter with her sister Lilly in Brisbane. Most of the family on both sides had turned up to wish her well. Charlie was particularly attentive, ensuring they had everything they needed. His love of ships had finally persuaded him to take a break, and escorting his family to Australia on one made him doubly happy. He would return within the month on the next vessel, while Grace would stay on until the spring.

Saying goodbye nearly broke Jane's heart. Life would feel empty for the three older women until she returned. Jane kissed and hugged Tommy and Jaybee, leaving Grace until last. "I'm going to miss you."

"We'll be back in time for George's wedding in September," she assured Jane. "I'll have to be. Charlie is best man, and Jaybee is one of the flower girls, along with one of Florence's nieces. You will design me something new, won't you, Janey?"

"Of course she will," answered Brigid. "Don't you fret none. You just come back restored to health is all we ask. I'm sure the warmer weather will do you good." She too hugged and kissed and fussed over the family as they lingered at the foot of the gangplank. "And here's an extra parcel of lace for Lilly. She'll know what to do with it."

"Love you all," shouted Grace, blowing kisses from the deck to everyone standing waving handkerchiefs and hats on the dock, but all too soon the ship put to sea and the family returned home.

"Will you come to the Arts Society exhibition with me tonight?" asked Gwenna. "It might help take your mind off things for a while."

"What's on? I haven't been following it much lately."

"It's their annual exhibition. I hear there are a great number of portraits this year."

"I'd like that. I enjoy portraits, you can see into the character of a person when you study their features."

And indeed, the exhibition had given Jane more ideas, and she started sketching new designs for the more modern woman who wanted none of the restrictions of earlier fashions.

Loose-fitting, sleeveless evening dresses, worn shorter with rows of long tassels, or ribbons trailing from a sash around the hips. Some were heavily beaded and bedecked with feather boas or strands of knotted pearls. Black had become a fashion colour for evening, decorated with silver and gold, while muted pastel shades like blush and aqua led the trend for daywear. Day dresses were also looser in style, with long V-collars and pleated skirts worn with strings of beads.

Jane wasn't sure she liked the close-fitting cloche hats so much. She had always been a fan of big hats, herself, which she believed offset the ensemble better, but her drawings were selling so fast she could barely keep up. She never neglected her theatre work but her enjoyment waned with the escalation of her fashion designs.

The winter months sped by and spring heralded Grace's return.

"My darling girl," sighed Jane when Grace visited her cottage in early September. "I'm so pleased to see you – and looking a lot perkier than the last time I saw you."

"Hello, Janey. I missed you, too. And yes, I'm so much better," said Grace, hugging her. "Lilly was so amiable. I'm not absolutely sure why, but she was. She's changed since losing Joseph. I like her a lot better now, and she is a great asset to the store, I can tell you."

"Will she marry again, do you think? It's been, what, eight years now?"

"No. She won't. She's married to the store. It's like she has become the matriarch since Mrs Browne passed. Papa Phillip delights in her and indulges her outrageously, but I fear she neglects Phillip Junior. He's no more than ten, but then Lilly's mother-in-law has taken him under her wing, so maybe that has something to do with it. Those two women do not see eye to eye at all."

Jane and Grace talked for hours about the fashions in Brisbane and what Grace had seen to inspire her, but soon their attention was taken by George's wedding at the end of the month.

"I drew this for you," said Jane, handing her a sketch.

Grace studied it for a moment, her face lighting up with pleasure. "How do you do it? This is fantastic. I'll be better dressed than the bride."

Secretly, Jane hoped she would be but thought better about saying so.

After insisting she not be invited to the celebrations as Gwenna wished, Jane agreed to attend the church service, if only to see Grace in her soft blush dress, coat and hat, and Jaybee in the ridiculous over-frilly and out-of-date primrose coloured flower-girl's dress Florence had chosen. But then the bride's dress was a flouncy affair trimmed in lace and flowers and nothing like the sleeker and more stylish fashions of the day, so Jane wasn't surprised.

As she stood watching the photographer prance around and give instructions where people should stand, she hoped someone would think to have one taken of Grace and Jaybee. Then she could request a copy, but she couldn't get close enough to whisper her thoughts to Grace. Collecting photographs had become something of a passion for Jane, and she looked for every opportunity to add another to her hoard.

Throughout the unseasonably wet spring months, Jane and Grace had followed the Miss New Zealand pageant. Hundreds of girls had applied, and local and regional voting had reduced their numbers to the final eight – two each from Otago, Canterbury, Wellington and Auckland. The final would be judged in November at His Majesty's Theatre, and Jane had tickets ready.

Still buoyed by the fun of the Miss Auckland competition the night before, Jane, Gwenna, Grace and hundreds of others lucky enough to get tickets sat through the various vaudeville acts preceding the main event. Outside, hundreds more gathered in Durham Lane and Her Majesty's Arcade hoping to hear the outcome.

"Isn't it all so exciting," said Grace, practically bouncing on her seat, just like she had when she was a young girl. Jane's eyes misted over at the memory, glad the girl had recovered her spirits.

When Miss Otago, 19-year-old Thelma McMillan, was crowned Miss New Zealand, the thunderous applause threatened to shake the plaster off the ceiling, and hundreds of streamers were thrown onto the stage.

"I've supplied some of my lollies and chocolates as prizes," shouted Gwenna, clapping along with the rest of the audience. "Small tokens in comparison to the lavishness of some of their gifts, but it gets my name in the papers again."

It took some time to extricate themselves from the theatre. Once outside, scenes of chaos greeted them as crowds of well-wishers trying to catch a last glimpse of the girls brought traffic to a standstill. The three women continued to chatter about the event until they went their separate ways, promising to meet up again soon.

Back in her cottage, Jane pasted the tickets into her scrapbook and wrote in her diary as she did every time she enjoyed any occasion with Grace. She had been pleased to recognise several of her designs amid the parade, including Miss Auckland who wore one of her Bernadette designs. One day she would give her collection to Grace, but until then, no one knew about her habit or her secret other self.

Jane's workroom once again took over her life as the programme of revues for December was presented to her. She and her team reorganised the racks, instigated a regime of repairs and alterations, and began work on a range of new costumes, but the night of the 3rd of December was the beginning of the end.

She had finished tidying up and laid out her designs for the morning, checked the costumes, variously pinned to mannequins or on hangers, before she turned out the light. The music and laughter from the show in progress echoed through the building as she made her way towards the stage door.

"Goodnight, Mr Singe," she called to the stage manager as she left, receiving a wave in response, before Mr Diamond, the scenic artist, stopped her to ask about needing some fabric.

"I'll see what I can find for you first thing in the morning."

At home again in her cottage, Jane had barely turned out the light after her night-time routine – changing and donning her favourite beaded wrap and sketching some new designs before retiring – when the sound of bells clanging roused her.

The clock said twenty minutes after eleven, and she wondered what was happening to bring the fire brigade out. She threw on a skirt and her outdoor coat and made her way into the street, finding it full of people heading towards Wellesley Street. She shut the door behind her and followed in their wake, seeing flames illuminating the night sky. As she turned the corner, she gasped in horror.

Flames were bursting through the upper-storey windows and dome of the Opera House, where she'd been no more than two hours earlier. She stood rooted to the spot. Thick black smoke enveloped anyone close by and billowed into the sky. The hot, choking air stung her eyes and made her cough as she watched the firemen break down the door and aim their hoses at the inferno. She covered her ears to block out the crashing, screeching sounds as parts of the building fell in. But the screams and the oohs and ohs from the throng watching still pierced her senses, and an agonising ache settled inside her. After a time, she heard cheers from the spectators as the extra fire hoses directed at the stage section adjoining Elliott Street slowly gained control and still she stood, mute and unable to move.

"Let's hope it doesn't spread," yelled someone beside her.

"We got out in the nick of time, I can tell ya," said another man. "Can't have been more than a half-hour or so since the show finished. It must have started straight away."

"Anyone know what caused it?"

"What's going to happen to the theatre now?"

Speculation mounted, but until the damage could be seen in the light of day, no one could say. Except Jane knew the inner workings of the theatre and couldn't imagine how anything could be saved.

The crowds started to drift away, once the raging inferno was brought sufficiently under control, but Jane held vigil until the last fire truck had gone.

The next morning, as the sun streamed through the piles of debris and charred beams still emitting wisps of smoke, people could see the extent of the devastation. The upper circle and stage were complete wrecks. All the scenery and curtains were lost, and in the orchestra pit, the grand piano and harp stood as skeletons of twisted metal and wire amid the ashes. Water lay more than ankle deep in the basement, where crates of costumes released dye into the blackness. Members of the dance troupe sloshed around looking for personal possessions, hoping something might be salvaged. Some of the sodden garments were saved and taken away by the performers.

"Management says they will pay for the laundry to dry them. And I can help with repairs," said Jane, although her heart wasn't in it.

She had lost her entire workroom. How the performers would continue their tour, hastily shifted to Prince Edward Theatre, another of the Fuller Brothers' many holdings, Jane would never understand. She was far too distraught to consider salvage.

A few days later, Fullers announced a blown fuse in the electrical box on the stage had caused the catastrophic fire. Thankfully, there were no deaths, and the only injuries were to Mr Diamond, who received some minor burns as he escaped the blaze.

"However," they said to the assembled employees, "we will not be rebuilding the Opera House." Groans of worry and despair interrupted the bigger news. "Instead, we will look for a suitable site to build a larger, grander and more modern theatre. We plan to be open in less than two years."

The managers tried to make it sound like an adventure with enormous prospects. For many, the time frame was too long.

Within the week, Jane's career was over.

29

UNRAVELLING THE PAST

February 2019

In the two weeks since her birthday, when she wasn't working on her photography, Katie spent every spare moment working through the discoveries at the cemetery and the list of names and dates Jared had given her. The revelation of a shared ancestor spurred her to discover who, and how, she and Jared were connected. Whatever the outcome, surely they couldn't be closely enough related to affect their relationship, could they?

She had spent hours loading them onto her online family tree and could see it gradually taking shape. "I think I've got most of it sorted now," she told Jared, pointing to her page relating to her grandparents' marriage. "I've checked all the birth, death and marriage certificates, and it looks like Granna Katy's parents *are* Grace and Charles Price. The same couple you have in your tree, which makes the baby Susan I found in the cemetery Granna's sister."

"What a great find," said Jared, peering over her shoulder and studying the dates and names, comparing them with his records. "Your gran was a marvel, working out how to make sure you ended up in the right cemetery at the right time – and so many years beforehand."

Katie's mind drifted back to the days when her grandmother was an intelligent, vibrant woman, who loved music and flowers, rather than the lost soul of her later years. She'd have known exactly what she was doing.

"What else?" asked Jared, pulling Katie back to the present – or was it the past?

"I've also found the records for a brother, Thomas Charles. He was their firstborn and was killed in World War Two. A daughter, Jane Brigid, was born in 1919, nine years before Granna, which all matches what you gave me," replied Katie. "On the headstones, the name Jaybee appears in brackets beside her full name, and there's a Jaybee in the journals, so she's got to be one and the same person. This Jane Brigid was briefly married to a Jack Ellingham in 1940, but it looks like he was killed in the war too."

Jared picked up the thread of her discovery. "OK, so if Charlie is Gwenna's half-brother, and we can trace him back to Bethan and George Price, it looks like dear old however-many-times great-grandfather George is our common ancestor. Well done. You've gone back five generations in your line and six in mine."

They high-fived each other with huge grins, knowing any connection that far back would not affect their relationship.

"But who is this Grace?" asked Jared.

Katie shrugged and refreshed the page. "Good question. I can't find a birth certificate. I even tried the Australian registers, since their marriage certificate says she was born in Brisbane, but drew another blank. The marriage certificate lists her mother as a Brigid Price née

290

O'Brien, but no father, so a Price marrying a Price makes for a confusing life."

They laughed at the corny rhyme and talked about the various branches, twigs and possibilities, and followed the likelihood of children being given the names of parents or grandparents, but could find nothing to prove their theory.

"Like your mother being named Susan, probably after baby Susan."

"OK, so, with Thomas Charles ... one name after his father, the other a grandfather maybe? But Jane Brigid? Where did that come from?"

He shrugged. "How does this Brigid fit in?"

"Don't know. I don't understand how she is connected but she definitely is somehow. I've traced her tree as much as possible. She left Ireland in 1886 for Brisbane. I'm not sure when she arrived in New Zealand, but a Brigid O'Brien married a Thomas Price in 1890 in Auckland." She paused. "Could he be the one Grace's son is named after? I wonder ..."

Jared shrugged. "Don't jump to conclusions. Thomas was a common name."

Katie scribbled a note on the pad beside her to remind herself later to check it out further, then returned to the screen. "Brigid was a lacemaker and the owner of Miss Brigid's, a boutique lace and fashion store. A daughter Lilly was born in 1893. She married a Joseph Harrison-Browne in Brisbane. There was a prestigious department store of that name there at the time. Joseph died in the First World War. They had one son, Phillip Junior, who was killed in the Second World War. Poor woman. You have to feel for someone who loses a husband and then her only son to two wars. Lilly died in Brisbane, listed as the owner and general manager. The store was then bought out."

"Why do you think this Brigid is connected then?" asked Jared.

"The photos."

Katie got up and stood in front of the wall unit she'd recently purchased to showcase all Granna's old portraits. "Granna Katy talked a lot about a Mórai. Thanks to my brother Tom, I found out it's an Irish term for grandmother, and then I discovered this picture of Miss Brigid in the newspaper, and then there's the photo you gave me of my Granna when she was young, with Mórai." She pointed to the various frames.

"And she appears here," said Jared, indicating another one, "with your lookalike and the woman we've identified as Grace. You're right. There's a connection."

They stood looking at the images, searching for more clues, pointing to this one and that. Katie tapped the one of Mórai and her lookalike. "I want to find out who this woman is. There's got to be a connection there somehow too. It's impossible for us to be such spitting images if we aren't related. But how?"

"So, what are the options?"

"Tell me my eye is wrong, if you like, but take a good look at these."

Katie rearranged the frames on the shelves so she had the mystery woman in a row of photos, starting with Mórai as the earliest, one with Grace, Grace and Lilly, a few others, Granna Katy and finally one of herself taken for her twenty-first birthday.

"What do you see?" She pointed to Mórai and Lilly, to Mystery Woman and Grace, to Grace and Granna Katy.

Jared's eyes flicked back and forth, he picked one up and turned it to the light to get a better view, and peered more closely at another couple. "A striking family resemblance from whoever to you. Since you've proved this Grace is your Granna Katy's mother, then she has to be your great-grandmother, and she looks like it. And I'd swear this mystery woman is Grace's mother, not the other one you call Mórai. But the resemblance between this Mórai and Lilly is uncanny too. They are mother and daughter in my opinion."

Katie nodded. "That's what I thought. Look at this." She handed Jared the photo she'd taken of Janey O'Neill's headstone, printed to 8 x 10 to make it easier to read.

"I think our mystery woman is this Janey. Why else would so many of the family names be there? But who's this Elizabeth? She's a new name. Is she the one I'm looking for? The one in Granna's will? Granna used to talk about a Janey as much as Mórai. I've a Grandma Gwenna and a Granty, a Breeda and an Aunt Sally, and I haven't attached real names or legitimate connections to most of them yet. Gwenna must be the same person, even if she's Charlie's sister not his mother, but I don't have a clue who Elizabeth is."

Katie stopped chattering as she became aware of Jared's stillness. He peered intently at the wording on the headstone then looked up at the photos again. "What's the matter?" she asked.

"I'm not sure. But ..." He shook his head and handed the print back to Katie. "It's not possible."

"What's not possible? One thing I'm learning about all this family tree stuff is *anything* is possible. Through all the scrapbooks and diaries, the same names keep coming up – these women are connected, either as friends, mothers and daughters, or marriages, or something."

Jared pulled out his phone. "I'm sure it's here somewhere," he said, scrolling through his photos until he found what he was looking for. He held it up before her face. "What do you see?"

"Who is she?"

"Never mind for the moment. What do you see?"

"Granna Katy – well, not exactly, but there are similarities. Who is it?"

Jared didn't answer. He scrolled a few more times and brought up another one.

"Is that your Grace? Gosh, she looks like the other woman."

"I hadn't spotted it before, but looking at all these photos reminded me of something. The name Elizabeth sparked my memory."

"And ..."

"My Grace's mother is Angela. Her mother was called Elizabeth. She's gone now, and I'm not sure Grace remembers her, but the first photo was Granna Beth."

Katie was dumbstruck. Was Jared's daughter Grace Granna's missing heir? Surely not. The idea seemed preposterous, but she couldn't avoid the evidence stacking up. "Are you telling me we've stumbled across the link Granna Katy stipulated in her will? But I don't understand. How ...?"

"I'm not sure I understand either."

Jared had trouble recalling the details and admitted he'd need to do more research, but one thing he did remember – Granna Beth was adopted. "I remember Beth said something about her mother being her aunt so it could all be kept in the family."

"When did she die?"

"About ten or eleven years ago, and Ange's father went a few years earlier. He was quite a bit older than Beth, I think."

Jared offered to ask his ex if she knew anything more about her grandmother's history but didn't hold out much hope. Her older brothers might remember, but he'd had nothing to do with them for years.

"But a couple of things come to mind. Think about the possibility of an adoption, or at least an informal adoption within the family. And what are the chances of any of these people appearing on the ship's register alongside your Brigid? Didn't you say you'd found out she emigrated to Australia? And the term Granna is different from the usual forms for grandmother. Idioms like these often run in families and get handed down."

Katie never thought she'd be frustrated by having too much work; work that took her away from her family tree research. But she was loving it.

Rosemary called to confirm two clients. "A word of warning," she said. "One of the ladies will not last long, so prioritise your time. We need to have her album ready."

Katie had to take a minute or two to rationalise what she was doing, now someone was actually going to die. In one way, it seemed macabre to be photographing people in preparation for death, but her second impulse confirmed her instinct: families would welcome the keepsake after their loved ones were gone.

"I have also told a couple of colleagues what we're

doing," said Rosemary. "They were quite interested, so you may get a call."

The following day, both of Rosemary's contacts had called and set up times to meet with Katie. She couldn't believe her little business was expanding so fast.

In the middle of sorting photos, she came across one of Jared. After staring at it for a few moments and thinking how much she loved him, she realised they hadn't seen each other for days. She picked up her phone. "It's been ages, and I haven't had time to do anything on the tree since you were here last," said Katie. "How about dinner? We need to catch up. Do you want to bring Grace?"

Although she and Jared talked on the phone every day, some weeks catching up in person proved more difficult. Between the hours he worked, both at the bakery and meeting the increasing orders from his website and Grace's commitments, pitched against Katie's workload, days could go by without them seeing one another.

"Great idea. What's in your fridge?" Jared heard the hesitation. "Never mind, I'll pick some things up on the way. Six OK?" There was a pause. "And Grace says thanks, but no thanks. Not tonight."

The first time Katie met Grace she'd been terrified, wondering what on earth she would say to the girl, but she needn't have worried. Grace soon broke the ice.

The weekend before Katie's birthday, the three of them had met at Mission Bay.

"Katie, I'd like you to meet my daughter Grace," said Jared.

The young girl looked so much like her dad, with dark eyes and her light-brown wavy hair hanging long over her shoulders, but there was also an air of familiarity about her that Katie found comforting.

"I'm pleased to meet you, Grace," Katie said, shaking the outstretched hand. "I've heard a lot about you."

"If Dad's talked about me as much as he's talked about you, then there's not a lot you won't know. Eh, Dad?" She smiled up her father, and Katie could see the bond between them. Katie's anxiety melted away when she realised Grace was not the surly teenager she'd expected. On the contrary. Katie liked the girl on sight – just like her father.

"Well, why wouldn't I talk about my two favourite people?" Jared asked, grinning and hugging his daughter.

They walked along the beach chatting about a lot of nothing, and then sat in the park eating ice creams while watching the little kids play in the fountain.

"Thanks for doing my dad's website," Grace said out of the blue. "It's done him wonders. He's busy doing what he likes now and is in a much better mood." She'd poked her tongue out at her father's raised eyebrow, but then just laughed. "But you might have a lot to do with that," she added.

More than slightly embarrassed at the girl's forthright manner, Katie mumbled about it being a pleasure. "I'm glad the website is working out. I enjoyed doing it. It's how we met. But you know that already. And I've been looking forward to meeting you since he told me about you." She hoped she wasn't rambling.

"I'm glad Dad told me about you, too. He doesn't have to pretend he's not dating someone any more. Honestly, he's hopeless at it. Tell me about your work. Dad says you take great photos."

Katie had explained about some of the tricks she used, what she liked to photograph best and the work she was about to start. "Especially people and flowers. I like capturing nature's perfection in the small things."

"I want to be a botanist or specialise in something like that," she said. "Can you teach me how to take photos of plants?"

The two talked for ages, almost to the exclusion of Jared who sat legs extended, arms behind him propping him up, listening to their chatter and wearing a silly grin.

Since then, Katie and Grace had spent a few happy hours going on photo tours together. They'd shared some girl time at the manicurist and discovered a similar taste in girly movies.

"Thank goodness!" Grace rolled her eyes. "Dad's movie taste is atrocious."

Katie laughed. "I couldn't agree more."

One day, Grace surprised and touched Katie. "By the way, I love your work. Your photos of the old people are amazing. I can see so many stories in them."

"Thank you, Grace. What a lovely thing to say."

"Do you enjoy what you do?"

"Very much. More than I expected."

"That's important, isn't it?" Grace looked pensive and Katie wondered what she was thinking. Maybe about her own work? One of the things Katie had discovered was that Grace could draw. Some of her botanical sketches were outstanding. Perhaps she should encourage her to expand her skills and consider an exhibition.

30

THE PAIN OF LOSS

June 1940

Instead of writing in her journal, Jane sat poring over her portfolios and let memories block out the pain of her most recent trauma. There had been so many sad events over the years, but this latest one rocked her.

She wondered where all the years had gone. One day she'd been young and eager and thankful for the opportunity to work and play – and hide – at Abbott's Opera House, and then suddenly she was old and tired, two years past her sixtieth birthday, and her beloved Opera House was long gone.

The night it burnt to the ground was the end of her career as the costumier. She could have stayed with Fuller Brothers and followed them into the new St James Theatre in Queen Street, when it finally opened towards the end of 1928, but Grace's pregnancy changed her mind.

Jane would never forget how terrified Grace had been ...

"I'm so scared, Janey. I don't want to burden Mam or Aunt Sally with my worries, and Charlie is over the moon at the thought of another baby, but what if something goes wrong again? I can't face losing another. I can't."

Jane recalled her words over and over, and her own heart shattered with sorrow. She couldn't find the right words to comfort the girl, but she could do something far more practical. She'd rashly promised, "Nothing bad will happen. I will care for you day and night until your child is safely delivered."

Grace had been thin, too thin, and while past the early miscarriage stage, she didn't look strong enough to carry a child to full term. The best preventative measure was bed rest.

The burden of caring for her fell on Jane, but neither Brigid nor Sally wanted to be left out. Between them they managed; even though Brigid, the family's big sister, mother, mentor and strength all rolled into one, had more than enough on her plate keeping up with Tommy and Jaybee, and the once-vibrant and vivacious Sally had turned into a wizened old lady in her late sixties.

Throughout the following six months, the women ran the household, cooked the meals, attended to the children, and kept up a regimen to care for Grace and keep her entertained and relaxed. On occasions, Gwenna took her turn. Grace was never left alone.

Whatever else was happening in the greater world mostly passed them by. They listened to music on the radio, and sometimes kept up with the daily report. Occasionally, Charlie would bring news but was told not to share anything that might upset Grace.

Two events in particular gave Jane the opportunity to keep Grace distracted. "The Duke and Duchess of

York, Albert and Elizabeth, are visiting again, and there's to be a second Miss New Zealand contest."

With Grace propped up in bed with lots of soft pillows supporting her and Jane in the comfy armchair facing her, the two talked endlessly about the celebrations: the decorations, the cars, the flowers, the illuminations and everything else to do with both events. But they talked fashion and design more than anything else. Jane brought fabric swatches, and they compared one with another for fall and movement. While Grace didn't have Jane's imagination for composition, she had a sharp eye for colour and style. During the months of her confinement, the two became closer than at any other time.

"Can I let you into a secret?" said Jane. "It must remain something between just you and me."

"Of course. I love secrets. I promise not to tell. But why? Why don't you want the others to know? Is it bad?" Grace's eyes goggled at the thought and she put her hand to her mouth.

"No, not bad," said Jane with ease. "Just private."

Jane handed across a folder containing many sketches. She watched Grace study each one in turn, waiting for her to say something.

"These are extraordinary, and I'm sure I've seen some of the gowns, but I've not seen these sketches before." She looked again at the drawings and then at the signature just about hidden amongst the comments in the bottom corner. Jane heard the gasp. "These are by Bernadette. Oh, my goodness. Are you *the* Bernadette?"

Jane smiled and passed her a second folder.

Grace checked the signature and squealed. "You're Mademoiselle Maree too. How amazing. I love her - I mean *your* – designs. I saw some made up in Brisbane. They are so elegant. You've been doing this for years, haven't you?"

"A long time ago, I needed extra money so I started selling designs I wasn't using for the theatre. I bought my cottage with the proceeds and now I have a tidy nest egg. I didn't tell anyone because I was afraid I'd get into trouble."

"Why should you be in trouble?"

"I had an employer who paid for my time."

"But you did these after work? I remember you always did your designs at night, wearing your beautiful beaded wrap. And anyway, I know Mademoiselle Maree's designs are of the latest fashions so you must still be designing. You haven't worked for anyone in the last year or more."

"I'm still designing and I still can't fathom where all my ideas come from, but I just see them develop on the page as I start to draw. Most of the time, I see *you* when I'm sketching, and I just fatten you up a bit so it'll suit the average woman."

Grace laughed at Jane's confession. "You must tell everyone. You must."

"Maybe, now I'm working for myself, I could. But I've kept it a secret for so long, I'm not sure ... but don't you think the mystique about not knowing who the designer is adds to the value?"

"Of course! How clever of you to think of that."

And so the winter months passed, and Grace blossomed again like she had with her first two pregnancies, although they still confined her to bed. Once spring arrived, she was allowed to sit in the kitchen with the old women, or walk in the garden. Sometimes Charlie took her for a drive for a change of scenery and to enjoy the summer air, since they were experiencing the first year with the extended summer daylight hours.

Then on 10 February 1928, Kathleen Grace Price was born, the girl who would become Jane's favourite person of all, coming close to surpassing her mother.

"What wonderful news and the best birthday present any grandmother could hope for," said Brigid, whose sixtieth birthday fell the next day. The celebrations amongst the family within the confines of their home that night exceeded any New Year celebrations with all the bands and brightest fireworks. Little Katy won the hearts of everyone present ...

Jane picked up her pen but still couldn't bring herself to write the words she knew she must. Instead, she thumbed through the journal, stopping at odd times to read random pages – some with fond memories, others not. She read about the time Laura completed her qualifications and became a lawyer. They'd celebrated her success, even though it had taken years longer than Laura had hoped. Her involvement with the war effort had interrupted her studies, but she'd been determined to finish. The degree gave her the momentum to challenge the status quo and continually fight for the rights of women. Since then, she'd become a force to be reckoned with, winning many a case for downtrodden and beaten women, and leader or member of any and every group involved in the betterment of women. Laura's name would go down in history.

Over the years, Jane had often written about Gwenna, her best friend and confidante. Like Sally had been to Brigid. Those two women, Gwenna and Brigid, were cut of the same cloth – determined women who succeeded in business, worked hard and took people under their wing. But Jane had never seen Gwenna so undone as when her Hugh died, six years earlier. The light had gone from her eyes that day.

"I've known Hugh since my teenage years," she said. "He worked for my brother in those days, and he loved me and protected me even then. Although I didn't realise it at the time."

Jane had commiserated as best she could but knew she hadn't reached her friend.

"He's been my life, my strength. What am I going to do without him?" Grief etched deep shadows on Gwenna's face.

But in time, Gwenna rallied, as she always did, and continued running her Sweet Treats business with an iron fist. With her son George as partner, she needed to, thought Jane.

The page opened on yet another sadness.

Aunt Sally's passing, eight years earlier, virtually broke Brigid's heart. Jane spent many hours sitting beside Sally's bed to give Brigid a break, or with Brigid in the kitchen listening to her endless stories about their life together.

"Do you realise we've been friends for more than forty years, and more like sisters than anything else? We've lived through everything together. What shall I do now without her?"

"You've been more devoted as friends than Laura and I have as sisters," said Jane, somewhat regretfully. It would have been nice to be closer to Laura, but they were distinctly different people. In truth, Laura was different from all of them and found her niche with others like herself. They hardly saw her these days.

"How true. You're right, dear Jane. Sally and I hit it off on the ship all those years ago and have stuck by each other ever since. We've had some great times. And some sad ones."

Brigid soon had Jane crying and laughing alternately with each memory, some of which Jane shared, many of which were only between the two friends.

Brigid rarely referred to their life in Australia, saying the distance between Brisbane and Townsville had kept them apart, until her cousin Jamie brought Sally, Maggie and the girls to Mrs Browne's doorstep. Jane remembered their eventful journey too well but chose not to dwell on it.

"That event, thanks to dear Mrs B, sent us to New Zealand where our new life truly began," said Brigid.

But in her delirium, Sally had talked a lot about what had happened. One night, Sally grasped Jane's hand. "Don't you fret none, young Jane. Your father will never harm you or anyone ever again. He's gone for good. Gone to the bottom of the gully. I was there."

Jane tried to ask questions, but Sally had drifted off to sleep. She never woke again and Brigid refused to answer Jane.

"What's in the past belongs in the past. Nothing will come of raking over old coals."

After Sally's passing, Brigid seemed diminished. Tiny as she was, she appeared to shrink even more in size and in disposition. She took little interest in anything other than her daily routine around the house, and Katy. She always had time for Katy.

But now Brigid, too, was gone.

A month since Brigid's funeral, and Jane felt more bereft now than the day of her passing.

The tears began again as Jane thought of what Brigid had meant to her. The pain was indescribable as she recalled how many times Brigid had rescued her, supported her, encouraged her and listened to her. Jane was now the matriarch of the family by default. She didn't feel at all matriarchal.

She wrote the bare facts in her journal.

Brigid Kathleen Price (O'Brien) born in County Clare, Ireland, 11 February 1861. Died Auckland 27 June 1940 as another war escalates in Europe and thousands more men and women will die.

Many of Jane's memories captured in her diaries and journals collated over her lifetime held sadness and regret. Pain and hardship had dogged her personal life, while success lifted her professional life. Most people saw the success. Brigid alone knew the pain.

In the darkness of the midnight hour, Jane bewailed her loss, while in the brightness of the daylight hours, Grace and young Katy were her joy and she could smile once more.

The time for another visit had arrived.

"Janey, Janey, you're here," said Katy, flinging herself into Jane's arms the moment she stepped through the door. The other children called her Granty – short for great-aunt – and she loved the name. But Katy had only ever called her Janey, just like her mother Grace.

31

VALIDATION

March 2019

Katie pushed 'print' and waited for the words she'd found on the screen to appear on paper.

Jared had told her to search the Papers Past website through the National Library archive and see what she could find. "Especially marriages. They tended to go into detail about who attended and who wore what and the colours and stuff like that. And death notices. You may turn something up. And it wouldn't hurt to google some of the names either."

Katie's instincts told her this time she'd found the answers to many questions.

The first item she'd found was a fairly recent academic essay by a student at the school of fashion design. Skimming over the descriptions and analysis of the designers Bernadette and Mademoiselle Maree, and their importance to the fashion industry of the time, Katie reached the part where the student surmised there was an affinity between the designs, which indicated they were by the same person.

The next section talked about theatre costume design.

During the clean-up from the fire at the Opera House in Wellesley Street in 1926, several designs from earlier shows and many of the sodden costumes were salvaged. Some pages were water-stained or singed around the edges, some had nearly half a page burnt away, while others were totally lost, but from it all came a collection the owners had the wisdom to preserve.

These sketches and many of the costumes have since been digitally recorded, and from studying the designs, it is this author's conclusion that the costumier of the time, Miss Jane O'Neill, could also have been the fashion designers known as Bernadette and Mademoiselle Maree.

Miss O'Neill worked for what was then called Abbott's Opera House, from 1894 until the fire destroyed the building. There is no evidence Miss O'Neill did any further design work for any theatre company post 1926, but the two named fashion designers continued their work until the mid-1940s, when the effects of World War Two curtailed the fashion market.

The paper continued to analyse the sketches and moved on to other designers, but Katie could find nothing to add to those few lines of speculation.

Except. Katie already knew the two fashion designers were the same person. She had the original signed sketches in the suitcase the lawyer gave her. But she had not made the connection with Jane O'Neill before this, although dozens more unsigned theatre costume design sketches lay in the files.

And she'd not been aware of any historic collection either. That was a bonus. She clicked on the link and saw the few black-and-white images held by the archives and recognised them in an instant. No wonder Granna Katy had wanted the collection catalogued and put on show.

What an amazing gift – a true legacy. A thought struck her then – that's what she'd call the collection: The Costumier's Gift.

A rush of ideas started falling into place.

The printer stopped, and Katie reread the indistinct black words from the newspaper columns. *The author didn't do their research very well if they missed this gem*, she thought. She'd found it under the In Memoriam notices, along with several others, some of them years apart, but this one wasn't signed.

JANEY O'NEILL, BERNADETTE, MADEMOISELLE MAREE
All three was she
In secret, at her behest.
Now she is gone
The truth will out
The world will know her as
Designer to the best,
And my unsung mother.

Whose mother was she? Katie thought she knew the answer, but she'd not found any marriage records or birth records to confirm it.

Jared had been right. A search of the ship's records showed a Michael, Maggie, Laura and Jane O'Neill left Ireland on the same ship as Brigid O'Brien back in 1886. They disembarked in Townsville, along with a Jamie O'Brien and a Sally Forsythe. Brigid had continued her journey to Brisbane. Could it be the same Jane O'Neill? And Laura and Sally? And how did they all end up in Auckland together?

Sometimes, thought Katie, her searches brought confusion rather than clarity.

She still had so much to discover, and she might never learn about everything her ancestors did, but each find added to her knowledge, and every time she read the journals more and more of what was written made sense.

While googling names, she came across a Laura O'Neill who had been a lawyer, women's advocate and leader of a recognised women's organisation of some note, and made a name for herself. Katie still had to place her in the tree, but a Laura fitted somewhere.

And she scored a hit when she discovered a J B Ellingham had worked in the botany department at Auckland Museum and the Wintergardens. An Elizabeth Ellingham became a botanical artist, who published many fine books and became a stalwart in her field.

If she remembered correctly, Jared thought Granna Beth had kept her Ellingham name professionally after her marriage, so it was more than likely the same person.

Even if they were not exactly direct links, Katie could at least connect the women whose names appeared on the various headstones.

She looked at the tiny notices appearing on the other printed pages and knew she'd found gold – and could now confirm all her suspicions.

Forsythe, Sally: 1932 –The best friend anyone could wish for. Missing you. Breeda (Mrs B Price).

Price, Brigid (née O'Brien): 1940 – Never forgotten and greatly missed. The best Mam a girl could have. Lilly (Mrs J Harrison-Browne, Brisbane) Grace (Mrs C Price, Auckland). Móraí to Thomas Price (dec'd), JB (Mrs J Ellingham) and Katy (Mrs R Bridges).

O'Neill, Jane: 1950 – Beloved Janey to Grace and Katy (Mrs R Bridges), and Granty to Thomas Price (dec'd), J B (Mrs J Ellingham) and Elizabeth. A second mother, friend, confidante and unparalleled fashion designer. Gone from our lives but never forgotten. Greatly missed. Mrs G Price.

At what sounded like her door being kicked in, Katie opened it to find Jared, his hands full with brown paper grocery bags, and his laptop bag slung around his neck.

"Here, give me one of those," she said, taking a bag from him and dumping everything on the kitchen bench. "I've got so much to tell you. I'm so excited, I've found them. They were all there in the newspapers, as you said."

Jared threw his arms around her waist, picked her up and twirled her before putting her down and kissing her. "Clever you. I knew you would. If you keep digging, this stuff finds its way through. You have to persevere until you understand it all."

While Jared happily banged around the kitchen cooking up a stir-fry, Katie talked non-stop about what she'd found and how it connected and what she still needed to prove. "Brigid is Móraí! I found Granna Katy's Móraí. She was her adopted grandmother – informal more than likely, just as you suggested. I almost missed it in the tiny print, but there it is. See?"

She showed him the printout and looked again at the familiar photograph of Móraí and her lookalike, and felt as if she'd come home. "Brigid was definitely Lilly's mother, but the best news is ... I found Janey."

Janey was Jane O'Neill, Bernadette and Mademoiselle Maree. Janey was Granty. Janey was ...

Katie looked at the photo again as certainty filled her innermost self.

"Janey was Grace's mother. I'm absolutely sure of it. And therefore, any child of Grace's, like Granna Katy, or grandchild, like my mother, is a direct descendant of Jane O'Neill, the costumier. Which makes me her great-great-granddaughter."

Katie's face flushed as a sense of fulfilment and belonging flowed through her such as she'd never felt before. At long last, she had put some of the 'known as' titles to real names.

"Just as we suspected. Great news. Who was Jane married to?" said Jared as he handed her a glass of wine and clinked his against it.

"I haven't discovered that yet. In fact, it doesn't look like she ever married."

"Woo-hoo. Looks like another scandal in the family, but it wasn't unusual in those days for the grandmother to raise a child born out of wedlock. Never mind, it's still worthy of celebration," said Jared.

"I think you're right. If I had to take a guess, I'd say Brigid raised the child."

Katie's stomach rumbled at the delicious aromas coming from her kitchen. "Something smells yummy. I'm starving."

"Won't be long now. So where to from here?"

Katie's spirits sank slightly. She still had to meet the last condition of her grandmother's will before she could claim the larger part of her inheritance. A tiny piece of information she'd not yet explained to Jared. "Finding Granna's long-lost daughter and proving who her descendants are."

Granna Katy had been specific about some details

but left out so much other information, Katie was finding it hard to prove.

The sketches and journals Katie found in the suitcase, and the shawl, belonged to her, during her lifetime. And now that Katie had discovered they had been drawn by the famous costumier, Jane – or Janey, depending on who was speaking – she understood why Granna wanted to have the drawings curated and recorded. Granna left instructions allowing them to go out on loan to a museum or art gallery, but they were not to be sold or leave the family's possession. Ever.

At least that much was clear and simple to follow.

Another clause said, if Katie had a daughter, the drawings would pass into her possession upon Katie's death. Which made sense, even if Katie never intended to have children, but the next clause had thrown her completely.

If Katie didn't have a daughter, they were to 'pass into the hands of the last female descendant of her daughter Elizabeth'. Whoever she was.

Katie had no idea Granna had another daughter. As far as she knew, her mother Susan and her Uncle Mike were the only children. So when Jared showed her the picture of a woman he called Granna Beth, who looked so much like Granna Katy, and then one of young Grace, who looked so much like her Granna Beth, the surprise could not have been greater. But she was even more surprised when she learned Granna Beth's maiden name was Ellingham.

"The question remains, was this Elizabeth Ellingham, the supposed daughter of J B Ellingham, one and the same person. If so, how can she be the daughter of both Granna Katy and her sister Jane known as Jaybee?" Katie paused, her mouth agape. "Oh, my goodness. I've just realised. J B – Jane Brigid. She was named after Jane the costumier, her real grandmother, and Brigid, her móraí, her adopted grandmother. How dumb of me not to notice before."

She scribbled down some more notes and cleared most of the paperwork to one side as Jared carried two bowls of steaming stir-fry to the table.

"Another tick. But thinking about Elizabeth. What about the idea of another informal adoption, like I suggested?" asked Jared. "It looks like that's what happened in Grace's case: Jane's child raised as Brigid's daughter. Could this Jaybee have raised Elizabeth as her own, when in reality she was her sister Katy's child?"

"It's an idea. But how do I prove it? I can't find a birth certificate for Elizabeth under any name. And they won't let me into the adoption records."

"Grace's mum might be able to, but, as I said, I'm loath to ask her."

Katie shook her head. "Let's leave her out of it for now. I think we have enough complications as it is."

"But you still think this person you're looking for might be my Grace, don't you?"

She nodded. "Except it seems way too far-fetched. What are the chances of two people getting together and finding they have a common ancestor on the paternal side of the family, to then discover a direct line on the maternal side as well? Come on. That's impossible, isn't it?"

Jared got up and filled a couple of glasses with water and brought them back to the table and then refilled the wine glasses. "Before I started all this genealogy stuff I would have agreed with you. And if your grandmother hadn't named names, I would also agree with you. But how many Elizabeth Ellinghams are there? Especially those who are the daughter of J B Ellingham, or Kathleen Bridges, who was also the daughter of a Grace and Charlie Price?"

Katie was forced to agree. "So, if we're looking at name patterns, where did Angela, Grace's mum's name, come from?"

Jared shrugged. "Her father's side maybe? But Elizabeth Ellingham was Angela's mother, and Angela is Grace's mother. That much I'm certain about."

Trapped between doing what her grandmother wanted – which she'd have to do sooner or later to claim the bulk of the estate – and burying it all in the past until she sorted out what she and Jared were doing, Katie dithered.

Was there a future for them? Between his work, her work, Grace and all this family tree stuff, she wondered if they would ever live together as a couple like they'd planned.

Katie had told Jared about setting up a series of self-funding annual lump sum grants available exclusively to female students. Now the names of those grants – the Janey O'Neill Award for advanced students of art and fashion design; the Grace Price Award for advanced piano studies, and the Elizabeth Ellingham Award for botany – made a lot more sense.

But there was more to it. Katie had also told him about the design collection she had to establish, and that she was looking for the descendant of Granna's previously unknown daughter, Elizabeth. What she hadn't told him was that if Grace proved to be the long-lost descendant of Elizabeth, then Grace would inherit a large sum of money. Nor had she told him that she would then inherit her grandmother's estate, once everything was confirmed. There was too much money involved. How would she tell him and how would he react?

If what she'd discovered so far, and what Jared had told her was true, then the young Grace Price met all the criteria.

She was Granna's great-granddaughter.

32

Until her dying breath

March 1950

Jane never thought she'd live long enough to share the happiest day of her life with those she loved the most. Her precious Katy would wear Jane's final design as she walked down the aisle to marry Robert Bridges, a fine man who loved her Katy as much as she did.

Some years earlier, Jane vowed she would never design another gown under any name. Since the second war in her life had caused so much heartache to so many, she'd lost her innate flair.

Jane doubted her ability too. Her hands had become arthritic, and she lived with more pain than she confessed to, which clouded her thinking. The design for Katy's dress had required considerable thought and effort, but thankfully, Grace had intuitively opted to choose a ready-made dress.

After Brigid passed away, ten years earlier, Grace insisted Jane give up her cottage and move in with her and Charlie and the family. They'd first invited her after Sally died, nigh on two decades before, but she'd not been ready then. She felt ready once Brigid had gone.

It had worked out perfectly for them all in the generous house Charlie had purchased to accommodate everyone, but now they had another empty room.

Tragedy had stalked Grace through the years and struck once again. Her only son had been taken from her. She was not alone, of course: the war devastated millions worldwide and tens of thousands in New Zealand, but Jane cared most about those closest to her. She remembered the strength Brigid had shown and tried to emulate her, until the numbers started to multiply and her heart could take no more.

Gone to early graves were Thomas, Grace's eldest, Phillip Junior, Lilly's child, and Jack Ellingham, Jaybee's delightful husband, before they'd got to know him properly. Gwenna's sisters lost sons, and Tillie's daughter lost her husband. Everywhere Jane turned, she met another distraught, broken woman.

The war, the one after the Great War, the one to end all wars, that failed in its promise, had once again taken so much from so many.

While Jane sat in the church waiting for the bride to arrive, her thoughts returned to late 1944 when nothing but sadness engulfed them. Life works in mysterious ways sometimes, and it worked to her advantage then as the war drew to a close.

"Janey, help me," said Katy sitting upright in the chair, constantly pulling at the handkerchief she held in her hand. "I've done something terrible."

"Whatever it is, nothing is insurmountable and nothing is so terrible we can't deal with it. Not after what we've already suffered. Now tell me, my darling girl. What's your problem?"

The problem was an American soldier.

Over the last two years or so, American soldiers, taking respite and recuperating from the battles in the Pacific, or new troops arriving to replace those sent home, could be found occupying camps throughout the country. Several were set up in Auckland.

The Yanks were used to a different way of life. One with far more entertainment and liveliness than the closed shops of Auckland offered, and they had far more money to spend. Since the tents and huts they lived in offered little in the way of comfort, the boys found warmth and comfort elsewhere and created their own entertainment. Parades, dances, music and alcohol created a party atmosphere in a city worn down by the rigours of war. Many people, mostly women whose husbands and sons were still overseas, opened their homes to these soldiers, giving of their hospitality and kindness freely, in the belief another woman in another country would do the same for their menfolk. In return, the women of Auckland were showered with nylons and chocolates and many other delights usually out of reach.

While working with the Red Cross, Katy met several soldiers, either because she was helping with their recovery or as a partner at the various dances. One young man had become particularly attentive, and Katy had fallen for his charms.

"Oh, Janey. What have I done?" Katy began sobbing again and Jane put her hand over the girl's and held it tightly. "I didn't mean for it to happen, but he was so nice to me, and so persuasive. And now I'm ... I'm pregnant, but he's been sent home and doesn't know. I haven't dared tell anyone. I'm so scared."

Blotchy red eyes stared at Jane, begging her to come up with an answer for her problem.

"Leave it with me, my darling. I have an idea. I'll talk with your mother."

"Aren't you shocked? Mama will be? And Da."

"There's not much can shock me, Katy darling. I've seen too much in my life to feel outraged any more. Don't fret."

The conversation with Grace went better than she anticipated.

"Are you sure?" asked Grace, gravely concerned with Jane's proposal.

"I am. I want to see some of this country before I die and now is as good a time as any."

"But there's still a war on and rationing and ..."

"I'm aware of all that, but I have money and a car, and there will be plenty of women willing to open up their homes to an elderly woman and her young companion for a few extra shillings in their pockets."

Finally, Jane persuaded Grace and Charlie to let Katy travel with her to see the sights of New Zealand before it was too late. Jane hated lying to Grace, but she'd do anything for Katy.

"I'll write and tell you where we are and what we're doing but I plan to be away for several months."

"My dearest Janey, you always were one to dance to your own tune but you have truly become quite eccentric as you've grown older. But very well, I can't see any reason why Katy shouldn't go with you and make sure you don't get yourself into any trouble. She might save me a lot of worry."

The two women, the old and the young, set off shortly after Christmas with few plans where they would go. While on the road, Jane taught Katy to drive, which relieved her of the task. She was not a natural driver, having given in when Gwenna persuaded her into a car when her knees began to trouble her. Gwenna had been delighted with the news her long-time friend was heading off on an adventure, as she called it.

"About time you did something for yourself, Jane. You've always given more of yourself to others than you have received in return."

Jane couldn't agree. Brigid had done more for Jane than ever she'd done in reverse. This was her way of making amends.

They'd gone north first and investigated as far as they could where the roads led them, then headed south through the Waikato and west to Taranaki, before retracing their steps to head east to the coast then south to Wellington. Along the way, when they had car trouble, a friendly man would help them find petrol, or repair whatever needed repairing, or change the wheel and fix a puncture. They met some lovely ladies glad of the company of a kind-hearted woman taking her widowed granddaughter on a tour to take her mind off her loss.

"Poor girl," she'd whisper to her hostess, casting surreptitious glances towards Katy, head lowered and fiddling with a newly purchased narrow wedding band. "Married a matter of a few weeks before her husband goes missing, presumed dead. And the one thing she has to comfort her is the wee babe growing inside her." Jane would shake her head in sorrow and move on to the next town.

True to their word, she and Katy wrote to Grace from every town, describing the scenery, the people and the sights they'd seen. They didn't mention the days when Katy was nauseous, or teary, or plain down in the dumps. They didn't mention the new dresses Jane bought to fit

Katy as the months passed, nor the baby requisites. They didn't mention their plans, although Jane knew where she wanted to be, when and why.

Jane arranged to store her car in Wellington while she and Katy boarded the passenger ferry to Picton. The town offered a quiet respite from their travels, and kindness from strangers. After several weeks, Jane decided to return to Wellington and her timing couldn't have been better. Katy was admitted to the maternity hospital, where she gave birth to a daughter less than a month after VE Day.

"Clever girl. Now wasn't it all worth it?"

"She's so beautiful. Thank you, Janey, for saving me from the scandal and embarrassment, and ... oh, everything. But what happens now? I can't just turn up at home with a baby in my arms. But I don't want to give her up. Do I have to give her up?"

Despite Katy's tearful agitation, Jane remained perfectly calm. "Don't you fret, my pet. I have an idea."

After a two-week stay, Katy was allowed to leave the hospital.

"I've given up my place at the guest house," said Jane, escorting the girl to the car. "It's time to move on. It'll still take several weeks to get home. You need time to recover. Now, listen to me my girl. I've written to your sister."

"Jaybee? Why?"

"Listen." During their months away, Jane had come up with a plan. "Our story is, I befriended a war widow we stayed with, who was expecting. Unfortunately, the poor woman died in childbirth and without any other family of her own, I rescued the newborn."

"Who are you talking about?" asked Katy, genuinely confused.

"Someone who doesn't exist but will solve our problem."

"Won't people be suspicious? Why would you adopt a baby?"

"I'm not going to. We have an infant in need of a mother – one who is not you. You must never admit she is your child. Not if you want to make something of your life and marry well in the future. Do you understand? This child is not yours."

Looking totally dejected, Katy nodded.

Satisfied, Jane continued to outline her plan. "Waiting for us in Auckland, we have a pitiful excuse for a woman still mourning the loss of her husband, and in need of something to focus on. Why not put the two together?"

"But Jaybee wants to be a botanist."

"And she still can be if she wants it badly enough, but I don't see any evidence of it so far. She's lost six long years to the wretched war. It's time to help her take her life back."

"And you think a baby would do that? Would Jaybee take her for me?"

"Not for you, dear. Remember – no one must ever learn the truth. But to answer your question – yes, for the child's sake – the poor orphaned mite that she is. I believe she will. And this way you can see the child any time you want to and become her 'Katybee', her special aunt."

Katy perked up at the thought her child would be so close. "You are so clever, Janey. I do love you so."

Jane nodded but she hadn't finished. "And I love you, my sweet. Now, I want you to do something for me in return. You must finish your piano studies and become the teacher you'd always wanted. Your mother regretted not following her dreams to teach. Don't you do the same thing. Promise?"

Letters passed back and forth between Jane and Jaybee, until the younger woman agreed to adopt the baby they named Elizabeth, after the Princess Elizabeth.

The organ interrupted Jane's memories.

The congregation stood as the beautiful bride walked down the aisle on the arm of her father Charlie, into the hands of another man who would care for her.

Behind Katy walked her flower girl, five-year-old Elizabeth, Jaybee's daughter, followed by Jaybee herself as matron of honour.

Jane's heart swelled with love and pride. She had done all she could. She would die happy.

33

JUST WHEN THINGS ARE LOOKING UP

March 2019

"I've applied for some uni courses for next year," Grace said quietly as she and Katie set the table while Jared cooked his famous stir-fry. "I'll take whichever one I can get into."

"Does your dad know?"

She shook her head. "Not yet. He thinks I'm doing a gap year first."

"I think he'd prefer to have you close so he can keep tabs on what you're doing rather than overseas on your own, anyway. He was never comfortable with the gap year idea."

"Wasn't he? That's news. But then he's always allowed me to make my own decisions – with heaps of guidance. He usually keeps asking questions until I come up with the right answers."

"Clever Dad. So, you've decided on botany then?"

"For now. I'd like to study native ferns. They are quite fascinating and such amazing shapes."

"You draw them so well too. Have you ever considered studying art?"

"Nah. Not yet. Maybe if there's a call for drawings I might; meanwhile I'll take photos. Quicker too."

Pity, thought Katie. But it had nothing to do with her.

"You're creating some wonderful aromas there, my talented cooking angel," said Katie as she returned to the kitchen.

"Nearly ready – are you?"

"Most definitely."

Over dinner, Katie and Jared caught up with each other's latest activities. Katie told him about the passing of one of the residents of the home and the additional work coming her way. He updated her about the stats on his website.

"Wow. It's turned out better than I thought possible," she said. "Looks like we're both doing well in our new career paths."

He pushed his bowl away and tapped the side with his chopsticks. "Which brings me to what I want to say while I have my two favourite girls paying me full attention."

"Dad, stop with the holding court nonsense. Neither of us pays you any attention unless it suits us."

"Don't be cheeky, Miss," he reprimanded without any hint of reprimand.

"Did you want to say something, Grace?" asked Katie, hoping she might tell her father her news, but the girl shook her head.

"Nope. Other than I've sold a couple of the photos you helped me take."

Katie smiled, remembering the day she and Grace had sat together and submitted some of Grace's photos to stock sites. "Well done. You have the eye for it. You see tiny plants I miss."

Grace shrugged away the compliment and returned to picking at her meal.

"Grace. Pay attention, please. This concerns you."

Grace placed her chopsticks over her bowl, sat back in her chair and folded her arms. "What?"

Jared looked at her sideways but ignored her mood. "I've been thinking lately. Since Dazzling Desserts is proving popular, I'd like to expand it a bit further. I've had enquiries to do home demonstrations and home deliveries. I'm not so keen on the deliveries. It would take too much of my time."

"You wouldn't do them. You'd employ someone else. Like me?" said Grace with a touch of hope in her voice.

"You don't have your full licence yet, so it can't be you."

"Well, someone like me then." Her face dropped. "A student in need of money. It can't be hard."

"No, but it could be dangerous."

"How?"

"Going to a stranger's home on your own."

"Honestly, Dad. Get real. As long as there's no money changing hands, delivering something is perfectly safe – especially if the customer is waiting for something they've ordered."

Jared sighed. He was obviously getting grumpy with the change of conversation.

"Anyway, that's not what I want to talk about right now. What I want to say is I think it's time to quit my job at the bakery and do DD full time."

"I think it's a great idea," said Katie straight away. "I've never regretted quitting my job. Must be coming up twelve months now." And what a year it had been too. "Things were a bit tight financially in the beginning, but

327

I always found some work to keep me going and now look. I'm loving this new role."

Her photography work was going from strength to strength and she was busier than she'd ever imagined. She was being paid well too. She got over her initial anxiety. No, that wasn't the right word – wariness – about intruding on people's lives, was a better way of putting it. But so far, all the families had welcomed the albums. Whatever she was doing, she was obviously meeting a need since she was visiting three other rest homes as well. Not all the residents were dementia patients, or close to death, but the relaxed atmosphere of having professional photos taken in their own space was building a larger platform.

Her health was better. She was fitter, and the endless irrational tears had dried up. She still had so many loose ends to sort out, but most of them were wrapped up in what the man sitting beside her decided to do. Like now.

"It'll be a bit of a financial risk, and I will have to hire more permanent premises, but I feel the time is right."

"So, what's it to do with me?" asked Grace.

"I've seen a property which might fit the bill. It's in a semi-commercial area, but there's a generous two-bedroom flat above and a retail space below. I could fit out a kitchen downstairs and ..."

"You want to move!" demanded Grace. "What about me! What will I do?"

"You'd come with me, of course, but yes. It would mean selling the townhouse and investing in the property – or one like it. This one is brand new ..."

"I don't care if it's brand new. What about me? I still have to finish school."

"There's nothing stopping you. You can still go to the same school. There'll be more travelling involved, but ..."

"I don't want to move and I don't want to travel."

Grace's reaction was so unlike her, Katie wondered what the cause was, but she detected fear in the girl's eyes.

Katie held her tongue while this exchange went on. She could see both sides of the argument. Jared did need to work full time on his business and not be distracted by labouring for someone else, but disrupting Grace wasn't practicable either. But she had no intention of expressing an opinion.

"Help me, Katie," said Jared.

"No ... no way." She held her hands up in front of her to fend off further involvement. "This is between you and Grace. It's got nothing to do with me."

"Well, yes it has, actually. That's why I wanted you both here."

He took Katie's hand and rubbed his fingers over her knuckles in his usual way. "I want us to be together more than we are. Some weeks I scarcely see you. I know we've only been with each other for a few months, but I knew from the minute I first met you, you were the girl for me."

Alarm bells rang. He'd used the same phrase about meeting his ex-wife and look where that had led him.

Unaware of her disquiet, Jared took a deep breath and reached across to take Grace's hand as well. She gave him a funny look but didn't withdraw her hand.

"So here goes." Jared looked at each of them in turn. "Katie, I want us to get married. Grace would you mind if Katie joined our little family? Katie, will you accept me and my daughter into your life?"

She'd expected a conversation about living together, but she hadn't expected a marriage proposal. Not so soon or so suddenly. And definitely not in front of his daughter. What could she say?

Grace withdrew her hand and glared at her dad, looking just about as stunned as Katie – and furious. Katie's heart sank. Their future was over before it had begun.

She wished Jared had talked to each of them alone first, instead of putting them both in this awkward situation.

"Say something, one of you."

He removed his hand from Katie and started to polish his glasses, a sure sign of his nervousness. When he began tapping his nails on the table, Katie and Grace simultaneously reached over to clap a hand on top of his to stop him. The three-handed clasp reduced the girls to giggles and the tension was broken.

Grace fidgeted in her chair and stared at the floor. "If you're asking my permission to marry Katie," she said, "the answer is yes. But if you want me to live with the two of you, the answer is no. Been there, done that. Doesn't work."

Jared blushed. He turned to Katie and shrugged his shoulders in entreaty.

"Sorry. She's a bit too blunt for her own good sometimes." He scowled at Grace. "Watch your manners. There's no need to be rude."

Grace folded her arms and glowered at him.

Overwhelmed, both by Jared's proposition and Grace's acceptance, Katie strived to raise a smile as her heart lifted and her eyes shone brightly. "Grace, I'm thrilled, truly thrilled you're happy for me to be part of your dad's life. Thank you. And I understand your reluctance to be a third cog in the wheel, but I promise never to come between you and your dad. That relationship is too special to break." Katie left Grace to think about what she'd said, knowing it would take time to sort out the logistics. "And Jared," she said, facing him, "I want to spend my life with you too. I couldn't think of anything I want more. But ..."

"But, what? Go on, what's the but?" asked Jared, not looking at all confident.

"Are you expecting me to move into this upstairs apartment with you and Grace?"

"Yes, of course."

"Then we have to talk a lot more about your living arrangement ideas."

"Oh yes!" Grace punched both arms straight up in the air.

That made Katie smile.

"In any case, I can't see me giving all this up," waving her hand around her apartment and the view, "and moving into a flat above some commercial unit in a semi-industrial setting, can you?" She kept her voice light. Grace needed time.

Jared dropped his head and shook it. "No, I can't." He looked up at Katie and took her hand again. "Sorry. I didn't think it through properly, did I? I can really mess things up sometimes. I can't expect Grace to live somewhere like that either, can I?"

He glanced at Grace who solemnly shook her head.

"Let's leave it for now and think on it," said Katie, wishing for a much more intimate and romantic occasion to discuss their future. "There's got to be a better answer."

"Yep. There is," confirmed Grace. "Honestly, Dad. You are dense sometimes. But I love you."

"Oi, Miss. Enough of your cheek."

No amount of thinking or talking solved the problem. As the days slipped by, Katie began to feel like a commodity in need of placement, or a stumbling block to be removed. Grace and her Dad argued constantly, which put them both on edge and in bad moods. Whatever romantic outcome Jared had hoped for had turned into a messy obstacle course.

"I have no choice but to sell the townhouse," said Jared gloomily several days later.

They sat in Katie's lounge, gazing out at the view with a glass of wine in their hands as he tried to sort out his dilemma. "I need the money to invest in somewhere with a suitable kitchen, otherwise I can't take Dazzling Desserts any further."

"Well, selling's not such a bad thing, but isn't the hire kitchen working?" asked Katie.

"Yeah. It's OK, but it's a lot of driving and I can't crash there when I'm done."

Katie couldn't think what to say. She understood his one-eyed focus on what he wanted. That's why he'd come to the agency in the first place. And to achieve set career goals, you had to be ambitious and driven and not let anything get in your way. She'd done that once, but now she wanted more from life. She thought he did too, but maybe their timing was wrong.

"It never worried you before. What's changed?"

"You. Me wanting to be with you. Grace. How the three of us can live together."

The suggestion she sell her apartment had not come up, not since Jared's first clumsy attempt, but her thoughts kept turning to buying somewhere else as the solution. She could easily solve their problem, but would Jared accept the idea now she was much wealthier than him? She doubted it.

And she needed to be certain they were fully committed to each other.

Grace came first in Jared's life. She'd understood that from the beginning. And while she and Grace had become friends in the last couple of months, it was still early days, and living in the same household would put a different strain on their relationship.

And then there was the rest of the inheritance.

So many thoughts ran through her mind, she was on the point of telling Jared they should put everything on hold until Grace left school at the end of the year.

Dare she mention the conversation she'd had with Grace? Was that only yesterday?

In her inimitable way, Grace had done her research. "Can you talk to Dad?" she'd pleaded. "I need to finish Year 13 first, but I'm pretty sure where I want to do a combined fine arts and science degree which'll open up a few extra doors for me. But it means moving to Sydney."

"I'm sure he won't mind," said Katie, thrilled Grace had added art to her degree plans. "Can't you talk to him yourself?"

"Thing is, it's not for another year. You and he can't carry on like you are for another year."

Katie started to bluster but Grace butted in. "Don't pretend. It's not working out. So, I've been thinking."

Katie wasn't at all sure Grace's thinking would line up with her father's, but she was seventeen. By the end of the year, she'd be making her own decisions, whether he liked it or not.

"I've found this place. A bit like the one Dad talked about but within school zone. It's small upstairs, but there's huge space for a kitchen and a walk-in chiller and all the things Dad needs."

"So how does a studio help us?" Katie was thinking about her comparatively spacious one-bedroom apartment. It worked for two but not for three.

"I could live there while I finish school. Dad could set up his business. It's central, and after I'm gone, he could rent it out for extra income." She wrinkled her nose and shrugged. "It'd mean he'd have to live at your place."

"You mean you'd live there on your own!"

Grace nodded, grinning, hopeful, and Katie's brain automatically answered, no. She couldn't see Jared going for it. But she wouldn't mind if he moved into her place. "Let me think on it."

And think on it, she had. Maybe she should take the opportunity to talk to Jared now, since there was just the two of them.

Deciding their moody silence had gone on long enough, Katie got up from the couch and washed her glass in the sink.

"Did Grace talk to you last night?"

"What about?" asked Jared, suddenly alert. "Is there something I should know?"

Intuitive parents! thought Katie. Now she'd got herself in a mess. "I don't know exactly, just …"

"Just what? Come on, spill."

"She said she had an idea."

"And she ran it past you first? Must be serious."

334

34

PASSING ON THE BURDEN OF SECRETS

September 1950

Within the year, Jane became so riddled with arthritis she could not move without pain. She spent most of her days on the daybed in the living room where she could see the garden and listen to the birds. Grace attended to her needs, and she looked forward to visits from Jaybee, Elizabeth and Katy, who arrived with gossip to fill her mind.

Jaybee had joined the local botanical interest group and spent endless hours helping at the Wintergardens in the domain and had applied to work at the museum.

"Little Beth is developing a passion for plants similar to mine. It's amazing to think how nurturing can be passed on. Thank you, Granty, for guiding me to where I am today. I couldn't live without Beth. I love you. I still miss Móraí, even after all these years, but you stepped into her shoes and cared for us like we were your own."

Tears filled Jane's eyes, and she hugged the young woman who she felt would make an impact on the world after all.

Katy reported on her students and her love of music, having fulfilled her promise to Jane to become a piano teacher. "There's so many concerts and musical events to attend I don't have much time left. And my students are a delight. I've the odd one or two I could crown sometimes, but I'm loving it all – but I'm going to slow down soon." Katy turned to make sure no one else was close to overhear her words. "I'll let you into a secret, Janey. I'm expecting. I haven't told Robert yet. I wanted to tell you first."

The news was another fillip to Jane's sad, weary heart. All she ever wanted was for her girls, all of them – Grace, Jaybee, Beth and Katy – to be happy; and Lilly, for Brigid's sake.

Grace had matured into a remarkable woman, active in the community, a graceful hostess, supportive of her husband Charlie, whose left arm had completely withered from lack of use over the years, and a wonderful mother to her two girls. Jaybee was happy again, with plans to forge a career for herself. Beth had the best of mothers, watched over by her 'Aunt' Katy, whom she called 'Katybee'.

The future looked brighter than it had for decades. There'd been far too much misery in the world during her lifetime. Only the 1920s had offered any degree of optimism, until the stock market crashed, creating further worldwide misery. Jane hoped the next generation wouldn't suffer the way hers had.

"Janey," said Grace cautiously one day as autumn turned to winter. "Are you up to going out, do you think?"

"I don't think so, love, if it's all the same to you. It's too cold."

"Are you in a lot of pain today?"

"Not so bad today, but why do you ask?"

"It's Gwenna. Charlie tells me she's sick and has taken to her bed."

"Gwenna's never been sick in her life."

"Maybe not, but she's sick now. The doctor says its pneumonia."

Jane's body sagged. Women of their age didn't often win the battle with pneumonia. "Gwenna's younger than me, she'll fight it."

"I don't think she will, Janey. Please, let me take you to her. Wouldn't you rather see her while she's alive than go to her funeral?"

Grace didn't need to be so blunt about it, thought Jane, wishing the truth didn't hurt so much. She nodded.

After some difficulty hobbling on her sticks, Jane got into the car and out again at George's. With help, she made it to the comfortable armchair beside the bed which they'd turned around so she could face Gwenna. The family had moved Gwenna downstairs to the living room where they could care for her more easily. Although in Jane's mind, George and Florence wouldn't be the best of caregivers under any circumstances.

Gwenna had little strength to talk and often ended up in a fit of coughing when she tried. Jane held her hand, smoothing the wrinkled skin with her thumb. "You've been the best of friends, Gwenna dear. Now rest. I'll do the talking. I'll remind you of all the good times we've shared and the secrets we've kept."

Jane fell asleep after a long, one-sided conversation, with Gwenna squeezing her hand in answer when needed or raising a chuckle now and then. Time passed while she slept, but no one disturbed them. As soon as she awoke, she noticed how Gwenna's hand lay soft and gentle in hers, but the lifeblood had gone.

Jane continued to hold her hand, remembering close to fifty years of friendship. One didn't give up on friendship without sadness, just like one didn't give up their own flesh and blood without heartache. Like she had. Like Katy had.

"I'd like to go home now," said Jane when Grace returned to check on her.

She took to her bed that night and didn't get up again, not even to attend Gwenna's funeral. Nor could she pray for Gwenna's soul. Jane didn't think she believed in God any longer. Not after all the misery in the world. Brave, devout Brigid would scold her for such impiousness, but nothing mattered any more.

Spring came and still she waited for God, or whatever being granted peace to broken hearts and minds. She wondered if she'd see the pōhutukawa trees flower again but didn't think she would. Nor would she see Katy's new arrival, but she had one last thing to do before she joined the people she'd lost. She needed to leave those behind her with the truth: and a legacy, she hoped. A gift.

"Grace, my darling. Do you remember when Katy was born, I showed you my sketches?"

"Shh. Don't talk. Save your strength."

"What for? I'm not done just yet, and I need to tell you something."

Jane asked Grace to fetch the old suitcase on top of her wardrobe. Inside were folders and folders of sketches. She had never thrown any of them away. Her will was also in the case, alongside her journals and her shawl.

"I want Katy to have my sketches and my journals. One day she will understand. Once it comes out who Bernadette and Mademoiselle Maree really were, there are some around town who will be most surprised. The designs could be worth something in themselves in years to come." She chuckled to herself. She might become famous after all. "My savings and the money from the cottage I've divided equally between you, Jaybee and Katy. Invest it wisely, please, dear Grace. That money has to last more than the lifetime it took to save it. It's my way of asking for forgiveness."

"For what? There's nothing to forgive."

"There is much to forgive. I want you to forgive me for lying to you your entire life. And for not having the courage to own up to my mistakes and letting Brigid take responsibility."

"I don't understand. What has Mam got to do with it?"

"Everything. Just like I took Katy away, Brigid took me away. Many years ago, I went with her and Lilly to Brisbane and when we returned, Brigid had miraculously had another baby. You."

Grace gasped and total disbelief crossed her face as put her hand against her mouth.

Jane lay back against the pillow and momentarily closed her eyes. A sense of completion flowed through her and she opened them again. She couldn't give up now.

"I was young and ... It doesn't matter how it happened now. Brigid took charge. She took my baby as her own ..."

"What?"

Jane ignored the question. "Your Mam was the best person in the whole world, and I miss her terribly."

"I miss Mam too."

This time Jane let her eyelids close.

"But I'm confused," she heard Grace say. "Are you saying *you're* my mother? That Mam is not, was not ..." Jane could hear the shock in Grace's voice but could do nothing to ease her pain. "I don't understand ..."

Gentle sobs reached her ears but Jane kept her eyes closed. "I'm being selfish," she said, "but there's a purpose in my confession. Brigid wouldn't let my life be ruined by my mistake. I was seventeen. By doing what she did, she saved my reputation and my career, and I still had you in my life. I've lived with the guilt ever since – but there's something else you need to know."

"What more can there be?" wept Grace, anger creeping into her voice. "You've turned my life and my thinking on its head. You and I had a special bond. One that came naturally but ... but ... I never for one moment thought Mam wasn't my mother."

"And neither should you." Jane opened her eyes and fixed Grace with a glare. "She was your Mam in more ways than one. I simply gave birth." The two women continued to stare at each other. "Think, Grace. Who, and how, do you love? And then think why, then you'll understand what I'm talking about. Love comes in many disguises."

A few moments passed before Grace spoke. "Yes. Yes, I think I know what you mean. Mam was always Mam, and you were my Janey, and I loved you both," she paused. "But who was my father?" she asked, as it dawned on her that Brigid's long-deceased husband could not be.

An icy stillness invaded Jane's body and she clutched Grace's arm, leaving red finger bruises on her white skin. "No one of any importance, and no one you need bother about." She released Grace's arm and lay back on her pillows, clenching at the blanket covering her spindly legs.

"But why?" asked Grace.

"Because he was a wastrel. He's dead now."

"Oh. So I'll never ... I still want to know his name.

What was he like?" Her voice took on an edge of desperation. "How did you meet him?"

"No, Grace. No. I am not going to tell you. Ever. So don't ask again. He was neither a decent man nor a kind man. You have not inherited anything from him, so consider yourself fortunate. He matters not one whit. I shall never speak his name. Now, shall I continue?"

Grace nodded, clearly not convinced.

"The next part of my confession concerns Beth."

"Beth?"

Jane looked at Grace's distraught face and wondered if she was doing good or harm, but she'd come too far to back out now. Grace deserved the truth. One way or another, she'd lost four children, the hardest of which was her firstborn son to the war. The least Jane could do was to give her the gift of a grandchild.

She pushed herself up in bed, wincing at the pain. "When I took Katy away with me, I was following in Brigid's footsteps. Saving a girl from disgrace."

"What?" Grace rose and backed away from the bed. "No. I can't believe I'm hearing this. You took Katy away to have a baby without telling me? How could you?" Grace's face flushed with anger.

"Don't judge me badly, or Katy, because I wouldn't change a thing, and I would do it again if I had to. Come sit down beside me. I need you near."

Grace sat and Jane reached out for her daughter's hand, grasping it tightly.

"Enough years have passed for you to forgive. For your own sake. But you mustn't tell anyone. Do you understand me, Grace? No one. Katy is safely married and about to have a new baby. Jaybee is happy and moving on with her life, thanks to Beth. But my darling girl, Beth is your granddaughter. My great-granddaughter. Who would ever have thought? But promise me, you must never tell her or you'll break Jaybee's heart. Promise?"

Again Grace nodded when words would not come, her face bleak and her eyes troubled.

"Thank you," said Jane, relieved her ordeal was over.

Grace automatically began to rub Jane's crooked joints. The two women sat in silence as time ticked by, each coming to terms with Jane's confession and what it would mean in the future.

"I love you, Grace. I've loved you more than I can ever say. Brigid was right to protect you – and she continued to shield you for the rest of her life. Society would have crucified us both and ruined your life for my mistake. I did the same for Katy. I didn't trust that society wouldn't ruin her life either – I still don't."

Her energy drained, Jane paused. "I couldn't leave this world without making sure my flesh and blood are watched over. I'm sorry to do this to you. It's not easy living with secrets, but if it protects the ones you love most, then so be it. It is your turn to carry the burden of my confidences and safeguard those we love. Promise me, Grace, you will keep our secret."

"Oh Janey, I don't know what to think or feel right now," said Grace, utterly drained and bewildered. "But I've always trusted you and I love you, so I'll keep your secret safe within my heart until the time comes to pass it on."

Grace let the tears trickle down her face as she rested her head on Jane's lap. Gentle hands smoothed her hair. Mother and daughter had found each other, and Grace's life took a new turn.

35

ALL GOOD THINGS MUST COME TO AN END

April 2019

As co-executor of the will, alongside the lawyer, Katie spent far too many expensive hours with him trying to establish the award criteria Granna had insisted on. The first grant could not be awarded until the following year, as a trust had to be set up and formal documents put in place first. The lawyer wouldn't distribute the initial tranche until six months after probate either, which was still more than a month away.

Utterly overwhelmed by all the detail, Katie was grateful for his expertise, but he had not been at all helpful when she tentatively outlined her thoughts about young Grace.

"I'll need more proof, Miss Anderson. Hunches are not sufficient. I need certificates. Evidence."

Stymied on that account, Katie mulled over the problems which seemed to mount at every turn.

As she'd expected, Jared hit the roof when he heard about Grace's idea of living alone, which led to a huge fight, which meant they hadn't been talking to each other for days.

"That's not good," she said, when Jared called. "You and she have a great relationship; don't wreck it over me."

"It's not over you. It's about a seventeen-year-old child controlling my life."

Oh, dear. This doesn't bode well, thought Katie.

"Jared. Calm down. She's not a child. She's a very intelligent, capable young woman trying to help you move on. And it is about me. Or else the two of you would have moved to somewhere more suitable by now. Now, please. Tell her you're sorry you yelled at her and restore some of the harmony you so famously boast about."

She could see the problem more clearly than he could. He was bordering on exhaustion, still getting up at a ridiculous time to work the early shift at the bakery, and then working all afternoon and weekends to meet the demands of Dazzling Desserts. It meant the rhythm of family life had changed completely.

He'd given in to Grace's idea for deliveries, and she organised the packing and the drivers, but he wouldn't let her drive: another bone of contention leading to more disagreements. The business had reached the stage where it needed his full-time attention and extra staff. He should have been over the moon with the result, but while he stubbornly clung to the idea of one home for three people, with a commercial kitchen, and couldn't or wouldn't see past that, nothing would change.

Katie sat busily working away on the albums for Heart's Home when she heard a knock on the door. "Hello, Grace," she said, surprised to see the girl arrive mid-morning. "What brings you here?"

"It's holidays and I'm bored. Dad's working, and anyway, he's so filthy lately, I'm avoiding him."

"What, no friends to go gallivanting with?"

Grace shrugged. She threw her jacket on the back of the couch and flung herself onto it with one leg dangling over the arm.

Katie itched to grab the jacket and hang it where it belonged but thought better of it. "Juice? Or fizzy?" she asked, heading to the kitchen to see what she could feed the girl. If she remembered her teenage years properly, bad mood equalled junk food. Her pantry revealed nothing of interest so they ended up making grilled cheese on toast together.

The ice broken, Grace relaxed and began to chatter. "Got any decent colours?" she asked. "I need to paint my nails. See?"

Katie looked at Grace's hands and took one in her own, fingering the girl's ring.

"Where'd that come from? I've never seen it before."

"Dad gave it me. A peace offering, he said. It belonged to my gran. Cute, eh."

"Which gran? And how did he have it?" asked Katie rather too sharply.

"Granna Beth," Grace looked nonplussed. "She gave it to him years ago. Before she died, but after he and Mum split. He was supposed to give it to me on my 18th birthday – he skipped a few months. Why?"

"I've seen something like it before somewhere."

Katie's brain searched for the where she'd seen it – Claddagh rings were unusual at the best of times.

"It's engraved. Look." Grace slipped the ring from her finger and held it up.

In tiny, worn lettering Katie read: Tommy & Brigid 1889.

Her brain clicked. A photograph. "Come with me."

Katie opened her laptop and scrolled through the file she'd set up with her grandmother's photos. Now that she knew who people were, she soon found what she was looking for. In the early days of sorting out her grandmother's things, she took close-ups of any jewellery she spotted in case she ever needed to identify a piece. Like the St Brigid's cross she'd found in her mother's drawer. She'd identified that from a print of Móraí Brigid wearing the identical brooch.

"There. Isn't it the same ring?" Katie pointed to a woman's right hand wearing a Claddagh ring.

Grace peered over her shoulder, and compared the ring with the picture. "Could be. Yeah. I'd say so. Whose was it?"

"Her name was Brigid."

"Who's she?"

Now she had to identify Brigid, she found it hard to describe her to Grace. "I think the best way to describe her is your grandmother's adopted grandmother."

"How do you know her then?"

Now came the moment of truth. "She was my grandmother's adopted grandmother too."

"Huh? You're kidding, right? No way – that doesn't make sense."

Katie couldn't agree more. The generations were wrong for a start, and how did she explain such a convoluted family tree to someone else? "Sometimes families adopted other family members amongst themselves, without any formal paperwork, especially in the old days. I'm told your Granna Beth was adopted. Did you know?"

"Yeah. Dad's into all this old history stuff too."

"Well, I think my grandmother's sister, Jaybee, adopted your grandmother Beth from my grandmother Katy."

346

"What?"

Seeing the confused look on the girl's face, Katie changed tack. She guided Grace to the shelves of photographs and pointed to the people she was talking about. "Let's start from the top down. Brigid, here, adopted a child called Grace. Grace had two daughters – my grandmother Katy and her older sister Jane Brigid, known as Jaybee. I don't have a picture of that Jane, but she adopted her sister Katy's child, Elizabeth. Elizabeth was your Granna Beth. Got it?"

Grace nodded. "Cor. Are we related then?"

"Sort of distant half-cousins several times removed, I think, but it's too hard for me to work out."

"And I'm named after that Grace," she asked, pointing to the photo.

"Yes, your great-great-grandmother."

"So why would this Jaybee adopt her sister's child?"

"Probably because Katy wasn't married."

"So? Lots of kids' parents aren't married."

"Today, yes, But not then. Being illegitimate was a stigma on both mother and child. They'd be ostracised."

"Well, that's stupid," said Grace.

Katie had done her best to explain the relationships, and the more she explained it, the clearer the connections came in her own mind. She wondered if she'd found the solution to one of her problems. "Can I take some photos of your ring, please?"

The only way Grace could have the ring was the same way she had the St Brigid's cross. Handed down from mother to daughter through several generations. She had the jewellery and enough written proof to show the connection from Brigid to young Grace, and Brigid to herself. Would the lawyer accept it as evidence?

A few days later, she came away from the lawyer's office in two minds. He'd said yes. The photographic evidence, the graph she had drawn and copies of enough certificates to prove lineage had convinced him even without formal evidence of Elizabeth's birth or adoption certificate. She should have been happy. She should be rushing to tell Jared she'd met the conditions of the will and, thanks to him, found her grandmother's other daughter, traced her family and filled out all the branches and twigs on the tree. She should be telling him about Grace's inheritance.

But she couldn't.

They had another problem which she hadn't yet shared. And they were still at odds after the last row.

"No. It's got to be equal or nothing," he said, after she offered to buy a suitable unit for his kitchen. "And it won't solve the problem. I want the three of us to live together."

Katie had given Grace's suggestion a lot of thought. The place was exactly what Jared needed, if you took her out of the equation. He could quit his job, he and Grace could continue to live at their townhouse and rent the upstairs to offset costs or use it as a crash pad until Grace went away to university.

And then maybe, just maybe, the two of them would have more time to spend together. Their relationship was suffering as things were.

"It solves lots of problems," said Katie, "in so many ways, and you know it. I'm not offering you money as such. Think of it as a partnership opportunity. An investment. Something temporary until you sort out what's best. Quit your job and get the business established. Take time to sell your place and get the best price. The two of you can live there until Grace decides which university to go to. It's only for a few months. Don't rush things. You can't force the issue with Grace, so stop being so stubborn."

They argued back and forth but Jared remained adamant.

"I'll pull my own weight or nothing. And I still want the three of us together."

"Oh, for goodness' sake. What's got into you? Why won't you listen?"

But he wouldn't give in. He kept working and working himself into the ground.

"I'm worried about Dad," said Grace over the phone a few days later.

"So am I. But have you got any ideas? He's not listening to me."

"Me neither. But something's got to change."

Katie knew what that change could be but hadn't had the gumption to put it into words, not while Jared was tearing himself apart. But time was running out.

"Has he handed in his notice, or put the house on the market, or done anything?" asked Katie.

"Nope. And he says he won't until I agree to live with the two of you."

"Well, the two of us don't live together," said Katie. "You two do, so he's talking nonsense."

"I'm sorry. I didn't mean to come between you, but ..." Grace sounded so despondent, Katie felt quite angry towards Jared.

"Don't be sorry and don't explain. I understand. It's a big thing to ask of you, especially after your mother's situation turned sour."

"It's like he can't wait to get me out of his hair," Grace muttered, her voice full of anguish.

"That's not true, Grace. Never, ever believe that. He loves you so much. And anyway, blame me. I'm not sure I'm ready to compete with such a beautiful, switched-on young woman about to embark on her own life." She heard Grace's shaky chuckle and could visualise the embarrassed smile. "Your Dad's being unreasonable. Let time take its course."

"OK, but something better happen soon," she said.

They chatted for a while longer but then Grace had to go, and Katie hung up.

They'd backed each other into a corner, and there was no way she would put Jared in the position of having to choose between her and Grace. She had to break it off and let him sort himself out. There was no other choice.

Her heart shattered.

36

FOND FAREWELLS

December 1950

For the second time in three months, Grace stood beside a newly dug grave to say her farewells to someone she loved. Charlie stood silently next to her, but she knew he was as distressed as her, although he didn't show it. Not like he had when they buried Gwenna such a short time since. No one else in his life had ever been as important to him as his sister. Not even herself, Grace admitted. But she'd understood and never felt less loved. And now they were saying goodbye to Jane. Her beloved Janey.

Her two beautiful daughters, Jaybee and Katy, sobbed into sodden handkerchiefs as the minister intoned a prayer. Grace moved to put her arm around each of them to share in their grief for Granty, their Janey and – as Grace alone knew – their grandmother; her mother. She would keep her promise to Janey and never reveal her secret, until or unless she believed passing the secret on would help the receiver – like it had her. Eventually. Grace would never forget the sacrifices Janey had made, and she was so grateful to her for telling the truth and giving her the gift of a grandchild.

Thinking back over her life, Grace realised her mam Brigid and her Janey had been with her throughout the happiest and blackest moments in her life: during two miscarriages and when she buried baby Susan. Then later, Janey was there on the day she buried her mam, and when she buried her son Tommy, lost to the war so soon after Brigid had gone. How was she going to live a life without either of those women to give her strength?

Their courage had come from hardship, of grin-and-bear-it times, when life was what you made of it. They had learnt life wasn't fair and wasn't even-handed, and they fought for what they wanted from it. Just like Jane's true sister Laura who stood alone on the far side. Grace's relationship with Laura had never developed beyond childhood. Laura remained the intense, driven being she always had been, aloof from emotional understanding. Laura would continue to live her life peripheral to theirs.

Jane's resilience she learnt from Brigid, who learnt from necessity. Gwenna's, too, came from necessity. Grace's own courage had come from loyalty – loyalty to Janey mostly but also her mam who had taught her well. Her girls, Jane Brigid named after two exceptional women, and Katy, Kathleen Grace, who took Mam's second name, would inherit the genes from both Jane and Gwenna, through her and Charlie, and would learn to find strength in adversity. Grace's duty was to show the next generation of women, and the one after, how to live a life of fortitude.

The minister finished the service and people began to drift away.

"Shall we go, my dear?" asked Charlie, coming to Grace's side as she threw the last handful of rose petals over Jane's coffin.

Grace nodded and linked her arm in Charlie's. Pride filled her whole being as she watched Jaybee and Katy lead Beth towards the car. Despite the solemnity of the occasion, the young child bounced along between them, holding hands with both. Joy shone on the girl's face, and Grace's two daughters smiled and laughed at something she'd said. Grace smiled too. The girl was flourishing under the care of Jaybee, who herself had flourished since Beth had come into her life, and her 'Katybee' would remain, like Janey, the favourite aunt, confidante, mentor and anchor. And they had Jane to thank for everything.

Grace instinctively knew Jaybee would not have children of her own. She would never remarry, even though she'd been married such a short time before her husband became a casualty of the war, like so many. Jaybee would dedicate her life to Beth and to her love of all things botanical.

Now that Katy was married, Grace hoped for further grandchildren, but none would ever take the place of her firstborn. Sometimes she was torn between telling Charlie, so he too might share her joy, and remaining loyal to her Janey. For now, she held her tongue. She wanted to hold the truth within her heart for the time being. The reality was still too new and too raw to share – and there would be too many questions to answer.

"What a touching service," said Grace to Charlie when they returned home. "I felt I was reliving Janey's life story as people talked about what they knew of her. I remembered her little cottage, and the times she took me to the theatre or listened to me playing piano – and her costume designs were the best in every way. Every momentous moment in my life, Janey was always there beside me. So many happy times. I'm going to miss her so."

She put the kettle on, and they settled at the table by the window where Jane had spent much of her time over the last three months.

"She certainly had a full life," said Charlie, remembering through five decades, to when he was no more than eight years old and Jane and Gwenna had first become friends. "I didn't realise half of it, if truth be told, but she was good to me."

"Janey was good to everyone," said Grace. "In the next few days, I'm going to sort through those sketches she gave me. I want to read her journals and let everyone in on the secret: my Janey was Jane O'Neill, the famous costumier at the Opera House for over three decades, and she was Bernadette and Mademoiselle Maree, two of the most sought-after fashions designers for many more years after that. The girls will love it when they find out."

"Make sure they understand how important it is to pass the gift on, Grace dear," said Charlie. "In time, those drawings will be a treasure in someone's hands."

"I will, Charlie. I will. I am also going to give Mam's St Brigid's cross to Katy, now she's married, and her Claddagh ring to Jaybee, with instructions to hand them on to their daughters." Now she only had two secrets to keep – the truth about herself, and about Beth.

3

GRACE SAVES THE DAY

May 2019

Katie never got the opportunity to tell Jared her decision to put everything between them on hold, at least until Grace had finished school. Instead, she received a hysterical phone call around ten one evening.

"Dad's been in an accident. He's at the hospital. Come quickly. Please," sobbed a distraught Grace.

Katie grabbed her keys and drove as fast as the traffic allowed, tooting her horn and swearing profusely at every hold-up. The pitch-black night and torrential rain made driving more difficult, and Katie could feel her nerves twitching as she ground her teeth. She wished she'd asked Grace for more details.

She got lost trying to find parking at the hospital, and ran from the car to the emergency department on edge and feeling dizzy and light-headed. Grace was hovering anxiously in the waiting room and immediately threw herself into Katie's arms, sobbing and gabbling about what happened and she didn't know any more. She'd not been told anything for ages.

Bit by bit, Katie disentangled her garbled explanation.

Jared had driven into a tree in the dark and had been knocked unconscious. There was no other vehicle involved but the car was a write-off.

"Don't let him die. Please don't let him die," begged Grace. "I'll do anything he wants but don't let him die."

"I'm sure it can't be that bad, Grace. You'd have been told if it was anything serious."

"Will you stay? Please?"

"If they'll let me."

At Grace's request, they allowed her and Katie through to sit with him.

"It could have been a lot worse," said the nurse, "but he's recovering well after surgery to his leg and we are monitoring any concussion he may have. He'll probably sleep now."

Through the long night, Katie and Grace listened to the whir and beeps of machinery, the squeak of shoes on polished lino and the quiet whispers of staff observing the patients, waiting for Jared to wake up. They hadn't talked much – both were too emotionally and physically drained to make unnecessary conversation – but an understanding grew between them about the future.

"What happens if he doesn't wake up?" asked Grace.

"He will. Have faith, he will," Katie assured her. "He's just sleeping at the moment. We'll know more in the morning."

Although Katie said the reassuring words, she wasn't sure she believed them herself. She was as scared of losing Jared as Grace was.

"You won't leave me, will you?"

"Of course not, Grace. I wouldn't dream of leaving you on your own." Taking pity on the girl, she added, "Until we can organise something more suitable, would you like to sleep on the couch at my place while your dad's laid up?"

Grace nodded, looking relieved. She found an extra chair to put her feet on and slid down enough to rest her head. She plugged her earphones into her phone and retreated into her world to await whatever the morning brought. Katie laid her head on her arms at the foot of Jared's bed, wanting to touch him.

From time to time, as they awakened from their awkward doze, one of them would seek out yet another cup of coffee, pulling a face at the bitter taste, leaving it to go cold in the cup. The sandwiches were marginally better. As dawn arrived, they stretched, paced a short distance up one way and back watching the hospital come to life, until a movement and sound brought both of them to Jared's side.

Unable to understand what he was saying, Katie guided the straw in the water glass to his lips. He sucked gratefully and cleared his throat. "Grace?"

"I'm here, Dad," she said taking his hand.

"Sorry. I'm so sorry."

She burst into tears and laid her head on his chest while he smoothed her hair.

"I thought I was going to lose you," whimpered Grace, fear and worry blotching her face.

His eyes sought Katie and he smiled. Her hand found his. Everything would be all right.

A nurse arrived. "We have some checks to do. Go home and freshen up, get some sleep if you can, and come back later to see the doctor."

Jared had been lucky. There was no obvious sign of concussion but a badly broken leg would keep him in a cast for several weeks, and the numerous nasty cuts, grazes and bruises would take time to heal, but otherwise he'd come out of it with minimal damage.

The relief brought tears again, and anger. "You scared me to hell," said Grace. "Don't you do anything like that again."

"I'm sorry. It was all my fault," he admitted. "I was too tired. I shouldn't have been driving. Must have fallen asleep."

Katie didn't need to voice her thoughts, Grace said it all for her. She insisted something needed to change.

And it did. Jared's accident forced them to adjust their thinking. This time the decisions came without any of the angst they'd previously struggled with.

Katie and Grace agreed; after Jared left the hospital he would move into Katie's place while he recuperated. At least for a while.

"But you have to come up with something better, and soon," she said, glaring at her father. "I don't want to sleep on the couch for the rest of my life."

"We will, Grace, I promise," said Katie, trying to calm her. "But you have to let your father recover first. You heard what the doctor said, no stress and lots of rest. They are still a little worried about some mild concussion."

"Rest is one thing, ignoring the obvious is another," she snapped, still angry with her father for scaring her so much.

After a few days, Jared began to move around more comfortably on the crutches, and Grace returned to school. While they'd fallen into living together by default, squashed into Katie's apartment wasn't the best solution for any of them, even if her and Jared's relationship had improved remarkably. It didn't take long to discover he wanted more of her attention than she had bargained on and often interrupted her while she was working.

"I love you, Katie," he'd whisper in her ear and the photos on the screen would fade into the background.

But Grace was right – something had to change.

While they settled well into living together, Katie's place was just too small for any of them to have any privacy.

"Jared, we can't only think of ourselves," said Katie as they lay in bed one morning. "It's not fair that Grace should have to sleep on the couch when she has a perfectly comfortable bed in her own home."

"I don't disagree, my darling, but it feels so good being here with you." Jared snuggled up to her again, but Katie pushed him away.

"I have work to do, even if you don't. Rosemary says there're clients waiting for albums."

"How's it all going?" he asked.

"Better than I could have wished. And I'm loving every moment of it. I could never have imagined such good fortune could come from Granna's ill health, but it has. But stop changing the subject. We have to talk to Grace."

And Grace had agreed with Katie. "I didn't want to be rude to Katie, Dad, so I didn't say anything before, but I would like to go home, please. All my stuff is there."

So Jared and Grace had returned to their townhouse a week after the accident.

A matter of days later, when Katie arrived for dinner, Grace brought their situation to a head once again.

"Look at this," she said, plonking down on the couch beside them and handing her laptop to her father.

She'd found a three-storey building with two retail spaces at ground level, two one-bedroom units on the first floor and a three-bedroom apartment on the top floor with an outdoor area which offered a peep of the water.

Grace had it all worked out. "Dad. You can fit out one of the shops to suit Dazzling Desserts and sell your delicacies both online and from the shop. You rent out the other shop space, which will pay for the fit-out and bring in an income. You and Katie get the top floor apartment. I'll live in one of the smaller units, and you can rent out the other, which will help pay expenses."

Katie and Jared laughed until their sides ached. How could they possibly let a seventeen-year-old organise their lives? *But someone needs to do some planning*, thought Katie. Grace didn't know the half of it. Neither did Jared.

"Oh, and by the way," added Grace, "I've changed my mind, and decided to go to uni in Auckland after all, so you're stuck with me."

"Doesn't sound like you've left us with many options, does it?" answered her father, not looking at Grace, but staring adoringly at Katie.

The three of them talked it through, what the future looked like and how it would fit into a lifestyle for three. They were finally on the same wavelength, except for Grace wanting a place of her own.

"I won't know where you are or what you're doing," Jared complained.

"For Pete's sake Dad, I'll be eighteen soon. You can't keep me at home like a little girl any more – and I'll be on the next floor if you buy that place. And it's not that I want to get away from you, but you have your life with Katie now, and I need to work on what my life is going to look like without getting in your way."

Katie thought the girl had a far more mature head on her shoulders than her father gave her credit for, but she could tell from the look on Jared's face he wasn't convinced.

"Give us a bit more time to think about it, and do some research, Grace," said Katie, more enthused by the idea than she'd owned up to so far. "It's a great find, but we may find something even better, but credit where credit is due, it's a lot better than my place."

"Sorry, Katie," said Grace. "My bright ideas probably mean giving up your gorgeous place, and I should have asked you first. Exciting, though, isn't it?"

More exciting than she realises, thought Katie.

Grace disappeared back to her room, leaving the two of them sitting on the couch. Katie curled up beside him. The time had come.

"I've got some important things to tell you and I don't want you to say anything until I've finished. OK?"

"OK. But why so serious?"

"Because it's going to have an effect on what we do next."

Jared frowned but said nothing as he wriggled to get more comfortable and put his arm around Katie as she settled to her story.

"I went to the lawyer's with everything we know about Grace and her Granna Beth, and showed him what certificates I had and the photo of the Claddagh ring, and he's accepted that Grace is the person stipulated in Granna's will. So that means Grace will receive her inheritance once she turns eighteen. During our conversation, I realised Grace will qualify for one of Granna's university grants. It's going to make a huge difference to how and what she decides to do with her future." Katie stopped and raised her head to look at him. "I'm so pleased it's worked out the way it has."

"That's going to be a lot for Grace to take in, but wow. You're right. She has the freedom to choose whatever she wants to do. Damn. She might go and study overseas."

"She might – or go travelling for a while until she can work out what she wants. Or, she might just make it work for her right here. She's an extremely level-headed girl, even if she does get mad at you."

Jared laughed and kissed the top of her head. "You're so good for me, you know that?"

"There's one more thing I need to tell you," said Katie.

"What more can there be?"

She stood up and paced, feeling unrealistically nervous at what she was about to reveal.

"Now that's all settled and I've completed the tasks Granna set me, I'm about to come into a lot more money."

When she'd finished explaining the details, and why it had taken her so long to tell him the last part of the story, Jared took his glasses off and polished them. He neatly folded his handkerchief before he spoke.

"I don't know what to say. It's almost too much to take in."

Katie agreed. "It's taken me a long time to assimilate everything and come to terms with what it all means, which is why I didn't tell you earlier. But it does solve one problem – we don't have to worry about where the money is coming from to buy us a decent future."

"But that's your money, not mine."

"Don't be so old-fashioned, Jared. It doesn't matter where the money comes from – we need a new home and you need a new kitchen, and Granna has given us the means for both. We should be happy."

She still needed to tell him her other news, but she decided he had enough to take in for the time being.

Despite Jared's reservations, over the next few days their discussions produced results. There'd been no more disagreements on whether they should get married – just when – and no arguments about finding somewhere more suitable for them all to live. Jared finally gave up the fight about using Katie's money should they find something that fitted the bill before he'd cashed up.

But they couldn't agree on when to tell Grace the news of her inheritance.

"I don't want her to know until her birthday," said Jared. "I don't want her distracted while she's studying for her exams."

Frustrated with his constant resistance to her new-found riches, Katie said, "You never quite give the girl the credit she deserves, do you? How do you know she'll be distracted? How do you know she won't make a better decision about her studies for next year if she knows about everything now?"

"She's my daughter. I know."

Katie had no response to that obvious and direct put-down. "I think I'd better go home and let you think about it. We'll talk later."

A sour taste settled in the pit of her stomach as she realised they still trod a fine line between success and failure.

"I'm sorry, Katie," said Jared when he phoned the following morning. "I shouldn't have spoken to you like that."

"I'm sorry, too, for landing everything on you at once. And I know Grace is your daughter, but you aren't the only one who cares about her."

Katie had taken to going to Jared's place several evenings a week. He still did the cooking, but Katie was glad he and Grace had time on their own without her constantly in the middle. He'd mastered getting around his place quite well, and Grace was happily back in her own space with her music, her studies and her art.

"Yay, about time," said Grace over dinner when Jared announced he'd quit his job at the bakery.

"And because of this stupid broken leg, they've released me from working my notice."

"Well, that's good news, isn't it?" said Katie.

"But I've had to put a hold on the Dazzling Desserts orders until I can stand unaided and without pain. Which leaves me without an income," he said. "I don't want to burden you, Katie. I want to pull my weight."

Katie sighed. Money. Again.

"You're on ACC, Dad, so get over yourself. But half the time in the cast is over already so it won't be long. I'll get my full licence next month, then I can drive for you. You'll be sorry you said you wanted to pull your weight when I'm done with you."

"And besides," said Katie, "isn't there some clause in relationships about 'in sickness and in health'?"

Jared grinned and leaned across to kiss Katie. Grace quietly slipped out.

One evening, Grace started to head out the door, saying she was 'going out' with friends.

"Whoa up, young lady," said Jared. "Which friends? What are you using for transport? What time will you be home? And going out where exactly?"

Grace rolled her eyes, and in that tired, condescending voice only teenagers can perfect, ticked off the answers. "School. Parents. Midnight. A live show. Honestly, Dad. I'm not a child."

"And Katie," she said in a more genial tone, deliberately ignoring her father, "I've had another idea. You should open an art shop in the other shop space and sell your photos on canvas. I might try selling some of my drawings if you did."

Katie held back her laughter and tipped her index finger in acknowledgement, but the girl had already turned and was heading out the door.

Katie said a silent thank you to her grandmother who'd sent her on the quest to discover her family tree. She'd found her great-great-grandmother Jane, the costumier, and generations of women leading to herself and young Grace, and the amazing legacy Jane had given them all.

She'd found Jared – her one true love – on the day of her grandmother's funeral and, coincidentally, the date of Jane's death, as if guiding hands had brought them together so they could discover their past and their future side by side.

Grace Price had inherited a bucketload of talent and an equal amount of ambition from a string of talented, ambitious and determined women. *Lucky girl*, thought Katie. *She'll not fail at anything she sets her mind to.*

Alone for the first time since his accident, Jared took advantage of the moment and kissed Katie deeply. So much had happened in such a short time. They'd been

365

shaken to the core and nearly torn apart. There was no need for words, just love and passion and reconciliation.

Later, lying in a tangle of sheets spent from their lovemaking, Jared said, "Sometimes, I wish I could turn the clock back. I wish we could go back to those fun times we had over Christmas and New Year before any of this happened, and I could have another go at getting things right."

"You're not doing that badly. Just let Grace grow up and make her own decisions, and don't get yourself into any more scrapes."

"I love you, Katie, my darling. I love you more than I've ever loved before. I want to spend the rest of my life with you, and I'm happy you care so much for my Grace. I hope you two will be the best of friends. But my clumsiness, stubbornness and stupidity got us into this mess – and my pride. Will you ever forgive me?"

Katie's heart swelled. She loved him so much. "Only if you'll forgive me."

"I'd forgive you anything, my darling, whatever it is, if you'd agree to marry me now. Please say yes and we'll set the date. How about tomorrow?"

It's all happening too quickly again, thought Katie. They should wait until Grace had finished school but Katie couldn't hold back the march of time. Nor could she resist teasing him a little longer.

"So soon? What about Grace? What about your career and my career, and where will we live? And what about all that horrible money?"

He chuckled, but his eyes were serious. "After what we've been through, nothing is insurmountable. We'll find a way. Hasn't Grace just come up with an idea already? Say yes. Please."

"Tomorrow might be a bit soon, but yes, I'll marry you."

Putting her hands over her ears in mock horror, she wouldn't have been at all surprised if Grace said she'd heard his whoop from wherever she was. She couldn't wait to ask Grace to help her plan and invite her to be her maid-of-honour.

"Well, if that's all settled ..." said Katie as Jared put his arm around her and she snuggled up to him again. "We'd better take a good look at the property Grace found. We're going to need a lot more space in a few months' time."

At one time, Katie had sworn never to have children, but it seemed Granna's guiding hand was still guiding her – as though she knew something Katie herself had never thought possible. Granna wanted her grandmother Jane's gifts to be passed down from mothers to daughters through the generations. And now there was another generation to add, and both of them would be Jared's girls.

She still had much to do to fulfil Granna's wishes, but all that could wait. They would do it together when the time was right.

Katie placed his hand over her stomach.

"Are you telling me ...?" asked Jared, eyes glistening with elation.

She giggled. "Yes, my love. We're having a baby."

Author's Notes

Any book set in another time requires an enormous amount of research. How much of that research appears in the book defines it either as a non-fiction study or a fictional account. The story of *The Costumier's Gift* is fictional. However, the historical events the characters within the story lived through, participated in or knew about, did happen. Likewise, the historical figures mentioned by name were people of the time.

The Auckland Opera House, built by Mr H N Abbott, was opened in May 1882 on the corner of Elliott and Wellesley streets (now part of Smith & Caughey) and was commonly known as Abbott's Opera House. Mr Abbott died in November 1899, but the theatre continued under his name for some time, through the auspices of his wife, and was managed by Mr John McConnochie. Many of the performances were presented by recognised production companies of the time, such as Pollards, Rickards and Musgroves. In December 1926, the building was destroyed by fire. By this time, it was owned and operated by Fullers Brothers, and was never rebuilt. Fullers Bros went on to build St James Theatre in 1928.

Jane, the costumier, is loosely modelled on **Emily Nathan** Grundy (1859–1948) who began working for J C Williamson Ltd (who ran His Majesty's Theatre) in

Melbourne in 1881. She acted as chief wardrobe mistress for 56 years until she retired. An interview with Emily Nathan after her retirement in 1937 can be read in Trove National Library of Australia. *https://trove.nla.gov. au/newspaper/article/229444090?searchTerm=Emily%20 Nathan%20Grundy&searchLimits*

In this story, Laura is a 'work colleague and friend' of the true-life **Ellen Melville** (1882–1946) and aligns her activities and beliefs with her associate. Laura is also fictitiously 'employed' by the actual Devore and Cooper legal firm where Ellen Melville began her career (as did Āpirana Ngata). Melville was well known as a suffrage activist. In 1906, she became the second New Zealand woman to be admitted to the Bar and three years later, the second to establish herself in sole practice. She was heavily involved in the National Council of Women and other such groups promoting the welfare of women and children. *https://teara.govt.nz/en/biographies/3m51/ melville-eliza-ellen*

Madame Melba, as she was known in February 1903 (later Dame Nellie Melba), arrived by ship in Invercargill and toured the cities of Dunedin, Christchurch, Wellington, Wanganui, New Plymouth and Auckland. Her arrival by train was well reported in the newspapers of the time, as were the details of her Auckland concert programme in early March at the Auckland Opera House. Members of her entourage were as named in the story and the programme details were taken from PapersPast National Library of New Zealand.

The Great Strike, between October 1913 and January 1914, was one of New Zealand's most violent and disruptive conflicts. A relatively minor dispute at the Huntly coal mine and another one at the Wellington waterfront sparked a general strike. In opposition to the unions and striking workers, the government employed farmers and rural labourers to form a special mounted constabulary, known derisively as 'Massey's Cossacks'. Such actions led to many confrontations. The scene mentioned took place in Auckland between 8 and 22 November 1913. *New Zealand History – https://nzhistory. govt.nz/*

As with Madame Melba, the visit by the famous ballerina **Anna Pavlova**, in 1926, was widely reported in the newspapers. However, as she performed at His Majesty's Theatre, her relevance to the story of Jane at the Opera House was minor. Pavlova did famously hint that New Zealand audiences did not quite understand the artistry of her performances as well as overseas audiences. While not applicable to this story, the first-known recipe for the pavlova dessert was published in New Zealand in 1929. *New Zealand History – https://nzhistory.govt.nz/page/anna-pavlova-dances-new-zealand-first-time*

1926 was a big year. In addition to the tour by Anna Pavlova, the **Miss New Zealand Contest** attracted hundreds of contestants from all over the country. They were divided into regions: Miss Canterbury, Miss Wellington, Miss Otago and Miss Auckland (Anita Sutherland). Each winner was accompanied by her maid-of-honour. The final competition was held in Auckland in November: 19-year-old Thelma McMillan, Miss Otago, was crowned Miss New Zealand. Vera Jacobsen of the Auckland Arts Society was tasked with painting the girls' portraits, which were then put on display for the public to view at KK Footwear in Karangahape Road until the end of the year, at which time, they would have been given to the girls.

The Auckland Industrial, Agricultural and Mining Exhibition in Auckland in 1913 was as described, but another event in Dunedin in 1926 was not covered. Apart from the purpose-built entertainment sections, of which there were many and varied opportunities, the exhibition was designed to showcase the latest achievements in 'arts, science, agriculture, commerce and industry, and the marvels of wireless and telegraphy, astronomy, transport by air, sea and land ...' According to all reports, the Dunedin event was a great success, but the display buildings were later demolished. An image can be seen at *https://dunedin.recollect.co.nz/nodes/view/199744 (PapersPast, National Library of New Zealand)*.

Charlie's fondness for ships came from the visit of **HMS *New Zealand***, which was given by New Zealand to the British Navy in 1909 as an act of patriotic loyalty to the Empire. Completed in 1912, HMS *New Zealand* toured the country in April and May 1913. The ship was scrapped before the debt had been paid off. *New Zealand History – https://nzhistory.govt.nz/page/hms-new-zealand-begins-tour-nz*

Auckland's **Anniversary Day** commemorates the arrival of Lieutenant-Governor William Hobson in the Bay of Islands in 1840. The regatta first took place in 1842. It was replaced by horse-racing events until it was revived in 1850. Since then, the regatta has become an annual event and currently is quite possibly the largest in the world. While mostly for sailing vessels, powerboats were raced in 1903 and seaplanes flew in 1919. Today, waka (Maori canoes) tugboats and dragon boats can also be seen on the waters. *New Zealand History – https:// nzhistory.govt.nz/*

Between June 1942 and mid-1944, anything from 15,000 to 45,000 **American servicemen** could be found in camps in New Zealand. The camps were rough and spartan at best. The American lifestyle and attitudes were totally different from that of the residents of Auckland at the time, but their easy-going style endeared them to many who sought relief from the horrors of war. The arrangement of home visits became a feature of their stay. Inevitably, '... Romantic liaisons between American servicemen and New Zealand women developed. The soldiers were starved of female company, and many Kiwi women enjoyed the Americans' good manners and their offers of taxi rides, ice-cream sodas and flowers ..." Ask Katy what happened next. *New Zealand History – https:// nzhistory.govt.nz/war/us-forces-in-new-zealand*

The tradition of **open adoption** within families and villages was widely practised in the early Celtic world, with laws to support the system, at least until the churches changed many such customs. Illegitimacy as a concept didn't exist in ancient times. In the Maori world here in New Zealand, such open adoption is known as whangai. In all cases, the adoption was a three-way relationship in which the children understood they had birth parents as well as adoptive parents. Sometimes children were adopted by masters of a craft, whereby they could learn a trade and would return to their birth families at marriageable age. Only later, when the church influenced patterns of behaviour, did illegitimacy become a disgrace and adoption a secret.

* * *

I hope you have enjoyed this precis of historical events. I have not mentioned every one, or identified every individual, except for those who had relevance to the characters and storyline.

Vicky Adin

Principal Resources

Personal collection of *The Weekly News: Those were the Days* – hardback books highlighting major events of each decade taken from the original 'pink' *Weekly News* newspapers.

NZ Electronic Text Collection, Victoria University. *http://nzetc.victoria.ac.nz/tm/scholarly/tei-Cyc02Cycl-t1-body1-d1-d25-d2.html*

Papers Past, National Library of New Zealand – *https://paperspast.natlib.govt.nz/*

Te Ara: The Encyclopedia of New Zealand – *https://teara.govt.nz/en*

New Zealand History – *https://nzhistory.govt.nz/*

Trove: National Library of Australia – *https://trove.nla.gov.au/*

THANK YOU
I hope you enjoyed reading this story.

It would be most helpful if you could please visit
www.amazon.com/Vicky-Adin
and write a CUSTOMER REVIEW of the book.

Constructive comments are always welcome, and
if you would like to receive information on my new books
please email me on vicky@vickyadin.co.nz
with BOOK ALERT in the subject line.

* * * * *

Sign up for my newsletter to keep in touch
with things I'm doing
www.vickyadin.co.nz
and find my books on Amazon at
www.amazon.com/Vicky-Adin

**See my other books
on the following pages**

* * * * *

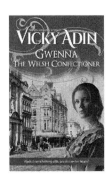

Gwenna
The Welsh Confectioner

Against overwhelming odds,
can she save her legacy?

(Set in New Zealand)

Amid the bustling vibrancy of Auckland's Karangahape Road, Gwenna Price is troubled. For all her youth, she has become the master confectioner in the family business since her father died. She promised to fulfil her Pa's dreams and open a shop, but with her domineering and incompetent stepbrother Elias in charge, the operation is on the brink of collapse.

In an era when women were expected to stay at home, Gwenna is a plucky young woman with uncommon ambition. She is determined to save her legacy. Despite the obstacles put in her way, and throughout the twists and turns of love and tragedy, Gwenna is irrepressible. She refuses to relinquish her dreams and lets nothing stand in her way.

Utter brilliance. I was captivated from beginning to end. Vicky really brings the characters to life and you can really engage with what it must have been like to be a young girl like Gwenna going into business at the turn of the century in a male dominated society. I was totally engaged with every character, each one contributing to make this a truly wonderful story; my only disappointment was when it ended. This is the first book I have read by this author but it won't be my last. ***** 5-star Amazon review

Winner Indie B.R.A.G medallion, Chill with a Book Readers' Award and Gold Standard Quality Mark

Brigid
The Girl from County Clare

Like making lace –
she pieced together a
new life from a single thread of hope

(Set in Australia and New Zealand)

Brigid is torn. If she stays in her beloved Ireland, she is another mouth to feed in a land plagued by starvation and poverty. If she leaves, she will never see her family again. But leave she must. There is not enough food.

Heartbroken, she boards the ship that will take her to a new life in Australia, comforted only by the knowledge that her cousin Jamie will make the journey with her. Her skill as a lacemaker soon draws attention, but life doesn't always run smoothly in the harsh new landscape. Brigid must learn to conquer her fears and overcome the stigma of being a servant, a female and Irish if she is to fulfil her dream.

A new start in New Zealand offers hope – until the day she encounters the man who seeks her downfall.

The historical aspects of the story are so accurate and described so perfectly that the reader will frequently need to remind herself/ himself that the story is fiction ... This is a thoroughly satisfying read. It is the kind of story that passes the test as a work of history, and is equally satisfying as a novel that will have your attention from first to last. **** 4 stars – Frank O'Shea, *The Irish Echo*, Sydney

Winner Indie B.R.A.G medallion and
Chill with a Book Readers' Award

The Cornish Knot

Can one woman's secrets change the life of another a century later?

(Set in Cornwall, Italy and New Zealand)

On the anniversary of her husband's unexpected death, Megan sits at home heartbroken and disconsolate. A mysterious package arrives containing a journal written a century earlier, which shakes her out of her self-imposed seclusion.

She embarks on a journey following in the footsteps of the journal's author, from New Zealand to Cornwall, France and Italy, uncovering a past she knows nothing about. She is pursued by a much younger man in Venice. She meets an intriguing fellow countryman in Florence and finds herself caught up in the mysterious world of art and captivated by a series of unknown paintings.

As she unravels her history and reveals its secrets, can she also find love again?

An engaging tale of grief, loss, love and family intrigue ... wonderful story, and a real page-turner, which leads the reader through all the twists and turns of a well-constructed plot. I loved the insightful descriptions of family relationships, the fully realised characters and the various locations in which the action takes place. Seldom have I read such a poignant and faithful account of the effects of bereavement. I can't wait to read more. **** 4-star Amazon review

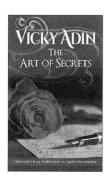

The Art of Secrets

Emma wants to forget;
Charlotte never can.
Together they remember.

(Set in New Zealand)

Emma is an enterprising young journalist with a bright future, but her life and career are falling apart. In a last-ditch attempt to save her position, she accepts the assignment to interview the best-selling author – Charlotte Day.

The ageing Charlotte has a reputation for being cantankerous and is highly secretive about her past, one she considers too painful to relive and too shameful to share. Preferring her roses to people, she is persuaded into meeting this girl who gets through her defences, forcing her to confront her past.

As Charlotte and Emma's relationship deepens, they find themselves enmeshed in a tangle of secrets that changes both their lives.

The art of great writing! ... Adin keeps a tight rein on her leading characters, their actions and reactions credibly grounded in genuine emotions. The change of tone from Emma to Charlotte, from young to old, works, helps the reader see behind the lies and half-truths they tell each other. Their progress from antagonists to friends is seamless, as the layers of the story peel back like petals, exposing the truth at the flower's heart. Bev Robitai, author of *Sunstrike*

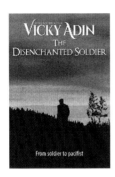

The Disenchanted Soldier

From soldier to pacifist

**(Set in New Zealand.
Based on a true story)**

In 1863, young Daniel Adin, a trained soldier, embarks on an adventure of a lifetime. In pursuit of a new life and land to farm, he travels to New Zealand to fight an unknown enemy – the fearless Maori.

A hundred and thirty years later, Libby is fascinated by the stories of Daniel, who looks down at her from the aged black-and-white photos on the walls. She wants to know more, to know what he was really like, but Daniel's story was more than she had bargained for.

A great insight into the lives of a family and what was going on around ordinary people in the early days of colonization.

– Ged Martin

I loved this book and so will you if you like historical fiction and family sagas set somewhere you likely know little about. This is beautifully and sensitively written. The characters are terrific. The fascinating part to me was how Vicky was able to take us on the family's journey in a thoughtful and non-judgmental way.

***** 5-star Amazon review

Printed in Great Britain
by Amazon